When I'm Not Myself

Also by Deborah J. Wolf:

With You and Without You

When I'm Not Myself

Deborah J. Wolf

KENSINGTON BOOKS
http://www.kensingtonbooks.com

KENSINGTON BOOKS are published by

Kensington Publishing Corp.
850 Third Avenue
New York, NY 10022

All Kensington titles, imprints and distributed lines are available at special quantity discounts for bulk purchases for sales promotion, premiums, fund-raising, educational or institutional use.

Special book excerpts or customized printings can also be created to fit specific needs. For details, write or phone the office of the Kensington Special Sales Manager: Kensington Publishing Corp., 850 Third Avenue, New York, NY 10022. Attn. Special Sales Department. Phone: 1-800-221-2647.

Kensington and the K logo Reg. U.S. Pat. & TM Off.

ISBN-13: 978-0-7582-1384-6
ISBN-10: 0-7582-1384-0

First Kensington Trade Paperback Printing: August 2007
10 9 8 7 6 5 4 3 2 1

Printed in the United States of America

For the countless unbelievably
amazing women in my life.
You know who you are.

And for Edward A. Wolf,
who believes I can do anything.
Silly bear.

Acknowledgments

I am blessed to have the most incredible agent in the world who despite his much more well-known clients, takes every one of my calls and stands unfailingly by my work. Thank you, Richard Morris, for every tireless minute you've put into this book and into building my budding writing career. My editor, Audrey LaFehr, has the uncanny knack of knowing exactly what input is needed to help turn things around, and at just the right moment. I am grateful for her continued sound guidance and direction.

My father, the president of my fan club, passed away just before the printing of my first book, *With You and Without You*. He never had the chance to read this one, but I have felt his presence whispered through the pages more than once. My mother, Janet Pretto, and my brother, Bill Pretto, have carried forth the tradition of soundly rooting on my cause. It's rather embarrassing, actually, but I am humbled by their belief that I could actually do this more than once.

I've had the most marvelous support from an ever-growing crowd of people who have sung the praises of my first book while encouraging me along with the second. They include those who hosted book club meetings and helped sell copy after copy of *With You and Without You*. (No doubt, some of them bought multiple copies themselves.) They are some of my closest friends and some of my newest acquaintances. I am constantly amazed when they introduce me as their "famous friend, the author" and I am indebted to them for their dedication.

For Kerry and Sherri, thank you for your years of friendship topped by acres of laughter and miles of loyalty. Somewhere in the pages of this book are the hints of weekends we've spent together, of secrets we've shared, and moments I'd never trade for anything in the world.

For Julie Ann Mardirossian, who embarrassingly enough was left off my acceptance speech the first time around. This is your fifteen minutes of fame. Use them wisely.

I am honored to call Frank Priscaro and David Hukari two of my dearest friends and confidants. For some reason still unknown to me, they've taken it upon themselves to provide that extra bit of confidence that sometimes still eludes me. It must be the years of wisdom they've got on me. They are, after all, much, much older. And wiser.

For Bradley, Andrew, Hannah, Colette, Ryan, Will, Lauren, and Megan . . . so you'll have something for show and tell. And for Jordan and Brodie, who still think their mom is pretty cool, I love you very much.

And finally, for Ted, this one is for you. Not a day goes by that I don't forget how damn lucky I am.

1

Cara's husband left her six months and twenty-three pounds ago. He turned her in for a new model, an updated Barbie. It wasn't that she was being cruel; her replacement's name was Barbie. Barbie was twenty-seven and quite pretty. Cara was in a position to know because she had spent enough time studying her from across the soccer field—the petite frame, narrow hips, pancake-flat stomach, and round, melon-shaped augmented breasts.

Cara turned forty-three this year, and although she was down three dress sizes since Jack had moved out, she'd lost the weight in all the wrong places. She was thinner in the face, but the lines were still there, the round curve of her belly still prominent. Cara had a closetful of clothes that didn't fit her and very few that did. She didn't think of the size 14s as her fat clothes; she thought of them as her married clothes, those that she'd peel off when Jack would still watch her undress. For that reason alone, she couldn't seem to part with them. They hung in her closet and mocked her silently.

They had four children together, Jack and Cara. The kids were the only things they shared anymore. Jack and Cara arranged to split their time with the kids evenly as if they were slicing a piece of pie right down the middle.

Katherine. Katie-girl, Kit-Kat, Kate, Kitten. Seventeen and a beauty, though, thank God Katie hadn't yet figured that out. She was tough at the surface, but soft and sweet if you scratched just beneath. Katie sided with Cara automatically, defensively; her first go at unconditional love. Jack, on the other hand, got a dose of love with more conditions than he could recognize or find names for. Katie went the first three months without speaking to him; she went longer without speaking to Barbie, regardless of the pile of endless gifts the poor woman futilely showered upon her.

William. Willie, Will the Thrill, Baby-Boy-Blue. Second in line, you'd never know it. Because of the distance between him and Katie—seven years—Will was more like a firstborn, and acted sometimes as if he was the eldest of the bunch. Independent and strong-willed, he suddenly needed neither his father nor his mother when Jack left, angry with the both of them for the cards unfairly dealt him. Unable to touch or control his own emotions, Will's outbursts came in long stretches that lasted days where he'd hurl discontentment like fast pitches on a baseball field.

Luke. Linus, Luke Skywalker, Lucas John Clancy. Two years behind Will, Luke stumbled through the third grade, stunned by what had befallen his family, and crawled so deeply into a shell it took nearly everything Cara had to pull him back out. For weeks, just after Jack left, she would find him each morning curled at the end of his bed and sucking his thumb, his sheets still damp from some middle-of-the-night accident. Luke hated to be left alone now and would do anything to avoid being so.

And, Claire. Claire-bear. Joy of joy, sweet little princess. The last in a series, only eleven months behind Luke, they might as well have been twins. Angel eyes, sweet and cuddly, Claire would never utter an unforgivable word toward anyone. She was the most moved by her father's disappearance, and wanted to talk about it every waking hour. Cara cringed and blinked back the tears as Claire's questions came like topics in a round of *Jeopardy!* She tried her best to answer her daughter's inquisitions, washing the venom from her mouth. Claire forgave Jack instantly and without repercussion, and was the only one to warm to Barbie, accepting her readily and crawling into her arms, unaware of what this did to Cara, how it tore her apart to see her daughter loyal to the woman who had stolen her husband.

Even with a full house, Cara never knew the loneliness would be so numbing. Jack left them with everything except his company.

He packed on a stifling Sunday afternoon in August, as if he was going on one of his extended business trips. He took the best suitcase and filled it with two weeks' worth of the underwear Cara had just folded and stacked neatly in two piles in the top right-hand drawer of his pine armoire. Briefs, for the most part, along with a few pairs of boxers. He took his black socks and two pairs of his good black wingtip shoes. He layered a few golf shirts in with his khakis and stacked a few T-shirts and jeans on top of those. He was a horrible packer; everything would be wrinkled by the time he got across town to Barbie's condominium. Everything but his suits and dress shirts. Still in the bags from the dry cleaners, he left those on hangers and looped them over the coat hook in the backseat of his 7 Series.

Cara watched him load the car. When he was done, he turned toward her and said, "Well, I guess that's about it." His sunglasses were perched on the end of his nose so Cara couldn't see his eyes, the blue eyes she had fallen in love with so long ago when they'd first met, but she had a feeling he wasn't looking directly at her, anyway. Coward. It was as if he'd been stripped of the features that had once made him so attractive to her.

"Really? Are you sure you have everything you need?"

Jack dwarfed her. She felt nearly invisible in his presence now.

He stared at her awkwardly with a crooked eyebrow, not sure what to make of her concern.

"I mean, that's it? This is how it ends? This can't be the way it ends. This is just pathetic. Me standing here in the driveway in my shorts and sweatshirt and you driving off with a carload full of clothes from the dry cleaners? They're not even neatly folded, Jack. Everything's going to be a mess by the time you . . . Well, I mean, wouldn't you like me to fold them for you?"

He tilted his head and stared straight through her. "Yeah, Cara, I think that's it," he said, sensibly. "I'm not really sure what else there'd be."

He settled himself behind the wheel as if he was driving off to work, then pulled the seatbelt tight over his wide chest and buckled it. The sun stretched in long bands across the sky, bleeding. Cara thought about what a beautiful sunset it would be, about how this would be the last sunset she would remember with Jack.

"Wait! Wait!" Cara screamed after he'd backed out of the driveway and started down the court they had lived on for fourteen years. She tore after the car the way Katie used to when she didn't want him to go. Halfway down the block he stopped the car. Cara stood on the sidewalk parallel with his car and stared at him, trying to catch her breath. The pavement beneath her bare feet was hot, as if she was stuck walking through a bed of coals. She shifted her weight from foot to foot, bouncing lightly on the balls of her feet.

"You can't go, Jack," Cara said. "Please, you can't leave."

He took a deep breath, then calmly said to her. "Why not?"

Cara's hands fell to her sides and she felt naked, as vulnerable as she had the first time she'd given a speech in junior high school. He stared at her, waiting on her answer. Trouble was, she didn't have one. There was no good answer, no real reason for him to stay. There was so much that had passed between them, so many weeks and months, years even, of distance that had grown like weeds between who they were.

"Why not?" he asked her again, impatiently.

She couldn't answer him. There was nothing left, really. He was right about that, about this being all that was left, an awkward silence that spanned the distance between them, from the sidewalk to the hot pavement where his car sat idling. She stared at her bare feet, discontented with the way her toes looked, the week-long stubble that angrily stood at attention on her legs. She'd let herself go, there was little attractive about her. She'd become who she thought she would never become, so disinterested in taking care of herself, of putting herself first, that he'd lost interest in her along the way.

He drove away then, slowly at first as if he was afraid she might come after him again, before accelerating sharply and taking the corner with an embarrassing screech from his tires. She stood watching the back bumper of his car, the turn signal blinking urgently, until it disappeared from sight.

After Jack left, Cara sat as still as she could in the bedroom that had been theirs together and listened for the first sounds of the house to come back to life, for familiarity to breed itself back into the room. Jack had purposely sent the boys and Claire to Cara's sister's house. Katie was out with some of her friends. From the bedroom, Cara could hear the Whitneys's sprinklers kick on next door, a dull *chuck-chuck-chuck* followed by a thick spray of water. A block over she could hear a dog barking at kids passing on their bikes. But inside there were no real sounds of life. All that was left was the pierce of silence that screamed in wailing cries from room to room, haunting the halls. Sadness crept into Cara's house, the house that was now hers alone, easing its way in, seeping into the paint on the wall, into the fabric on every piece of furniture. Like the stench of the poison left behind by a smoker, sadness grew on Cara like a debilitating cancer.

When Katie arrived home Cara was sitting at the kitchen table, a square box of tissues surrounded by nearly two dozen balled up, crumpled, snotty used Kleenex in front of her. Cara's eyes were bloodshot and swollen; she'd been crying in waves for nearly three hours.

She couldn't think of an easy explanation for her daughter when Katie said to her, "Mom, what's wrong? What's going on? Where's Daddy?"

"C'mere, sweetie," Cara said in a slur, drunk on the exhaustion and nausea that had washed over her. She yawned big, her body convulsing involuntarily, and patted the side of the chair, though clearly there wasn't enough room for the both of them.

Besides, Katie, with her feet planted firmly on the floor in an old pair of grimy tennis shoes, wasn't willing to budge from the very spot that welded her to the floor. Instinctively she said to Cara again, slightly more in control and with an edge in her voice this time, a thin line of distaste running through her vocals, *"Where's Daddy?"* Women's intuition.

"He left, sweetie. He left this afternoon . . . Um, he moved out. I think he just finally needed some space. All the arguing we've been doing, you know. He didn't see much way around it, I guess. We've been disagreeing on things for a long while now."

The color drained from Katie's pink cheeks, her eyes changed from their usual lustrous green to a dark, dead brown. "He *what?*" she asked Cara in a tone that accused no one but the man who was not there to stand in his own defense.

Cara plucked a fresh tissue from the box in front of her and blew her nose with effort. She pulled herself up from the kitchen table and pushed the chair out from behind her, letting the harsh scraping sound fill the room. Her daughter was frozen, rigid with hostility. She meant to take Katie into her arms and hold her, but she didn't have anywhere near the strength required to do it. Cara took a step toward Katie but her daughter backed away, cold.

"What do you mean, 'He moved out'? Where the hell did he go?" Katie took the backpack she had slung over her shoulder and heaved it across the room and into the foyer. It slid, then came to a halt near the base of the stairs, taking out a pair of Will's shoes in its path. Katie's temper was known to flare; she was easily angered, especially these days when there had been so much anger in the house, so much screaming and yelling and arguing. She was resentful and moody, the anger playing out in small Broadway shows that were most often negatively reviewed.

"Katie," Cara warned her, though she was hardly in a place to be strict with her. "Can we sit down? I want to talk to you about this. I want to make sure you're okay. Dad would want to make sure you were okay. You know how much he cares about you, honey. He always has."

Katie looked at her with disbelief and shook her head, disgusted. How could her mother defend him?

"Okay, okay," Cara said and moved even closer to her daughter, invading Katie's personal space, "if he wanted to make sure you were all right, he'd have been here to tell you himself."

"Where'd he go, Mom? Tell me where he is." Her thick dark eyebrows narrowed, a wrinkle forming above the bridge of her nose.

Cara stumbled. *DAMN, Jack. Damn, damn, damn.* He'd left this for her to clean up, for her to make right.

"He's staying with a friend, honey." Cara picked at a button on her shorts, avoiding Katie's eyes. She didn't feel like she owed Jack anything, certainly not the least bit of dignity, but she did want to spare her daughter the ugly truth, the lies that would come crashing down on her soon enough. Besides, she wasn't sure Katie was altogether strong enough to tolerate the truth, not the enormity of it in its entirety.

"Where?"

"Um, I, well . . ."

"He's with someone else, isn't he?" Katie asked, and then when Cara didn't answer her right off, barked at her, "*Isn't he?* Tell me, Mom. He went to stay with that woman, didn't he?"

At seventeen, Katie was keen to pick up on the scent of another woman. She'd been through her first heartbreak, the first boy who had disappointed her, and so the feeling now was not unfamiliar, though far more grave coming from her father. She shuffled across the kitchen floor until she reached the bakers rack in the corner. One-handed she picked up a small, framed photo of her father and her at a dance taken years earlier. In it Katie was twelve; her leg was in a cast and she was on crutches. It was the year she had fractured her ankle skiing but insisted on going to the father-daughter dance anyway. Jack was holding her as if she was his bride and he was crossing the threshold, her white-cast leg swinging wildly in the air.

Katie was ages different now, harder and unforgiving. She had lived through the unraveling of her parents' marriage, the broken promises, the ugly disagreements followed by stretches of silence and discontentment. She had learned from both of them that life didn't work out the way it was supposed to, that commitments weren't always kept.

"DIDN'T HE?" she screamed, not at Cara, but at the silent room, before she hurled the photo against the far wall, glass shattering in shards across the floor.

The sound caused Cara to jump, startled, and made her feel sick, her stomach churning in giant waves. Cara shivered even as the breeze blew warm air through the room, stirred the used Kleenex on the table.

Cara took a long, deep breath and tried to steady her voice. "Yes. He is. There is someone else he wants to be with, someone besides all of us. He's staying with her for now. I can't answer for him, sweetheart, I can't tell you what he's thinking; he's going to have to do that. And I'm sure he will, in his own time." She said this to Katie in a whisper. Never had she sounded, never had she felt, quite so dead.

Katie crossed the kitchen floor with determination and picked up the cordless phone that hung in its nest on the wall. She punched in the numbers and waited, her eyes focusing on nothing in particular. Subconsciously she gnawed on her fingernails, the black nail polish chipping off with each bite. Muffled, the outgoing voice mail greeting on Jack's cell phone clipped out of the receiver. The beep tone pierced through the still air in the room before Katie began hurling obscenities and left her father the last words he would hear from her until nearly Thanksgiving:

"YOU ASSHOLE. BASTARD. HOW DARE YOU DO THIS TO US. IF YOU THINK YOU CAN JUST WALK OUT OF OUR LIVES AND EXPECT US TO BE OKAY WITH IT, YOU ARE MORE STUPID THAN EVEN I GIVE YOU CREDIT FOR. I DON'T KNOW WHO YOU THINK YOU ARE, BUT I WANT NOTHING TO DO

WITH YOU. DON'T FUCKING COME AROUND THIS HOUSE OR ME OR MY BROTHERS OR CLAIRE OR MOM EVER. EVER AGAIN. DO YOU HEAR ME? DO YOU HAVE A GODDAMN CLUE ABOUT WHAT YOU ARE DOING?"

Jack would be furious with Katie's disrespect. Cara silently wondered if such a rage existed somewhere within herself, some untouchable place she hadn't yet found. Somewhere that she'd eventually be able to find and use. She was never more proud of Katie, never more in awe of her than while watching her berate her father on his voice mail. Cara hoped he'd play Katie's message on his speakerphone, Barbie poised in the front seat of his car with her lips pursed as if she'd bitten into a lemon.

Cara sat at the table, and tucked her legs up under her behind. She knew she had a role to play—the parent—but she was so tired, so done with life, that she couldn't find the strength to take Katie aside to talk with her, reason with her, even punish her for the outburst she'd just had. Katie slammed the phone back in its cradle before she made her way back to Cara's side. She stopped to run her hand down her mother's spine, kissing her on the top of her head lovingly before she stomped down the hall and out of sight to the back of the house, her bedroom, her refuge.

Katie was fragile, just barely on the mend. Surely Cara could find the courage to remind her that they could all deal with this, that a drink wasn't the solution. Katie had lost herself so many times in the bottom of a bottle; Cara couldn't bear to think of what this might do to her.

Cara put her head down on the long kitchen hardwood table and dozed off.

What seemed like forever later, she heard the front door swing open and close firmly and listened for the footsteps that would follow. She made her way out of the chair she'd been molded into and toward the entrance hall, convinced it must be Jack who had realized his stupidity. She prayed that he'd come to his senses.

Either that or he'd gotten Katie's message and was ready to stand battle.

She cut the corner at the dining room, and came face-to-face with Melanie. Their eyes met just as Mel began calling Cara's name. Melanie's hair was swept up in a long but simple heavy black braid; she'd been at the gym. Dressed in her workout clothes and her cross trainers, she seemed longer, more graceful than she already was at six feet. Her legs went on forever. She was without makeup, but sheer beauty, confident and calculated, and she took Cara in with her exquisite, piercing eyes.

They slumped on the polished marble floor together; Cara's cleaning lady had just mopped and high-gloss waxed it the day before. The tiles were cool and they dissolved against them in a heap. Heaving, heavy sobs racked Cara's body until there was nothing left. Mel held her, wordless and comforting. Then she asked Cara if she was done, if she'd had enough. Melanie said it just like that, too.

"Cara, for God's sake, are you done now? Have we had enough of this already?"

"How did you know?" Cara asked, confused. Mel lived in San Francisco, nearly an hour away, and she rarely ventured south of Market Street unless she absolutely had to. It had to practically be a life-or-death emergency for her to follow the freeway south of where the bay cut inland, separating the Peninsula from Oakland and the East Bay hills.

Melanie cleared her throat purposefully. "Kate called me."

Across the foyer, Katie made her way down the hall toward her room, convinced she'd done the right thing. She'd changed her clothes and brushed out her hair and, in a pair of holey jeans and a tank top, her hair loose and cascading around her shoulders, she looked much younger than she had only an hour ago when she had been screaming obscenities into the phone at her father. Her eyes were dark, circled in eyeliner and heavy with mascara. She jammed her hands into the back pockets of her jeans and waited, watching them.

Melanie's tone was reassuring but short and clipped. Cara

knew Mel would have no sympathy for Jack; there would be no mourning period. Never friends to begin with, Mel and Jack had tolerated each other for Cara's sake. Jack had moved in on Melanie's territory, stole her time and diverted Cara's attention. Mel was here to stake claim on what she thought had been unjustly taken from her.

Melanie lifted Cara to her feet, steadying her and, allowing her to rest her head under the arm she cradled around her as she led Cara back to the kitchen table. Immediately, Cara felt cared for, protected, the way she had always felt when Mel was around. Melanie then went to the bar, reached for two scotch glasses and filled them generously with tequila before she returned to the table and sat opposite Cara's chair, the half-full bottle between them. She set the glasses on the table and sighed, waiting for Cara to say something.

"I don't think I can drink that," Cara said to her, because the same nausea that had been with her all afternoon had washed over her again. The smell of the tequila rose up to burn Cara's nostrils even before she reached for the glass. From the back of her throat Cara tasted bile.

"Suit yourself," Mel said and reached for her glass, "but it would do you some good, it would help."

Cara stared at the shot, the honey-colored liquor that filled the bottom one-third of the glass. The smell was pungent, strong.

"He's gone, Mel. Walked out."

"Yep, sure is."

Melanie tipped back the glass and took the booze into her mouth in a single swig as if she was taking a long drink from her water bottle. She placed the glass back down on the table and wrapped her hands over Cara's, encapsulating them in her own. Mel's hands were warm, and she laced her long fingers within Cara's.

"He ain't coming back, Cara. You know that, don't you? You've known that for a long time; that once he left, he wouldn't be back," Melanie said matter-of-factly and without fear of repercussion. She wasn't particularly concerned with hurting Cara's feelings any more than they'd already been damaged; she simply wanted Cara to recognize what she knew would come to unravel over the next few days and months.

Cara nodded her head slowly, her eyes glazed and very far away. She felt like she should cry again, like there would never be enough tears to be done with it all, but nothing came this time; no loud sobs, no whimpering sighs.

"Cara? I mean it. Look at me." Mel's eyes darted across her face. "He ain't coming back," Mel said again, sounding out each of the syllables in the words. "You know this because you knew he was leaving. You've known all along that he was going to go." She spoke slowly and clearly, allowing Cara to absorb the words. She wasn't vindictive or vengeful, just factual.

Cara was used to Mel's approach. It might have seemed cold, heartless, but it wasn't meant to be. It was just Mel's way.

A buzz collected in Cara's brain like a swarm of bees round a hive.

"What do I do, Mel? Where do I even begin?"

"At the beginning, the new beginning. Oh, baby, you start from this place—this one right here—and move forward," she sighed. "Sometimes it's going to feel like you are moving backwards. Sometimes it'll feel like you're being sucked backwards and you can't go on another step, but you will. You'll see. You start at the beginning, Cara. You can do this; you're going to be fine. Without that bastard, you're going to be better than fine."

Cara knew Mel thought she should have left Jack long ago; Mel had been reminding her about it for years. But then again, Melanie would have never allowed herself to be in a relationship like Jack and Cara's, married for so many years, dedicated and loving and nurturing in the beginning, truly partners. Cara's mind flashed to the good times that dotted the canvas of her married life like fireflies in the night. You never knew quite when they were going to appear, but they were like a special treasure when one of them went off, something to be captured and held on to in a jar as if they might live on forever. In the past few years they'd become more rare, leaning toward extinction.

Melanie dropped her friend's hands and poured herself another shot. Cara said to her, "Really, Mel, you can drink mine, if you'd like. I can't stomach it right now." She stared at the glass, and nudged it toward Melanie. "I just never thought he'd go. Really, in the end, I just didn't think he would actually go."

"He left a long time ago, Cara. He just packed today."

Cara sat with those words for a minute, turning them over in her mind, shuffling them like a deck of cards. Mel was right. Jack had been unfaithful the bulk of their marriage, bouncing from one relationship to another, timing them at the most inopportune moments—just after Katie was born, then later when Cara was pregnant with Will. They'd nearly separated then, but Cara had clung to the notion that things would improve, that the kids would bring them closer together, that Jack's new job would satisfy the craving within him that Cara couldn't seem to fulfill. Then Luke and Claire nearly back to back, which had sent Cara spiraling and drove Jack further away, rather than closer, from all of them. Jack succeeded in the firm, made partner, spent less time at home, until finally his indiscretions were so obvious, he didn't seem to mind the number of times he was caught. Still, Cara had never stopped loving him, never stopped believing she could bring him back, to all of them.

"Fool," Cara whispered, barely audible, shaking her head at the memories of all the times she had known, all the things she'd disregarded.

"Uh-uh. No way, Cara, I won't let you do that to yourself. This was not your fault. This was not something you caused or did or had any control over. This was Jack, this was all his deal."

"Such a long life to be looking the other way."

"You always knew where you stood on this, Cara. You knew what Jack was doing. You never once looked the other way; you were always honest about his infidelities. You do not deserve to be punished for trying to keep your family together, for trying to keep your marriage together. It was an admirable effort, even if I thought you should have given up on it a long fucking time ago."

"At what cost, Mel? Look at me. I'm forty-three and I've got four kids, who I'm assuming will all stay right here with me, right here in this house, where every memory of my husband exists. This is the consolation prize? This is what I get?" Cara spread her arms wide and looked around the kitchen at the memories, the artwork hanging on the refrigerator, the corkboard covered with notes and a calendar full of activities. Signs of life, of family, were sprawled everywhere.

"No, babe, you get to start over. It's hardly a consolation prize if you think about it. You get to do this the right way. You get to take all the stuff you were doing right about this, all the good you have done for your kids, all the love and unselfishness you've poured into this family, and you keep going, you keep doing that. And then? You start over, you get to a place where life's about you and the things you need, the things you deserve. Not Jack. Not figuring out how you're going to make this better for Jack, how you're going to turn things around so Jack is happier. Now you get to see what makes this better for you. 'Cause you deserve that. You deserve to know what it's like to get something back. You deserve that and so, so much more, Cara. So good riddance to Jack. Good riddance to his midlife crisis and his affairs and his piss-ass attitude around this house. Good riddance to all of that, Cara. This is your chance to make a life of your own, one that counts for something more than what Jack handed you."

Cara pushed the shot of tequila across the table so hard that it sloshed and dripped down the side of the glass, and set in to form a ring on the table. Everything about her was unkempt, droopy. She couldn't remember when she'd become so droopy. Her eyes were red-rimmed and swollen, her cheekbones puffy. Her bobbed sandy-colored hair was limp and lifeless like straw. She was out of tissues, the cardboard box before her empty. She pushed her chair back and made her way to the bathroom for more.

She should be mad, she thought. Angry, angrier than she'd ever been. She should be disgusted with Jack, sick with what he had done to her, done to their children.

"And don't tell me you didn't know he was leaving, Cara," Melanie hollered after her. When Cara turned to look at Mel she was staring at her glass, turning it round and round so the light from the window bounced off the crystal. When Mel met Cara's eyes again, she said just a bit softer, "Don't tell me you didn't know he was leaving. You've known it all along. At least admit that. You'll feel better about things if you're honest with yourself. Trust me on that, Cara. Trust me on that."

Cara nodded, plodding back to the table.

"How's Katie taking it?" Mel asked, craning her neck toward the foyer, and down the hall toward the bedrooms. "She sounded fairly angry on the phone."

"Oh, she's pissed off all right. If I wasn't so worried about what she might do next, I'd think it was kind of fabulous, actually." Cara snorted, recalling the message that her daughter had left on Jack's machine. "But you know how quickly Katie can swerve off course. I know there's something I should do, I'm just not sure what it is."

"Let me check on her, Cara. I'll see how she's doing before I head out."

Cara agreed, nodding her head and blowing her nose at the same time.

In the hall, Mel knocked firmly on Katie's door and didn't wait for her to answer before opening it. Inside, Katie sat on her bed, propped by pillows, her knees pulled up to her chest. She'd put on a zip-up sweatshirt and her black Converses. There was a large hole in the left knee of her jeans and she sat pulling at the threads, staring at nothing.

"Kate?" Mel asked.

Katie stared ahead, her shoulders hunched and her mouth curved into a frown.

"Katie-girl?" Mel asked again, waiting to get a rise out of her.

Katie raised her eyes to meet Mel's. "Yeah."

Mel leaned against the door frame as if it was there to support her. "Your mom seems to be doing a little better but it's going to be rough going for a few days."

"Huh. Really? I can't imagine why."

"Kate, you get it, right? You know this may take a while for her to bounce back from. No matter how bad they'd been fighting. Well, your mom, she wasn't really prepared for him to go, even after all this."

"Uh, yeah, Mel. Yeah, I think I get it."

"How are you doing?"

Katie rolled her eyes but didn't meet Mel straight on. "Huh."

"Your mom thinks you're pretty angry about all this."

Katie shrugged her shoulders in response.

"You want to talk about it?"

"Not really."

"You want a drink?" Mel asked her. She wasn't used to not getting a response and quite frankly, it was annoying her.

Katie's eyes shot up, open wide. She couldn't tell if Mel was altogether serious, but it wouldn't have surprised her. Mel was always up to something and Katie was almost certain that she could even smell tequila on her.

"I'm not kidding, Kate. 'Cause if you want a drink, and I'm sure there's a part of you that does, well, let's just get it over with. Let's just march right out to the kitchen and pour you one right now. Quite frankly, I'd rather watch you drink it than leave and wonder about what you're going to do next. I'd rather you have it right here with your mother and me than sneak out of the house and go stand in the shadows over at the liquor store, waiting for someone to ask to buy you some beer."

Mel wasn't far off. The fact of the matter was that Katie did want a drink, preferably something that wouldn't sit well, like Jagermeister. But Katie hung her head and shook it quickly, a mix of embarrassment and shame washing over her.

"All right, then. Listen, I'm going to go. You can call me, just like you did. You can call me anytime you or your mom needs me over the next few days. I'll be down later in the week to check on Cara. And to check on you, too. But you can call me. It was the right thing to do."

Katie nodded and when she did, Melanie realized that tears had filled her eyes. Mel hoped she hadn't shamed Katie into feeling bad about wanting to drink, about coming clean with the fact that it was a weakness for her and that Melanie understood that weakness and how much, how easily, it could consume her. It hadn't been Mel's intention to embarrass her, only to give her an out. Who could blame the girl if she went off the wagon? Mel bet that Cara's glass was still sitting on the table, untouched. Who would blame Katie for one shot?

Mel knelt at the side of the bed and pulled Katie toward her. She was shocked at how thin Katie had gotten, how knobby her legs felt as if she was a tiny, undeveloped adolescent.

"Oh, Katie, sweetheart, come on now. We've had enough tears today."

Katie sniffled and sucked up the snot, wiping her nose with the back of her sweatshirt. She nodded at Mel, taking a giant gulp of air and trying to catch her breath. "I know. I know."

"This isn't your fault, you know. It's not your fault or your brothers' fault or Claire's. This has nothing to do with you. This is your dad's deal. When it comes right down to it, this is something your dad has to own up to."

"But why did he go, Mel? Why would he leave all of us? I just don't understand how he could do that. He's turned his back on all of us, Mel." She took a deep breath then, anger still sneaking in. "Bastard. God, he is such a *bastard*."

Ghosts filtered in and out of Mel's head, memories that haunted her, chasing her. She had sounded the same way once, so long ago. She had wondered the same things when her mother had taken off, and she was left to fend for herself. *How could her mother have done that to her?* She shook her head, chasing away the demons.

"I know, sugar, I know. There's a lot of it we won't understand right now. There's some of it we may never understand." Mel spoke from experience.

"It's just so unfair. What he's done is so unfair. And it sucks, Mel. It just sucks."

"Yes. Yes it is," Mel said, rubbing Katie's legs.

There was nothing else Mel could say to her, no magic answer that would end her suffering.

Mel sat close by her side for a few minutes, rubbing the back of her hand. "You and your mom are on your own tonight, okay? I called Mary Ann and asked her to keep the little guys. There's no reason for them to come home tonight. Let your mom catch her breath."

"I doubt it'll only take a night, Mel," Katie said, sounding very adult.

"I know; you're right. But she needs a night to get it out, at least the beginnings of it. When Claire and your brothers come home, she'll need to pack some of that away and be strong for them."

In the months that followed Jack's leaving, the thing Cara remembered feeling most was numb. It was as if someone had corseted her two sizes smaller, cinching her waist so tightly that the circulation in her arms had been cut off and she could barely move, hardly wriggle her fingers. She often found herself breathless and suffocating at the end of the day, panic setting in as if she'd been weighted down and had to remind herself how to breathe, slow and purposeful.

Ritual sustained her. School, birthday parties, playdates, soccer, baseball, ballet, homework, laundry. All the things she had done when Jack was there, his presence at the end of the day like an interruption.

The holidays lined themselves up one by one, each of them taunting her, heartily ridiculing her as they trounced by. Halloween with its memories of nights of trick-or-treating with the kids, Jack carrying one of the kids over his shoulder, sick from too much candy, too much excitement. Thanksgiving, with its built-in day of grace, that went on to span four days of family and merriment. Christmas with its glow, its warmth, an embrace all its own.

And finally, the New Year, the worst of them all. Jack's first real attempt at winning back his children, he took them skiing and Cara was left alone—really alone—for the first time. Without pause she took two Ambien at eight o'clock sharp and slept well into the Tournament of Roses parade midday on the first of January, waking to Melanie's shrill voice on her answering machine.

"Cara, you are scaring me now. Pick up the goddamn phone!"

"I'm here, Mel, I'm here," Cara said drowsily into the phone, peering across the empty bed to check the time on the alarm clock that still sat on Jack's bedside table. She hadn't altered a thing; hadn't moved a piece of furniture or changed a habit since Jack had left.

"It's the New Year. Get up and make something of it," Mel said to her.

Cara fell back on the pillow, her head still groggy from the drug. She closed her eyes on her room, on her life, hoping that when she opened them it would, in fact, feel like a New Year, like a new beginning.

Jack was gone. Mornings, Cara would wake and for a split second before the sun broke through the blinds, believe her life hadn't changed, that things had remained as they always had. But then she would roll to her side, reach next to her to find one of her sleeping children who'd snuck in sometime during the night, and everything would roll backward in time, backward to the day when Jack had packed his things and simply left.

She saw him often, actually. Stopping by to pick up the kids or collect the mail that hadn't been forwarded properly to his new address. He was cool and aloof, careful to keep his distance. They were polite to each other but short in their greetings. In the end there was nothing really to talk about, anyway.

Mel and Cara had known each other a long, long time, which wasn't to say that Mel was the best at handling Cara's particular flavor of depression. Like everything else she tackled, Melanie did it in the only way she knew how, her own. Mel pushed Cara, forcibly at first and with little regard for the years Jack and Cara had spent together. When Cara couldn't take Mel's brusque demeanor anymore, she'd call Leah. Leah was there when Cara needed to have a good cry, someone to tell her that, despite all the affairs he'd had, Jack had loved her and that, in some way, he always would. Leah listened to Cara's endless chatter of memories played over and over again like a broken record, letting her relive pieces of the good times she'd shared with Jack. Then she'd softly remind her of those times when things hadn't been so breezy, when isolation and rejection had been all Jack had given her, gently easing her into reality.

Paige brought casseroles. Lots and lots of casseroles. As if someone had died, they came rolling in one right after the other. Spaghetti. Chili. Some sort of hamburger-laden corn thing Cara had a recipe card for but hadn't made in years. Chicken and broccoli smothered in cheddar cheese and cooked until it was crisp. One Saturday morning Paige called and told Cara she was making a double batch of enchilada pie and asked if she could have back her oblong white 2½-quart Corning Ware dish, the one with the glass lid, so she could bring them dinner. In sweats and stockinged feet, Cara rummaged through her cabinets and found six casserole dishes she recognized as Paige's. She stacked them neatly for Paige's husband, Dennis, who was coming to claim them.

When Dennis greeted Cara at the door, wide with a smile, he held a plate with two dozen oatmeal chocolate chip cookies stacked on it.

"Dennis, tell her to stop. She's done too much already," Cara said to him at the door, not feeling the least bit self-conscious about how ragged she looked. Her unwashed hair was pulled up in a sloppy, stubby ponytail, her Friday makeup still crusted around her eyes, the mascara smeared in dark circles under her eyes.

"You know how she is, Cara, she loves to do this." A boyish grin spread over his face; his cheeks were freckled and sun-kissed. He maintained a genuine sense of love and warmth for his wife. "I'll bring the enchilada pie later this afternoon. Do you have plans or will you be around?"

"Dennis," Cara said, spreading her arms wide to the side, "you're looking at my plans."

Paige's casseroles came with cheery notes attached to them

written in perfectly printed penmanship on engraved cards with her initials:

> *I'm thinking of you, Cara.*
> *Let me know if there is anything I can do for you, Cara.*
> *You've got a friend, Cara, if you need one.*
> *Don't forget how much we all love you, Cara.*

"Can't she tell you're not eating them?" Mel asked one afternoon, grabbing a handful of the waist of Cara's jeans, bubbling in the back and cinched tightly with a black belt. "Look at you, Cara; you certainly haven't lost all this weight eating those Hamburger Helper noodle fiascos." Mel was right; Cara hadn't been eating them. Or much of anything, for that matter. She hadn't been this thin since before she'd had Katie. She was desperately in need of new clothes but had little desire to go shopping.

Cara shrugged her shoulders. "What difference does it make?"

"I just don't see what . . ." Mel started in again.

"It's what she does, okay?" Cara snapped. "You don't make casseroles, Mel. Hell, you don't even eat casseroles. But it's what Paige knows, it's what makes her feel like she's doing something to help."

Melanie settled onto one of the bar stools in Cara's kitchen and rolled her eyes. She dug out the March issue of *Cosmopolitan* from the pile of mail that sat on the granite countertop and began leafing through it, flipping the pages in rapid succession so that Cara knew she wasn't really reading anything.

"I'm sorry," Cara said, immediately feeling guilty. "Look, Mel. I'd haul off and throw you through the front of Jack's car window if I had the chance because I know you'd have the biggest impact. I know you'd shatter the glass from here to the end of the Earth. Leah's no good for that. Leah's good for a long talk and a good cry. And Paige? Well, Paige is good for casseroles, okay?"

"I just don't see the point, Cara. That's all I'm saying. I just don't see the point."

"That's because you don't need any casseroles in your life, Mel. You are 100 percent casserole free."

"What's that supposed to mean?" Mel asked her, knowing full well what Cara meant.

"It means that you're a survivor, Mel. You can pick up and move on, unlike the rest of us who need to sit and think on it for a while, that's all. There's nothing wrong with that, Mel; nothing at all. But the rest of us need a little time, you know. The rest of us occasionally need to sit and stew over a good, hearty, home-made casserole."

Mel shook her head and rolled her eyes, again flipping the pages of the magazine. Under her breath, Cara heard her say, "He cheated on you, Cara. How long do you need to stew on it?"

"What?" Cara jerked her head around. *"What did you say?"*

"I said, 'He cheated on you.' That's it, plain and simple."

"I know what he did, Melanie. Who do you think has been living with it for all these years? Who do you think has spent the better part of their entire marriage—eighteen years—trying to figure out what part of her wasn't good enough, wasn't sexy enough, wasn't whatever enough to keep her husband interested? Who, Mel? Who? Newsflash: it wasn't you. So I'll beg your pardon if I spend a little time wallowing in the good support of my friends who take the time to do something nice for me. I'll beg your pardon if it feels good to have someone bring me over a Crock-Pot full of stew."

2

"Shit. Who schedules their annual exam on Valentine's Day?" Cara moaned. She searched her oversized bag for her car keys; she'd had them in her hand only moments earlier and now she was late.

"Someone who clearly doesn't stand a chance of getting laid," Leah answered, affectionately. "Don't feel too sorry for yourself. I'm still married and it's not like I have any hot plans, either. No knight in shining armor at my door. No four-star restaurant reservation. Andrew is somewhere between here and New York. It's not like he'll be home before midnight, anyway. And I'm sick of sitting here waiting for the florist delivery truck to pull up with my dozen roses. As if *that's* likely to happen."

Cara checked in at the front desk of her OB/GYN with a curt smile from the receptionist who begged her insurance copayment before dismissing her. The chairs were hard-backed, uncomfortable and not made for waiting. There were two women ahead of her in the waiting room, both pregnant, one so far along that she looked like she might be experiencing the early stages of labor. She sat with her feet braced against the small coffee table, one hand absentmindedly rubbing the swollen basketball in front of her. The other woman had three small children in tow, one of whom she was bouncing wildly on her knee while she tried to read to the other two. The baby hiccupped, belched and sprayed a stream of cream-colored spit-up down the front of his overalls and onto the woman's jeans. Cara shuddered, remembering the day the OB had announced she was pregnant with Claire, her fourth, only a few months after she'd given birth to Luke.

From the inner office the door to the waiting room opened abruptly, slamming against the back wall.

"Will the first week in April work for your next appointment?" the receptionist asked the woman who had bolted through and stood teetering on stilettos.

"Yes, that should be fine," the voice said and Cara froze from behind her magazine.

She knew that voice; had committed its off-key pitch, its slight twang to memory. Panic churned her stomach over on itself and rendered her paralyzed.

"They'll do an ultrasound at that appointment," the nurse said cheerfully. "You'll be able to find out the sex of the baby, if you want to know."

Cara's legs and arms went numb, her stomach lurched, and perspiration began to dampen her pits. Her mouth was instantly dry. *No, impossible. It's impossible to think God could be this cruel.* The woman made a note in the Day-Timer she stuffed back into her petite handbag and then zipped it shut in one simple motion before she turned to leave the office, her lips pursed into a thin, flat line. She was even thinner than Cara remembered, taller and in better shape—if that was possible—but the color in her face was washed out as if she'd been spooked good. She did not appear to be pregnant, not a bulge or a bump or anything that would indicate she was, in fact, carrying a child.

For a second Cara thought she was free, still propped squarely behind the magazine, her fingers clamped shut on the pages so that the newsprint beneath her fingers smeared across her skin.

"Cara Clancy?"

She heard someone call her name, distant, but in a clipped tone that meant business. The nurse stood in the doorway, dressed in green scrubs and holding a thick, beaten-up folder Cara knew was her chart. She smiled at Cara through wire-rimmed glasses, tapping her pen on the chart, and held open the door with her back until Cara felt the weight of the whole room staring at her, waiting for her to get up. Her legs were impossibly gel-like and she couldn't find the floor beneath her feet until it rose up to meet her, spinning. Somehow she struggled to stand, vertical.

Barbie stopped at the exit, rigid, car keys in hand, cell phone propped under her chin, but she never turned, never looked back. She was frozen, and for a split second, Cara almost felt sorry for her. Almost. Then she clip-clopped out of the door and down the hall. From behind, her perfect size 2 ass appeared perky, as if she was skipping.

In the exam room Cara barely heard the nurse's questions: *"First date of your last period? Any changes in your diet? Any medications? Still taking the same birth control? Will you need a refill today?"*

"Huh?"

"Are you okay, Mrs. Clancy?" the nurse asked her.

"Um, yes. Think so."

"Okay, then, everything off, gown ties in the front. The doctor will be in to see you in a few minutes."

The nurse dropped Cara's chart into the clear plastic tray bolted to the front of the examining room door and closed the door behind her, leaving Cara alone in the room, the edge of her butt suspended on the cold metal examining table. Outside a barren tree branch rocked gently in the afternoon, the bare tips of the brown limbs scratching against the window. Cara watched it sway and bounce against the tinted glass. There was a sharp ringing in her ears that she couldn't control, a constant pitch she could neither command nor dismiss. It continued while she began to unzip one boot, then the other, kicking them under the leather side chair in the corner of the room.

Barbie. In *her* doctor's office. On the same day she was due to see him. Barbie. Perfect and petite. And *pregnant*. Jack had been gone only a few months, hardly long enough for Cara to get used to sleeping alone permanently. She still had to remind herself he wouldn't be coming home; setting a place for him at the table, then clearing it away before one of the kids could come in and ask her who was coming over. The house was still trapped with his things—shoes, clothes, books, movies, pieces of artwork they had collected together, pictures from places they'd visited together or as a family. She'd barely rid the bedding of his scent, barely packed away his CDs. And now Barbie. Here. In her doctor's office.

Cara was only half-undressed. She stood in her bra and thick black knit stockings, folding her skirt with precision, when Dr. Bremmer knocked three shorts raps and opened the door before she had a chance to answer. Cara turned abruptly, caught like a stripper when the lights go on. He expected her to be dressed in the white paper gown and seated in her usual spot on the examining table, and was clearly stunned when Cara whipped around and held her skirt to shield her body like a junior high school girl changing in the locker room for the first time. She blushed fiercely.

"Oh, Cara, I'm so sorry, I thought you would have been undressed by now. I'll give you a few minutes." He eyed her up and down before looking away, pretending instead to focus on the chart he was holding in his hand.

She felt the blood rush to her cheeks. "Okay," Cara said, because she could think of nothing else, and being caught in the process of undressing was nearly as unnerving as having intercourse for the first time. When he backed out and closed the door gently, Cara ripped off her stockings, unhooked her bra, and dove into the paper gown in less than half a minute. She positioned herself on the end of the table and waited, her body convulsing in waves from the frigid temperature in the room. It was twenty more minutes before the doctor dared knock again, and waited this time before Cara was forced to manage, "Come in!" in an audible pitch from inside the room.

He apologized again quickly, "Sorry about that . . ."

"No worries," she answered, watching him sidle up to the

counter and rest half a butt cheek on the silver metal rolling stool, avoiding her eyes.

"How many times have I told you to get a woman gynecologist, Cara, how many times?" Cara could hear Mel's shrill voice playing in her head. She'd been after her for years to switch.

"So, let's see. Mmmm-hmmm, looks like you've lost some weight, Cara," he said to her in an accusatory and not-so-friendly tone, peering over the top of his rimmed glasses. "Nearly twenty-five pounds, that's quite a bit." He eyed her again and she pulled the gown around her neatly, covering herself.

"Not on purpose, exactly."

"No?" he asked, barely looking up from the scribbles on her chart. "Everything okay?"

"Separation."

"Oh. I'm sorry to hear that. Recently?"

"Been about six months."

"Divorce?"

Cara swallowed hard at the sound of the word, so final and complete, so empty and hollow. She pushed back the lump in her throat, thinking about Barbie, about losing Jack to the woman teetering on three-inch heels in the waiting room, the size 2 who had taken her husband away. "Looking that way."

"Are you seeing anyone?" he asked, looking up at her for the first time now, piercing brown eyes focused on hers.

She shrank under his question, uneasy. "Um, no, not yet. I, um, I really don't think I'm ready for that."

"No, no." He smiled. "I meant, are you seeing someone to talk about what you're going through? A therapist, maybe? Someone who could hear you out?"

"Oh. Um, no, I hadn't really considered it."

"You've got to go in and see someone, Cara, get this shit out. Go talk to someone. Trust me; it'll do you a world of good." Mel's voice again. She'd be smug with credit.

"You might."

"Okay."

"How're the cycles? Still having all the irregularities?"

He began to pull out the stirrups, the shiny metal covered in fuzzy socks so that they almost look inviting, and guided her back, positioning a pillow under her head and instructing her to scoot as far toward the end of the table as she could. Cara stared at the dotted ceiling tiles and listened to him rummage around on the table of gynecological utensils, tongs and pokers that reminded her of something you'd use to crack crab.

"No big changes there," she said, ready for the battery of questions she knew would follow.

"Heavy bleeding?"

"Yes."

"Long cycles?"

"Yes."

"Heavy cramping? Clotting?"

"Mmm-hmmm." Cara clasped her hands, laced her fingers and laid them over her stomach, cringing as he started to dig around.

When he was done, he pushed the paper that covered her waist down between her legs and told her to sit up and push back toward the middle of the table, which she did in one swift move. He peeled off the latex gloves from his hands, one, then the other, dropped them into the stainless waste pail in the corner and let the lid slam closed. Cara waited, her legs hanging off the end of the table.

"Here," he said, ripping off the top sheet on his prescription pad. Cara studied his slanted, illegible writing. "I know it's probably the last thing you're thinking of right now, but stay on the pill, okay? You never know what might happen. And I'd hate for you to find yourself unprepared." He raised his eyebrows and winked at her before he clicked off the pen, stowing it in the front pocket of his white lab coat.

She was beyond humiliated.

"Besides, I still think it's helping with your cycles, at least a little bit. And I doubt you're ready to talk about a hysterectomy at this point in your life."

Cara swallowed hard and shook her head. "No, not yet," she answered him, and blushed even deeper, wrapping her arms around her waist and pulling the paper gown closer to her body. Her legs swung wildly from the table.

He closed the chart and tucked it under his right arm, ready to leave the room. "Look, Cara," he said to her, placing a hand on her knee. "I see this kind of thing all the time. It'll get better. You're young, well, look at you, you've practically got a whole new life ahead of you."

When he opened the door to go, Cara cleared her throat and clenched her butt cheeks together tight and figured she had nothing to lose. She wanted to grill him about Barbie; she wanted to know everything about her, anything that he was willing to share. "Dr. Bremmer?" she asked, her voice hovering.

He turned and looked at her squarely, waiting on her question.

"The woman who was in before me? Your last patient? Has she been coming here long?" Cara steadied her voice, trying instead for confidence.

"I, I'm sorry, but . . ." he trailed off and confusion clouded his eyes. A deep crease formed in his forehead as if he was trying to remember the last woman who had come through. He ran his forefinger and his thumb over the bridge of his nose, pinching it slightly.

"The blonde woman, late twenties? I, I think she may have been pregnant, but very early on. She was leaving as I was coming in."

"I'm sorry, Cara, but I can't discuss another patient with you. You know that. Each patient's history is highly confidential." He frowned at her, disappointed, before saying, "I'm sure you can understand."

"Oh, right. Of course." Cara recovered. She was prickly from the embarrassment that rushed over her. "I . . . just thought I knew her from somewhere, that's all." She shrank back against the table, her shoulders sagging under the weight of his admonishment.

He smiled weakly at her before leaving the examining room, and when he closed the door he did so firmly, indicating he meant business.

Was it possible that Jack had sent Barbie to Cara's doctor? No, that was giving Jack far too much credit. Jack would never have remembered the name of Cara's gynecologist, the man who had delivered all four of their children. Surely, it wasn't Jack, but what possible other explanation could it have been? Coincidence? Imagine the odds; too great.

Cara fiddled with the keys in the ignition and turned the engine over just as there was a tapping on the passenger window, which scared her nearly senseless. Barbie peered at her through the tinted glass, sunglasses perched on top of her head. There was mascara smudged under her eyes and in the corners, and her face was blotchy; she'd been crying.

"Can I come in?" she mouthed through the cracked window, as if she was buying movie tickets at a booth. She pointed to the empty passenger seat next to Cara. "Just for a minute."

Go away, go away. Cara stared at her, dazed.

"Pleeeease, Cara. This isn't easy."

She mispronounced Cara's name, saying it 'Caaara,' and to Cara the sound was worse than nails on a chalkboard. She wondered if Barbie had never heard her name before. Was she simply "Jack's wife" to her? Had Jack never used her first name when referring to the woman he had been married to for so many years, the woman who had given him four children and years of clean clothes, cooked meals? For Christ sake, she couldn't count on Jack for anything. Would it have been too much for him to make sure his lover knew how to pronounce his wife's name?

"It's Car-a," Cara said to her, plainly, definitively, pronouncing her name slowly.

"Hmmm?" Barbie put an ear to the window opened only a fraction. "I'm sorry; it's hard to hear you out here with all the noise." She waved her hands at the expressway just outside of the parking lot where the midafternoon traffic had picked up. A slow line of cars crept by, shuffling through the timed lights. Cara imagined the men and women on their way home to celebrate Valentine's Day together, dinner reservations in hand.

Reluctantly Cara pressed the electronic lock on the armrest. The lock released and Barbie took the opportunity, quick as she could, to pull open the door. She was careful not to bump it against the white pickup parked in the next spot and shimmied into the seat, pulling the door closed behind her, bringing all of her perfumey self with her. Cara recognized the scent; she'd picked it up on Jack's shirts many times before. It was strong and overpowering and caused Cara to crack open the window on her side of the car.

"Hi, Caaara," she said again, her voice an annoying and uncontrollable high pitch, squeaky.

"It's Car-a," Cara repeated, this time with emphasis, though Barbie stared at her, clueless. "My name. It's pronounced Car-a. Like an automobile. Car, then a. Car-a."

"Oh."

"I guess I thought you'd have known that."

"I'm sorry."

"Is there something you wanted?" Cara asked, looking at her watch. "Because if not, I really should be . . ."

"Oh, oh right." Barbie came alive. "Yes, yes, actually there is." She paused and smiled; teeth and gums that gleamed and positively glowed, they were so white.

Her lips rolled back and her mouth was big, not horsey, exactly, but big. Cara thought she must give an awesome blow job; Jack would love that.

"Imagine the coincidence of ending up in the same doctor's office, Car-a," Barbie said awkwardly, carefully, slowly working to ensure she got Cara's name correct this time. "I just can't believe it." She raised a hand to her throat and played with an oversized aquamarine that sat at her collarbone. She was fidgety and nervous.

"Completely ironic," Cara said to her, deadpan, and watched Barbie's face cloud up before she realized Barbie didn't understand what she meant. She found it implausible, almost, that Jack would have migrated to this woman, gone willingly and anxiously to her side, to her bed. It confirmed her suspicion almost immediately of a radical midlife crisis.

"Well, I was wondering if, well . . ." Barbie shifted in her seat, visibly uncomfortable, and then stopped. She bit on her bottom lip, drawing the slightest bit of blood, then subconsciously dabbing at it with her pinkie finger before she went on. "Well—"

"I'm sorry, Barbie," Cara interrupted her suddenly, a little more loudly than she intended to be, "but I really need to get going. Is there something that we needed to talk about?" Cara waited; calm spread across her face. Much as she wanted Barbie to leave, she was enjoying watching her squirm.

"Yes, well, Cara, I was just wondering if, I mean, I'm sure that you must have heard the receptionist in the waiting room. I didn't realize you were there, you see. You have to understand that, I never even saw you sitting there until that nurse called your name and then I was just so taken aback . . ." The words poured out of her in a purr, a confession of sorts.

Before Cara could get a word in, Barbie continued. "I mean, I was really, really surprised to see you there, you know? You just can't imagine how uncomfortable that was for me." Barbie paused and Cara guessed she was waiting for an apology.

"Actually, I suppose I have some sort of understanding of how that must have been for you," Cara said and let the slightest snarl unfurl itself from her upper lip. Barbie didn't seem to notice because she carried on.

"Well," she said with a harrumph, "I suppose you must have heard what that receptionist said to me, about the *ul-tra-sound* and all." She looked perplexed, annoyed, as if it had been Cara's fault for eavesdropping in the first place.

Cara didn't want to admit what she'd heard; she would have given anything to avoid the conversation altogether. There was little space in the front of Cara's van, precious little distance to look away and concentrate on something, anything, else. But Barbie was persistent, her eyes studying Cara's face so intently that Cara couldn't break away to stare down at the cuticle she'd found a way to start picking. She shook her head slowly, her mouth gaping just slightly and a light, "Mmm-hmmm . . ." escaped and ran free within the confines of the van.

"Well, that's great," Barbie whined, as if she believed Cara had gone searching, snooping, for this particular bit of knowledge. "Just great." She sighed long.

"I'm sorry," Cara muttered, because for the first time, she was. She really didn't want to know any of this. She would have given anything to have disappeared, to drive off and never speak of this again.

"Well," Barbie started again. "I don't suppose there's anything I can do about that now. But, Car-a"—she broke up Cara's name into two purposeful syllables, each with their own equal emphasis—"I guess I need to ask you a favor. And I don't suppose you have any reason to do M-E a favor, but I'll ask you anyway, because I suppose maybe, just maybe, well, you being a woman and all, just maybe you'll understand what it is that I need you to do, what is so very important and all . . ."

Jesus Christ, Cara thought, *Claire speaks the English language more proficiently than this woman.* She stared openly at Barbie, gaping, waiting.

"It's just that, well, Jack doesn't *exactly* know that I'm pregnant. I haven't told him yet. And so you can imagine how embarrassing it would be if, well, if he heard it from his ex-wife and all. So, again, I'm just wondering if you could do me this itsy-bitsy, teeny-weeny little favor and not mention this if you happen to be talking to him. It'd be best, actually, if you just didn't mention that we ran into each other at all, if you know what I mean."

"Wife."

"Excuse me?" Barbie asked in her perfect high pitch, and cleared her throat with a twitter that sounded like something that might have escaped from a small bird.

"Wife," Cara said again, more clearly and pronounced this time. "You said, '*ex*-wife.' I'm still Jack's *wife*," she corrected Barbie, her arms clasped tightly over her chest. Cara sat up a little straighter, a little taller in her seat, and faced her body toward Barbie head-on. "We aren't divorced yet."

A nervous gasp escaped Barbie's mouth in a quick little huff, a

sigh of sorts. "Oh, of course, um, 'WIFE,' " she said slowly, cor-
recting herself. "Just a formality, of course."

"No. Just a fact, actually."

Barbie's face grew scarlet, hot and flushed with hives that
started at the base of her neck and spread in giant blotches as if
she had swallowed something she was desperately allergic to.
"Of course," she said, because she had no choice but to admit the
truth. Jack and Cara were not yet divorced.

"Don't worry, Barbie." Cara reset her body parallel to the
wheel and fiddled again with the keys. She turned the engine
over and the van came to life, idling in place for a minute. "Your
secret's safe with me." She gripped the wheel tightly, ready to
back out of the space, and turned her head to dismiss the woman,
but Barbie was immovable, simply wouldn't budge. She caught
her reflection in the vanity mirror on the back of the visor, fid-
dling with her hair so that it was just so.

"Oh, I just knew you would understand, Cara." She mispronounced Cara's name again. "I just knew the minute I walked
out of that doctor's office and back down the hall. I said to myself,
'Oh, no, she wouldn't be *that* kind of woman. Certainly she'll understand what I need her to do. I'll just have a little talk with
her.' I knew it was a good idea to wait here for you so we could
have this little chat."

Cara wasn't sure who that *kind of woman* was. She laid her head
down on the steering wheel, melted her chest right into the oversized rim and sighed, watching Barbie as if she were a caricature.
She smiled weakly at Barbie and willed her to vacate the front
seat of her car. *Please, oh, please, oh, please . . . Leave this car N-O-W.*

"Okay." Barbie's breasts heaved a long sigh and relief flooded
her face. She looked for a minute as if she might settle in. "*Whew,*
well I just feel so much better about all of this." Her gummy,
toothy smile was wide. Cara studied the fillings that lined Barbie's back teeth; deep silver crosses that cut through her back
molars.

Barbie clasped her hands together in a cheerleading clap, a
deep, full echo that hung in the air. "Okay, well, I suppose I

should go now, then. Yes, that's probably a good idea." As careful as she was in getting in the car, she was equally haphazard in getting out, and banged the door wide against the truck still parked next to Cara's car. Cara leaned over to inspect the damage and spied a black crease in the valley of a small dent that Barbie had left in the door of the truck.

"Oh, sorry about that."

Cara nodded her head, dismissing it immediately. She was done with the small talk, not interested in spending another minute with her. She put the car in REVERSE before Barbie could get the door closed.

Barbie squinted her eyes, leaning back into the front of her van. "Oh, and Cara?" she asked, a high pitch rising again in her voice.

"Huh?"

"Have you lost some weight? You look really fabulous. Almost skinny." She smiled at her then while Cara put the car in DRIVE and sped away.

3

It was too good to keep, of course.

"Okay, so who do you think is pregnant?" Cara asked her friends.

Leah and Paige turned to stare, full gape, at Mel, accusingly.

"Good God, no. You have got to be kidding. I've already made that mistake. Holy Christ, you two, don't curse me." Mel looked positively ill.

This made Cara laugh; giddy. She swung her legs back and forth on the bar stool and ran her finger over the salt on the rim of her margarita glass. She had drained two already and the tequila and Grand Marnier hummed softly in her head, keeping time with the music playing on the bar's speakers. She hadn't had this much fun getting drunk in a long time.

"Who?" they asked in unison, their eyes dancing. They had settled in, each on her own bar stool. Around them the bar buzzed, men in suits done for the weekend.

Cara looked into the face of each of her friends, savoring the anticipation. She almost didn't want to tell them, longing to keep such a luscious secret to herself as she had the entire week. It had taken her a day and a night to get used to the idea, but when she did, she relished it, amused by the fact that Jack would be saddled with a baby—clearly not in his plan when he packed his bags and headed off to silicone island.

"Barbara Jean."

Paige looked positively pained; Leah stunned, her mouth hanging open in mock horror. Only Mel whooped it up, rubbing her hands together and throwing her head back. Clearly the news had made her day.

"You have got to be kidding?" Mel laughed openly, clenching her fists together in victory. "Perfect. Just absolutely perfect. God is a woman; this is proof." Mel's emerald eyes twinkled, the long lashes blinking rapidly in succession as if she was flirting with someone.

"Mel," Paige nudged her. "Have a little decorum. It's no reason to throw a party." She reached across the round terra-cotta-tiled bar table and took Cara's hands, holding them tightly. Paige's fingers were long, delicate, and her hands were warm. Genuine concern washed over her face and her forehead crinkled at the temples. "Cara, I'm so sorry. Are you okay? My God, what in the world did Jack have to say for himself? He only just moved out."

A wicked smile formed across Cara's lips. "Actually, Paige, Jack wasn't the one to tell me. And you can't tell anyone else, for that matter." She wagged her finger at each of them, warning.

"Then who?" Leah looked at her, confusion washing over her round face. "Did one of the kids tell you? Katie?"

"No. I ran into Barbie. At my annual, if you can believe the chances in that. What do you think, couple hundred gynecologists in all of the Bay Area, and I wind up at the same doctor, at the same time, in the same office, as the girlfriend of my ex-husband. Oh, no wait; I beg your pardon. We're still married, right?" Cara looked to Mel for confirmation.

Mel shrugged her shoulders, nodded her head and quietly muttered, "Technically, yes . . ." under her breath. "Oh, Cara," she said and rubbed her hands together again, smiling broadly. "Honestly. You have got to be kidding me."

"Nope."

"So, what? How far along? Could you tell? What did she say when she saw you?"

Cara recounted the story, the fact that Barbie's perfume still clung to the fabric in her van despite a second trip to the car wash where they doused her carpets and upholstery with jasmine air freshener. She had sulked on the details for two days, dour and morose and mourning, before she found the courage to shrug off the way Barbie had made her feel. Once she did, it was as if she had been freed, a first tiny baby step in reclaiming her independence. She wondered if Barbie had come clean with the news, if she had told Jack yet, and if so, what his reaction had been. He had never wanted four children, never mind five. He would have been perfectly content to stop after Katie. So Cara had no doubt that it would be more than just a bit of a shock for him. She wagered that he might have even been angry, pissed. Maybe even enough to pack his bags and move home. Maybe.

"What do you think they'll do, Cara?" Sitting across the table studying Paige's deep blue doelike eyes, Cara had no doubt that Paige was already considering the future of this unborn child, when she said, "Your poor kids, Cara. I'm so sorry they'll have to go through this."

Cara considered Paige's comment carefully, imagining the reaction from each of her kids. Would Katie be angrier and come out swinging? Would Claire be happy at the thought of a real, live baby doll to play with? Would the boys slink further into despair, pull back and cower, feeling unloved, unwanted?

"I have no idea what they're going to do. I can't imagine a baby was in Jack's plans when he moved out. He sort of had that taken care of at his previous residence. But I can assure you of one thing, Paige: I'm not the one who's going to tell the kids. Not this time. I've done that. He can explain his way out of this one."

When Jack finally called, Cara was fighting evening traffic, weaving her way through a particularly hilly area not far from the home Jack still paid the mortgage for, and the cellular reception wasn't good. The phone line cut in and out, but despite the static

Cara could make out the high pitch in his voice, the abandon-ment to joy.

"Cara? How are you?" he boomed.

"Fine, Jack. And you?"

"Good, good. I'm great, actually. Well, Barbie said she ran into you a couple of weeks ago." His words came quickly, as if he was bursting with a great, giant secret he couldn't contain.

"Oh. Right, yeah." Cara was careful not to let on too much, still unsure of what he knew.

"Well, c'mon Cara, what do you think?"

She considered her answer; baiting him, wondering how much he really knew. "What do I think about . . . ?"

He never let her finish. "It's crazy, isn't it? A new baby. I mean absolutely insane. Maybe the most out-of-this-world thing I've ever done, you know? But here's the thing, Cara. I really think I can do this *this* time. I mean I know I wasn't always there for you and the kids, but I think I can be different about it this time around. The thing is, I think I might be really great at it."

Anger flooded Cara's every nerve, the blood pulsing through-out her brain. Cara let the silence burn its way into the receiver until Jack was forced to ask, "Cara? Are you still there? Can you hear me?"

"Yeah," she answered him, flatly, her voice dead.

"Um, well," Jack sensed the change in her voice, deflated. "Well, what do you think? I mean isn't it just crazy?"

He laughed then, sending a shiver down her spine. *Was he seri-ous?*

Silence.

"I really wanted to share this with you, Cara. You know, I thought maybe you would understand that this was just meant to happen. I mean, after all, why else, why now? Why would some-thing this crazy come along if it just wasn't meant to happen that way?"

Silence.

"Cara?"

Silence. Was he looking for her approval?

"Cara? Can you hear me? Cara?"

"Yeah, Jack. I can hear you."

"Well, isn't it great? A father, all over again."

"Again?"

"Yeah. Again."

The silence did little to rattle him, let alone break him. Cara counted slowly, holding her breath, careful not to explode.

"I didn't know you were done being one."

"Huh?"

"A father. I didn't know you were done being one. You know, in time to start all over again." In the dead air between them, Cara could make out the sports report on his radio, the college basketball scores rattling off one by one.

"Goddammit, Cara, you know that's not what I meant," he said, finally, frustration seeping into his tone.

"What did you mean then, Jack? 'Cause, correct me if I'm wrong, but I seem to remember four kids you aren't done with yet. Or have you forgotten?"

Cara knew what she was doing wasn't fair. Since he'd moved out, Jack had not been a bad father, not by a long shot. He'd kept his end of the bargain, and been as much of a father—maybe even more—than he was when he was living in the same house with them. But it was all Cara had so she used it. Wedging this new child between the two of them bought Cara little; wedging it between him and his kids filled Jack with contempt. Cara figured he'd hate her for it later but she didn't much care.

"I'd have thought you'd be happy that I was moving on, Cara. You always struck me as a woman who could see through to find the bright spot in something."

"Is the sun shining, Jack?"

"I thought so."

"Oh."

"Well, anyway, I just wanted you to know."

"I did know, remember? Surely Barbie told you about our little chance meeting? Our little talk?"

"Uh . . ." He seemed perplexed, confused.

"The doctor. Imagine how much fun that must have been."

"Right."

"So . . ." She waited for him to offer an apology. She thought, perhaps, that was the least he could do.

"So?"

At a stoplight she pinched the bridge of her nose, closing her eyes and breathing deeply. Was it possible that he'd lost his mind and all of his senses with it? "Will you be telling the kids soon?"

"Oh, right. I guess so. Soon enough, anyway. I'll let you know when."

"You do that."

"Bye, Cara."

"See you, Jack."

4

Katie was late. Katie was nearly always late, lumbering down the stairs with her backpack slung over one shoulder and her headphones hanging from her ears into an iPod buried somewhere inside her Hollister sweatshirt. Cara laid on the horn loudly, waiting for her daughter to appear through the garage door. When Katie finally arrived, Cara had already backed out of the garage, left the car idling and was stomping her way back into the house. Cara tapped her watch pointedly and threw Katie a look, which her daughter promptly ignored.

Cara was used to the constant banter; the pitch of four voices, each trying to outdo the other with a concern that they thought required Cara's immediate attention. Katie sat in the front seat, slumped low as if she could barely tolerate being seen with her mother, never mind her little brothers and sister. And in a van. *A van.* It was so uncool.

"So," Cara said, interrupting the chaos, "how was the weekend with your dad?"

"Lame."

"Boring."

"I made cookies with Barbie, but she threw up twice when we were making the batter. She said it has something to do with the raw eggs making her sick." From the backseat Claire offered exquisite detail, a blow-by-blow description of Barbie's current condition.

Cara knew that Jack had broken the news to the kids; their reaction had been resounding juvenile disgust, which Cara secretly cheered. Only Claire had shown a remote bit of interest in a new sibling, and Cara had a sneaking suspicion that would pass once the new arrival made his or her presence known.

"Yeah, Claire got to make cookies. The rest of us spent most of Saturday hauling crap out of the house and cleaning the garage to make room for *the baby*," Will offered.

Cara raised an eyebrow at her eldest son. "Crap?"

"Sorry. Garbage. You know, Barbie's stuff. And, man, Mom, she's got enough of it to fill an entire dump. We should know; we took three loads."

"How 'bout you, Katie?"

Katie shrugged her shoulders and hid behind the thick binder she held in front of her chest.

Cara waited to see if Katie would continue on her own without any prodding, but her older daughter remained silent, brooding. She circled the parking lot at the elementary school and put the van in PARK. On cue, her three youngest children unbuckled and collected their things, scampering out of the van and into the fray of the schoolyard.

"Bye," Cara called and they waved her off, Claire stopping to blow her a kiss before skipping off to find her friends.

"Was it that bad, honey?" Cara asked her after they had pulled out of the parking lot and the van grew quiet.

Katie shrugged her shoulders again and stared out the window. "It was like every other weekend there. Dad gushing all over Barbie and pretending like everything is normal; Barbie acting like we're one big, happy family, like she's actually interested in what's going on in our lives. It's totally lame, Mom."

Cara took a deep breath. It had been like this for a while now, Cara taking stock of the time the kids spent with Jack as if she was tallying up the war wounds she would have to deal with later. Katie's scars were particularly visible from the explosion.

"Once that baby comes I doubt he'll have time for us any-more, anyway. His *old* family."

"What do you think, Kitten? A new baby? Maybe it won't be so bad." Cara tried to sound upbeat, just to see if she could en-gage her daughter. Maybe Jack's new baby was something they could share, if only to dismiss it as a bad idea.

"Oh, c'mon, Mom, it's disgusting. Dad's way too old to have a *baby*. God, he could practically be a grandfather. I don't know what he thinks he's trying to prove. He barely sees the four kids he's got. Not that I need to spend any more time with him than you already make me." Katie's dark eyes were circled in too much eyeliner, her mascara thick and chunky. She was hard, tough-skinned, which was a good thing. If she risked crying, she'd have been one black mess.

"I don't *make* you spend time with him, Katie. He's your dad. You can let him know that you'd rather stay home than spend time with him and Barbie. That's your choice."

"Right, Mom. Like I actually have any choice in any of this," Katie said, and opened the door when they pulled up to the high school. Kids in low-slung jeans and oversized sweatshirts swarmed the parking lot, dashing around the van. Katie zipped up her pull-over and grabbed her backpack, slinging it over her right shoul-der. She slammed the door hard and never looked back at Cara.

Cara hadn't watched her kids so closely since they were in-fants, when nearly every move they made left her paranoid, afraid that they might take a tenuous step and fall the wrong way, crashing into the corner of a coffee table or the fireplace hearth. Now she was not only protective but possessive. Part of her rel-ished the fact that Katie wanted nothing to do with her father, that her boys found themselves bored spending an entire after-noon cleaning out Jack's girlfriend's garage. Their weekends in purgatory became a source of entertainment for her. Still, even after all Jack had put her through, put all of them through, she couldn't bear the thought that his own children would want noth-ing to do with him.

The boys had lost the sweet part of themselves, the part she'd always loved most about both of them. Avid sports fans, tough and tumble, true boys through and through, they'd always had a soft side, a gentle nature that made them special in Cara's eyes. But lately, that part had simply disappeared, replaced in Will with a sarcastic, snippy attitude and a mouth to match. Superseded in Luke by a lackluster desire to do much of anything. Just last evening she'd pinned Will down, forcing a thin line of liquid soap over his tongue in response to his off-handed comment to Claire.

"You little shit," he'd exclaimed confidently, standing over her with his fist raised in the air as if it might come crashing down under her eye or across her chin at any moment. Sure, she'd pulled the bottom card from the house he'd been building, practically a fortress in the making, and sent the entire castle folding in upon itself. But that gave him no good reason, certainly no authority, to threaten his little sister, half his size. She stood boldly in his shadow, her eyes glaring back until she couldn't stand it anymore and she crumbled herself, dissolving into tears. Will had always been her prince, her hero. Never had he taken such a tone with her.

Cara didn't think he'd really strike her, not really. But for a split second she wasn't so sure, and perhaps that's what frightened her the most.

"William," Cara whispered harshly. She hadn't raised her voice, she hadn't needed to. He unclenched his fist, dropping his arm to his side, but he continued to stare her down, his top lip trembling in anger. "I think you owe Claire an apology."

"Sorry," he muttered, his shoulders still stiff, his body rigid.

"Oh, Will, me, too," Claire wailed and threw herself at him, wrapping her tiny arms around his waist, wanting all at once to be forgiven for the mean prank she had pulled. She hadn't really meant to do such harm; she hadn't realized the impact that removing one small piece of the base would have on the entire structure.

Will pushed her off, unwrapping her arms from his waist and stepping back from the table. And Cara had moved in, a translucent dab of liquid soap on the end of her index finger. She ran it across his lips and when he opened his mouth to spit it out, forced her way to find the tip of his tongue.

He pushed past her, reaching the sink and spitting over and over again, saliva dribbling down his chin. "God, Mom," he choked out, coughing and wiping his mouth with the back of his sleeve. "Geez, sorry. I didn't mean to say it."

Cara stared at him, guilt washing over her as it had the first time she'd used the same variety of punishment years earlier when Will had come home from school exposed to an entire new dictionary of expletives. She gripped the back of the chair and swallowed back her disgrace, praying to stay strong. Since Jack had left, discipline had taken on a whole new meaning for her; she was playing both roles.

"I won't have you using language like that. Not in this house." She worked to steady her voice. "And keep your hands off your sister, too. Do you hear me? Keep your hands to yourself, Will."

Will rinsed his mouth for the second or third time. When he was finished he threw the kitchen towel across the countertop, glaring at his mother, and stomped out of the kitchen without another word.

But for all his bravado, it wasn't Will that Cara was most concerned with; it was Katie.

Katie had always been Jack's favorite. Oh, sure, they weren't supposed to have favorites; no one was. But it didn't take much to detect Jack's preference for his eldest daughter, his selective nature when it came to just about anything Katie was involved with. Jack had always been over-the-top proud. He delighted in her successes; he mourned with her when she failed, and he had always been there to pick her up and brush her off. Always, that is, until now.

No doubt, Jack had cheated on Cara. But the thing she feared even more was the way he had deceived Katie. She was their time bomb, set to go off at any moment.

* * *

Katie had started drinking a year or so earlier. It hadn't started particularly slowly; she hadn't worked her way into it. Katie had simply poured her first drink—a tall Grey Goose on the rocks from her father's bar—and never looked back. At first, Cara and Jack were too busy arguing to admit there was an even graver problem, a product of their own issues, brewing right under their noses. They chose instead to look the other way, to chalk it up to teen exploration.

Not even Mel confronted Cara about it at first, and Mel hardly ever let something go. She and Leah and Paige had seen pieces of the bad when Katie's drinking had gotten so out of control that it had become painful for Cara; so burdensome that Cara had no choice but to confide in her friends. There was the Monday morning when Cara couldn't wake Katie up, couldn't even get her to move. Cara was so shocked by how shallow Katie's breathing had become that she called 911. There was the pool of vomit Cara had found her lying in one night; blood caked around her nose and mouth. When things got really bad, there were DUIs, phone calls from the police station, the impounded car. There was the vodka Cara found stashed in Katie's dresser, the gin in her water bottle, the beers she had stuffed into her backpack. Katie didn't have a favorite flavor. It wasn't the booze she fancied; it was what the drink did for her.

Cara had dragged her daughter to a half a dozen shrinks, drove her back and forth to AA meetings, sitting obediently in the parking lot of the high school until the meeting was over and she could drive Katie home again, silence settling over the car. The situation improved some, on and off, and Cara convinced herself they were finally on their way to sobriety.

But Katie was a highly functioning addict. Her grades had declined, but she wasn't failing; and her demeanor was, for the most part, manageable. And that made it harder and harder to know when she was using again. She'd get clean and stay that way for a month or so and then, like a bad habit, she'd go back to Jack's bar and start all over again.

* * *

Cara picked up her cell phone, doubled around the block and dialed Mel's number.

"'Lo?"

"Bella?" Cara asked Mel's daughter, her only child.

"Hey, Auntie Cara. Whatcha doing?"

"Hi, sweetie, not much. What're you doing over there?"

"Laundry. I can't stand that damn Laundromat, you know, and I'm down to my last pair of thong underwear."

"Too much information, Bella, too much information. Those things'll give you yeast infections. Do yourself a favor and buy some granny panties." Cara imagined Isabella standing in a thin T-shirt and her last pair of thong underwear, iron-flat stomach, long legs like her mother. Beautiful, stunning Bella. Tall, thin— almost too thin—almost, if you weren't so taken with every other aspect of her. She was Melanie all over again, only with every advantage, every option Mel never had. Isabella had graduated from Stanford with an art history master's and at twenty-two had only just moved out of her mother's flat.

"God, Auntie Car, as if."

"Where's your mother, child?"

"Hang on."

"Hey, lady," Mel's voice singsonged into the receiver, settling Cara instantly.

"Tie that girl up, Mel, tie her up."

"I know, I know." Mel sighed, sinking down into her favorite chair, a worn leather library lounger that sat in the corner of her loft under soft reading lights. Mel went there sometimes to review her proofs, sheets of photos that she had spent the day taking. She said she liked studying them under the loop with the softer light; that it told her how a shot might hang in a room somewhere, the way it might change with the light. "What's up?"

"The usual. Four lunches, four sets of homework, four crabby kids who spent the weekend maneuvering the land mines between their father and his hormone-laden girlfriend."

"Cara, you know what you need?"

"What?"

"You need a night out."

"Mel, I need a life out."

"Does Jack have the kids this weekend? Come into the city. Bring Leah and Paige. It would do you all some good."

"I cannot argue with that."

"Cara," Mel said softly, very much unlike herself, "you know something else? It wouldn't kill you to start seeing someone."

"Enough with the black leather couch, Mel. I don't know what drudging all this up with some shrink is going to buy me." Cara bristled at the suggestion she couldn't quite get her head around. She'd taken Katie to enough counseling sessions to know that she wanted no part of it. Besides, she was trying to move on from her relationship with Jack; she really had no desire to talk with anyone about it.

"No. I mean, yes. Yes, I think you should see someone. A therapist, sure, absolutely a great idea. But that's not what I'm talking about. I mean, *see someone*. Go out on a date, for Christ sake. Meet somebody. Get dressed up; go to dinner, maybe a movie. You'll be amazed at how much better everything looks and feels and seems."

"Four kids, Mel. I got four kids. I got three loads of laundry to do before I clean up the house, pull a bunch of shit together for the PTA and bake cookies for Claire's Brownie meeting. Later I get to untangle fourth-grade word problems and glue together pieces of Styrofoam for Luke's project on the Milky Way. After that I get to haul Katie and her A+ attitude over to another AA meeting. A *date?* You want me to go on a date? I can barely find time to shave my legs and pluck my eyebrows. Besides, who in the world do you think would find me remotely attractive?"

"It'd do you some good, Cara," Melanie said smugly, for the second time in five minutes. "Anyway, about Saturday. See if you can make it happen."

5

"You cannot possibly be serious." Leah stood firm, tennis-shoed feet planted squarely on the hardwood floor in Mel's flat. She had yet to remove the jeans jacket she was wearing—ancient by anyone's standards—but had already started to complain about their plans for the morning. Her auburn hair had been cut shorter than normal and she pushed it back away from her face, running her fingers through it to spike it up a bit.

"No, I'm not kidding, and don't even bother taking off that jacket, sister; we're leaving. I'm not canceling my wax appointment. Even for you guys. We'll be in and out in fifteen minutes." Mel turned on the heel of her Bettye Muller pump and headed into the kitchen to ditch the coffee she was drinking. "On second thought, Leah," she yelled from the kitchen, "for Christ sake take that ridiculous jacket off and go find something in my closet that's slightly more presentable. Something out of this decade, would you?"

When Mel poked her head out from the kitchen, Leah was staring down the front of her pink cotton blouse and fidgeting with the oversized silver buttons on her jeans jacket. Mel had hurt her feelings, something it seemed she was doing on a regular basis. Leah flaunted indignation, but sauntered down the narrow hallway toward the back of the flat and came out a few minutes later in a camel-colored soft suede jacket Mel knew she'd been envying. It was cut too long for Leah's short frame, but no matter, the new jacket was a dramatic improvement. Leah felt a bit more fearless, walked a little taller as she slung her chocolate leather bag over her shoulder, her sunglasses perched high on her head. She stopped in front of them and turned twice as if she was on a runway.

"Much better." Mel nodded her head in agreement, a hand on her hip. "Okay, ladies, we're outta here. I've got a ten o'clock appointment with Macey."

"Seriously, Mel, what is it you find necessary about the whole waxing thing?" Cara reached in her bag for the oversized key ring that was weighed down by two plastic photos: soccer pictures of each of her boys. She dangled the keys noisily in her hand, waiting on an answer as they all walked out of the flat.

Mel had regaled her friends for years with stories about her bikini waxes. Cara was both curious and repulsed at the same time. Despite how hard Mel had tried she had been completely unsuccessful at recruiting any of her friends to go with her.

Mel threw her head back. *"Shaving! God, my friends are still shaving! And DOWN THERE. Ladies, honestly you have got to come of age!*

"How many times am I going to have to explain this to you, Cara, before you fling off your panties and try it for yourself, huh? Nothing to it, really. A million, zillion times better than that damn pink disposable razor you're probably still using every day. God, those things are so archaic. What if you cut yourself down there? It's not exactly somewhere you could put a Band-Aid." She shuddered at the thought. "One day you'll have a wax and walk out of Macey's salon feeling like a sexy new woman. I'm telling you; you'll be hooked on the first visit."

"It's not even summertime, Mel, that's what I don't understand," Leah said as they all piled into Cara's van. "It's not even like you're sporting a bathing suit right now. Jesus, I go half the year without shaving at all. Bush city."

"Oh, God, Leah, it's not about wearing a bathing suit. It's

about sex, for Christ sake. It's about feeling your absolute most sexy when you're in the moment."

"Like that's something I need to be concerned with. Hardly. Andrew's in town long enough to drop his dirty clothes on the floor and repack the wash I've done. He doesn't look twice at me, never mind my crotch." It was true that Leah and Andrew had grown apart, never much of a couple to begin with. She saw him infrequently, his job keeping him on the road more often than he was at home.

"Okay, Mel, you get your way today. I'm game." Cara smiled as she pulled out of her parking space. "Today I'm in your capable hands. How bad can it be? I'll give it a shot."

"My girl! Really?" Mel screamed, delighted. She threw herself back against the seat, kicking up her heels and startling all of them so that Cara swerved in the middle of the narrow street. "I knew you'd come around one of these days. Okay, Cara, first the wax, then some new jeans, for God's sake. I don't even want to know where you got that pair, but Christ, they are out. Wax, lunch, then shopping at the Centre. Certainly we can find you something, anything, better than those pathetic old *blue* jeans. They're actually BLUE, Cara. No one wears jeans that are *blue* anymore."

Cara stared self-consciously at her jeans, both comfortable and familiar. They were faded and broken in in all the right places; she'd had them for years. Cara shook her head. She should have figured Mel would have an issue with something she had on, Mel nearly always did. She ran her hand over the fabric, thinking about how many times Katie had pleaded with her to buy some new clothes, something somewhat more fashionable that wouldn't embarrass her when Cara dropped her off in the mornings or showed up on campus late in the afternoon.

"P-L-E-A-T-E-D! Cara, my God, they are PLEATED. Absolutely no one wears pleated pants anymore."

"You're going to try to get me to wear those ridiculous low-rise jeans, aren't you?" Cara asked. "The ones that barely cover your hips and expose your butt crack. Those damn jeans that Katie and Bella wear, huh?"

"Hello. Welcome to this century. Of course. It's not as if you can't wear them, Cara. Especially now. Look at you, there ain't nothing left to your poor little body. You are thinner than you've ever been."

"Amazing what a separation will do for you."

"Well, for Christ sake Cara, it's not doing you any good in *those* jeans. God, enjoy it. Make the most of it, Cara, *flaunt* it. Put it to good use; you might actually find someone who appreciates it."

"Okay, Mel, here's the deal. You can take me wherever you want. You can pull whatever you want off the racks. I'll try on twenty pairs if you want. But I'm telling you right here and now that there ain't a pair of low-cut jeans—blue or not—in all of San Francisco that are going to look good on this body. You have no idea what those damn things do to me. My butt grows wider, my stomach flabbier. They pinch across my midsection and cut off my circulation. They are doing a disservice to women. All women. There's not an adult out there who can wear them," Cara complained, but stole a sideways glance at Mel, who would look absolutely perfect in exactly the pair Cara had described.

"*You* can wear them, Cara. And I'm going to prove it to you. Little low-cut number, a new belt, a clingy little top and you're all set, woman. Trust me on this."

"Forty-three, Melanie. Don't forget. I'm forty-three."

"Uh-huh." Mel let out a long, drawn-out sigh. "Forty-three. Check, I got it. Forty-three. Not to be confused with sixty-three."

"Um, Cara?" Leah chirped from the passenger seat.

"Hmmm?"

"You know it's a rare day when I actually agree with our resident psychotic who still thinks she's eighteen years old, but I'm with Mel on this one. You realize she will have you transformed within the day, don't you?"

"Of course, Leah. Why the hell do you think we're here?"

* * *

When they arrived at the studio Macey looked positively fabulous in a black tank top and jeans that landed six inches south of her navel and were held together by a pink belt with a rhinestone butterfly buckle. She was tall, unbelievably thin, and everything about her was manicured, from her eyebrows to her toenails. Macey smelled of organic fruit, sweet and ripe. She bent and flowed like water when she moved, graceful and giving. Her face actually glowed when she opened the door to the loft on Union Street, and something about her made you instantly want to befriend her. Candles and incense burned from the shelves and the small round tables were littered with copies of *W, Esquire, Essence*, and *InStyle* magazines. Macey was quick to embrace Mel, then stood back and took the rest of them in.

"You've got to be Cara," she said, pointing out Cara. "Mel talks about you all the time."

"I am, yes."

"I'd have known you anywhere. I swear, Mel"—she looked over and nodded—"you weren't kidding; she looks fabulous."

"I told you." Mel was quick to go to Cara's side and wrap her arms around her friend's waist, hugging her tightly, possessively. "She won't believe me, though, Macey. I'm dragging her straight to the Centre for an extreme makeover after this. I mean, look at this figure. And look at these *jeans!*" Mel shook her head, refusing to let the jeans issues go. "By the time I'm done with her, she's going to be transformed. Oh, and we might even be lucky enough to convince her that a good wax can change your entire perspective on life. You up for a virgin?"

"Oh, Cara, really? I'd love to. It would be an honor, really," Macey exclaimed with a little squeal, giving Cara the once-over before continuing the hugging with Leah and Paige. "There's tea there, ladies. Or water, if you'd rather. Make yourself comfortable; we won't be long." She took Mel's hand then, warmly. "Let's do this, Mel," she said to her, fondly. "We have plenty to catch up on. C'mon . . ."

The walls in Macey's reception area were painted the palest honeydew green, accented in an electric orange that normally would be a shock to the system. Here, in the small room, where sliced lemons, oranges, and limes floated in a pitcher of ice water and the smell of gardenia floated in the air, everything felt welcoming, even warm. Mel had been coming to Macey for a couple of years; her studio had become something of Mel's second home. These days Macey knew more of Mel's secrets than even her closest, oldest friends did.

Leah shuffled her weight anxiously from her left foot to her right, and Paige sat rigidly, cautiously, on the edge of an oversized chair in the corner, her right foot tapping wildly with the music, and not quite sure what to do with the rest of her moving parts.

Mel shrugged off her lambskin jacket and tossed it on a chair. "Let's go," she said.

Macey took that as her cue and they set off, locked arm in arm, down the narrow hall to a room in the back.

From over her shoulder Mel called to her friends, taunting them, "You can watch. If you want, that is."

Cara shrugged her shoulders at Leah and Paige. "Why not? I might as well know what I'm in for." She ducked behind Mel into the treatment room and squeezed into the far corner. The room was tiny, not made for three people, never mind Paige and Leah, who had abandoned the idea of diplomacy and made their way to stand just inside the door frame. Despite a small table fan that worked to stir the air, the room was stifling. White weightless chiffon curtains swayed ever so lightly. The windows overlooked the quaint, eclectic shops on Union Street, but only streaks of sunlight crept in through the narrow strips between the windows and the blinds.

"Just leave the door open," Mel said. "It's too hot in here to close it. God, Macey, it's always so hot in this room." She peeled away her clothes without another thought, dropping hot-pink cargo pants and black lacy thong panties in the chair in the corner. Mel's legs were endless, toned and tan. She was an exhibitionist, comfortable in nothing more than her own skin.

"God, Melanie, I never tire of looking at that thing." Macey motioned at Mel's backside where a gorgeous vine ran from the base of her ass up her sacrum. Absentmindedly, Melanie ran a hand over it, tracing the outline, the area that had long scarred over and left behind nothing but an imprint.

She had acquired the design one afternoon in the Haight. She was seventeen, the spring of their senior year, and she and Cara had cut school early, taking the train into the city, hell-bent on tattoos. When they got there, Cara had chickened out, but there was nothing she could do to convince Mel otherwise.

"Above my bikini line," she had told the stringy, long-haired tattoo artist who'd clearly had plenty of practice, his own body covered in more colors than there were names for. "Make sure you can see it if my T-shirt lifts like this," Mel instructed him, inching up the tight-fitting cotton tank top she was wearing. She didn't want it to be missed, not by anyone who might be looking.

The tattoo artist had eyed her hungrily, and positioned his large, grimy hand just above her ass, steadying her body. His thumb ran inside the thread of her thong, pushing it down.

She blinked back the tears the minute he touched her skin with the needle.

Mel hiked herself up on Macey's table and sprawled out as if she was ready to spend the afternoon sunbathing in the nude. Leah shifted her weight from one foot to the other, visibly uncomfortable, and tried to find something else to divert her attention. Paige concentrated on the canisters of cotton balls, Q-Tips, and a very tall jar of colored gumballs that Macey handed to Mel. She took two, a pink and a green, and popped them in her mouth, chomping down to break their hard shells.

"Gum's a good idea," Mel said to Cara. "It helps to have something to chomp on when that first rip goes."

Cara shuddered and swallowed hard, immediately regretting her decision. She wondered if it would be too late to change her mind.

"Don't let her fool you, Cara," Macey said encouragingly. "She's a pro."

"It's not that bad, guys. You know me; I'm a wimp. Do you think I'd do this if it hurt *that bad?* But c'mon," Mel said, full frontal, "it's worth it, you'll see."

Macey coated Mel's crotch with baby powder, then dipped the flat wooden stick, a tongue depressor, into the tub of purple wax and painted it on her pelvis, adjusting her legs and moving her body this way and that. Macey placed a long, thick white strip over the purple wax, told Mel to breathe in, and then out. They all leaned in, holding their breath in unison, when Macey ripped away the strip of paper. Mel winced, then relaxed, before she let out an audible growl.

In her right hand, Macey proudly displayed the long white strip covered with the remnants of the purple wax and Mel's thick, wiry dark pubic hair. "See!" She smiled proudly holding it up like a trophy.

"Oh, my God, Mel, you have got to be kidding," Leah said. "OH. MY. GOD. What in God's name prompted you to try this heinous act of self-inflicted pain? Lord, that's gotta hurt." Leah was breathless. "I swear to God you have got to be insane."

"Oh, sweetie, that was nothing." Macey laughed. "We're just getting started."

The torture went on for another seven or eight minutes, this ritual of hot purple wax followed by thick strips that, with some effort, left Mel smooth and hairless. Occasionally Macey reached for her tweezers, bent in close to Mel's crotch, and plucked a stubborn errant hair that she couldn't seem to get with the wax. Macey moved Mel back and forth spreading her legs open, then closed, all the while talking her ear off. Macey knew Mel's history; she'd heard all of her stories. They were comfortable in each other's presence, perfectly at home with each other. Mel's lifetime friends listened in as if they were eavesdropping, learning new things about their friend.

Macey proclaimed victory on Mel's manicured front side, her

bush neat, tidy and compact. Cara, Leah, and Paige circled the area like vultures preying on their lunch. They cocked their heads in close until Mel lifted her pelvis and thrust it at them.

"It looks like a Frito," Leah proclaimed. "A scoop, actually. One of those Fritos Scoops that you could just pick up and dip something with. Who would have guessed that Mel's crotch could look exactly like a snack food?"

"What do you think, Car? Nice, huh?" Mel asked proudly, ignoring Leah's comment and glancing down at her crotch, admiring Macey's work.

"Okay, ladies, step back. We're far from done. C'mon, Mel. Flip," Macey commanded. Mel rolled over, climbed up on her elbows and knees, doggy-style, her butt in the air, and only inches from Leah's face.

"Good Lord, Melanie," Leah muttered. "What the hell are you doing now?"

"What?" Mel glanced backward at the room. "I told you if you're going to do this, you gotta go all the way."

"How much hair have you got back there, Mel? Is this really necessary?"

"Have *you* ever seen what's between your ass, Leah?"

"I can assure you that I have not. But I can also tell you, from this vantage point, that Macey's got her hands plenty full. Thanks for the flash."

"You're welcome," Mel answered her. "This is full Brazilian. Can't wear a string bikini without it."

"The possibility that I might actually, at any point in time in the remainder of my life, wear a string bikini—or, for that matter, any kind of bikini at all—is absurd," Cara said and shook with laughter. "What, exactly, is the purpose of this, Mel? For me, I mean? No one got this close to this part of my body when I was married. Who, in God's name, am I trying to fool now? This is ridiculous."

Mel gripped the sides of the table as Macey ripped another strip from underneath her backside. Her body convulsed, then released and relaxed. "You never know, Cara," Mel said. "You just never know."

"Okay, girlie," Macey said finally, "you're finished."

She sprinkled some baby powder on the areas she'd just waxed and Mel hopped off the table and stood in front of the three of them, long muscular legs, narrow hips. They formed a semicircle around her like football players in a huddle and stared at the work. Paige cocked her head to the side as if she had never seen anything like it and studied the area carefully. Finally, absently, she reached out to dare touch the tender skin that had turned an angry pink from the treatment but stopped short of actually making contact.

"It's just a masterpiece, isn't it?" Mel held up her arms in victory.

Cara crinkled her brow and shook her head as if she was trying to talk herself out of it one last time before she finally said, "What the hell do I have to lose? Okay, I'm game." She unbuttoned and unzipped the condemned jeans and flung them carelessly on the one chair—empty and abandoned—in the corner of the room. When she turned around to whip off her panties, Mel was staring at her crotch. Speechless.

"God, Cara. Je-sus."

"What?" Cara turned quickly, self-consciously. She looked herself over and studied her midsection in the mirror, running her hands over her belly. Immediately she felt unveiled, on display. "Now what's wrong?"

"Those, those . . . God, those *underPANTS*." Mel tsk-tsked, shaking her head, her arms crossed over her chest. The crease in her forehead deepened and she rocked with dismay. She had seen underpants like those before, cotton briefs that rode across the hips and cut the stomach in half. She just didn't expect to find them on her best friend. Honestly, the woman had lost all sense of anything sexy, romantic, even fashionable and efficient. No wonder she suffered from visible panty lines. No wonder her asshole husband had switched her out for a younger version. Mel had set eyes on Barbie only once, but she imagined the woman did not own a pair of under*PANTS*.

For a minute the room was quiet, save the hum of the small fan in the corner that rotated.

Cara stood with her hands on her hips. "What?"

Leah, Paige, even Macey all stood staring at her, trying, without success, to hide their laughter.

Leah cracked first. A snort escaped her, unanticipated and obnoxious, and forced her to catch her breath. She covered her mouth with her hand and turned her back to them, her wide shoulders shook up and down with laughter.

Paige tried to suppress a giggle, but it finally caught her in tiny bubbly hiccups until she was doubled over. She apologized once, then twice and finally a third time. "I'm so sorry, Cara, I don't know what came over me . . ."

"Fine." Cara ripped off the panties and flung them slingshot style at Mel. Mel ducked and they landed in the corner, forlorn, turned inside out. "Just fine. Friends? You people say you are my friends? Uh-huh. We'll see. Make fun of my panties, will you? I'll show you."

"Under*PANTS!*" they all cried in unison, while Cara hiked herself up on the table.

"C'mere, Cara. Just ignore them." Macey's soothing voice guided her to lie on the table while she adjusted the overhead light so it shined on Cara's crotch. The snickering finally started to die down but Mel went on about lecturing her.

"You can't wear low-cut jeans with those, those high-waisted, ladies under*pants*. You just can't, Cara. My grandmother used to wear those things. I'm adding a trip to Victoria's Secret, too. God, pathetic. Just pathetic. What size are they? XXL? Honestly! They've lost their elastic, as if that was a selling point in the first place. They practically hang down to your knees and they sag." Melanie picked up the cursed underpants from the pile they lay in, holding them up for everyone in the room to see. "For sweet sake, Cara, you are a fortysomething single woman and you are walking around in those underpants. You simply can't be afraid to spend a little money on yourself. You deserve it, Cara. You can treat yourself to something that might actually make you feel just a smidge sexier."

"I told you, Mel, I can't wear those damn jeans. Period. So it won't matter, anyway. But fine, you want to buy me some slutty little black piece of butt floss that is supposed to do the job those hardworking panties do, well that's just fine. Worthless, but fine."

"Okay, Cara," Macey interrupted. "You ready to do this?"

"Macey, you see the unbelievable support I'm getting from my so-called friends? I don't know how more ready I could get. Could I get some of those gumballs?"

"Oh, sorry, of course." Macey handed her the canister and Cara took two, chomping on them until the sugar seeped into her teeth and ran down the back of her throat. She reclined on the table, her head supported by a thick, stiff pillow, and sighed deeply. She didn't know what she had gotten herself into now. What in the world was she doing here? She looked from one friend to another, poised and waiting on her.

"Melanie, come over here and make yourself useful. I need something to hold on to," Cara ordered and Mel appeared at the end of the table, quite near Cara's right ear and lent her hands. Cara gripped them tightly, her palms sweaty. Upside down, she glared at Melanie in jest.

"Okay, Cara, ready? Deep breath in and let it out, and . . ."

"HOLY SHIT!"

"OH."

"MY."

"GOD."

Cara took a deep breath, her toes curling at the other end of the table. She let out the breath slowly, counting in her head and waiting for the sharp pain to subside.

"Oh, my God. Oh, my God. Oh, my God," she repeated over and over again, panting, then laughing hysterically as if gripped by a bad case of the giggles, as if she had taken her first hit of pot, her first swig of a beer. "You have got to be kidding. Come on, Mel, you have got to be *kidding* me."

"Bravo," Mel exclaimed. "Excellent! That was the worst part, Cara, trust me, it gets better from here."

"Good, Cara, good. I know how much that hurts, but way to go," Macey encouraged.

"*Better? It gets better from here?* You people are insane. You must be fucking kidding me. You do this for pleasure, Mel? Good Lord that hurt." Before Macey could get another layer of purple wax on her, she sat up and examined the area that Macey just ripped the strip from. Little red bumps stood out against a patch of hairless skin as if someone had taken a lawn mower and run through the first section of a yard.

Leah and Paige moved in. Cara turned on her right hip so they could get a better look, proud all at once of her accomplishment. They nodded their agreement; suddenly Cara felt a surge of independence, the feeling of having accomplished something she never thought she would have done. As silly as it sounded, it gave her a feeling of power, of truly conquering something.

Leah took one step back, crossed her arms over her chest and shook her head in disbelief. "No way you'll get me up there. Don't even ask," Leah assured Mel, just in case she was considering encouraging her to climb up on the table next.

"What do you do now, Leah? You know, to take care of the area down there?" Macey asked her curiously, the tongue depressor with purple wax poised in her hand ready to go at Cara again.

Cara settled back on the table and took Mel's hands again, gripped them even more tightly this time.

"I shave. Same thing I've done all my life. Seems to be working just fine for me."

Macey refocused her attention on the mission at hand, but Mel shook her head back and forth, annoyed. "It's so archaic, Leah. Every day, you gotta shave that. And what do you do underneath? How do you get all that?"

"First of all, Melanie, there is no reason I *have* to shave every day. And for your information, I don't. And furthermore, I don't worry about what's under there, if you must know. It doesn't seem to be too much of an issue for me."

"But what about the beach, the pool? You're always at the club. What do you do at the club?"

"I don't give a crap. If anyone is staring at that part of this body for that long, well something's just really wrong about that, that's all I gotta say. It just doesn't happen that way anymore," Leah answered her firmly, dismissing her immediately. "And before you go asking me about my feet, I don't get a pedicure in the winter, either."

Macey gave Cara no warning for the next rip; she went at it with a vengeance. Cara took turns alternating between holding her breath and clenching her teeth just before she anticipated Macey would pull off the next strip. Finally, Macey proclaimed her done on the front by saying, "I don't know, Mel, maybe we just ought to go with the bikini wax this time and break her in slowly. A Brazilian might be a little over-the-top for her first visit."

"What? What do you mean?" Cara asked, a high pitch escaping the back of her throat somewhere. "Not do the back?"

Macey rested her hand on Cara's shoulder and rubbed it back and forth gently. "You're a total trooper, Cara, you've done really well this time, but . . ."

"But nothing. I'm doing this. The whole thing. I've come this far; you can't just leave me hanging here. Besides, it's not that bad," she reasoned, shaking her head. Instantly she flipped over, butt up in the air.

"You heard her, Macey, have at it," Mel said, pride seeping into her voice. She might not be able to convince Leah or Paige, but she'd gotten to Cara. The transformation had begun.

Poised on her hands and knees, Cara's butt was eye level with everyone in the room. Macey said from behind, "Okay, Cara, you gotta arch your back a little more."

Cara followed Macey's instructions and curved her back like a frightened cat.

"No, not that way, the other way. Drop your chest toward the table and really stick it out there, Cara."

"Good God," Cara said to Mel, shaking her head. "Honestly."

Mel smiled; satisfied.

* * *

The San Francisco Centre was hot and crowded. In Victoria's Secret, Mel convinced Cara to purchase eight pairs of thong underwear in enough colors to light up her lingerie drawer: purple, lime green, red, white with little cherries, two black, and two beige. On Nordstrom's fifth floor Mel insisted Cara try on a pair of Seven jeans.

" 'Jeans for all Mankind,' " Cara whined, reading the label on the pants. "All mankind except this one. It's the cruelest tagline I've ever heard. It's like, *If these don't fit you, baby, there ain't no hope.*"

Cara rested her weight on one hip while Mel pulled pair after pair of jeans off the rack and held them up to her friend's waist. She put a few back, then literally dragged Cara along the rack until she found what she was looking for. She wouldn't risk Cara's escape; Mel was determined.

"What size are you these days, anyway, Cara?"

"I don't know. Eight, maybe," Cara answered her. "But it's in all the wrong places, though, Mel. I'm telling you. Don't expect any of these to fit me like the way you think they're supposed to."

Mel put up a hand to silence her, and grabbed one more, an indigo pair. In all, they had a dozen pair, the hangers tangled and dangling from Mel's left arm. A sales associate met them halfway to the dressing room and unloaded the haul in one swift swoop.

"Put us in the bigger room in the back," Mel said to the woman, smiling.

Cara whipped off the condemned jeans, the underpants right behind them. She reached in the small pink shopping bag from Victoria's Secret and pulled out the red thong underwear Mel had convinced her to buy, despite her loud protests. She yanked off the tags with one swift pull and, just before she was about to put them on, stopped when she heard Mel say, "Ladies, I ask you, is that not a work of art?"

Mel motioned toward Cara's crotch until she stopped and modeled her new wax, the area still raw and pink, but perfectly shaped, perfect in every way. They were all crowded into the dressing room, Paige huddled on the little chair and Leah on the floor. No one dared miss the modeling of the new jeans, they were all curious to play witness to the next stage in Cara's transformation.

"Don't worry, Cara, you're always a little sensitive the first day, but by tomorrow, you aren't going to believe how great it looks. And how great it feels."

Through the mirror they all stared at her. "It does look great, doesn't it? Okay, Mel, you win. It wasn't that bad and I feel like a whole new woman." Cara pulled on the thong underwear, adjusting the thin G-string backward and forward, yanking at it until she could find a way to make it work. She circled the dressing room as if something was creeping up her ass because, as it happened there was. "Oh, shit, these things are so uncomfortable I can hardly stand it."

Mel ignored her and answered her smugly. "Now, put on those jeans so I can gloat a little more, would you? I swear, Cara, one of these days you are going to learn to trust me. One of these days."

Cara chose the last pair of jeans that Mel had picked up. On the hanger they looked shameless, but the material was soft and inviting. Cara put them on, sliding in her right foot first, then her left, and pulling them up.

"They feel all wrong," she said when they stopped just above her hip bones, nearly five inches below her navel. But they looked fabulous. Not just good, but great, in every sense of the word. She buttoned, then zipped them easily and stood as far back from the mirror as she could get. She couldn't believe they fit. Oh, sure, they were long—much, much too long; they would need to be hemmed before she could wear them, but by God, they fit!

"Whoa, baby, stand back." Leah whistled.

Mel shook her head in a when-will-you-start-believing-me, I-told-you-so sort of way. She forced Cara to turn around twice, then bend over, and then bend down. She told her to put on the slim fitted T-shirt that barely covered her midsection and a new belt that she had chosen and watched as Cara studied herself in the mirror.

"I don't know, Mel, I just don't know if I can pull it off."

"What do you mean you don't know if you can pull it off? Are you crazy? You look fantastic. Jesus, Cara, look at yourself."

It took Cara a few minutes to become familiar with her own image in the mirror as if she was studying someone she didn't know, someone she was just meeting for the first time. She didn't feel anything like herself; she wondered who she was pretending to be. But then something happened. Most definitely, something happened. Some sort of something took over and lent her a bit of the confidence she'd lost, the confidence that left the day Jack packed his bags and moved out. Some part of her—a part that he'd left stranded the day she watched him back the car out and pull away—began to ease its way back into her soul, into her body. She stood in front of the mirror with her hands buried in the back pockets of the jeans, barefoot and cracking her toes on the worn carpet in the dressing room. She couldn't believe the reflection, the person she had become. She wondered where the woman she was had gone, where she was hiding.

"Okay, they'll pass," she said, trying not to look too shocked, remaining calm. She hadn't felt like this in years, like a teenager. But she contained herself, wanting to jump up and down, but refraining.

"God, Cara, curb your enthusiasm, will you?"

6

Cara was suffering a headache, the ill effects of one too many glasses of wine. The phone had bolted her awake and she sat up in bed, rubbing sleep from her eyes.

"Hello," she croaked.

"Cara?"

Jack. Fucking Jack. What in God's name did he want at this hour? She brushed her hair from her face and leaned back against the pillow, shading her eyes against the bright light that filled the room.

"Yeah. What's up, Jack? Is everything okay?" Her throat was dry, sore, probably from snoring all night. She snored when she drank; Jack had told her that. It was one of the things he found darling about her when they'd first married, and drove him crazy years later in their marriage. He'd told her that, too.

"No. It's Kate."

Cara's stomach lurched, her heart beating alive. "What's wrong?" she asked with alarm. "What's happened?"

"She was taken in last night. She and a few kids she was with out on Highway 9." Jack took a deep breath then, quieting his voice.

Cara imagined he was trying not to wake the rest of the house, especially their other children. She imagined him standing in sweats in the kitchen, a cup of coffee steaming on the counter in front of him. Jack was incapable of doing anything in the morning before he had his first cup of coffee. Calling Cara would have been impossible for him before the caffeine started pulsing through his veins.

"What happened?" Cara asked again, because this wasn't enough information. She needed more. She needed to know every detail, every inch of the story. She needed to know that Katie was all right. Why hadn't he called her earlier? God, where was Katie now?

"She was arrested for another DUI. It's not good, Cara. They found coke on one of the kids she was with. She swears she didn't know about the coke and hadn't done any of it, but it doesn't matter much either way. With her record there was no way they were going to let her off with a warning and a slap on the wrist. They hauled her in faster than she could get an explanation off."

Cara's hand covered her mouth, open and gaping. "Oh, God," she managed. Katie needed her. Katie needed her and she was not there. Katie needed her and Cara was not there because Katie had been at her father's house. It was Sunday; she was Jack's responsibility. She couldn't get dressed fast enough, pulling on her new denim jeans in one swift move, holding the phone to her ear, begging Jack to fill in the details.

"She was stopped for a minor violation, a burned-out headlight, then questioned, then given a Breathalyzer, then hauled in. Her blood alcohol was .08, she was right at the limit. They probably would have just called one of us and slapped her with a warning if it hadn't been Katie, but the cop called her license in and it was over from there. She's violated her probation, of course, so they didn't have much choice after that."

"Damn it, Jack, where were you? What was she doing out last night? You know you can't let her go out like that, to some random party. How many times have we been over this?" Cara's anger flamed instantly. "This never should have happened. If you can't keep an eye on her, you shouldn't have her on the weekends. You know how easily she can get into trouble." Cara was quick to blame him, even quicker to drag his departure out into the middle of the room as if it was his fault.

On the other end of the line, Jack was quiet. "When can you be here?" he asked, finally.

"I'm getting dressed now."

"You'll have to see about getting her out."

"*What?*" Cara asked accusingly. "Today? You mean you didn't bail her out last night?"

"They wouldn't let her go, Cara."

"Why not?"

"She violated probation. You get that, right? She vi-o-la-ted probation. She's seventeen, she was driving on a suspended driver's license, she has two previous DUIs, and they've got a record on her. What do you suppose they should have done with her?" Jack cleared his throat. "What part of this aren't you getting?"

Katie's arraignment was scheduled for Monday at 11:00. Despite Cara's pleas with both the juvenile detention center and Katie's probation officer, they were holding her at the center until she was scheduled to appear in Room 108, the Juvenile Justice Agency. She wasn't permitted visitors prior to that, so, spending time pacing the long, cavernous hallways at the courthouse—the hallways Cara had grown all too familiar with—wasn't going to do anyone any good. So she went home.

In her house Cara felt protected, safe. She could scream and no one would hear her. She could carry on with her laundry, get her other children off to school, rearrange paperwork, do the dishes, watch television, shower and fix breakfast as if nothing was out of the ordinary. She could talk to herself in long, drawn-out, rationalizing sentences, reminding herself that everything would be okay. *Everything will be okay, everything will be okay.* She repeated this over and over again, deep breaths, in and out.

She was on her third cup of tea of the morning, Earl Grey. Nothing was helping to calm her jittery nerves, certainly not the tea. She had spent the night lying as still as she could, listening to the familiar noises her home made, the way it settled this way or that. Near two AM Claire had padded into her room in her pajamas shaking from a nightmare that had left her damp with perspiration.

"Mama," she whispered, "when will Katie be home?"

"Soon, sweetie. I hope she'll be home soon." She lay next to Claire and stroked her back softly with the tips of her fingertips, the way Claire liked it best, until her daughter was breathing softly and evenly again.

Cara heard Mel's car in the driveway around nine. She had already ushered the children off to school and was sitting at the kitchen table staring at the gray, colorless morning. She took a deep breath and opened the heavy oak door before Mel knocked. Cara was wearing sweats and an old T-shirt. She was disheveled and worn, tired to the bone.

Mel would have an opinion about what she should do, of course, and she wouldn't be afraid to offer it. Cara wasn't sure if she was ready for company, never mind Mel's viewpoint, which would come whether or not she was ready.

Cara threw open the door. "Hello."

Mel had brought Leah, and they both stood anxiously on her front step as if they were debating about who should ring the doorbell. The morning sun was bright and the reflection off the wide copper porch beams blinded them when they approached. Cara sucked in the dewy morning, the sweet smell from the jasmine that bordered her front walk. She smiled a wide, fake smile when she greeted her friends, as if nothing was wrong, not a thing out of place. Her bottom lip trembled when they walked past her but she swallowed hard the lump that formed at the base of her throat.

"Hi, babe," Leah said to her with concern and stopped to hug her tight around her neck, planting a kiss along Cara's rigid jawbone. Her embrace was quick, rehearsed.

Cara felt rigid, embarrassed at her daughter's latest episode that had landed them on her front step first thing Monday morning.

"She's not here. They're keeping her at the juvenile detention center until her court arraignment later this morning. She's on at eleven, so it's not likely we're going to know anything before then." Cara pushed her honey-colored hair back behind her ears and crossed her arms over her chest.

Leah pulled Cara close again, wrapping her arms around her waist and not letting her go. "I'm sorry we didn't see this coming, Cara. I'm so sorry we're right back here again."

Cara shook her head hard. "Katie's a really good liar, Leah. When it comes right down to it, lying might be one of the things she does best." Cara cleared her throat. It was unlike her not to defend her daughter, not to find some justification for her latest antics, but even she'd had her fill this time.

Mel agreed with Cara immediately, broke the silence and clipped across the floor, nodding her head vigorously all the while. "Damn straight she is, Cara. Damn straight." In a huff, Mel disappeared through the double French doors in the wood-paneled library and out to Cara's English garden. From the pocket of her black trench coat she pulled out a pack of Camels and positioned one between her pursed lips, cupping her hand to light it and inhaling deeply. She exhaled the smoke in great billows around her, tilted her head back and stared skyward, pacing the yard like a new puppy with too much energy.

"Damn straight," Cara scoffed, mimicking Mel. "Christ. As if I need her to remind me."

She shook her head, crossed her arms over her chest and headed toward the kitchen. Leah followed her double-time, trying to keep up, making excuses for Mel as they went.

Leah apologized for Mel immediately. "You know that's not what she meant, Cara. Mel's just that way. She didn't mean to hurt you; she's just worried about Katie. You know how much Katie means to her, to all of us. You know how she can get."

Cara stopped in front of the refrigerator, opened it and pulled out a sparkling water before she slammed it closed. "No, how can she get, Leah? Are there any limits? Any boundaries she's not willing to cross?" Cara replied sarcastically, her words cutting through the dead air. Leah stood helplessly watching her work the cap off the water bottle, twisting and turning it in her fist. "Does she have to have an opinion about everything? About my marriage? About my kids? Can't she just support me one time? Just one time. That's all I'm asking."

"I do support you." Mel's dry, throaty voice poured into the kitchen long before the wafting smell of fresh nicotine followed her. "You just don't see it. You never have."

Cara felt her face grow hot, red with shame, caught like a child in a lie. Scarlet washed over her pale skin, crept its way down her neck.

"What are you going to do with her this time, Cara? What's the magic cure this time?" Mel continued, wedging her way in between them and propping open the refrigerator door, reaching for a Diet Coke. "What's your solution this time?"

Cara shrugged her shoulders, "I, I, well, I guess I'm not sure yet. We're going to have to see what the judge says. What kind of program . . . ?"

Mel cut her off immediately, refused to hear anything more. "And Jack? What's his opinion?"

"We haven't even talked about it, Melanie. I don't know yet."

"Why not?"

"We haven't had the chance. He had to deal with the rest of the kids yesterday when everything fell apart. He dealt with them and I dealt with our esteemed juvenile justice system."

Melanie let out a deep breath and shook her head back and forth vigorously. "It figures," she said, curling herself into the cushion on the window seat, pulling her long legs up under her like a cat.

"You're not helping, Mel," Cara fired back, her voice shaky and erratic. "You're just not helping."

"*You're* not helping *her*, Cara. Don't you understand that?" Mel stared at Cara, willing her to make eye contact. "*YOU* are not helping *HER*. Neither one of you. You refuse to see what's right before you, what's going on with your daughter; and Jack . . . Christ, Jack barely knows who she is these days. He picks her up for dinner on Wednesdays and drags her over to a three-bedroom condo so she can waste away the weekend. When was the last time Jack sat down to talk to her? When was the last time you sat down to talk to her? I mean really, really talk to her?"

"As soon as I get my hands on her, I will, Mel. She'll be back in a full program with Dr. Levine. Back in school with no car privileges, no dating, no weekend parties, nothing. I've got my eye on her."

"You've had your eye on her, Cara. It hasn't worked."

"Jack is going to have to step things up, too. She's going to know we're serious this time. She doesn't have a choice."

Mel stared at Cara long and hard for a few minutes, looking her over. "Listen to yourself, Cara," she said. "Listen to exactly what you are saying. At what point is Jack going to talk to her? Over a quick dinner at fucking Bakers Square? Or while they're painting the nursery for the new baby he and his model girlfriend are going to have? And when he does talk to her, what is it that you think he's going to say to her? What profound thing do you think Jack's got rolling around in that midlife crisis head of his that would possibly make sense to the daughter he barely recognizes as his own?"

Leah started to interrupt. She had been a witness to Mel and Cara's bouts before, hundreds of times. They could start like a fire; one of them would set the other off like a match and before you knew it, an inferno had erupted over the room, burning like tinder through a dry forest. And they could get nasty quickly but were nearly always resolved in laughter. Still, they made Leah uncomfortable, fidgety. She was usually left on the sidelines, watching.

"Leah?" Cara whispered quietly without turning her head, staring through Mel at the wall behind her. "I think it's probably best if you go. Both of you. I could use some time by myself before I have to go down to the courthouse. I'll call you later."

"Bullshit," Mel answered her, stopping Leah from gathering her things. "Bull. Shit."

"What is it that you want me to do, Melanie? What is it that you want me to say to you?" Cara asked her slowly. She was tired, more tired than she'd felt in a long time. And she couldn't defend herself against Mel, not today, not in this condition. Couldn't Mel understand that? Couldn't she see that Cara wanted what was best for her daughter?

"I want you to tell me that you'll get your daughter some help. Stop covering up for her, Cara. And for God's sake, stop covering up for Jack. Stop thinking you can handle this, that you can make it better. Stop thinking that you'll just ground her for the weekend, or that taking the goddamn car away, or even taking her back to that ridiculous psychotherapist, is going to fix her addiction to booze, her dependency on drugs. She's an alcoholic, Cara. Tell me that you will admit to yourself, to me, to all of us, and especially to Katie, 'cause she can't do it for herself yet, but tell me that you'll look her in the eye and say, 'Sweetheart, you've got a problem, we need to get you some help. Some real help.'"

Cara yawned audibly. She was weary from the ordeal and tired of arguing. She took a deep breath before she addressed Melanie again, more collected. "I know she needs help, Mel. I'm doing my best; really, you have to know that."

"I know that you *want* to do your best for her. I know that you want what's best for her, too. But what you've been doing ain't working. We gotta find something else." Mel's voice was kinder this time and had softened just a little. "We all love that girl, Cara. Lord knows I love her like I love Bella. But what you've been doing, well, sweetheart, it's just not working. Not this way."

"But what? What else is there?"

"I don't know," Melanie said to Cara. She uncurled her legs, stood and walked over to face her. Mel's height dominated, she was nearly a foot taller than Cara, and she cupped Cara's face in her hands, pulling her into her chest like a mother would hold a child. "I don't know what it is, sugar, but I can tell you this. I can tell you that we'll find it."

*   *   *

Jack called just as Cara and Mel were walking into the court-house. Cara had to dig through her bag to find her cell phone while Mel stood next to her in the long sterile hall, intolerant and impatient, hot-tempered. Cara took a few steps down the hall for privacy but Mel followed close behind like a loyal pet.

"Cara, I got your message," he barked when Cara answered the phone. "Listen, about me picking up the kids after school today. It's impossible; I'm buried in meetings and there's just no way."

"But . . ."

"But, nothing. It's just not feasible. I can't make it work. I suspect you'll be out of there before they get out of school, anyway."

Jack was short-tempered and uncompromising. He had called with one thing in mind and it was this. Cara knew it had less with him being available to pick up the kids and more with him not being ready to deal with his daughter's latest episode. Katie's illness—and Cara could finally bring herself to call it that—had hit Jack the hardest. It had not only been especially embarrassing to him, but personally devastating. He'd lost his little girl in a way he'd never expected. Cara had spent enough time thinking about it to know that Jack could have stomached Katie's addiction to a first love, a sweet, puppy dog romance. He wouldn't have liked it, but he could have gotten through it. He'd just never expected her first love, the thing that pulled her away from him, to be the bottom of a bottle, or a line of coke. He had no conception of how to compete at that level.

Cara took a deep breath, measuring her words carefully. "Can Barbie get them?"

"No," he answered her flatly. "She can't fit all three of them in her convertible." His answer was rehearsed, practiced.

"Of course," Cara answered. She was fuming and had to work to keep her voice calm. "I'll take care of it, Jack." She clicked off her cell phone and checked her watch. Nearly eleven o'clock and her stomach was a mess of nerves.

"What's so important?" Mel asked Cara, disdain crossing her face.

Cara shook her head, shook Mel off. She clipped down the hall at a quickened pace, not wanting to be late for Katie's proceedings. "Someday that bitch is going to be forced to drive a van," Cara answered. "Someday."

Katie sat on the hard wooden bench in the second row of the courtroom, dressed in plain, conservative clothes Cara didn't recognize: a white blouse and a jeans skirt that hung loosely around Katie's petite frame. Her hair had been washed, parted down the center of her head and combed straight on either side of her shoulders in the simplest way, as if she'd been forced to let it air-dry. Without the excessive black eye makeup she usually wore, she looked softer, sweet, almost angelic. She slouched carelessly on the bench, barely glancing at her mother and Mel as they entered the courtroom and settled into the row second from the back of the room. Cara's right foot twitched nervously, keeping time with an imaginary beat. She willed Katie to have better posture, to sit up straight and look interested in her own well-being.

Cara never took her eyes off the judge; the woman who held her daughter's future in her hands. She tried to read the judge's intense demeanor, the way she shuffled papers back and forth and constantly cleared her throat. Just before Katie was called to the bench, Cara leaned over and said to Mel, "This isn't the judge we want, Mel, she just doesn't seem like she'll understand Katie."

"Katherine Lynn Clancy?" the bailiff read from the clipboard.

Katie shuffled to her feet, flanked on her right side by Lucy Johnson, the attorney Jack had hired the first time Katie had found herself sitting on the hard wooden bench, facing a judge. Lucy held Katie tight at the elbow, guiding her. It wasn't that Katie needed the direction; she had this drill nailed. She sauntered, head up, through the wooden gate that separated the courtroom and the judge's bench, her hands buried low in the pockets of the baggy skirt.

"Miss Clancy?" the judge addressed her, and continued. "We haven't had the pleasure of meeting, but I see you've been a regular with some of my neighbors here at the courthouse." The woman removed her glasses and peered at Katie, waiting for her to make some sort of response.

Lucy Johnson stepped forward just slightly, her black suit jacket folding open, and handed a few loosely clipped papers to the bailiff. "Yes, your honor, Miss Clancy is somewhat familiar with the proceedings."

"And why is that, Ms. Johnson? Explain to me what we are doing wrong here on mahogany row to keep Miss Clancy from paying us a visit on Monday mornings? Because as I look over these papers, I'm really at a loss as to why she has now appeared in my courtroom."

Katie slumped lower to one side and shifted her weight so that her right hip was sticking out, her weight resting on her left side. Cara willed her to stand up straight, to stop fidgeting. But Katie looked bored with the whole episode, as if she could have cared less.

Before Lucy could answer, the judge turned to Katie and addressed her directly. "Miss Clancy, do you have any idea why you are in this courtroom today?"

"Yes."

Pause.

Dead air.

A defiant stare.

Over and over again in her mind, Cara pleaded with her daughter to answer the judge respectfully. Silently she prayed that Kate would realize the heap of trouble she'd found herself in this time.

"Would you be so gracious as to explain it to me?" the woman directed at her again.

"I can try," Katie said, clear as a bell. "I was pulled over on Saturday night. The cop gave me a Breathalyzer and I failed it. I'd been drinking."

"I see."

"Really, that's all there is to it. Not much more to the story than that."

Lucy cleared her throat, hoping to quiet Katie before she said anything further, tugging on her wrinkled white blouse and holding her tight at the elbow again.

"Oh, I'm sure there's plenty more to the story. I'm reading your file, Miss Clancy. I see that this is the third time you've been to see us in a year. Is that correct?"

"Um, yeah, I guess so."

"And am I right to assume that you are driving on a suspended license?"

"Yes."

"So I suppose suspending it is a bit pointless."

"I don't know that you could, actually," Katie said to the judge.

"Excuse me?"

"I just meant"—she paused and started again—"it would be fairly difficult to suspend something that has already been suspended."

Lucy Johnson cleared her throat again and shifted in her black pointed stilettos, visibly uncomfortable. On the clock, she was $275 an hour. But even she looked as if she wanted this to be over.

The judge perched her thin wire-framed reading glasses on the end of her nose and the courtroom fell silent while she rifled through the paperwork.

"Are your parents in the courtroom today, Miss Clancy? Your mother? Or your father, perhaps?" Her eyes lifted from the paperwork to rest on Katie before she began to scan the room.

Cara swallowed hard, suspended on the end of the bench, and gripped the leather handbag tighter in her lap. Mel placed her hand on Cara's shaking leg, steadying her.

Lucy glanced toward the bench and urged Cara forward with a nod, but Katie never met her mother's eyes. Instead she said to the judge, "My father isn't here, but my mother is."

From behind, Mel pushed Cara forward a little until she found her feet and somehow her legs knew how to support her. She stood, cautious at first, weak with uncertainty, until she seemed to gain her balance and courage, and approached the wooden gate that separated Katie, Lucy, the bailiffs, court stenographer, and finally the judge.

"Mrs. Clancy?" The name seemed foreign to her, disassociated and unattached.

"Yes, your honor. Katie's my daughter."

"Is there a reason, at least one you can think of, why I have the pleasure of your daughter's company in my courtroom this morning?"

"Nothing other than what is stated in the report, your honor."

"And may I ask, just for curiosity's sake, what it is you expect me to do with her, Mrs. Clancy?"

"Well." Cara paused. "I was hoping you might release her to her father and me so that we may continue with her treatment program. She has been seeing a psychologist and has been attending regular AA meetings. It would be my hope that we could continue that program."

"Mrs. Clancy, does it appear to you that these programs are working on behalf of your daughter?"

Cara fidgeted with the buckle on her bag, clipping it and unclipping it nervously. "Well, your honor, I can assure you that Katie has been working very diligently on her program. We have been seeing to that on a daily basis, and her fath—" Cara stopped short before she finished her thought, thinking of Jack, how much she would have to lie on his behalf. She started again. "I have personally been responsible for seeing to the fact that she has been attending AA. I drive her there myself."

"Mmmm-hmmm," the judge answered her, not looking directly at Cara, but jotting notes on the papers in front of her. "Again, does it appear to you that the program you have set out on your daughter's behalf is working for her? Am I to believe that this visit here today is part of your so-called *program?*"

Cara blushed furiously, hot with embarrassment and anger. She felt the weight of every person in the courtroom, all eyes staring at her, evaluating her, judging her. She gripped the wooden gate that separated the two sides of the courtroom until her knuckles turned white. Her legs buckled, and she shuffled her feet.

"Mrs. Clancy. I am sure that you and your husband have your daughter's best interest in mind, but I'll ask you again. Do you feel that this program you have set about for her is working in her best interest?"

Slowly Cara began to answer her. "No, your honor. I would have to say these programs don't seem to be working for Katie. Otherwise, I'd expect this is the last place you'd find us today."

"Very well." She dismissed Cara with a nod, her mouth a thin line.

As Cara tripped back to the bench where Melanie sat, she stared ahead with her back arched, her shoulders squared, her jaw locked. Cara was rigid when she took her seat again, and Mel scooted in close next to her.

"Breathe," Mel whispered, and Cara continued to stare straight ahead.

The judge gathered the papers together, signing them one by one, and handed them to the bailiff before she addressed Katie. "Miss Clancy, I do not wish to see you in this courtroom again, do you understand that?"

"Yes."

"In order to assure that that happens, I am remanding you to a ninety-day court-ordered live-in drug rehabilitation program. You will check into this program tomorrow morning. The facility will handle the transfer of your scholastic studies. You are still attending classes, are you not, Miss Clancy?"

Cara took a sharp breath that nearly cut her in two. Her hand went to her throat and she was frozen with fear. *A live-in program. Ninety days.*

Katie started to answer the judge but Lucy cut her off, stated clearly to the judge that Katie was still in school, in an excellent accelerated program and couldn't the judge, no, *wouldn't* the judge take her academic performance into account and, perhaps, allow her to continue the treatment she is receiving under the care and supervision of her parents?

"Ms. Johnson, I think it's a bit obvious to all of us that the care Miss Clancy has been receiving under her parents' watchful eyes haven't done her a bit of good. I'm hoping this will." The judge turned toward Katie. "Miss Clancy, when you are finished with this program we will revisit your status and the best course of action at that point." She stapled a final group of papers and shuffled them into Katie's file, before saying to her, "As I said, check in tomorrow. I've requested regular monitoring of your progress and reports on your academic status. I want you clean and sober. Do you understand what that means?"

"Of course."

"Clean and sober. Ninety days. See if you can manage it, Miss Clancy."

Cara never thought it would come to this. Taking her baby away. Sending her off to get *clean and sober*. The words echoed in her head over and over again and ridiculed her. Immediately she felt like a failure, absorbing all the responsibility for Katie's addiction. She had failed her daughter and she would barely be able to look herself in the mirror for it.

"Clean and sober. Ninety days, Miss Clancy. See if you can manage it."

7

Katie's addiction hadn't started out of weakness, but rather from the stubbornness that she'd been born with. She was angry. Angry with her father for his extramarital affairs, the way he had abandoned their family. Angry with her mother for standing back and allowing that to happen. She was out to prove she could control something in her life, even if everything else in her life had become completely uncontrollable.

Cara believed Katie had willed the addiction to life, as if she had taken her first drink purposefully and never looked back. It was as if she had been born to achieve the status *addict* and so she did so with drive and vigor, putting everything she had behind it. She was an excellent scholar, a master at getting drunk.

Cara had tried to reason with her daughter, explaining to her the downsides of drugs and alcohol as if she was reading from the script of a TV after-school special. But by that point, Katie was long past a lecture. By that point she knew how to tap into Jack's liquor cabinet, refilling his gin bottle with just enough water so that he wouldn't notice. She knew how to tap the shoulder of an unsuspecting college student, look him in the eye with a promise of something more, and get him to buy her beer. She knew which kids to hit up for pot, which ones could get her the best cocaine, and which could, on request, get her something stronger like ecstasy. She knew that she could lift prescription painkillers from the medicine cabinets of her friends' parents, and she knew which ones would leave her feeling like she was floating and which ones would leave her feeling like she'd been hit by a truck.

Katie wasn't so much bothered by the court-ordered lockdown. As far as she was concerned, it was three months away from her morose mother; thirteen Wednesdays and thirteen weekends away from her idiotic father and his bubble-headed blonde bombshell. Katie could survive anywhere; she didn't think she needed help. She believed she could shut off her desire to drink, the craving for drugs, anytime she wanted. She just didn't see the need to want to.

Cara and Mel had been arguing about the lockdown program from the minute Katie walked through the heavily alarmed doors at the rehabilitation facility, away from both of them.

"She's going to hate it in there," Mel said, shaking her head and lighting a cigarette as they walked back toward Cara's car. "But it's the best thing for her, Cara. She's strong enough to survive this." She inhaled deeply and held the smoke in her lungs, then blew it away from her.

Cara glared at her friend. She loved that Mel could speak her mind; it was one of the things she admired most about her. But not now; not where Katie was concerned. Where Katie was concerned, Cara wished Melanie would keep her opinions to herself.

"It's extreme, Mel. It's far too extreme," Cara said, shaking her head.

Mel held strong. "It's what she *needs*."

Cara cringed at the sound of Mel's words—they weighed heavily on her shoulders. She hated the way Mel confronted the subject, as if she was ripping off a Band-Aid to reveal a scab that hadn't quite healed. "I know what she *needs*, Melanie; she's my daughter. I recognize she's screwed up. God, I get that. But honestly, don't you think she deserves to be home in her own bed, home where she can have the support we can give her? Certainly that would be more productive than, well, the next thirteen weeks of awful cafeteria food and self-humiliation sessions with *these* people."

Mel closed her eyes to Cara's words and took a deep breath in and out. Like it or not, Katie was now part of the group her mother so lovingly referred to as *these people.*

Jack didn't visit his daughter in rehab. He managed every excuse, every justification, like he was juggling balls in a circus act. He asked Cara for regular progress reports every time he picked up the rest of their brood, and made his own summarizations from there.

"They didn't have visiting hours that day."

"I was stuck on a conference call all afternoon."

"You said Katie's mood wasn't all that up right now, so it just didn't seem like the right time to visit her."

"Given what you told me the therapists there said, by all accounts, she's doing much better."

Jack hadn't been able to handle it: his pride and joy drowning herself, self-medicating. What he didn't have to see, he didn't have to internalize, he didn't have to feel.

Cara went to visit her daughter every day they'd let her, which was three times a week for an hour each visit. When her mother was there, Katie would clam up, cross her arms over her chest and stare at the television set droning on in the corner of the visiting room. She bit her nails and paced the room like a caged tiger, ready to pounce. She gave her mother little information to go on, saving her deeper conversations for someone who might actually enjoy having a meaningful conversation. Those conversations were usually reserved for Mel.

Mel saw Katie at least once a week, sometimes twice. She and Katie had an agreement that Katie would not mention to her mother that Mel had been there and, in turn, Mel would not mention it to Cara. That way, what passed between Mel and Katie stayed between them. Neither of them was left to answer

Cara's incessant barrage of questions or betray the confidences that had been built between the two of them all these years.

Katie could do what her mother could not. She could admit that she was an alcoholic; she readily acknowledged it to Mel. She told Mel she drank because it helped fill the emptiness she felt in her life nearly every minute of the day from the second she woke up. She'd started drinking because it helped her cope with every uncontrollable thing in her life; she kept drinking because drinking had become the thing she did, it was part of who she was. When her friends described her, they used terms like *wasted* and *hosed* and *plowed*. She'd lost a sense of the little girl she was before she'd started drinking, of the person that existed somewhere deep within her, the person who could survive a day sober. Katie claimed she was strong enough to survive a day without taking at least one drink; she just hadn't done it in a long, long time. Mel knew she had it in her but that it would be a hard, long road before Katie found that person again.

Katie loved the way alcohol made her feel—fearless. It numbed her head and dulled her senses and afforded her a warm, soft space that was hers alone. It was as if she was falling but would never hit the ground. It was as if she was spinning but never felt sick. It was as if she was awake but never left the dream. Her mother could be yammering at her in that incessant whine that meant Cara was unsatisfied with everything in her own life, her father could be slobbering over his girlfriend, and still Katie could survive it all. She chose to live in a drunken-filled world whenever she had the chance, self-medicating her way through the hours.

In the early days when her mother was naive and didn't believe Katie had ever touched the stuff, she'd stashed beers under her bed, in her drawers, at the back of her closet. Cara never bothered to look; she refused to acknowledge that her daughter could be the type to drink in the first place. Later, when Katie's moods began to swing and her grades began to suffer, Cara was forced to own up to what she had known all along. By then Katie's drink of choice was Absolut and the evidence much less easy to spot. Kate was a pro at concealing the goods; in her shampoo bottles, rolled into the bottom of her sleeping bag stuffed in the rear of her closet, back behind a stack of DVDs in the media room. Finally, as if she no longer cared, Katie began drinking straight from her father's bar in the study; long, full draws on the bottle as if she was hydrating with Evian after a long run. When he questioned her about stealing his booze, she readily admitted she had done so. When he locked the cabinet, she broke the lock. When they finally cleaned the house of any bottles, she bought her own.

Mel sat with Katie in the sterile visitor center at the facility. The brick walls were covered in posters with cheery sayings, like:

WE CANNOT CHANGE YESTERDAY.

WE CAN ONLY MAKE THE MOST OF TODAY,
AND LOOK WITH HOPE TOWARD TOMORROW.

Katie fingered the pages of a book she was reading; flipping the pages back and forth.

Remarkably Katie's eyes were brighter, her hair shone with more luster. Her face was fuller, she had put on a few pounds that sat on her hips and helped fill out her skeletal frame. Mel watched her carefully, taking in every movement, every breath Katie took in and let out. Mel was happy to see her looking more like the child she remembered but hadn't seen in a long while, but didn't quite trust that she could maintain the changes in her appearance.

A comfortable silence settled between them as if they were friends, peers. Katie had never thought of Melanie as her mother's friend, probably because Mel had never treated her like her friend's daughter. Katie sat in a wide wicker chair in the corner with her legs pulled up under her butt. She played with the ends of her long, bone-straight hair. Mel wore tight jeans and a crisp white blouse, great shoes and a long sterling silver chain. She didn't mind visiting Katie so much; people everywhere were smoking, lighting up one cigarette after the other as if they had exchanged one addiction for another. Mel could smoke freely here without any repercussions. No one here, not even Katie, chastised her for her nicotine habit.

"Do you think you'll drink again? You know, when you get out of here?" Mel asked her, blowing the smoke from a newly lit cigarette away from their conversation. Mel kept one eye on Katie, eager to see if she could read her face. Mel could nearly always tell when Kate was lying.

"Yes," she answered, staring Mel straight in the eye. "I can't imagine I'll make it the rest of my life without ever drinking again. I mean it seems sort of far-fetched. Don'cha think?"

Mel nodded her head. Katie's words didn't frighten her; she was glad Kate was in touch with reality and hadn't been brainwashed into believing it was so easy to quit. Mel told her as much.

"It's a long, long time. You've got a lot of life left," Mel answered her.

"We're supposed to take things one day at a time."

"Yes, I've heard that. But I think it's good that you know what you're up against."

The hum of the ancient air conditioner filled the room, a faint, dull drone that proved all too ineffective.

"Do you think you'll want a drink the minute you walk into your house?" Mel was testing her, pushing her. She wanted to know how honest Katie could be with herself; she wanted to know if Katie had had time to think it all through.

Katie paused for a minute, thinking. "Maybe. Don't know yet."

"You can call me, you know that. You can call me anytime you want to; anytime you think you might need to take a drink."

"I know." She paused and looked down, studying something in her lap. "I have a whole list of people I can call. I have a sponsor."

"I know."

"I should probably call her first. She'd know what to tell me. She'd probably talk me down off the ledge."

"I suppose. But if she doesn't answer, you can call me."

"Okay."

Mel studied the outline of Katie's face, the lines that had appeared much too early on such a young girl. The alcohol had taken its toll on her body, already. Katie had missed her awkward phase and gone straight from cute to hard. At seventeen, she looked hard. It reminded Mel of her stepfather, how the alcohol had aged him so much in such a short period of time, how Dermott's skin had ceased to glow and his eyes had stopped shining. She remembered how alcohol had become so much a part of his life, as if he was swimming in it, taking the rest of the family down with him. She didn't want Katie to get to that extreme, to wither away from her right before her eyes. Mel longed to pull Katie back; to save her from what would certainly kill her if Katie wasn't careful.

Cara interrupted their visit, just as Mel was gathering her things and readying to leave. She came into the room in a sweep of emotion and concern, her bag flying open and various items scattering about.

"Oh, sweetie, they told me you were in here." Cara's voice echoed through the hollow room. "They told me someone was here to see you, but I couldn't imagine who you'd . . ."

Mel didn't have to turn around to know that Cara had stopped when she saw her. Mel knew Cara's mouth had fallen open and then pressed into a hard, thin line of discontentment as if she had stumbled upon Jack cheating on her.

"Oh. Mel," Cara said, looking from Mel to Katie and then back again, as if they were hiding a bursting secret from her. "What are you doing here?" Cara's voice was strained and clipped, displeased. She sensed that they had been deep in conversation, something she couldn't manage with her own daughter. Jealousy blanketed her, shielding her from hurt.

"Just on my way out, actually. I came to check on our girl," Mel answered her. "She looks so wonderful." Mel winked at Katie, grabbing her hand and holding it tight before embracing her quickly and giving her a peck on the cheek. "I know she can't wait to get home. Soon enough," Mel said.

Katie was all of a sudden awkward and stilted in her mother's presence. The air in the room felt thicker than it had, choking. She longed for Mel to stay, longed for her mother to disappear so that she could sulk back to her room and think on her conversation with Mel.

Cara stood pigeon-toed, untying a silk scarf from her neck. She draped the scarf on the table before asking Mel, "How long have you been here? Don't let me run you off."

"Not long," Mel lied, checking her watch, "but no worries. I know you and Katie have things to catch up on. I'll call you later." Mel leaned in and kissed her friend, hugging her tight at the waist to allay her sudden fears, the jealous mistrust Mel was all too familiar with.

Cara fidgeted, wanting to feel as if she was on equal footing with Melanie. Instead, all she felt was inadequate, not worthy of the same intense discussion, the same secrets, and with her own daughter. "I'm meeting with Stewart," Cara said quickly, abruptly changing the subject, and hoping to cut through the tension before Mel left. "Tomorrow morning. He didn't waste any time calling me back just like you said he would be."

Mel smiled broadly, two straight lines of white teeth gleaming back at Cara. "Fabulous, Cara. That's great. He'd be lucky to have you. And don't think he doesn't know it, either." Mel hugged her friend again, tightly and warm.

8

Stewart Weaver was a bona fide hugger. Not just your run-of-the-mill squeeze; we're talking all-out, take no prisoners, warm bear hug that cut across your rib cage and left you feeling good all over. Cara was standing in the open foyer of his agency when he tore down the wide, newly refinished staircase and wrapped his arms around her. Instantly she disappeared against his broad chest. Then he held her at arm's length before he kissed her on each cheek, exuberantly. His cheeks were ruddy, his face beamed. Stewart's teeth were crooked, but his smile was infectious. He was thrilled to see her.

In his small, crowded office, he offered her coffee and a job at the same time.

"Do you need some coffee, Cara? A late-morning pick-me-up?"

"No, Stewart, I'm fine."

"Then come and work for me, Cara. Come and work *with* me. I've been waiting for you to come back to work for years. Clearly I'm entitled to first right of refusal. I don't see how you can deny me that."

Cara laughed, warmed by his eagerness. "Geez, Stewart, how about a little foreplay?" she joked with him. "A girl can't be expected to be ready right out of the shoot, you know." Cara settled against the modern angled chair and crossed her ankles. She'd bought a new outfit for the meeting, a caramel-colored suede suit that fit her perfectly.

"Right out of the shoot, my ass. How long have I been begging you to come to your senses and come back to work? As long as I can remember. Wasted talent sitting at home with those four adorable children of yours. Honestly, what more do I need to do to seduce you?" His English accent was charming, sweet and alluring.

"Don't remind me. I haven't had a day among the creatively gifted in years." Cara cringed, reached for the stress ball on his desk and squeezed it tightly. Stewart's office was cramped. Stacks of creative boards—rejected ads, layouts, and sketch boards with ideas flowing across them—were piled haphazardly in the corners. His bookshelves were dense: back issues of design magazines, small awards, framed pictures of his daughter, a collection of Marvel Comics plastic superheroes. Cara scanned the decorated walls, the framed artwork that hung proudly in his office.

"Let's not go that far, Cara. It's only advertising. But, say you'll do it. Haven't you had enough of this mommy stuff? Say you'll come back." Stewart's eyes pleaded with her from across the desk. "I need you. I need someone who won't get caught up in her panties over this crazy business. You know how it can be. It will eat you alive. I need someone who can roll with it. I *need* you."

Stewart wasn't exaggerating; he had been begging Cara for years to come back to work with him. It had always been flattering but not particularly enticing. And completely unnecessary. Jack, for all his faults, kept a healthy bank account and there was no financial reason for Cara to work. And after she became pregnant with Luke, she petered out, telling herself she could take on consulting jobs as they came, work from her home office. That had been over eight years ago.

This time it was different. Cara needed a job. Money aside, and even with the alimony Jack would surely be paying her, she'd still need more. She longed to feel like she was important again, as if she had the ability to make a decision about something and have people listen to her. Since Jack had moved out, she'd begun to wish for more adult contact, for people who praised her for something other than the suggestions she made at the PTA meetings. More than that, she desired a new identity, to share her new life with people who didn't connect her with her old life. Going back to work just might provide her the anonymity she was looking for.

Mel had arranged for the meeting. She and Stewart had a history together. They'd been lovers briefly but friends for what seemed like an eternity. Stewart's agency was Melanie's first repeat client. They'd brought her in when she first started shooting, giving her a shot at the jobs she'd never have gotten anywhere else. Stewart allowed her to trip and stumble but never let her fall, and for that she was eternally grateful. Word spread and Mel's work was immediately in demand, but when Stewart or someone from his agency called, she'd practically drop everything, work double-time, rearrange her schedule to make something work for them. If nothing else, Mel was loyal.

Stewart ran Weaver Sinclair Advertising solo. He and his former partner, Madeline Sinclair, parted company the year after they'd opened, leaving him with a client roster too long to handle on his own, though somehow he had managed to do so. Madeline had been homesick for London and left him like a bad divorce. He retained her name in the agency, promising her that if she had ever wanted to come back to the States, he'd have her back in a minute. Rather, she married, had three kids and moved to the country. Christmases, Stewart would receive her smiling family photo, hang his head, pour himself a scotch, cover his eyes and have a good cry. He'd worked with some of the best talent since Madeline left, but no one gave him the same groove, he said. No one struck the same vibe with him.

"Do you have a job for me, Stewart? I mean a real job. Because I don't want your pity, just for the hell of it, you know. I won't be your pro bono charity case."

"Oh, for God's sake, Cara, we'll figure out the details later. Just say you'll do it."

For no reason in particular, Cara stalled, eyeing him over an arched brow. "It's been a long time, Stewart. A really, really long time. I'm not sure I'm any good anymore."

"Trust me on this, Cara, you'll be fine."

"That sounds like something Mel would say," Cara answered him.

"Brilliant. She's the smartest woman I know. And you can tell her I said so. C'mon, there's someone I want you to meet. New suit I hired. Best in the business. Maybe he can convince you to come to your senses and come do this with us."

"He's good?"

"Good? He's fucking fabulous," he said sincerely, jumping up from his leather chair and pulling Cara by the hand. "I stole him from New York but he was born and bred here in San Francisco. Maybe you know him? David Michel?"

Cara shook her head. "I've been out of the game too long, Stewart. I don't know anybody anymore."

"Oh, you'd be surprised, luv. There are plenty of us still left in this crazy business. It's a young person's game, no doubt, but there's a bunch of old loonies that can't seem to hang it up. But David? He's . . . Well, he is a bit, shall we say, younger."

"A kid? You hired a kid?"

"He's good, Cara. Smart. Bold. Unaffected. Charismatic and charming. He is exactly what we needed. Inspiring and enthusiastic. Just an infectious attitude. You'll see."

Stewart steered her through the agency, practically pushing her along. Glass offices—some with two or three desks to a room—bordered the row of windows, but large, open workspaces with whiteboards and kitchen table–sized conference tables filled the middle of the spacious building. The ceilings were high and unfinished. The place actually buzzed, humming with energy. Cara felt a surge of energy run through her body, a bolt like nothing she'd felt in a long while. She felt her body come alive; she craved everything about the intensity of the place.

David Michel's office held the same glass desk, the same small, round conference table as Stewart's. Sparse and minimal, there were few stacks of papers, fewer framed ads or art. He sat with his back to them, a wireless earplug in his ear. The ends of his impeccably trimmed hair brushed the top of his suit jacket. Cara heard him before she saw him. Softly but convincingly, he was working a client over on the phone, defending the work they'd shown at an earlier meeting, but carefully listening to what it was the client was looking for.

Stewart cleared his throat and David wheeled around in his leather chair, motioning for them to wait just a moment more.

Cara took him in. Olive skin with perfectly oval-shaped brown eyes. Long legs sprawled beneath the desk. Good shoes, an even better suit. Great hands, long nail beds. No wedding ring.

No wedding ring.

It was the first time Cara remembered noticing such a thing in a long, long time. She admonished herself for doing so, blushing furiously in his company.

God, Cara, pull it together.

Cara shifted, one Marc Jacobs heel to the other, clutching her leather bag. Stewart had lost interest in waiting and wandered outside David's office, stopping to chat it up with a twentysomething who looked as if she was fresh from the art academy. The young woman studied him attentively, hanging on his every word as if he spoke the gospel. Stewart had a wonderful reputation and ran an incredible agency, but this looked as if it was more than that, as if she might jump into bed with him at any minute, if she hadn't already. Working here at such a young age was a dream and this girl knew it.

"Hello, hi," David Michel said to Cara as he removed his headset. "You must be Cara. Sit, please." He extended his hand to her and she took it, firmly. She tried her best to concentrate on her purpose, smoothing her skirt and ignoring his charming good looks.

She took the chair on the other side of his desk, altogether self-conscious and jittery at once. *What's your problem, Cara?* she thought to herself. *A kid, my God, he's a KID.*

"Good to meet you, Cara. Finally. Stewart has been talking

about you since I started," he said to her and laced his long fingers together. He rested on his elbows, moving in close across the desk. He spoke quietly, forcing Cara to listen carefully.

"Ah, you've met." Stewart's British boom filled the room from behind Cara. "And haven't killed each other yet. Good, good. This woman has held out on me for years, David. She is the biggest tease I know."

"So I've heard." He tilted back in the leather chair so that just the tips of his shoes touched the floor. Calm and sexy as hell, he made Cara nervous the way he looked at her, right into her as if he could see into her soul.

Cara recovered quickly. "Oh, Stewart, get over it already."

"Come to work with us and we'll consider it," David Michel jumped in, pulling Cara's eyes back to him.

"Geez, you two. Foreplay, David, foreplay," Cara teased back. "What is it with you men? Get out of here, Stewart, and let me talk to your boy. Let's see what he's got."

With Stewart gone, David walked to the door and closed it firmly so that it echoed. He was wide at the shoulders and narrow at the waist; his pants hung nicely on him. He took the chair next to Cara's, crossed his legs and balanced his chin on his fist. "Okay, Cara Clancy, let's see what *you've* got."

The room filled with electric energy. Cara could feel it radiate from David's eyes, the way they danced and smiled and made her feel welcome all at once. She shrugged her shoulders playfully at him, and wondered if she was on an interview or a first date. "What do you want to know?"

"Why are you here?"

"Ah, the open-ended question of the year. Hmmm, okay." She paused, trying to decide if she trusted him, what he made of her. *Oh, hell, why not?* "I need a job. I can't stand to go another day without working."

He smiled, shuffled his legs and shifted his weight from his right to his left side. "What? Nothing else to occupy your time?"

Cara laughed. "Four kids and all the assorted nonsense that goes with them, but, no, that's not doing it for me these days. Not even close. I'm getting divorced, I'm afraid. I need something to get my mind off it, something else to pour my heart into."

"Four kids? My God, Cara, who has four kids anymore?"

"Me. Temporary insanity. But I love them to death. They're fabulous. Seventeen, ten, eight, and the baby; she's seven. Girl, boy, boy and another girl. You have kids?" she asked and eyed his ring finger again.

"Nooooo. No, no, no, no, not me. Declared incompetent, actually. They'd never give me a license."

"You'd be surprised."

"And your husband?" he asked boldly without wincing or cringing the way so many other people had.

"He's on baby #5 with girlfriend, um, soon-to-be wife #2."

"I'm sorry."

"Don't be."

"Okay. I won't."

Killer smile, full killer smile. Quiet settled on the room, thick and chunky, leaving her studying the walls, wishing to find something that could take her eyes off him just for a minute. Still, he continued to study her.

"Can you have lunch with me, Cara?" He glanced briefly at his watch before he raised an eyebrow at her. "Do you have the time?"

He'd taken her completely by surprise and she fumbled. "Oh? Um, well, ah, I guess, well, I'm not sure. Do you know what Stewart has in mind? Um, maybe I should check with him first . . ."

He stood and began to check the growing stream of messages on his computer. She collected her things and waited uneasily, as if she was unsure of what to do, where to go. He glanced up from his computer and caught her eye.

"Just give me fifteen minutes or so. I need to make a few calls. Tracy can show you to a conference room." A sea of electric current passed between them and left her weak at the knees.

David Michel was hitting on her.

DAVID MICHEL WAS HITTING ON HER. And by all accounts, he wasn't done.

Cara followed his assistant to a glass conference room, and asked for directions to the closest ladies' room. Inside she peed and punched out a text message to Mel from her cell phone.

David Michel is hitting on me. Going to lunch with him now. Help!!!

Mel's reply message came back immediately.

Just don't sleep with him before he offers you a job.

Cara fired back.

I swear to God, Mel, I'm not kidding you. He's hitting on me. What do I do?

What's he look like?

"Oh, for God's sake, Melanie, what do you mean, 'What does he look like?'" Cara barked into the phone when Mel answered. "This is supposed to be a job interview. What the fuck do I care what he looks like?" She flushed the toilet with the heel of her shoe and scooted out of the stall, crouching to check the vacancy of the stalls next to hers praying she hadn't spilled her guts in front of the office gossip.

"Well, he looks like *something*, Cara, what?"

"That's beside the point," Cara whispered harshly as she made her way back through the long hall toward the conference room.

"No, it's not. Is he worth it? 'Cause you can't sleep with Stewart's number-one guy before he offers you a job. Unless, of course, it'd be better to sleep with him than work with him."

"We're not even talking about sleeping with him, Mel. It's lunch, for Christ sake. Get your mind out of the gutter." Cara was exasperated with her friend; she sighed deeply into the receiver.

"Look, Cara, you want this job? If so, you'll have Stewart cumming all over himself. He's been begging you for years to come back to work so he could have you all to himself. Go to lunch. If David Michel's as good-looking as I think he might be, go ahead and hit back. What have you got to lose? All I'm saying is that I don't think Stewart will hold it against you."

"Jesus, Mel, why do I call you? What in God's name do I think I'm going to gain by checking in with you?"

"You haven't answered my question."

"What question?"

"What's he look like? Tall? Short? Dark, blonde? Old, young? He's supposed to be a kid, right? How old is he?"

"Thirtysomething. *Early* thirtysomething. Jesus Christ, Melanie, he *is* a kid. He'd be better off dating Katie. I've got years on him."

"He's got you all tangled up in knots, Cara. I can hear it in your voice."

"Does not."

"He does. I can tell. You sound just as smitten as you did in ninth grade. Denny Spangler."

"Don't be ridiculous."

"Uh-huh."

"Stop it. I'm hanging up now. I don't know why I bother with you, Mel. I have no idea, really I don't. You are absolutely no help."

"Uh-huh," Mel said again, smugly.

"I'm hanging up now." Cara sprinted back into the conference room without being seen.

"Call me later," Mel cried. "I'll want a full report."

David Michel opened doors. Car doors, restaurant doors, the lobby door of the agency. You name it; he was a door opener. He and Cara collided the first time when Cara started to push her way through the revolving glass door and he stepped just in front of her to catch it first. She wasn't expecting him to be such a gentleman; it had been a long time since she'd been in the company of a man who opened a door for her.

"Sorry," she said, nervously, too quickly.

"No problem. After you."

He assisted her into the front seat of his Mercedes, literally taking her arm and settling her into the soft leather as if he was helping his mother to her seat. It wasn't as if he was so young and Cara was so old, but something about it left Cara feeling cared for, as if he was escorting his grandmother out to lunch. She told him this, in a fit of giggles, when he finally tucked himself behind the steering wheel. But then she realized this had nothing to do with age; David Michel was a well-kept secret of a man.

Cara couldn't remember the last time Jack had opened a door for her. She couldn't remember what it was like to have him listen, really listen to her response when he asked her a question. In fact, she couldn't remember the last time Jack had asked her a question that didn't sound something like, *Did you pick up my laundry?* She couldn't remember a time when Jack had made her feel so special, even when she wasn't feeling well or when a day with the kids had taken its toll on her.

David ordered wine with lunch. Over salad, Cara learned he was first-generation American, and that both his parents had grown up in Paris. He spoke fluent French, the only language he was permitted to use when addressing his parents. He pronounced his last name *Me-shell* with the sweetest hint of seductive femininity that Cara had ever heard.

"Okay, Cara Clancy, let's hear it." He touched the edge of his glass with hers. "Why've you put Stewart off for so long?"

"Uh-oh. The inquisition."

He nodded, leaning back against the hard wood chair and crossing his legs so that his body was parallel with hers. Dark, nearly black, charcoal suit. Pressed pale-pink striped shirt. Black square-toed shoes. A fabulous tie. He'd tucked his dark clip-on frames in the front pocket of his suit jacket; they peeked just over the rim of the pocket as if to be eavesdropping on their conversation.

"I lost the drive to work, I suppose. We didn't need the money, and when my second child came along, I just decided to give it all up for a little while. It just seemed so much easier, I guess." Cara laughed, then shook her head.

"How so?"

"Oh, I don't know. Playdates and diapers versus uptight clients and ridiculous deadlines."

He paused, swirled his wine in the glass and watched her. "Kind of the same thing, don't you think?" After a minute, he said to her, "So?"

"So, what?"

"So, is it time for you to join Weaver?"

"Maybe."

"How do we go about convincing you?"

She turned his question around and asked him, "Why'd you go to work with Stewart? What drew you back to San Francisco from New York?"

"That's easy. For the great work. You can't get better work than you'll get at this agency. Period."

Cara nibbled on her pecan-crusted halibut. She found that she liked David Michel. She liked everything about him. His confidence radiated through his eyes, his smile, his demeanor.

"You should work with us, Cara. It would be great, great fun. I'm fairly sure it would be the next best thing in your life."

Everything he said, everything about the way he said it, made her want to do just that.

Later, Cara told Mel that Stewart had let out an audible sigh, something almost sexual, when she finally accepted the job.

"Wicked, Cara," Mel said. "You are absolutely wicked. Teasing my boy like that. I can't imagine where you learned it."

Cara smiled at her friend. It was the first time she had remembered making a decision—one that really mattered—for herself in a long, long time.

They had agreed to the terms of her contract in a meeting back at the office, at the end of which David Michel walked her to the front door, and held it open for her to walk through. This time she was ready for him, and scooted through with confidence and grace. He lit a cigarette and offered her one. She declined and dug around in her oversized black bag for her car keys.

"He was watching me, Mel. I could feel his eyes on me the entire time I was digging around in that damn bag."

"I told you to get rid of that thing. For God's sake, Cara, get a small clutch. Christ, you were probably pulling out a bunch of those ridiculous McDonald's toys that get stuck at the bottom of that ratty old bag."

Cara ignored her comment. "I mean, *watching* me, Mel. I could *feel* his eyes on me; feel the way he was dragging on that cigarette. Without even looking up. You know what I mean?"

"Uh-huh."

"He asked me to dinner. Saturday night. He said it just like that, too. 'I'd like to take you to dinner, Cara. Will Saturday night work for you?' "

"And? Are you going?" Mel asked her eagerly.

"I invited him to your party instead. Dinner was just so, so . . . full of commitment."

"And the party?"

"It's supervised."

9

Garin had canceled on Mel plenty of times before; it wasn't inconceivable. Through no fault of his own, of course, something would come up to keep him from whatever it was they had planned together. Mel never felt as if he chose something or someone over her, not any of the times he ended up canceling. But it never completely surprised her if she received a phone call that started with the words, *Baby, I'm really sorry, but* . . . And it never completely broke her heart, either. She was used to being alone. She actually preferred it that way.

They never would have lasted long living in the same city. Hell, they may not have lasted in the same state. Their arrangement was something Mel was comfortable with. Truth be told, it was something she required.

Mel had invited Garin to join her for dinner; that's how their relationship started. She was well aware of the fact that he was married and had children; he'd spent that entire day telling her all about them. She didn't care. After shooting him for his company's annual report, she wanted more time with him. Time alone, time when she wasn't behind the camera and he wasn't in front of it. After dinner, still more. After their first night of great sex at the Hotel Nikko, even more.

Mel had no desire to marry Garin, no desire for him to father a child of hers or buy a house with her. She didn't long for him on weeknights when he wasn't there, didn't go to bed lonely and wishing he was next to her. She liked what they had, the isolation of it when they were together and the freedom when they were apart. This way she never felt like she owed him something, never felt like she had to be someone she couldn't make herself be.

Mel had seen what could go wrong when you got too close to someone. She'd witnessed, firsthand, what marriage looked like, the so-called *exclusive* nature of it. And by her estimation, there was no such thing. Her mother's relationship had ended in divorce, and that wasn't even from Mel's father. Jack had been cheating on Cara for years; as far back as she could remember. And as far as she could tell that had resulted in nothing more than eighteen wasted years.

Everything about Mel was independent, sovereign. She wagered this was one of the things that Garin liked best about her, anyway. He had one white picket fence; there was no need for another.

During a brief phone conversation on her way to the caterer's, she'd told him about the party she had been planning. It wasn't meant to be an invitation but he'd taken it as such. For some reason, of late, he'd had the desire to meet her friends. But she had been putting him off. There was no reason to mix him into her life in San Francisco; nothing good could come of blending him into her circle of friends.

"I'll be in San Francisco this weekend, Mel. Why don't I come to the party?"

"Okay," she had said, much too quickly, regretting her answer immediately. She was in a rush and not paying attention and she had let her guard down for only a minute. For the last year, she'd kept Garin locked away; even Bella had met him only once, and that was a fluke, when they'd run into her daughter and some of her friends at dinner one night in the city. She just didn't see the point in integrating him into her daily routine, didn't feel like it was necessary.

"Don't you think it's time, Mel?"

"I don't know what time has to do with it, Garin," she snapped. "Yeah, fine, whatever. It's just a small party. It's not a big deal." She was stalling, downplaying her plans and hoping that by then he would come to his senses and change his mind. She had nearly forty people on the guest list. Forty introductions. Forty wide-eyed looks. Forty explanations about how long they had been going out and how they could possibly sustain a bicoastal relationship.

"All the better, then. No pressure at all."

"No, not really." She swallowed hard and pursed her lips, thinking about the crab wontons she wanted to make sure were on the menu. "None whatsoever." She paused then, trying to think on her feet. "Um, are you sure? You sure you want to do this?"

"Oh, Mel, for Christ sake, it's a party. Why the hell not?"

Cara was thrilled. For months she and Leah and Paige had been relentless about asking to meet the man Mel had been carrying on with for over a year. They relished Mel's stories; his sweet ways of showing up unexpected and staying for the weekend, of whisking her away when she needed a week at a Ritz somewhere fabulous. After all this time, Cara couldn't imagine why they hadn't met Garin. He had truly remained a mystery man.

On Friday, as Mel arranged two vases full of the Dendrobium Orchids she'd picked up at the flower market, she prayed he would cancel. She hated the uneasy feeling in her stomach and had been forced to chase it away with Tums, angry with herself for getting all jacked up. His visit meant nothing, she told herself over and over again. Meeting Cara, Leah and Paige didn't signify anything. They were no more a couple than they had been.

Near seven o'clock, the doorbell rang.

"Key?" she asked accusingly when she opened the door, wondering why he hadn't used the key she'd given him.

He shrugged his shoulders, bundled down with plastic bags, a sheepish grin on his face. The smell from Ming's Lemon Chicken mixed with that of Dried Braised String Beans made Mel's stomach growl. His familiar worn suitcase sat on the landing next to him.

"I brought dinner," he said to her, smiling.

She threw open the door wide, pulling him in, calmed immediately by his presence.

Without a doubt, Mel knew how to throw a party. Her flat vibrated from the street. Candles danced in the windows, shadows crossed the panes, and the cackle of voices sounded like something out of a university dormitory. On the front step two tall, rail-thin models whom Mel had shot recently stood in wool coats and high heels smoking clove cigarettes, the whispery ribbons of strong scented smoke swirling in the wind around their faces.

The music was excruciatingly louder and more vibrant inside the house. It reverberated off the walls and hardwood floors like a nightclub in full swing. Cara spotted Leah and Paige and rushed over in an instant, helping them with their coats and hugging them in one fell swoop. Cara had debated back and forth over her outfit, changing several times before she left for Mel's, but she looked fabulous in jeans and a jeweled black halter top that cut at her midsection. Her hair was pulled back from her face and, with just a tinge of lipstick and even lighter blush, her face was all aglow with mischief.

"You're late." Cara's eyes were large and glaring, but she hid a hint of laughter in her voice. She looked as if she was ready to burst forth with a secret she could hardly contain.

Leah smoothed her blouse and dropped her bag in the corner. "Okay, let's get this over with. Where's Mr. Wonderful? Let's have a look at him."

"Mr. Wonderful isn't here yet," Cara said, dismissing the comment immediately. "But that," she continued, and nodded to the man mixing margaritas in the stainless blender in Mel's kitchen, "that's Garin. Mel's secret has *finally* crawled out of the bag. Come on," she said, grabbing both of them by the hands, "you'll love him."

They gawked at Mel's mystery man. No one had laid eyes on him, not in the entire year he and Mel had been dating. They stood with their hands on their hips and stared at him until he must have felt their eyes on him, drawing him to look up. When he did, he flashed them a smile from across the room, a look that caused them all to dissolve into a fit of giggles, as if something had touched them off.

Garin was all salt and pepper. His features had, at one time, been defined and strong, his nose was sculpted, his eyes were deep set and piercing. But age had softened him; lines had set in around his eyes and at his mouth. He wore worn jeans, faded and broken in, a black button-down shirt and black sweater, pushed up to his midarm.

"He, he looks kind of sweet," Paige said. "Kind of, well, um . . ." Paige searched for the right words, struggling to find something considerate.

"He is sweet," Cara interrupted and nodded. "You're going to like him. Let me introduce you."

"Cara, you have got to be kidding," Leah choked out from under her breath, a staged smile on her face even as they made their way toward the kitchen. "He's like, an *OLD* guy."

"Leah!" Cara exclaimed. "He's far from old," she said in a harsh whisper, admonishing her friend, if only a little bit.

Cara had had a similar reaction when she knocked on the door earlier in the day and came face-to-face with Garin. He had welcomed her cordially and invited her in. Mel was showering and Cara immediately found herself in the kitchen, side by side with Garin cutting lemons and limes for the bar. They chatted casually, sharing similar stories about Mel, but Cara still hadn't felt she'd gotten to know him, not yet, anyway. She was hoping that now, with Leah and Paige, she might have a second chance.

"He's *old* for Mel, Cara," Leah whispered back. "Even you have to admit that. My God, he's like somebody's father. Mel doesn't date *old* guys. Mel dates young, hot guys. Mel dates twenty-four-year-olds, guys that take her to trendy clubs until four in the morning. This guy is *old*."

"Le-ah, please." Paige swatted her arm. "I'm sure he's perfectly delightful."

"Okay, shut up and listen to the details," Cara said. "Here's the skinny. He's fifty-four, Leah; he's not *that* old. He's out here on business this week, some conference he's speaking at, and he wanted to meet all of us. Mel says he showed up on her doorstep last night, brought her dinner and threw her whole schedule off today because he kept fucking her in bed all morning. Apparently the Viagra is working. Don't knock it until you've tried it." Cara relayed all of this under her breath and sent them further into a fit of hysterics.

Just then Mel came into the kitchen, wearing four-inch heels, jeans that barely covered the top of her latest wax and a thin black baby doll T-shirt. Her hair hung down her back in a straight sheen sheet and her emerald eyes were accented by thick, heavy black makeup. She commandeered the room and carried on multiple conversations while she introduced Garin to a group of people Cara knew from the agency. When her friends crowded into the kitchen, she turned her attention to them.

"Oh, for Christ sake, the three of you haven't even had a drink and you're already ready to pee your pants. What the hell is wrong with the three of you?"

This made them laugh harder.

"Nothing, nothing." Cara recovered first, then Paige, Leah still trying to stifle her giggles.

"You must be Leah," Garin said, surprising her. He reached across the bar to set a margarita in front of her.

"And I understand you're Garin," Leah said, hands on her

hips and giving him the once-over, top to bottom. They stared each other down until Garin flashed a warm smile and Leah was forced to turn her attention to the olives on a large antipasto tray. Even Leah had to admit there was something sensual about him, something that threw her for a loop. She watched him add more tequila to the blender, eyeballing it with confidence.

Paige waited her turn, until Cara finally said, "Garin, you haven't met Paige."

"Ah, Paige, yes." He offered his hand, grasping hers. "I'm happy to meet you. Mel has told me a lot about you. All of you," he added quickly.

Paige had never felt such soft skin on a man, his hands like velvet. She smiled at Garin, and his grin in return warmed her. She liked him instantly.

"What can I get you, Paige? Margarita?"

Paige surveyed the kitchen, the makeshift bar. "Just some mineral water, actually. If you've got some."

"Sure. Lime?"

She nodded, standing next to him while he poured her Perrier.

"How long have you known Mel?" Garin asked, handing her the glass.

"A long, long time," Paige said sweetly. "Too long to keep track, actually. She's a wonderful friend."

"Mmmm." He nodded and stirred the ice in his glass before he drained his drink. The skin around his eyes was soft, supple. Paige supposed some people acknowledged the lines only as age, but in their deep creases she felt wisdom, experience. He was tall, taller than she by more than a foot, but she felt comfortable next to him, sheltered from the noise and pulse of the party.

"Where's your cocktail, Paige?" Mel badgered her and stopped at Garin's side. She draped her left arm across his lower back and let it linger there. "It's a party, for Christ sake. You can have at least one drink."

"Oh, no, not tonight, Mel. Not much in the mood, I'm afraid. I think I've been fighting something off all week." Paige cleared

her throat purposefully, in an exaggerated fashion. She had debated about when to tell her friends that she was expecting,
when to break the news, partly because she was afraid they might
be able to read it, the thin line of apprehension that ran square
through the middle of everything. She knew they would be overwhelmed with joy, thrilled for her and Dennis. She expected tears,
exuberance. It had been a long time in coming and they had
been through so much defeat with her, so many failed attempts.

"Here, let me pour you a glass of red wine, just a touch won't
hurt."

"I, um, no, really, Mel, it's fine."

Mel tossed a striped dish towel on the small island in the middle of her kitchen. She stood with her hands on her hips, her
high-heeled feet spread wide apart. She wasted no time. "You're
pregnant, aren't you?" Mel announced, accusingly.

"*Mel* . . ." Cara admonished instantly, shock registering on her
face. It was the one question no one ever asked, certainly not in
public, especially not in a social situation like this where Paige
could fall apart, just dissolve in front of an entire crowd. They all
knew better and even Cara couldn't believe Mel would stoop
this low. The answer had too often been a disappointing *no*.

Mel had never understood the degree of Paige's disappointment in the first place; her sullen mood and the hell-bent determination Paige had to get pregnant. Mel had never had much
patience for the long, drawn-out discussions about infertility
treatments, the drugs that Paige had pumped into her body religiously. Mel had never comprehended the importance of this for
Paige, never recognized that everything about it signified failure
for her, that it was the one thing in her life that she had wanted
more than anything, and that it was the only thing in her life she
had ever been denied.

Mel stared at Paige, holding her gaze and waiting. She tapped
her foot impatiently, not willing to back down or let the moment
slip by as if she hadn't been so brazen. "You are, aren't you? I can
see it on you, Paige, come on."

Around them, music screamed out of the speakers, much too loudly for having an intimate conversation. Paige was perched on the edge of a stainless bar stool, condensation dripping down the side of her Perrier. She blushed furiously, feverishly, and silently cursed Mel for calling her out. If anyone would have, it would be Mel. Mel had given her grief about wanting a baby for as long as she'd wanted one. She had never understood Paige's desire, never stopped long enough to listen to what Paige really held in her heart. It had left Paige wondering if Mel understood anything about her, even after all these years. She knew they were different, surely that was obvious, even if you just stood them next to each other. But this was where the real division had cut, leaving Paige feeling on the other side. Leah and Cara waited uncomfortably, their eyes darting from Paige to Mel and back again. Behind them the party raged on, meaningless conversation lingered in the room around them.

"Mel, I don't know what you're out to prove . . ." Cara started in again, instantly furious and fiercely protective of Paige. There was a good deal they could all tolerate from Mel, a good deal of her judgment they simply let slip by, but this wasn't one of those things. Where Paige was concerned, Cara and Leah were quick to jump to her side.

"No," Paige said, stopping her suddenly. "No, Cara," she beamed, a smile instantly appearing on her wide mouth. "It's okay. Mel's right," she said quickly, quietly, and almost in a whisper. "I wasn't sure when it would be the right time to tell you, but she's right."

"She's *what?*" Cara and Leah screamed in unison and rushed to embrace their friend. They both placed their hands on her still-flat belly and searched for some sort of sign, a bump.

Mel never moved. She was frozen in the kitchen, waiting. An apology would be nice, she thought to herself. A smug, sly smile crept over her face. She had known it immediately, instinctively. She watched her friends fuss over Paige, and she watched Paige take it all in.

"Why didn't you tell us?"
"So, how far along are you?"
"When's the baby due?"
"How long have you known?"

They lobbed questions at her one right after the next, like smashing tennis serves that tore across the net and landed right in front of her. She couldn't get an answer out before the next one came crashing down on her.

"Okay, okay, give me a minute, will you? It's all a little overwhelming." She assumed her place on the stool once again and took a long sip of her water, swallowing and setting down her glass before she continued. "We've only just started telling our family. I'm barely twelve weeks. And you know how this could go, nothing is certain with everything we've been through." She shuddered, thinking about what could happen still. It scared her to think about the possibility.

"Oh, Paige, it's fabulous news," Cara gushed, turning her attention back to her friend. "I'm just so thrilled for you. Honestly, a new baby to spoil rotten. It's just what we all need." She threw her arms around Paige again, hugging her tightly.

"Really, Cara? Are you really okay with it all? Because I was so worried about telling you, you know, what with Jack's new baby and all. I just wasn't sure how you would take it, that's all."

Sweet Paige. It was just like her to think of Cara, to hold back her good news. Paige would never want to add to Cara's woe, she would never want to do anything to remind her of the obvious.

"Are you *kidding?* Come on, Paige, you can't even compare the two . . . This is just such wonderful news for you and Dennis. Jack's off fucking some twentysomething. It's not like he planned to have another baby, or even wanted his bleach-blonde girlfriend to pump out another kid for him to feed and clothe. But this? This is different. This is a miracle, sweetie. This is everything you've ever deserved."

"Ladies," Garin interrupted. "I don't suppose you might join me in a toast to our mother-to-be." When they turned he had popped a bottle of apple cider and poured it into Mel's finest champagne flutes. "Paige," he beamed, "congratulations and all good fortune to you and this child."

As if on cue, they clinked their glasses.

10

David Michel was a no-show at the party.

Cara had known early in the evening that he wasn't going to be there; she sensed it like she sensed a bad migraine coming on, like an argument with Jack that wasn't going to go her way. She was certain he had tucked away the scrap of paper on which she had carefully printed Mel's address without really meaning to come in the first place, and she felt foolish for having invited him. Maybe she'd misread his signs. Maybe he'd come to his senses and realized that she was a forty-three-year-old mother of four. Maybe he hooked up with someone in a bar the night before, someone thinner, younger and better looking. Her confidence waned and her self-esteem dropped.

Mel would hear none of it, not at first, anyway. She kept telling Cara she was overreacting, that she was worse than a schoolgirl with a bad crush. It wasn't until well past midnight, after Cara had finished off three double scotches, that Mel admitted maybe she was right.

"Men are the most unpredictable bastards on the planet. I actually thought this one might have some merit by the way you were going on about him, but simply bastards. He's not worth your time or energy, you know what I mean."

They were sitting on Mel's leather couch, a sectional that

wrapped around the outside of her front room. Cara stared out the large picture windows, watching the city lights blink below as if they held great promise. In the next room Garin was clearing plates and emptying glasses.

"Whatcha gonna do?" Cara shrugged her shoulders and crossed her arms over her chest, depression settling in. "We really shouldn't be surprised, Mel. He's a young, single thirtysomething in the city. I'm way out of my league on this one. Way out."

"You want to have a smoke with me?" Mel asked. "It might take the edge off."

"Nah," Cara slurred.

"C'mon," Mel answered her, "keep me company, anyway."

They stepped outside together, arm in arm, holding each other up. Cara's hair blew wildly and whipped around her face. The night was cold, damp and blustery, and the air helped to sober them up. Cara stood rocking on her heels and shaking, letting the frigid temperature seep into her bones. She watched Mel light a Camel, the smoke swirling around her head and dancing away from her. Mel sucked hard on the end as if it was a straw, the glow of the butt igniting in the dark night. The last of Mel's guests staggered down the stairs, people Cara didn't know. Mel hugged them with one arm as they left, the other held behind her, the cigarette between manicured nails.

"I think that's nearly the last of them. God, I don't even want to look at my place." She took another long drag and held the poison long in her lungs before blowing the smoke into the night. "Come on, sweetie, I've got your room ready. You can draw a bath before you go to bed if you want, Cara. Just blow that little piece of shit off."

Cara's eyes burned in the night. She desperately needed to sleep. "I'm ready for bed," She yawned wide, surveying the neighborhood one last time, looking up and down the street heavy with cars parked on either side. It was quieter now. She didn't want to talk anymore about David Michel, not tonight, anyway. She wanted to crawl under the covers and let the alcohol numb her head, send her buzzing into a deep sleep. Her ears rung from the noise at the party, the quiet in the flat just now setting in. Leah and Paige had left an hour earlier, Paige yawning indiscriminately and without apology now that they were all privy to her news.

Mel looped her arm in Cara's and they started up the stairs together. Cara let her head droop onto Mel's shoulder where it bobbed in rhythm with their unsteady steps.

"Mel." Cara stopped on the landing. "Garin is so hot for fifty-something. I gotta tell you when I first met him I was shocked that he was so much older, I think we all were. You *never* date older men. But really, he's so damn sexy. There's just something about him. Something that's so luscious."

"You have no idea," she answered. "He is unfuckingbelievable."

Cara studied her friend hopefully. Mel had never had a man in her life, not permanently, anyway. There had been plenty of dates, a multitude of meaningless relationships that had filtered in and out of her life, in and out of the flat, one right after the next. But never someone who had meant something to her, someone she truly loved, and who loved her back. It worried Cara, Mel's inability to involve herself with someone, to give herself to someone and allow him to love her back. Cara knew this was scar tissue, damage from the relationship Mel never had with her father, even more damage from the relationship she'd had with her mother. Her mother had vanished from her life, just up and left. And when Bea left, she left Mel with Dermott, her mother's husband. Everything after that marked everything in her life. It was her defining moment.

Cara wished for nothing more than to see Mel fall head over heels about someone. Surely someone could undo the damage that had been done. Surely someone could love away what had been taken from her. The walls Mel had built around her were tall, erected to keep out even the most painful memories. But certainly someone would dare scale them.

After all, Mel wasn't getting any younger, none of them was, and it was the right thing for her to do, to finally settle down. Enough was enough.

"I mean, really. Maybe this one's a keeper. Why doesn't he move out here? You should consider the possibility, you know. Maybe it's finally time for you to have someone in your life permanently. Maybe it's time for you to be with one person who really loves you. You have no idea how great it might be."

"He's not moving out here, Cara."

"Don't discount it, Mel. It might be the best thing in the world. You know, even if you didn't get married or something, maybe you could at least be together, really together. He really seems to love you. It's so great to see you so happy. You know, living in the same city might actually make things better."

"Good God, no, Cara. Why in God's name would we want to do that? We'd hate each other by the end of the first week he was here."

"Oh, c'mon, Mel, I really don't think so. He's soooo sweet . . . Look at how helpful he was tonight. And just charming as can be. He's interesting, bright, thoughtful, and, well, it's obvious that he's head over heels about you. All you have to do is watch him. I mean, really, Mel. He just seems like he's the perfect man."

"I'm sure his wife thinks so," Mel blurted to Cara deadpan, plainly, and without a second thought. She paused, staring out across the street, taking the last drag on her cigarette and blowing the smoke out into the black night sky. The wisps of smoke billowed around her eyes, her nose, and then drifted off before she threw the butt on the ground and stubbed it out with the toe of her shoe. Mel laughed. She threw her head right back and laughed, then straightened and exhaled deeply. The irony cut through the silent street and echoed back at them.

Cara stopped cold. She whipped her head up to meet Mel's face-to-face. On her feet she rocked, then stumbled backward, catching herself before she fell. She felt weak at the knees, as if the ground had come out from under her. *"What?"* Cara asked. *"What did you say?"* Cara grabbed Mel's arm, stopping her as if she was halting a child from doing something harmful. Cara's heart quickened and sunk, plummeting into her stomach. She was unsteady, dizzy.

"His wife. I'm sure she thinks he's Mr. Perfect, too. There ain't no doubt about that." Mel was drunk, slurring her words into one long statement. Beyond drunk, she was sloppy, and whether or not she had meant to, she had come clean with what she had kept locked away from her friends for over a year. She continued, her voice growing loud and uncaring. "Yep, he's a keeper, Cara. But he ain't mine to keep. It's not even in the cards. God, it's not even something I'd consider," she scoffed, unforgiving and insensitive.

Cara stared at her, disbelieving. The tone of Mel's voice shocked her and left her feeling ill. Stunned, she raised a hand to her cheek as if she had been slapped hard, and then released a gasp, a moan, like she'd been punched in the gut. She thought of Garin inside cleaning, righting the flat and disposing of the mess left behind by the party. He had seemed so wonderful, so sensitive and dedicated to Mel. And here he was playing some sort of game with Mel, some sort of heartless romp.

"Please, Mel, tell me you're kidding. Please, tell me this is some sort of sick joke."

Mel didn't have to answer her, of course. The look on her face said it all. Smug, almost proud, as if she had nothing to hide, despite the fact that she hadn't told any of them, not in the entire year she'd been dating Garin. She had been hiding it, without a doubt. She hadn't wanted them to know. But when Cara pushed her, even a little, she couldn't hold back. Enough of the secrecy, Mel was never good at keeping things to herself. It was just like her, just like her to light the fuse, stand back and watch it blow.

"Oh, my God, Mel, why? How could you?" Cara whispered harshly as if she was afraid someone might hear them. "What are you thinking?"

"What?" she scoffed. "Oh, come on, Cara, you can't be serious?"

"Why didn't you tell us? How long have you known?" Cara's

eyes pleaded with her. She was hoping that Mel hadn't known all along, that she had been fooled by Garin's dishonesty. At least that way, maybe Cara had a chance of helping Mel out of the relationship, of mending her disappointment and the broken heart that would undoubtedly ensue.

"Tell you what, Cara? That he's married? I've known since the day I met him. For God sake, it's not like it matters," she slurred, with a laugh that she croaked out. "It's not like I'm gonna marry the guy. Not like I'm even gonna get serious 'bout him. What difference does it make what he does when he's not with me? I don't want to be the one who is responsible for him."

Cara's head spun; the taste of bile in her throat, on her tongue. She choked it back, coughing. "But how could you? How? I mean, after all I've been through this year. Do you have any idea about the damage you're causing, Mel? Didn't you see how badly Jack's relationship has hurt me, hurt the kids? God, after all this time, everything you said about Jack. You're doing the same damn thing, Mel. The same damn thing."

"This has nothing to do with you, Cara. Don't confuse the two relationships." Mel's voice sobered quickly and her eyes pierced through her friend, careless. "What I have with Garin isn't anything like what Jack did to you all those years, all the lies and cheating and time he spent away from you. It's not anywhere close to the same thing. You wanted Jack; you had built something with him. The family unit, the white picket fence, Christmas trees and Saturday-night date nights and family vacations to Disneyland. I'm not that person. God, I'm so not that person. I've never wanted that with Garin."

Cara stared at the cracks in the cement steps, the long, thin lines that ran through the stoop and disappeared down into the city street below them. She felt as if she was being punished, mocked, and by her best friend, the person she had most often confided in. She shook her head to clear the loud buzzing that had settled between her ears. Everything around her felt foreign, her legs weak. She was unable to steady herself, dizzy. She shook her head again, squeezing her eyes tight as if to block out the world.

"But, but how can you think that? He's *married*, Melanie. He has a *wife*. It's exactly the same thing. He has someone waiting for him at home, wondering what he's doing when he's not with her, wondering if he's missing her. You have no idea what that feels like. You have no idea what it's like to be the wife. You have no idea about how lonely that is, to watch someone give their heart to another person, and not be able to do anything about it."

"It's not the same thing, Cara," Mel said again, more harshly this time. She was getting angry with Cara, unnerved by the fact that she couldn't convince her of the simplest differences between her relationship with Garin and Cara's relationship with Jack. It was so clear to her, so black and white. She'd never wanted Garin, not permanently, not in a way that would require her to give up her own independence, her own heart, her own soul. Certainly she couldn't give him her soul; it had been taken so long ago.

Cara grasped Mel's hands, holding them tightly, gripping them. "It is. It is the same thing. I don't see how you can look at it any other way." She pleaded with Mel, desperate.

"I don't want Garin, Cara. I don't want him on a full-time basis. He isn't mine to steal or keep or even plan a future with. I wouldn't have him even if he asked. That's what makes it different. I don't want something with this man that I know I can't have. It has never been about stealing him from some other woman. I wouldn't have a life with him even if he pleaded with me to give him that. I know he's got a wife. I'm viscerally aware that he goes home to her. And when he does, I kiss him on the cheek and send him on his way. You think this is about you. You think I've fallen in love with Garin the way Barbie fell in love with Jack, and him with her. But it's not. You can't see it because you're too close to it. Because you've been hurt by it. I'm not asking Garin to make a commitment to me. He's not cheating on his wife. Not the way Jack cheated on you, not the way he hurt you. But you can't begin to understand the difference. And trust me on this, Cara, there's a big difference."

Cara stood silent on the stoop. She had known Melanie a long, long time; one would qualify it as all their lives. And she knew that Mel's version of commitment had always been far different from her own, that when Mel's mother had left her it had made it nearly impossible for Mel to have a relationship, a real commitment of any kind, with just about anybody. She was afraid of being left, of being the one to be alone again. And up until now Cara had been able to overlook all of that. But now, even as she stood next to this woman that she had claimed as her best friend for as long as she could remember, she wondered if she had ever really known who Mel was at all. She wondered if Mel was the person Cara ever really knew her to be.

Cara tried again, emotion overtaking her, tears streaming down her face. The wind whipped at her hair and she pushed it back from her face, trying to tuck it behind her ears. "But when he leaves, Mel, when this little imaginary relationship of yours takes a break and he flies cross-country and goes home? Who do you think he's thinking about? Who do you think he takes with him? When he's gone and he's at home, maybe on a weekend when he's sitting around the house making breakfast or watching television, don't you think it's you that he's wishing would come down the stairs to say good morning to him? God, Mel, don't you think it's *you* he takes to bed with him when he's making love to her? Don't you get it? Don't you see any of that?"

The emotions ran through Cara's blood, crawled across her skin. She wanted to shake her friend, shake her until she could see straight into the logic of it all. "No matter what you think, no matter what you think he's capable of doing, I'm standing right here to tell you that he can't just turn you off, he can't leave you behind. Maybe you can do it, Mel. Maybe you can be the one to send him on his way and pretend that it's nothing more than a fling, but trust me, he can't. 'Cause every minute of every day that he's with her . . . The person he's really thinking about is you. The person he's really comparing her to is you. Trust *me* on that, Mel, Trust *me*."

Cara thought back on the days when she knew things with Jack had gone astray, the first time she remembered making love to him and knowing that he wasn't with her in the bed, not with his soul, anyway. She remembered what it was like to spend so many empty days and nights together when he simply had disappeared from their lives, left with his own daydreams of being somewhere else. She remembered the sick feeling she had when she knew he wasn't working late as he'd told her but rather holed up in a hotel room somewhere, dinner and a bottle of wine, and the remnants of great sex. She remembered when sex with Jack had changed, when it was something different than it had been. She remembered the night in her bedroom when she knew she was no longer sharing it with her husband but with someone else, someone he'd brought home with him. He had kissed her differently; he had made love to her differently, his body turning a new way, taking a new position that wasn't familiar to her. And she had been left to try and understand what had happened, how it had happened.

Mel reached for her friend. She didn't want to talk about this anymore, not like this, on the stoop in front of her flat where their shouts echoed in the streets and came back at them like a reflection in a mirror. "Come on, Cara, let's go inside. It's fucking freezing out here and I need to get some sleep. We both do. You're being ridiculous. We can figure this out later, but not now, okay? You're upset; I get that. David Michel didn't show tonight and your ego is bruised and we've all had a lot to drink. We should just go to bed and talk about this tomorrow. C'mon."

Cara avoided her touch, pulling back, defiant and bruised. She would have liked to be anywhere but there, with anyone but Mel. She felt sick to her stomach and nauseous. How could Mel cheat on her, cheat on her like Jack had cheated on her? Mel had hated Jack for what he'd done to Cara, she'd told her so, so many times. And yet here she was; the same loaded gun.

Mel opened the heavy oak door that led into the long hall, which ran the length of the flat. Somewhere at the end of the foyer, near the kitchen, water was running. Garin was rinsing the wineglasses, setting them in neat rows on a dish towel. He had changed the music; faint sounds of jazz poured from the other end of Mel's flat.

"Mel? Baby, are you okay?" His voice floated down the hall to them before he stepped out into the light.

"Fine. We're fine. We're coming in now."

There was no way to describe it but to call it betrayal. Cara felt betrayed by both of them, mocked and embarrassed. "I can't believe you, Mel," Cara whispered, seething.

"What?"

"You have no remorse, do you? You don't give a shit about his wife. What do you think this is doing to her? Do you think she doesn't know? God, Mel, I can't believe it. I just can't believe you would do this."

"Cara, honestly. What's the difference? I told you, I am not interested in a long-term relationship with him. I'm not interested in any sort of commitment whatsoever. He knows this, too. We've talked about it; it's what works for us. It's between us, okay? I'm not taking anything away from her. It has nothing to do with anyone else. He's free to go whenever he wants to. He owes me nothing. Honestly, honey, you've got to stop getting all worked up about this."

"Does he have kids?" Cara asked her in a harsh whisper, careful not to let her voice get too loud. A lump formed in the back of her throat, choking her. She thought of her own children, of the impact that Jack's affairs had had on Katie, how her boys had lost the man in their lives that they should be learning from, idolizing, how Claire was—how they all were—left to bounce between the two families like a Ping-Pong ball. Their wounds were like open sores, not quick to heal.

Mel sighed, annoyed and impatient. "Three," she answered Cara, much too quickly, dismissing her question as unimportant.

"Oh, God. Oh, Mel, really, how . . . ?"

"Cara. I'm goin' to bed. Come on, you need some sleep, too."

"You have no idea, do you, Mel? No. I take that back. It's worse than that. You do know." Cara shook her head. "You just don't care. You really don't give a fuck." Cara brushed past Mel in the doorway, leaving her standing in the door frame in her heels, still beautiful even at that late hour. Mel's guest room was the third door on the right, the last room before the back of the flat opened up to the kitchen and study. Cara inched her way along the wall, steadying herself on the wall, moving as quickly as she could, wanting to run. She thought if she could just make it to the room, she could lock out the world, lock out the whole memory of the hurt and pain and embarrassment she felt when she found out Jack was cheating on her, on their family. She prayed she could make it to the room in enough time; before she broke down and the tears came rushing forth again.

Garin stepped out from the kitchen just before she reached the guest room, a wineglass in one hand, dish towel in the other. He wore an apron—one of Mel's—over his jeans and sweater, but in stockinged feet he looked amazingly at home, as if he belonged here, as if this was his home, their home, together. Cara glanced at him briefly, barely able to make out the shape of his body through the blur that had become hot tears in her eyes and on her cheeks. She felt dizzy, hot.

She pictured Jack in Barbie's condo, what he must have looked like to Barbie's friends, how it must have appeared to the social circles he had assimilated into long before he had left Cara, long before he had moved on from his family. She thought of how he must have known where Barbie's dishes went, how she liked her coffee in the morning, where to place the newspaper when he was done reading it. All of this, everything, going on right beneath her own eyes for so long. And all this with Mel and Garin for so long and she had never guessed, never saw the signs that she should have been so acutely aware of. How had she missed them again?

"Good night, Cara," Cara heard him say, clearing his throat. "It was delightful to finally meet you."

She shut the door firmly; shut it on everything that ran the length of the hall between them. She heard Mel trip down the hall, the *clickety-click* of her stilettos on the cedar floor. She barely made out Mel's voice, the unmistakable confidence that purred out of her, begging him to abandon the dishes and come to bed with her. Cara lay on the bed and let it start to spin, everything in the room moving as if she was on a boat. She squeezed her eyes together tightly, then opened them just before she thought she might vomit.

In the morning, just as the first light broke through the thick fog that blanketed the city, Cara left Mel's house. The stench of alcohol and party followed her down the hall and out Mel's front door. She hadn't waited for Mel and Garin to wake and come out from Mel's bedroom, hadn't stopped to leave a note. Outside Cara gulped giant lungfuls of oxygen, breathing in and out deeply to avoid being sick in the street. The buzzing between her ears had subsided but had been replaced by a sharp, slick knife of a headache that cut deep across her temples and over the bridge of her nose.

She couldn't imagine a time when she'd ever want to see Mel again.

11

The day Mel's mother left was the first time Cara remembered having had a fight with Mel. To this day, she couldn't remember what they'd argued about, only that it was a cold and drab and lonely feeling, like a huge wedge had been worked in between her and her best friend.

They'd walked home in silence, each of them trying to outlast the other's stubbornness. Cara was just about to give in, to tell Mel to forget whatever it was they'd disagreed about when Mel opened the front door. The house smelled of desolation, of being abandoned. Drawers were open and empty; the pantry had been cleaned out, and most of the hangers in Bea's closet were vacant. Bea's car was not in the driveway. There was no note, no explanation.

It wasn't entirely surprising that she'd gone. Dermott had been unfaithful the bulk of his marriage to Bea, and Bea had put up with his nonsense long enough to know that he wasn't going to change. Melanie didn't blame her mother for leaving Dermott; it was the right thing to do considering the circumstances. But she was pissed as all get-out at her mother for leaving *her*. And for leaving her with Dermott. Simply unacceptable.

Truth of it was that Dermott was not her biological father. Bea had married him in a civil ceremony the week after Mel's fifth birthday. Mel had cried through the entire thing. She said she knew Dermott was bad news from the get-go.

Dermott had never bothered to adopt Mel or claim her as his own, either. She used his last name, Paulson, for convenience sake and because he was the only father figure in her life. Only her closest friends—Cara, Leah, Paige—knew the truth. She wasn't ashamed of it; she just didn't get around to telling people the difference. And leaving out the details meant she wasn't forced to come up with answers she didn't have.

After Bea left, Dermott's extracurricular activities followed him home like a stray dog. The women were hard looking and crass, vulgar and unrefined. The first climbed on top of Dermott one night while Mel was watching *Jeopardy!*—grinding her pelvis and hips into Dermott's lap, the two of them laughing and carrying on. The next left bottles of pills and pairs of thong underwear on the kitchen counter. Still another drank so much Mel would find her passed out half-clothed, on the living room floor, leftover from whatever Dermott had done with her the night before. The first moved in like a thunderstorm, quick and in a hurry to make an impact. The next one brought duffel bags and suitcases of inappropriateness with her. They would stay for a while, then quickly pack their bags and be gone.

Dermott stumbled in and out of the house, whiskey laced on his breath, fire in his eyes. He was angry with Bea for leaving, angrier yet at Mel for still being there. Everything about Mel reminded him of the woman who had left him, burdening him with the responsibility he didn't want.

The first time Dermott dared enter Mel's room, it was an unseasonably warm April night and she had left her bedroom window open. There was no breeze that night; the air was still and lifeless as if the world had been stripped of all sound. She sensed someone's presence, someone's eyes on her backside, and rolled over quickly, her heart quickening. She thought it might be an intruder, someone who had come through the open window, but instead, it was Dermott, standing with his hands behind his back, rocking on his heels, transfixed on her form in the bed. She could smell the mix of Johnny Walker and nicotine on every inch of him; he'd just finished a cigarette and the stench followed him like a snake, invading her room.

His round, hollow, bloodshot eyes rested on her. He was long and lanky and his Wrangler jeans fit him tightly. Finally, he took a seat on the empty twin bed opposite hers.

She opened her eyes and whispered his name in a breathless rush that came with urgency as if she was punishing him. "Dermott." She had never addressed him by his first name, but somehow "Daddy," the name she'd always called him, didn't feel right, not this time. It was as if she was speaking to someone she didn't know, someone she didn't trust. She was leery of him, frightened. She felt the perspiration bead under her armpits and the knot in her stomach grow.

"Yeah."

"What are you doing?"

"I ain't doing nothing. What do you think I'm doing?"

The moon moved through the cheap blinds that covered the window, throwing shadows across his long face, distorting his features. He was rough around the edges, stubbly and worn from too much work and even more drinking.

She swallowed down the fear, pushing it to the back of her mind. "Why aren't you in bed?" she asked him. She worked to control her voice, hoping she could fool him into believing she wasn't frightened.

He hesitated a minute, then smiled wickedly before he said to her, "I'm going." Then he shuffled out of her room and down the hall, his boots heavy on the wood floor.

One night she woke to him perched on the end of her bed staring into the dark at her. She had been dreaming that she was running, far across the expanse of the high school football field, as far as she could get, for no particular reason, only that she sensed danger. She woke with a start, realizing that someone had begun rubbing her feet methodically; then realized it was Dermott rubbing her feet. She couldn't stand his touch, the way his fingers ran over her toes and down around the bones in her heels. His hands were strong, rough and calloused, and they ripped across her skin. He'd clearly had too much to drink again, and the smell of nicotine and sour beer choked her.

She hadn't heard him come in, hadn't heard the usual turn of the doorknob, the noisy creak from the unoiled, worn screws in her door. She bolted straight up in bed, and curled herself into the corner nearest the wall, hiking the pink gingham sheet up around her neck as high as she could get it. Her skin was prickly, the hairs on her arms stood out amidst goose bumps.

He leaned back on one arm and scratched his day-old beard with his right hand. His long legs stuck out like matchsticks.

"What? What do you want?" She spoke in loud hushes, panic gripping at her vocal cords.

"You're jus' so pretty, Melanie, tha's all. Jus' so pretty," he slurred at her, reaching for her legs. Her knees were tucked under her chin; he couldn't get a hand on her. And she was prepared to kick him hard if he tried. He swayed and caught himself in the center of the bed, balancing on one arm.

"Dermott," she whispered harshly. "You've had too much to drink again. Get outta here. Go on to bed."

"Nah. Nah, I haven't had so much. I jus' wanted to tell you how pretty you was and all. You jus' so pretty. Jus' look like your mama. You know that? You look jus' like your mama."

Melanie swallowed hard, pushing back the bile that rose in her throat and kicking at his hand that crept her way across the worn bedspread. He recoiled only for a minute, hung his head and shook it from side to side. "Whassa matter, Mel? You don't want your old man in your room? You didn't use to mind so much when you were little. What happened?"

She shook her head hard, cowering against the chipped and scratched oak headboard so that it banged against the wall. "I don't know. You're scaring me is all. You've had too much to drink, Dermott. You can't keep drinking so much. You shouldn't be in here. Why don't you just go to bed? We can talk about all of this in the morning. Go on now . . ."

"You look just like her, you know. Just like her. Your mama. She had no right to go and leave me, you know. I didn't deserve to be left, Mel. She shoulda stayed here. Her place is here."

She felt her pulse echo in her temples. "Can you go now? Please? I'm real tired and I have school tomorrow. I need to go to bed. And you need to go to bed, too. It's too late to be talking 'bout all this stuff. We can talk about it tomorrow if you want." She let herself plead with him, cocking her head to the side and forcing her voice to sound soft enough that he might be convinced. She would do nearly anything to get him to leave, anything at all.

He was on her in a minute. She was gasping, begging him to let her go. "Dermott, you are hurting me. Dermott, let me go. God, please." She cried unsuccessfully for him to loosen his grip. His nails drove into her wrist, on the palm of her hand.

She kicked him with everything she had, bucking him as if she were a wild horse that couldn't be tamed, writhing and twisting her torso so that he'd fall to one side or the other of her. He was thin and bony and he dug his knee into the base of her spine and held it there, pinning the arm he'd been holding behind her back to her butt so that she was immobile on her left side. When she realized he was serious about all this, she stopped begging him to let her go and started screaming, piercing wails that rang through the house and shook the windows, deep and guttural and fierce.

"Noooo, God, noooo! Help me! My God, Dermott, stop, stop!" Her voice echoed throughout the room, echoed in her head and fired back at her, empty. When she began to scream again he covered her mouth with his right hand and pushed her head farther into the bed, suffocating her against the sheets.

When he penetrated her petite frame, he did it fiercely and with quick repetition, ripping everything innocent out of her. He forced his way deep inside her, pressing her legs open wide from behind and pushing her farther into the bed, farther into the soul of the darkness. She closed her eyes hard and prayed to stay conscious, prayed that she could get enough oxygen to sustain her.

He ripped at her hair, tore at her T-shirt until it was askew and then stripped it from her body. There was blood left behind, smeared across her legs and stomach.

When he was finished, he stood over her on the bed. She heard him zip his pants and cinch the buckle on the belt around his waist.

His face was scratched, deep red lines that ran across his rough stubble. She wasn't sure when she had gotten him but she was glad to see that she had succeeded, that he hadn't gotten away without something that would remind him of what he'd done when he looked at himself in the mirror.

He backed out of her room slowly, closing the door behind him and leaving her lying, discarded, in a heap. When he was gone, she locked her bedroom door. The next day she packed her duffel, stuffing it with everything she could manage, and went to Cara's.

12

David Michel swore to Cara that he had not stood her up. "Cara," he said, "I'm not sure I know what you're talking about." A blank, puzzled look crossed his face.

"Mel's party. I asked you to meet me there on Saturday night, remember? My friends were waiting to meet you."

As soon as the words had sprung forth from her mouth, she wanted to gobble them back up. Her face grew hot with embarrassment; she felt like a schoolgirl who hadn't gotten her way.

"Cara, I had no idea." He said this to her in his softest French accent. "I didn't realize you *expected* me to be there. I thought it was a casual invitation."

She forgave him immediately.

"Let me make it up to you. Can I take you to dinner? Just the two of us?" he asked her in what she deemed a purr.

"Well . . ." She failed miserably at being coy, she always had.

"We'll go tonight. I've got an idea about a perfect spot. Somewhere I'd like to take you. I'm sure you'll like it very much."

"Um . . ." She wasn't prepared to go out with him tonight. She had convinced herself she was due at least a week's worth of misery, that she would be angry with him for a long while before she finally just wrote him off. Besides, it had been a long time since she'd had a casual date, a long time since she'd had any kind of date. Did going mean she was too available? Did not going mean she wasn't interested? *Oh, stop thinking about it already and just do what you want to do*, she thought.

"You won't have been to this restaurant," he said to her confidently, baiting her with the idea.

She eyed him carefully, the way he waited on her response. He busied himself at his computer, working while she stewed on whether she should take him up on his offer. He looked as if he could have cared less whether or not she could join him, which made her want to go all the more. She gnawed subconsciously on her thumbnail, rocking back and forth on her heels. "How do you know I won't have been there?"

He stared at his computer screen but answered her nonetheless. "I know. You haven't been to this restaurant Trust me, Cara, I know." When he looked up, he smiled at her.

She was intrigued. And, more importantly, she was childless for the evening so there was no reason not to go. "I'm not changing. So you have to take me like this." She flung her arms wide, referencing the flattering black suit she was wearing.

He glanced up at her, his eyes running over her top to bottom. "Perfect."

She was all of a sudden tremendously self-conscious. She shifted from one foot to the other; unsure of what she should do next.

"Okay, then."

He waited for her to leave his office, which she did, backing out into the corridor, realizing that she had just accepted a date with the man she had spent the weekend convinced was the biggest ass in the city. She had been in a funk since Mel's party, angry with Mel and sad for those Mel was hurting, sad for what she had been through herself.

And now she had a date with him. A real eat-out-and-carry-on-a-conversation-between-just-the-two-of-them date, exactly what she'd been trying to avoid in the first place. She wasn't sure at all what she had gotten herself into. She wasn't sure at all that she should go.

Cara picked up the phone to call Mel no less than three times that afternoon. It was a natural reaction, a habit she couldn't quite quit. Under normal circumstances, it would have been the first thing she would have done. Mel was her sounding board, the one person she knew who could calm her nerves no matter what the circumstance. She shared everything with Mel; how could she possibly go on this date without a consultation?

The first time, she punched out the numbers to Mel's cell phone with her thumb, excitement bubbling over as she sat at her desk and stomped her feet on the floor. She was dying to tell Mel about her conversation with David. She knew Mel would be nothing less than proud of her, for putting aside her ridiculous feelings about being stood up and for snagging a dinner out of the deal. Melanie would have said to her, *Do you have on your best thong underwear, Cara? Just in case you end up in bed with him. Please, please tell me you took this into consideration when you got dressed this morning. My God, what are you wearing?* Melanie would have been just as excited for Cara as Cara was for herself. She would have wanted a blow-by-blow report of their conversation. She would have role-played the upcoming evening with Cara over the phone until the butterflies in Cara's stomach finally stopped dancing and fluttering.

But each time, Cara set the receiver back in its cradle, remembering Mel's selfishness. Mel would be holed up in her apartment with her married boyfriend, helping herself to what wasn't hers to have, what wasn't hers to taste. Cara could barely stomach the idea, never mind endorse it.

The truth was, despite what Mel was doing, the lie she was living, Cara had missed Mel ever since she had stumbled out of her flat on Sunday morning. It had been three days since they'd talked and she had longed to hear Mel's voice, she had longed to deconstruct why David Michel had stood her up. She'd never been very good at being angry with her best friend, her oldest confidante. But it was a longing that she pushed aside, and convinced herself that Melanie wasn't good enough for her. Mel had lied to her, without so much as ever opening her mouth. Mel had done to Garin's wife what Barbie had done to Cara. And the thought of it happening while Cara had been in such deep despair about Jack just about made Cara sick to think about it. Cara wondered how many times Mel had smugly laughed behind Cara's back, how many times she had pitied Cara for what she didn't know, for what was happening right under her nose. No, Cara couldn't call her; she simply wouldn't call her.

Cara was just bursting to share the information with someone, anyone who would listen and offer her some piece of advice. Cara finally called Leah near five o'clock, brimming with the news that she was going on a date. But Leah wasn't near as daring, not anywhere close to as adventuresome as Mel would have been. Leah made a lousy substitute.

"What are you thinking, Cara? Are you crazy? You can't go out with him; he stood you up. He never even called to say he wasn't coming. Do I need to remind you how miserable you were on Saturday night?"

Cara hated the sound of Leah's voice, the way Leah immediately made her feel as if she'd failed. "It's just dinner, Leah."

"Really? From the sound of your voice, I'd say it's more than just dinner."

"Okay, listen. I've already talked myself into it. And I've already told him yes. If things feel awkward, I'll excuse myself and head for home. I'm a big girl, Leah; I think I can handle dinner."

"Don't go to bed with him," Leah warned. "You're likely to go to bed with him, I can tell."

"I'm not going to go to bed with him. I hardly know him. God, Leah, you're worse than Mel."

"Ha. Mel would tell you to fuck him sideways and *not* to come back until you were good and done. And you know it. I'm telling you *not* to sleep with him, Cara. Take my advice on this one."

"Honestly!"

Just after eight, David Michel wandered casually into Cara's office, car keys in one hand.

She glanced at him anxiously. She had stopped working hours

earlier, her concentration shot since they'd talked earlier in the afternoon. "So? Where is this so-called restaurant I've never been to?"

"Hmmm? Oh. The Mission," he said, uninvolved. "We could go by cab, but it's not so far from where I live. I thought I'd drive home and we can walk from there."

"I'll need my car later. To get home, of course." She eyed him nervously from behind her desk. Leah's words came echoing back at her. *"Don't go to bed with him."*

She barely had his attention. He stood punching at the miniature keyboard on his Blackberry. Cara gathered up her laptop and bag, stuffed a few documents she needed to read into her briefcase and reached for her coat.

"Okay," she said firmly as if to alert him to the fact that she was ready. She swallowed back the hesitation she felt. She was beginning to regret her decision to go with him, unsure that this was a good idea.

"Okay, then. Shall we?"

With that, he turned off his electronic messaging device, took her briefcase for her and maneuvered her out the door. She relaxed, but only slightly.

He had been right about one thing: she had never been to the restaurant he chose. In the first place, she didn't eat sushi so it wasn't as if she would have ever wandered in there. In the second place, almost no one would have known it was a restaurant, save for the few people who had somehow stumbled on it. There was no sign, no discerning markings out front that would lead one in off the street.

"What is this place?" Cara asked him. There were four tables in the whole restaurant, each no wider than would fit two people. He held the door for her and ushered her inside, taking the brisk San Francisco fog-laden street with them. It was cold out and they had walked the few blocks from his building at a clipped pace to stay warm.

He shrugged his shoulders. "Not a lot of people know about it.

But I promise you, it's one of the best places you'll ever eat." He smiled at her assuredly.

The sushi chef came to greet him. "Hello, David," he said in perfect English.

"Shunichi, hello. I want you to meet my friend, the lovely Cara Clancy."

Shunichi bowed slightly to Cara, and led them to the only open table—a corner table where he pulled out the chair for her. He was short, no more than five foot two inches, and he had piercing brown eyes that danced when he looked at her. She smiled at him and took her seat.

"What's good tonight?" David asked the man, removing his jacket.

"Everything."

David laughed and patted the man on his shoulder before he took the chair opposite Cara. "Do you see, Cara? Shunichi serves the best. Well, have at it, then; we're starved."

Shunichi bowed one more time and shuffled off toward the back of the cramped restaurant to what Cara assumed to be the kitchen. He reappeared a few minutes later with tea and small teacups, placing them in the center of the table.

David reached for a cup, turned it over, and poured Cara some tea. "Be careful, it'll be hot."

"I have a confession," she whispered nervously, taking in the other patrons. "I don't actually eat sushi."

His eyes widened. "Don't? Or won't?" He looked disappointed but not entirely concerned.

"Well, to be completely honest, I haven't tried it. I know that sounds crazy, but just the thought of raw fish turns my stomach." She wrapped her hands around the small teacup and held it tightly for warmth.

He looked astonished. "*Never?* Well, that hardly constitutes as a reason not to eat it. Honestly, Cara, you live in San Francisco. Next to Japan, there are only a few places where you might find better sushi. You must eat sushi. Tonight you'll eat sushi."

She raised an eyebrow at him warily. "I don't think I have much of a choice, do you?"

"No," he said, firmly. "Not tonight."

She found him remarkably attractive and somewhat reassuring. She felt safe with him, even though he was years younger than she was. She even felt daring enough to try something she hadn't thought she'd eat, no matter how often people had teased her for it. Jack loved sushi; he'd eaten it at least once a week when they were married, sometimes even more. Cara had never given it more than a passing glance, the rolls topped with spicy sauces and raw pieces of fish, colorful fish eggs that glistened like pearls. Hamachi, magura, ebi. Jack had tried to educate her, tried to entertain her with the idea, but she'd turned up her nose, time and time again.

She shrugged her shoulders and sighed. "Okay, I'm in your hands. You do the ordering."

"There's no menu, Cara. Shunichi will take care of us. He'll only serve us the freshest fish you can find. I'm sure it came right off the boat this morning. It might"—he winked at her—"still be moving."

She laughed and gingerly took her first sip of tea, careful not to burn her tongue. He watched the expression on her face, which was pure adventure, pure abandonment, and he smiled at her. He liked Cara, the way she tiptoed into a room without realizing how beautiful she was. He liked that she was bright—smarter and more thoughtful than one would have thought had they just given her a passing glance. He liked that she was finding her way again, as if she had been given a second chance to define who she was to become.

"So, Cara," he said, "about this party. I think I should be very sorry for having missed it. All of your friends were there. Tell me, who did I miss?"

Cara inhaled deeply and settled against the bamboo chair. Her friends were not an easy bunch to describe. "Let's see," she started, "well, the big news of the night was from Paige. She is by far the sweetest of all of us—she always has been—and she's pregnant for the first time. At forty-two. It shocked all of us. Leah, Mel and, well, certainly me. God, we're all done having babies. It has been years for all of us."

"But forty-two is still an acceptable age to have a baby, especially these days. It's not that old, is it?"

Her eyes danced in the dim light. "It's not *old* at all. Yeah, sure, it's fine. But Paige and her husband, Dennis, have been trying for years to get pregnant. It's really a bit of a miracle if you want to know the truth."

He nodded his head. "That's great. Is she thrilled?"

"To be honest, I think she's still in a bit of shock."

"So, how long have you known Paige?"

"Oh, forever. Seems like it, anyway. I've known all my friends forever, actually. I go back the furthest with Melanie, of course, but we've all been very close since grade school. Paige was always the popular one; everyone loves Paige. She teaches second grade, and God, she's good at it. All the patience in the world. She'll make an excellent mother."

"Okay, so we've covered Paige. Next?"

"Um, Leah, I guess."

"And what's Leah's story?"

Just then Shunichi brought sake and David took the opportunity to pour this for Cara, too. She stared at the clear liquid in the small, thimble-sized cup and looked at David, confusion clouding her face.

"It's sake. Tell me you've had sake. Please tell me you've had sake."

"Yes, a couple of times. But it's usually cold. This is warm."

"You can drink it either way. I prefer it this way. I'll order it for you chilled, if you'd like."

She held up a hand to stop him. "No. This is fine. Like I said, I'm in your hands."

He laughed, watching her, the way she clasped her hands in front of her face, not quite sure what she had agreed to. "So, go on now, where were we? Leah, right? Let's get on with it."

"Right. Leah. Hmmm, how would you describe Leah?" Leah's words came back to Cara, her hesitation with Cara's date that evening, the warnings she had given as a way of protecting Cara from anything else that might have gone wrong. Leah would not be eager to meet David, not now, not after the way he had stood Cara up. Leah could hold a grudge, especially when it came to protecting her friends.

There was no easy way to describe Leah. Leah was more conservative, more afraid to take risks, more likely to stay in the loveless marriage she was in because it was easier than admitting she should move on. Cara chose her words carefully. "Leah couldn't be more loyal. Honestly, this year she's been there for me anytime I've needed her. She's a wonderful friend, the kind of person you want on your side, you know what I mean?"

David reclined a bit in his chair and crossed his legs. She had his undivided attention. Cara could never remember a time when someone had been so engrossed in a discussion with her. In the last few years, she and Jack had evolved into the couple that read the newspaper over breakfast, each with their own section, void of any discussion or human contact. Jack could have cared less about her friends; he'd known them nearly as long as Cara had, but that didn't mean he had any real interest in them, any real desire to know anything more about them. David was the exact opposite. David leaned in to hear her story, stopping her when he had a question or needed clarification.

"And so that brings us to Mel, right?"

"Um, yeah. Right. Mel."

"What's the story with her? Actually, given Stewart's stories, I think I might be afraid to ask."

Cara wasn't particularly interested in having a long, drawn-out conversation about Mel. What could she say? That she and Mel weren't speaking to each other? That they'd had a terrible falling out? That Mel was having an affair and that after a year—*an entire year!*—Cara and her friends had only just met him. Should she tell David about Mel's insecurities, her inability to really love someone and the history that brought her here?

"Oh, there's a story there, alright."

"Well, let's hear it. C'mon, spill it. I promise I won't let Stewart in on any of your secrets."

Cara laughed. "Oh, I'm sure I don't have to worry about that. Stewart's probably got a few secrets of his own when it comes to Mel. They were together, you know? A long, long time ago. And very briefly. But I'm sure Stewart could tell you a few things. Mel doesn't go far without creating a little drama wherever she goes."

Shunichi shuffled to their table with a platter full of delicacies Cara couldn't begin to name. He set down the plate in the middle of the table and, as if for her benefit, began to identify each item, pointing it out and enunciating the Japanese word slowly. The names were lost on Cara. She nodded her head as if she was perfectly comfortable with everything he was pointing out. Inside she was growing queasy.

"It looks great, Shunichi. Thank you," David said to him, and shooed him away.

Cara followed David's lead and ripped open the paper wrapper on her chopsticks. She pulled them apart at the base and watched how he rubbed the two ends together. She stabbed at the small scoop of green wasabi and mixed it in with a teaspoon full of soy sauce.

"Careful. How spicy do you like it?"

She eyed him, following his every move. "Why?"

"That's wasabi," he said, pointing at the mixture she was stirring. "Any more of that and your nostrils will be on fire. There isn't enough sake in this place to put that fire out."

She poured a little more soy sauce into the mixture to dilute it.

He pointed to a piece of fleshy, deep-pink fish resting on a square bed of rice. "That's tuna. You'll be fine if you start there. It's very mild."

She fumbled with the chopsticks for a minute and then managed to pick up the fish. She dunked it in the soy sauce and wasabi and brought it to her lips, praying silently that she could manage this, that the fish would somehow slide down her throat.

It would be horribly humiliating to have to run to the ladies' room, even worse to choke it down at the table.

"Well?" he asked her, when she'd swallowed it.

She paused for a minute, savoring the taste. "Better than I thought it would be. It's good," she proclaimed.

"Ladies and gentlemen, we have a winner." He smiled, satisfied. "Good. So, tell me about Melanie," David said.

Cara took a long drink of her water, trying to get used to the new tastes she was experiencing. She really wasn't in the mood to talk about Mel, but he wasn't going to let her off the hook. "Not much to tell about Mel. She's an original, that's for sure." Cara was careful to keep her temper even, not to let on too much.

"How was the party? Mel's probably the type to throw a great party."

"It was very much Mel."

"Is that a good thing? Bad thing?"

"It's just Mel. Everything is over-the-top with Mel. There isn't much she does in small form."

"And you've known Mel the longest, right?"

Cara nodded her head. "Our mothers were very good friends; the best. Mel and I met very early on. I think they used to stick us in one of those Port-a-Cribs together and sit around and play bridge together, drinking martinis. God, can you imagine. No one does that anymore; they'd be thrown to child protective services. But in the sixties"—Cara shrugged her shoulders—"in the sixties, no one thought about things like that."

"No one thought about much in the sixties."

"Now how would you know that?" Cara teased him. "You weren't even born then." She giggled under her breath when he threw her a nasty glare, crinkling his forehead.

"You and Mel . . . You have very different lives now. She lives in the city; you live down on the Peninsula. Do you still see her as often? Have you remained as close as you were when you were kids?"

Cara eyed him over a piece of hamachi. "We have, yes. She's

gone her way and I've sort of stayed much closer to home, to the place where we grew up, to more familiar things, but we still see each other quite a bit. Mel's daughter is a sweetheart, and my kids adore Mel to pieces, especially Katie, my oldest daughter. She and Mel are very close. Sometimes, I think . . ." Cara sighed. "A little too close."

"Oh? Why is that?"

Cara struggled to find the right words. How much was too much to tell David on a first date? Or was it that at all? She couldn't quite tell. Maybe his attraction to her wasn't what she thought it was. Maybe he was just set on them being friendly. She waved off his question, dismissing it. "Katie can just be a handful, that's all."

"Tell me about your children, Cara."

She looked at him across the table, waiting on more conversation, eager to know about her life, about what she was made of. He was not only charming but disarming. She could hardly relax, hardly get her footing.

"What do you want to know?"

"Everything. Tell me all about your kids. We know Katie's a handful, and I wouldn't think that should be too surprising to anyone. She's seventeen, right? Don't you remember what life was like when you were seventeen?"

Cara did. Her teen years had been peppered with experiments, drinking, certainly, and occasionally, some pot, but nothing like Katie's. Cara's parents had been married, her family intact.

"It's an interesting time . . ."

"And your boys?"

"Will and Luke. Will just turned eleven and Luke is nine. They're all boy. They play baseball and soccer and they're outside pretty much all summer long, riding their bikes or skateboarding. They're good kids, really they are." Cara paused. "It's been a hard year for them; hard for all of them. Watching your parents go through a divorce is not easy for kids."

"No. I imagine it isn't."

"It's not their fault. I think that's the hardest thing to help them understand. They really had nothing to do with it. They're just casualties of the war."

"How do you handle it? You and your, um, is it fair to call him your ex?"

"You could call him that, yes, although we're not officially divorced yet. That happens in another month or so. The kids are shuffled back and forth, I'm afraid. Jack lives now with his girlfriend in a condo. By all reports, there's not much room there but Jack has been determined to stay involved and have them stay with him. They usually have dinner with him midweek and go there on the weekends. I get them the rest of the time. It wasn't so bad when I wasn't working because I would see them much more often, you know, and be there to help with homework and after-school activities. But now it's much more difficult. I've got a nanny now, someone to keep the peace in the afternoon so they don't kill each other, and Jack and I are negotiating how we can each have some time with them on the weekends. It can get really ugly, actually."

"How do your kids feel about his girlfriend? What do they think?" David had finished his sake and left the last piece of sushi for Cara. She eyed it carefully, not quite sure what she was in for. When he noticed her thinking on it, he said to her, "It's eel. It might be a bit over-the-top for you, but I can't eat another bite. And, quite frankly, Cara, they say it's bad luck to leave any sushi behind."

Cara blanched. She'd been a good sport, trying everything that Shunichi had brought them. There had been a few things she wasn't too certain of, but nothing she couldn't handle. But eel? It gave her the creeps just thinking about it. She lined her chopsticks up on her plate and smiled at him. "Think I'm gonna pass on that one."

He laughed and smiled broadly. "Okay, Cara, no eel for you. Maybe next time."

"The kids; you asked me what they think about Barbie."

"Barbie? Please tell me you are kidding."

"No. I wish that I could. It's the worst cliché ever, isn't it? Just horrible."

"It's pretty bad."

"Oh, and she's all Barbie, too. Store-bought boobs, bleach-blonde hair, acrylic nails, fake tan. She's got to be five foot ten and a hundred twenty pounds soaking wet. Well, that is, of course, when she's not pregnant. Now she weighs one-twenty-five. It's so annoying."

"Surely you can't be remotely envious of that."

"No," she lied, hedging her answer. "Well, it is a little difficult. The woman did steal my husband."

David took her in, serious all at once. "Was she really the cause, Cara? Or were there cracks in the pavement before she came walking down the street?"

Cara was quiet, thoughtful. She wasn't sure she was ready for this conversation. Not just with David, but with anyone. It was the crux of why she'd avoided therapy, the knowledge that she'd have to come clean with the state of her marriage long before she had the opportunity to blame Barbie for the demise of it.

"I've upset you," David said, breaking the silence, and Cara's train of thought. "I'm sorry, Cara. I've overstepped my bounds and I shouldn't have."

"No. No, it's not that. I, um, well, I just haven't spent much time examining it. Not close-up, anyway." She was quiet then, before saying to him softly, "There were plenty of cracks, plenty of places where things had fractured. Bones don't heal well unless you set them, you know." She cleared her voice and watched as Shunichi came to the table to clear their plates. He frowned at the platter, adrift with one lonely piece of eel, before he looked from Cara to David and back to Cara again.

"She won't eat it, Shunichi," David said, outing her.

Cara blushed furiously, the weight of the sushi chef's eyes on her. "I'm sorry," she said, embarrassed and apologetic.

They both laughed, Shunichi's broad grin showing a mouthful of white teeth and David's laugh more a sly, underhanded snicker.

"It's okay, Cara Clancy," David said to her. "Next time."

Next time. His words floated out across the table, like a promise.

"My kids," she said. "I'd like to be able to tell you that they all hate Barbie, every last one of them. And, trust me, there've been plenty of shining moments. But for the most part, they've adapted." Cara shrugged her shoulders resolutely.

She shifted in her seat, nervously alternating from one side to the other, until he placed one hand over hers, gently leaving it there. She glanced up at him and he met her eyes then, holding her gaze.

"There's not much you can do, really. You have to let them have their own opinions. You have to let them figure it out for themselves."

"That you do."

David was wonderful company, comfortable in every way imaginable. They drifted in and out of conversations that revolved around work, about movies, books they'd both read. She was ten years his senior. Occasionally the generation gap would widen and, fraught with doubt, Cara would stare into the deep crevice, wondering again, as she had the first day she'd met him, when he took her to lunch and charmed her into taking the job at Weaver Sinclair, what he found remotely attractive about her.

After dinner they took a walk. He stopped her on Valencia Street, under a dim and flickering streetlight, and kissed her hard on the mouth. When he moved away from her, she touched her lips, the spot where his kiss had actually numbed them, to make sure that it was real. It was a minute before she remembered to breathe again.

"Are you okay?" he asked her gently, cupping her face so he could be sure of her answer. "Cara? Are you okay?"

"I think so." She wasn't. Not in that moment, and not in the one that was to come. It was as if something inside her had been awakened, something that had been dead for such a long time that she was hardly aware of it anymore.

He kissed her again, harder this time and with even more

force as if he didn't want to let go. And this time she was no less surprised, but she remembered to kiss him back. She remembered what it was like to kiss someone, really kiss someone, back. And when they parted this time, he stayed very near her mouth, very near her face, as if to watch how she might react again. She smiled, warmth growing over her like a blanket.

"Cara, I'd like you to come back to my flat. Can you do that?"

Leah's words hummed in her head like a warning: *Don't go to bed with him, don't go to bed with him, don't go to bed with him.* She pushed them away, annoyed at the intrusion.

"I, um, well, I'm not sure I should . . ."

"You don't have to stay. You can leave in a bit if you'd like. But I'm not quite done with you for the evening. And I'd hate to send you away just now."

Cara didn't want to leave. She laced her fingers in David's and let him lead her toward his apartment the way she would have if she'd been in college, at the university. He paused only one time before they climbed the stairs that led to the front door of his Victorian, and she had a fleeting thought that maybe he had changed his mind, but he hadn't. He held her by the hand tightly so that she couldn't get away, even if she wanted to, and led her up the stairs slowly, patiently.

Cara couldn't quite remember being kissed like he had kissed her, full of passion and selflessness. He had given her that kiss, like a gift, and asked nothing in return for it. She felt as if she owed him nothing, but wanted to give him everything. She remembered what it was like to be kissed by someone for the first time, the intense pleasurable feeling that rushed over her, leaving her dizzy. Jack's kisses—infrequent, quick pecks that were both rehearsed and mundane—hadn't been that enjoyable in years. She began to miss Jack less and less. He drifted away from her as if he was being carried down a river by the current.

David's apartment was spacious and sprawling. Intricate molding circled the ceiling in every room; chair rail ran the length of the grand front room. The wide cedar wood planks had been refinished and covered with gorgeous area rugs. He shared the entire house with her, taking her by the hand and flipping the lights on and off so she would know her way around. David was a minimalist. To no surprise, he had impeccable taste, far from the way her suburban home had been thrown together. She swallowed hard, thinking what he would make of her worn plaid furniture, the book bags and tennis shoes that lined the entry hall, askew in every direction, the stuffed animals and piles of books, the beanbag chairs sprawled across the floor, dishes stacked in the sink, piles of laundry, stacks of mail. She pushed her other life far away from her forcibly, filed it all away in another section of her brain where she didn't have to think about it.

He poured them both port in precious crystal glasses he told her his mother had brought him from Paris. He set these down on the petite table that sat between two angular chairs, then pulled her to her feet and walked her to the floor-to-ceiling windows that overlooked the city and bay bridge from the south end of the room. When he pulled back the paper-thin sheers that covered the windows, she gasped; the view from his parlor was spectacular. He cranked the side windows open just a small bit and stood next to her, letting the cooling city air force its way into the room. His world was too perfect, painted like a portrait that at first you find beautiful until you stare at it too long, then it becomes without fault, unreal.

Cara pushed Leah's voice from her head, the warning her friend had repeated over and over again, and let David take her by the hand and lead her down the long corridor to his bedroom.

They went to bed together quickly. David made love the same way he seduced a client, slow and methodically, purposefully. It was as if he realized it would take Cara a while to make up her mind about what she was doing and rather than let her come to her own decision, he was going to help her make it. Surely he must have known he was the first man she had slept with in a long, long time.

For her part, Cara let everything slip away from her. Her failed marriage; the countless years of sex with Jack even when she knew he was failing her miserably and cheating on her daily. Barbie's pregnancy. She let go of her children, her job, her friends, even the admonishment from her mother who thought she hadn't done enough to save her marriage. She let it all run out of her mind, away from her body, off the ends of her fingertips until there was nothing left of her. When she was void of everything that had consumed her, only then did she allow David to begin to fill her back up.

He started slowly until her body responded to the way he moved on top of her, to the places his tongue wandered across her belly, down between her legs. She arched her back in response to him, rose up on her heels and rocked and rocked with him, squeezing him with her hips, with her knees. He held her tightly, so tightly that she thought she might break, and then he eased off her, bringing her back down and allowing her to level off. He did this to her, with her, for an immeasurable time, until finally he let her have the pleasure that she longed for, the unbelievable release that she had so badly needed to let burst forth.

When he was finished, he cupped her breasts gently, kissing each of them over and over again, tracing her nipples with his tongue. Together they were sweaty and sticky and a tangle of parts, but he didn't move far from her, and she didn't want him to go. There was very little time between him bringing her to climax, and the point when they started over again.

David understood that Cara had been imprisoned in some way, that she needed to be unlocked. He had no interest in hearing what, or, more aptly, who had done the damage, but he was aware of his responsibility in untying the knots and he readily took on the challenge. They made love twice again that night until she finally called it good, and told him she couldn't go on. When she begged him off, he dropped to her side and smiled without saying a word.

She showered and walked the half block back to her car alone, despite his protests about her leaving to find her way alone in the middle of the night. The ends of her hair were damp and she pulled the collar of her wool coat tightly around her at the neck to keep the wind from blowing down inside her coat. During the forty-five minutes that it took her to get from the city to the Peninsula she never turned on the radio, never checked the messages that were on her cell phone, never even looked in her rearview mirror. She didn't want a single thing to interrupt what she had done, where she had been. She stayed very present and concentrated on the road ahead of her, the curve of the freeway that ran against the bay, lit by a full moon that danced off the water. She breathed slowly, in and out, in and out, until she regained the upper hand on the order that had been upset, the chaos that had been created.

She couldn't quite believe what she'd done. It was as if she'd become someone else, someone she hadn't ever met, someone she wasn't entirely sure she liked. And yet not someone she disliked, either. She didn't think less of who she was; certainly she was free to do whatever it was she pleased. But it wasn't as if she'd expected this type of behavior from herself. Surely Cara Clancy, devoted wife and mother of four, would never have done something like this, not in a million years. But maybe that was the point.

Cara had never had a one-night stand. Not in college, not afterward, certainly not in recent years while she had been married to Jack. A one-night stand was completely out of character for her, something she had sworn she would never do, something she had gossiped about when it came to other people, disdain crossing her face as she shook her head back and forth. It was something she had lectured Mel about, time and again.

She longed to call Mel. Mel would have been her first choice in confidantes. Mel would have calmed her down and told her that what she had done wasn't something to get completely sideways about. Mel would have understood what she had done, even if Cara didn't understand or accept it herself. Cara knew this intuitively.

* * *

Leah had waited two days before she called Cara. When she did, and Cara answered the phone, Leah said to her, "You slept with him, didn't you?"

"No." She had been practicing the lie, the tone of her voice and the measured weight at which she would answer. But even as the word sprung from her mouth, she knew Leah wouldn't believe her.

"Cara." She paused, waiting on her friend to crack. "Tell me the truth."

"No. No, I didn't." Cara let the guilt seep into her skin like moisturizer. She couldn't do it, couldn't fib to Leah no matter how badly she wanted to. "Okay, fine. Yes. Yes, I slept with him."

"Oh, Cara."

" 'Oh, Cara,' nothing. I did it. That's all there is to it." Cara hadn't felt particularly guilt-ridden about it. She'd spent the last two days wondering about it, letting David creep his way back into the recesses of her mind every now and then, but she hadn't poured over every little detail or let it weigh on her like heavy fresh snow.

Cara expected a full-blown lecture, but Leah waited only a minute before she answered. "Feel any better?"

"I don't know. Am I supposed to?"

"Well, Christ, Cara. If you're going to sleep with him, let's hope you at least got something out of it. Who the hell wants to start having sex with a man who can't frigging please you."

"I didn't say that."

"So?"

"Pretty damn great, Leah. Pretty fucking amazing. It had been too long . . ."

"Well, hallelujah for that."

Cara laughed. From behind her desk, she pushed her rolling chair back and put her head down on her desk and laughed. She didn't know what had come over her. What bit of insanity had caused her to temporarily lose sight of who she was. "God, Leah, I don't know what I was thinking. *What* was I thinking? I mean, never, never, never would I do this. You know that about me. I can't figure out what's come over me. I really can't. It was as if I needed something from him, some sort of rite of passage. Like I felt I had to get it out of my system."

"I hate to say I told you so, but . . ."

Cara didn't let her finish. She wasn't interested in a ten-minute dissertation about sex with a younger man. "It was pure rebound, Leah. Just a one-time thing."

"Are you sure?"

"Yes. Positive," Cara answered her, confidently.

"What was the morning after like?"

"I wouldn't know. I left the night before."

"And at the office?"

"He's gone. He's been gone ever since. He's away on business all week."

"Hmmm . . ."

"Trust me," Cara said, lowering her voice so that her office-mates couldn't hear her. "David Michel isn't interested in a relationship with me."

"How can you be so sure about that?"

"Come on, Leah. He's ten years younger than I am. He's single, very single. I don't think he's the marrying kind, quite frankly."

"Who said anything about getting married, sweetie? That doesn't mean you couldn't have more than one great night of sex with him, you know. He might be very interested in you. Look at you, Cara. You're beautiful, smart, energetic."

"I live in the suburbs and I have four kids, Leah. It's like a death sentence for someone like David Michel. What? He's going to drive down from San Francisco so we can order pizza, rent a movie from Blockbuster and sit on the couch with Claire between us? Forget it, Leah. We're worlds apart."

"Okay, Cara." Leah wasn't convinced, but she let it go.

Cara paused a minute, waiting on something Leah might add. When Leah said no more, Cara added quickly, "Not a word of this to Mel, understand?

"Cara. You and Mel have to patch up this thing between the

two of you, you know that, right? It's ridiculous. You're both being ridiculous."

"Talk to Mel, Leah. Maybe you can get her to take a look at her life, the decisions she makes. I mean, how do you think that made me feel, Leah? All this time she's been ripping Jack a new asshole about his affair, and she's been off playing the role of the other woman. For God's sake, Leah, she must have been laughing her ass off at me all the while."

"Highly unlikely, Cara. Even I don't believe that. And I don't think you do, either. Come on, you've had your arguments before but this one takes the cake. Can't you just let it go? Can't we all just move on?"

"Are you saying that I should be okay with the fact that Melanie is having an affair with a married man? That I should just look the other way like it isn't going on?"

"No," Leah admitted quietly.

After they hung up Cara stared out her office window at the stream of people who ran in and out of the ferry building below. Tourists, businesspeople out for a quick bite to eat on their lunch hour, lovers meeting to sit in the sun at the café and catch up. She watched them circulate through the building, in and out, in and out, until the color of their clothing, their skin blurred into one large maze.

Cara and David came face-to-face the following Monday afternoon just after lunch. Up until that point there had been no calls, no sweet e-mails, no sign that anything further might develop between them. And Cara had settled into a funk that had left her feeling rejected and undesirable. The more she tried to convince herself that David Michel was not someone she was interested in, the more he slipped into the back of her mind.

Neither one of them spoke right off, other than to mutter hello to each other and make their way around one another. David smiled broadly at Cara, and Cara smiled a lopsided grin back before they criss-crossed each other's paths and went their own way.

He meandered into her office later that afternoon, and slunk low into the leather-backed chair opposite Cara's desk.

"Would you like to have dinner with me, Cara?" he asked her openly.

She rested her elbows on her desk and studied him. It was the last question she had anticipated.

"Can't. I'm afraid I've got the kids tonight." She breathed deeply, grateful for the commitment at home. It spoke volumes about the differences in their lives.

"Ah, right. The kids."

"Ah, yes, the *kids*," she said again, with emphasis. She was intrigued that he had asked, but she felt it was her responsibility to remind him that she couldn't come and go as he did, her life wasn't nearly as flexible.

"Another night then?" he asked her, innocently enough, and she could tell that he meant it. He was testing the ground between them, looking for weak patches in the ice.

"David?" she asked. "Do you think it's a good idea? I don't want to sound cliché, but we've got work, the office, the agency, all the rest of this to contend with."

He smiled at her, calmly and confidently. "All the rest of this?"

"Well, certainly, my kids. And for that matter, my impending divorce. I'm not entirely sure you want to get wrapped up in any of that."

He laughed openly at her, his eyes dancing mischievously. "I'm not sure I understand what you mean."

She sighed, exasperated. She hadn't expected him to understand. How could he? But at the same time, she didn't appreciate being laughed at. "David," she started, "I'm not entirely sure you could comprehend what my life is like. The kids are a bit, well, um, how can I say this, demanding? They require quite a bit of my time, as you might imagine."

He sat with one leg crossed over the other, his hands clasped at his mouth, watching her. Not just looking at her, not in any way frightened by what she had told him, but watching her intently as if he was studying her, as if he wanted to know more, not less. He lingered in the chair, spreading his long legs out in front of him and lacing his hands behind his head. His scent was delicious, sweet and powerful, and it filled her office the same way his lanky frame did.

"So?" he asked, waiting on her. "When will you *not* have the kids?"

She shook her head and rolled her eyes. "Wednesday," she said to him. "The kids have dinner every Wednesday night with their dad."

"Wednesday, it is."

She had warned him.

13

Katie knew all the words to the Serenity Prayer by heart. She must have said it no less than a half dozen times a day.

God grant me the serenity

Her mother was due for a visit, any minute. On the weekends Cara liked to come early, after breakfast but before their first session of the day. It wasn't during regular visiting hours, but because Katie was a minor and because, when it came to her daughter, Cara was willing to push the envelope, Cara was afforded a more lenient schedule than were other visitors. Cara had managed to befriend the head counselor, a woman named Abigail, who was willing to look the other way when Cara needed an extra visit, or a few more minutes, just to feel close to her daughter.

To accept the things I cannot change;

Cara liked to make Katie's bed. She liked to pull up the sheet, tuck the corners under the mattress and smooth out the wrinkles. She hated the way the thin bedspread felt in her hands, cheap and fraying, but she pulled that tight as well, and then laid the quilt she'd brought from home over the top of it.

Courage to change the things I can;

"Mom," Katie said, "you don't have to do that. I'm supposed to be responsible for my own surroundings. It's part of the program. Besides, I've already made the bed once this morning."

"It just needed a little bit of a touch. You've got enough to worry about, honey. I can do this."

Katie was sitting in the only chair in the room, a short, square hard-backed chair with vinyl cushions. Her roommate, a nineteen-year-old single mother who had left her two-year-old with her mother when she checked into the facility for the second time, sat on the bed opposite Katie's, watching Cara and Katie as if she was watching a debate. They lobbed niceties at each other like they were lobbing a badminton birdie over the net, lightly and easily.

And the wisdom to know the difference.

Katie knew about Cara's disagreement with Mel but despite the probing, neither Cara nor Mel would come clean with the details. It was Claire who had told her, not in so many words, but enough so that with a few pointed questions to Will and Luke, Katie knew that something was significantly wrong.

Claire and the boys had been allowed to visit after the first month Katie was in rehab. They came on a stormy Saturday, which made it impossible for them to walk the grounds or play in the makeshift park that sported a climbing structure and a few swings. Instead, Claire, Will and Luke were forced to sit on the scratchy plaid couch opposite two straight-back chairs. Katie sat in one of the chairs.

"How are things at home, you guys?" Katie asked all of them at once. She didn't expect much of an answer and she hadn't gotten much of one from the boys. Will shrugged his shoulders; Luke turned his attention back to his Nintendo game.

Only Claire offered any insight.

"Horton keeps barking all day long while Mommy's at work. The neighbor says that he's going to call the cops if we don't get him to stop. Barbie's getting really, really big now. Oh, and Mommy and Auntie Mel are fighting. They don't even talk to each other anymore. I think it makes Mommy sad, but she says that, 'Auntie Mel needs to remember that she's not the center of the universe.'" Claire reported the sound bites, as if she was broadcasting the six o'clock news.

"What do you mean they're not talking?"

From the other end of the couch, Will piped up. "It was just some stupid fight. It's no big deal."

"When was the last time you saw Auntie Mel?" Cara asked.

They all reclined on the couch, fidgeting and squirming.

"Dunno," Claire answered. "I can't remember."

"Why are you and my mom fighting?" Katie asked Mel.

Mel narrowed her eyes, a wrinkle forming just above her nose, indicating she didn't particularly want to discuss the matter.

"C'mon, Mel, what happened?"

"It's just a difference of opinion, Katie. It'll blow over."

Katie wasn't so sure. She had asked her mother the same question early that afternoon. Her answer wasn't quite so dismissive.

"It has nothing to do with you, Katherine."

Her mother had called her *Katherine*. She used that tone only when she was very angry.

"What does it have to do with?"

"I really don't want to talk about it, honey. It's between Mel and me and, well, we just can't seem to see eye to eye on this one. I hope she'll come to her senses and understand that she's done a very unfortunate thing, and that she's hurting a lot of people, but I just can't be sure this time. I really can't be sure."

"Is she hurting you?"

Cara crinkled her forehead, confused. "Um, well, no, not exactly. But it's difficult to watch her hurt someone else."

"But why do you care? If it's not hurting you, then what's the big deal?"

"It's not like that, Katie. It's just; well, it's just very hard to understand is all."

Katie studied her mother. Cara was visibly uncomfortable; she looked like she would give anything to have the conversation behind her.

> *God grant me the serenity*
> *To accept the things I cannot change;*
> *Courage to change the things I can;*
> *And wisdom to know the difference.*

Katie let the words play over and over again in her mind like a song she kept hearing on every station no matter how many times she changed the dial.

14

It was raining the day Melanie showed up after fifth period, her worn, stuffed to capacity, black duffel in hand. When Cara's mother, Joan, opened the door and found Melanie standing in the downpour, her hair plastered to the sides of her head and shaking, she opened her arms wide and pulled Mel inside the house. Melanie would never forget how the woman's arms felt around her body, tender and comforting, protective, and the way they wrapped her entire body and drew her near, pulling her into the tiled entryway. She would never forget the smell of ginger and cinnamon that hung on Cara's mother like perfume, warm and inviting. It was as if the world had stopped spinning out of control for a split second and everything inside of Mel, everything that had been churning since the day she went home after school to find her mother had walked out the door, finally was still.

Later that night, Melanie told Cara she could never go back. They were lying next to each other in Cara's twin bed, the black night filling the room like ink spilling out over a clean piece of paper. Joan had made up the pull-out in the guest room, which doubled as the office, but Cara had snuck Melanie up the stairs to her room and pulled her close to her beneath the duvet. Their legs were intertwined and they held hands, their soft breath meeting somewhere in the middle of the bed.

"Does Dermott know where you went? Did you leave him a note?" Cara asked anxiously.

"No."

"But Mel, don't you think you oughta . . ."

"No, Cara. I don't want him to know where I am," Mel answered firmly, leaving no room for debate.

"He's going to figure it out soon enough. My mom will tell him, for sure."

Melanie stared at her friend through the dark, her eyes straining to make out Cara's features, the definition around Cara's strong jawline, her large, round eyes. She wasn't so sure Cara's mother would turn her in the way Cara thought she would. Something in the way Joan had held her when she opened the door told Mel that she was safe here, that she could stay for a while without being forced to go home. Something made Mel wonder if Joan understood, in some way, what had happened.

"She can't tell him. He can't know that I'm here."

"What happened, Mel?" Cara whispered through the darkness, afraid of the answer.

Against the pillow, Mel shook her head.

"You can tell me. I won't tell my mom if you don't want me to; I promise."

"Are you sure?"

"Yeah, of course I'm sure. I won't say a word to anyone."

Mel sat up, resting her weight on her left arm. She didn't say anything at first, but pulled her legs up to her chest and hugged them tightly, resting her chin on her knees. She shook her head as if she was trying to clear away a bad dream.

Cara sensed something had gone very wrong; it wasn't like Mel to be without words, speechless. Cara sat up and gently draped her arm around Mel's shoulder, kissing her lightly on the cheek.

"What happened, Mel? What'd he do to you?" Cara whispered, pleading with her.

Mel didn't answer, not at first. She swallowed down a vicious lump in her throat and blinked back the hot tears that burned in the corners of her eyes. She stared ahead, her eyes locked as if she'd been transfixed by a memory too wicked to bring to life.

"On your life, Cara? You can't tell a soul."

"I promise."

"He raped me, Cara." She whispered the words, nearly breathless as if saying them as quietly as she could would negate the act itself.

She wasn't sure she had confessed what had happened, not out loud, anyway. She wasn't sure what had come from her mouth was anything more than a hint, so soft that it was practically rendered inaudible. But when she looked up, she knew she'd been heard. For the first time, she'd told someone, her very best friend, the only person in her life she could trust at that very minute, that her life had been changed forever.

"My God," Cara whispered back, equally as softly, as if breathing a word about it would actually make it truer than it was. She flipped on the lamp and shielded her eyes, blinded instantly by the harsh light that flooded the room.

"No one, Cara. You can't tell a single soul. You promised me."

"My God, Melanie," Cara whispered again, trying to make sense of it, and at the same time trying to figure out what to do next. She'd have to tell her mother, there was no question about it. Joan would have to know. Joan would know what to do. She may have made a promise to Melanie, but this was beyond something she could keep to herself. An adult would have to know, someone who could do something. Someone who could help them. Dermott shouldn't get away with something like this, not something this enormous.

"Cara," Mel said to her more harshly, using her normal voice this time. She cupped Cara's chin in her hands and jerked her head toward her until Cara was looking at her, staring straight into Mel's eyes. Mel wasn't entirely sure Cara was looking at her; she appeared to be in a bit of shock, so she shook her again. She grabbed her by the shoulders and shook her hard until Cara came to. Pleading with her, Mel said, "Cara, *please,* you have to promise me that you won't tell anyone. No one can know about this."

"*But Mel.* He should be put away for what he did to you; he should be locked up for good. You can't let him get away with this; you just can't."

Mel stood up abruptly, pacing the area rug in front of Cara's bed like an angry child who wasn't being heard and needed to make her point. "This is not up for discussion, Cara. You can't tell anyone, do you hear me?" she asked, lecturing her friend. Panic crept over her skin and set her heart racing. "You can't tell anyone."

Cara sat on the edge of the bed, weak at the knees and nauseous. She wanted to run but she wasn't sure she could stand. And even if she could move, she was fairly sure Mel would tackle her at the waist and pin her down.

"Okay, Mel, I won't. I won't say anything to my mom or my dad. Or anyone."

"No one, Cara. Not a single person. Not Leah or Paige, no one at school."

Cara shook from head to toe, fearful. She nodded her head slowly, agreeing reluctantly.

When Dermott came looking for Melanie, he did so with fire in his eyes on a steamy weeknight just before school let out for the summer. Joan answered the door with a dish towel in hand. Dermott had been drinking; she could make out the distinct scent of Wild Turkey on his breath. He stared her up and down until goose bumps formed on her arms, but she stood her ground, sturdy in loafered feet.

"Okay, Joan, time to send Melanie home. I'd say she's just about overstayed her welcome."

Melanie and Cara were out running an errand for Joan, but she pulled the door closed behind her anyway and stepped out onto the front porch. She didn't want to be interrupted, or saved, should her husband feel the need to do so. This was between her and Dermott. After all, Joan was the one harboring the child he'd come looking for. The sun had left purple-gray streaks in the sky as if bruised by the day. Joan dried her hands on the dish towel and straightened her back as if she was readying herself to go a few rounds with him.

"She's not here, Dermott."

"Bullshit."

"I'm not lying to you; she's not here. Not right now, anyway. And even if she were I wouldn't let you take her. Not in this condition."

Dermott's eyes raged. "What the hell are you talking about? What sort of condition are you referring to?"

"You've been drinking. Certainly you shouldn't be driving." She nodded toward Dermott's well-maintained pickup, one of the few things he took care of. "Why don't you come in and sit for a while. I'll make you a cup of coffee and we can sit down and have a little chat. It would be good if we could have ourselves a little talk about all of this."

"I don't want your coffee, Joan. And as far as I'm concerned, there ain't nothing to talk about. I want you to send Melanie home. Tonight. You got it? Not tomorrow, not in a week or so. Tonight."

Joan sighed, unimpressed. "I don't suppose you've heard anything from Bea."

He bristled at her question, and then spat the words at her, "Christ, no. That woman is gone for good. I don't expect I'll ever hear from her again."

Joan took a deep breath, in and out. She could feel the pressure building at her temples, her head beginning to feel heavy, a migraine coming on. She wanted to close the door on Dermott, shut out his problems and his demands and go lie as still as she could on the sofa on the sunporch, the heavy shades pulled closed so that the room stayed dark and cool.

"I'll let Melanie know that you came by. And I'll tell her that you'd like to speak with her. But that's the best I can do, Dermott. Mel's welcome to stay here as long as she'd like. She's like another daughter to us, you know." She placed her hands on her hips and stood her ground, even-keeled and even-tempered.

His eyes grew to slits, tiny and hard. He looked as if he might like to come at her, but she held her own. "I could call the authorities, Joan. I could suggest to them that you're keeping Melanie against my will. I could suggest that she's a runaway."

"You sure you'd want to involve the police in all of this? Because I have a feeling there's a few things Melanie might want to let them in on, given a chance. And a little encouragement." Joan was bluffing, of course. She had a feeling something was amiss between Mel and the man who stood in front of her reeking of booze, but she couldn't be sure of it, not for certain. Try as she might, she hadn't been able to get anything out of the girl. Or her own daughter, for that matter.

But it worked, and she sensed her instincts were right on. Dermott backed away, if only a bit. And in a much quieter voice, he said to her, "Damn it, Joan, she ain't your problem. I'm warning you, I want her at home. You tell her she's got a day to pack her things and come home."

"Warning me, Dermott? Or threatening?"

"I think you understand where I'm coming from, Joan."

"And I'm almost certain you understand where I'm coming from, too."

She watched him strut across the porch, his bull-legged stride carrying him back to the truck. "It's time for her to come home. One more day, that's all she's got left. You need to send her home," he shouted on his way down the driveway, all too ineffective.

"Well, you finally fucking made it home."

Cara's mother had knocked on Dermott's paint-chipped front door the next night. He must have thought it was Melanie finally making her way home. When he answered the door he threw it back and greeted Joan with a surprised look.

"I beg your pardon, Dermott. That is a perfectly unacceptable way to speak to me." Joan eyed him harshly. She had known him a long time. She hadn't come to return his daughter; she hadn't even told Melanie, or anyone, for that matter, that she was coming to see him at all. She felt like she had to come. After Dermott's visit the night before, she felt as if she had to put a little more finality around everything, Dermott wanted Melanie home; Joan wanted to reassure him there was no way that was possible.

He looked her up and down. "What d'ya want, Joanie? Did you bring Melanie with you?" he asked, crossing his arms over his chest and leaning against the door frame.

A weak storm had blown through earlier, leaving a smearing of humidity hanging in the air, unusual for Northern California. Dermott's work shirt hung open at the waist, revealing the white sleeveless T-shirt he wore underneath it. He was damp at his armpits and his belt was unfastened and hung loose at his waist.

She glared at him in response. "No, Dermott. She isn't here. I told you she wasn't coming back here." Joan paused then, waiting for him to come undone. When he didn't, she asked him, "Aren't you going to ask me in?" Joan craned her neck around Dermott in order to better see inside the house, but it was dark, save for the television blaring the evening news from the corner of the room.

"You sure you wanna come in, Joan? It's sure been a long time since you've been over for a visit." He leered at her hungrily, but Joan ignored him. Dermott didn't frighten her.

He moved back and pushed open the front door for her with his foot. She stepped into the aging, cramped house. The leather couch was covered in random newspaper stacks that Dermott had left astray. She took in the clutter and made her way straight to the kitchen, surveying as she went. Dust hung in the air and the floors were filthy. The sink was full of crusted dishes, even more sat stacked in piles on the counter. The house was stifling, pungent and stale.

Joan stared out the back window and concentrated on the neglected, overgrown garden. A sprinkler that Dermott had jerryrigged in the yard sputtered but did little good to soak the brittle lawn, the area where weeds had taken root and were multiplying. Earlier in their marriage, when things had still been good, Bea had meticulously maintained the garden and filled the house with vases of flowers. But when Dermott had left and neglected Bea, she had turned on the yard. Now, no one tended to the flowing jasmine that desperately needed to be cut back, the heavily weighted eucalyptus, the rotting fruit hanging from the lemon and orange trees. Suddenly, Joan wasn't sure of her reason for coming, the thing that had brought her here in the first place. This house, the emptiness it posed without her friend, left her feeling depressed and incomplete. All at once she missed Bea desperately.

Joan looked around the room, taking in the disarray that was apparent on every shelf, in every part of the kitchen. "Looks like you're really keeping the place up," Joan said to him, smugly, baiting him. "It's disgusting, Dermott. You should be ashamed of yourself, living like this, letting Mel live like this."

"Are you passing judgment on me?" He looked her up and down through hard, squinted eyes.

"Look, I came to talk to you about Melanie."

"It's simple, Joan. It's time for that girl to come home."

"What's the point, Dermott? Why don't you just leave her be? Let her stay with us; she's no bother," Joan sighed.

"She belongs here; this is her home. She doesn't need to be burdening you or anyone else with her problems."

The mess in the kitchen was beginning to make Joan nauseous; she suddenly felt the need to break out some disinfectant and scrub everything in her path.

"What problems, Dermott?" Joan asked him inquisitively. She was fishing for something and he knew it.

Dermott fumbled, not sure of how to answer her question. "You got no business here, Joan. Not anymore. I can take care of my own household now; I don't need you coming round to check on me, to check on us. Melanie's mother left but she can't be dragging all of that over to your family to deal with. I can take care of her. She should be here." His voice caught as he said it, anger and emotion sweeping through. He stared at her, cold, waiting for her to meet his hard, angry eyes.

He lit a cigarette and inhaled deeply, holding the nicotine in his lungs, and reached for a glass sitting on the countertop that Joan hadn't noticed before. Lots of ice, filled to the top. Joan knew Dermott wasn't drinking water. She suspected Belvedere, Dermott's vodka of choice. He may live like a slob, but he had good taste in his liquor.

He saw her eyeing his glass. "Can I pour you a drink?" he asked her, smugly.

"No. No, thank you."

"C'mon Joan. One little drink? It's been a long time since you and I have had a cocktail together. We could always count on a cocktail together." His voice sent a shiver up her spine.

She stared at him, disbelieving. "No, Dermott. Not on your life. Not ever again." She swallowed back a spoonful of guilt, losing her composure briefly. She wondered if it had been such a good idea for her to come at all.

He swirled the liquor in the crystal glass, letting the tension between them build. The ice cubes clinked against each other and then settled. Dermott was lanky, skinny and bony. His parts were long all over. He leaned against the chipped tile countertop and sucked long on the cigarette he held between his finger and thumb. She couldn't stand it when he smoked; she had never been a smoker like Bea had.

Joan had had enough. She needed to leave the house before it came crushing down on her, before Dermott moved a step closer to her, closing her in. She cleared her throat and adjusted the silk scarf she wore loosely at her neck. "I suppose I should be going, Dermott."

"Yeah?" He leered at her. "What's your hurry? I don't expect Bea will walk in the door any minute. Jus' you and me here, you know." He laughed at her, his haughty, gravelly voice filling the kitchen.

"No, Dermott, really, I think I should probably be going." She rose and clutched her pocketbook against her hip, glancing at him briefly and letting him know that she meant business.

He caught her at the wrist, his long fingers easily circling Joan's fragile, small bones, and spun her so that she was facing him. He was taller than her by a head, but somehow he managed to come eye level with her. In his eyes, she saw the hatred that Melanie must have seen. In his eyes, she saw the anger that Melanie must have lived with. Joan shuddered thinking about it. She knew she could never send Melanie back, not now, not ever.

"I want you to send Melanie home, Joan." He spoke plainly, clearly. There was nothing friendly about his tone; Dermott was done negotiating.

Joan twisted her arm, trying to free herself but he held his grip on her. She did her best to keep her footing and thought about nothing but escaping the house, of running as fast as she could as far as she could. She cleared her throat and dared to meet Dermott's eyes again. "I hear you," she said to him. "I hear what you're saying."

For days following her visit to Dermott's infested home, Joan felt as if she couldn't get clean. She felt as if she couldn't get warm. She felt as if she didn't belong. It was as if something from the house had made its way inside of her and was staying put, and no matter how hard Joan tried to shake it off, she just couldn't lose the feeling. She let her mind wander to Bea and what it must have been like for her in that house, the lonely and incomplete feeling that had finally overtaken her enough to drive her away.

15

Claire swung her legs back and forth, back and forth off the end of the worn leather couch. On either side of her, Will and Luke sulked against the cushions, complaining. They were hot; they were tired and hungry. And above all, they were bored.

"What do you get to eat?" Claire asked her sister.

Katie shrugged her shoulders. "All kinds of stuff. But none of it has been very good. Sometimes we get spaghetti," Katie said to her, hoping to make it sound better than it was. Spaghetti was one of Claire's favorite foods and Katie didn't want her little sister worrying about her while she was locked in rehab.

Katie was annoyed with her mother; pissed off, actually. She didn't see the point in dragging her little brothers and sister to the rehab facility so that they could spend their Sunday afternoon on display at the center. And she certainly wasn't enjoying Claire's version of twenty questions.

"Where do you sleep?" Claire asked her.

Katie nodded her head in the general direction of the brick wing of two-bed suites that bordered the visitors' room. "Down there. I'm the second-to-last room. You can see my window from here."

"What's your room like?"

Katie shrugged her shoulders. "Nothing special."

"Do you like it here?"

"Not particularly."

"Then why don't you come home?"

Finally, a question she couldn't answer. Technically she had twenty-six days left, not quite four weeks. She didn't feel ready yet. Not really. She wasn't actually sure when she'd be ready. She just knew she didn't feel that way yet.

"Don't know, Claire-bear. I hope I can soon."

Cara had gone in search of sodas from the machine in the adjoining corridor. She came back with two root beers in one hand, a Sprite and a Coke in the other. She doled these out and collapsed into the chair next to Katie's. It had been a particularly grueling week at the office; she'd had a client fighting her on a campaign concept she knew in her gut was right for them, and nothing she or David had been able to do seemed to be working to convince the client otherwise.

"Mama," Claire asked with authority, as if she could change fate, "when can Katie come home?"

Cara didn't want to make promises she couldn't keep. She'd learned by now that the disappointment was far worse than the truth. "I'm not sure, sweetie. Soon, I hope." Cara reached for Katie's hand but her daughter pulled away, and turned her head to look out the window.

It was a particularly gray and colorless day. Lately, Cara hadn't been able to break through. Katie seemed angrier than ever, less cooperative and less willing to talk to her when Cara stopped by for her visits. The counselors assured Cara it was normal behavior, good signs, even. They thought it meant Katie was beginning to show signs of taking responsibility for herself and that it wasn't Cara she was angry with, but herself.

"Will and Luke, did you see the pool table? Pretty cool, huh?"

They all turned to stare at the middle of the room where two patients were silently sharing the table, involved in a game without words. One of the patients, a twenty-six-year-old named Javier, wore a long black braid down the middle of his back. He was in a head-to-head competition with Scott, an artist who wore square black glasses, shaved his head and carried an iPod shuffle around his neck. He reminded Cara of someone she worked with, a talented web designer named Bobby.

It was impossible to have missed the table; you had to walk around the edge of it to get to the other side of the room.

"Hard to miss, Mom," Will said and rolled his eyes. He kicked his feet up on the coffee table and slumped low on the couch as if someone from his middle school might spot him there and he'd be humiliated to be seen with his family.

"Sit up, Will. And get your feet off the table," Cara said to him.

He lifted his feet from the table one at a time and stomped them on the ground but he didn't push himself back on the sofa.

"You wanna play, Will?" Luke asked him, eagerly. "When those two guys are done? I'll take you on."

"Huh, yeah, right, Luke. Like you have a shot at beating me."

Luke shrunk back into the corner of the couch, disappearing against the worn leather.

Cara was ready to challenge Luke herself, willing to do just about anything to keep him from crying, which he looked like he was ready to do at any minute. Heavy, salt-laden tears sprang to the bottoms of his lids and were hanging there; fat and pregnant with emotion. "C'mon, Luke, I'll play you."

He shook his head firmly and turned his mouth into a tight screw.

"C'mon," Cara tried again, "I'll bet you can beat me at that, easy. I've got to be one of the world's worst pool players. You have no idea how bad I am."

Luke shook his head firmly again and Cara was just about ready to give up, furious with Will for teasing his little brother for the millionth time that day. She threw Will a look that should have sent him begging for an apology, but instead left him more annoyed than anything.

On the middle of the table, Cara's cell phone vibrated.

"Are you going to answer that, Mom?" Katie asked her.

"I'll get it later."

"Who is it?" Katie asked her.

Cara couldn't imagine. There were only two people that ever texted her: Mel, and she knew it wasn't Mel; and Katie, and Katie was sitting right in front of her. "I don't have any idea," she said to Katie.

They both reached for the phone at the same time, curious. Katie snatched it from the table, stopping the vibrating on the wood.

When will I see you?

"Who's David Michel?" she asked, pronouncing his last name, Mitchell.

Cara froze, her stomach lurching. She couldn't imagine what the message must say. She lunged for the phone and yanked it from Katie's hand, flipping open the phone and retrieving the message.

Katie's curiosity peaked, her intuition heightened. Her eyes narrowed and she stared at Cara, unforgiving. "Who's David Michel?" she asked again, more harshly this time, in an accusatory tone.

"Someone I work with," Cara retorted, snapping the phone shut.

When will I see you?

Could it be worse? Clearly her daughter had read the message and now Cara had to lie to her. Well, technically not a lie, of course. She repeated over and over to herself, we do work together; we do, we do.

When will I see you?

Cara's mind raced, her heart pounding in her chest.

"Someone you *work* with? Right, Mom."

Cara cleared her throat and looked up at Katie. Her daughter's eyes were waiting on her, full of hurt and mistrust. She didn't particularly feel like justifying her personal life, the one that existed outside of the life she had with her children, but then she realized there wasn't really any life outside of her life with her children.

"He's an account director," Cara started, steadying her voice. "We work together on a couple of accounts, one that is particularly difficult right now. And I suspect," Cara said, holding her cell phone in her hand and shaking it directly at Katie, "I suspect that David needs to speak with me about the client that has been giving us so much grief." She looked from Katie to Will, Luke and Claire, all lined up on the couch, watching her, mesmerized, like they were watching a favorite television show. "Now, if you'll excuse me for just a few minutes, I'll go check in and see what it is that he needs."

Cara stood up and dropped the coat she was holding in her lap into the empty chair. She smiled at them politely, trying to seem normal.

"Why didn't he just call you?" Katie asked, and Cara stopped cold, feeling the weight of Katie's stare on her back.

There was nothing she could tell her that would make Katie believe her. Cara stood still for a minute, then walked away from them at a clip.

"What do you mean, 'When will I see you?' Jesus, David, I'm with my kids."

"Hello, Cara," he answered her. He sighed, sounding tired, exhausted from dealing with their stubborn client, one of the agency's largest. Maybe she'd been right. Maybe he'd only needed her help with the client. Maybe she'd overreacted.

She waited on the line, unsure of what she should say to him.

"Cara?"

"Yes. Yes, I'm here." She took a deep, cleansing breath, instantly sorry for how she had reacted.

"I'm sorry, Cara. I didn't realize . . ."

She didn't let him finish. "It's okay. Never mind."

"I was thinking it would be nice to see you." He waited a minute, waiting for her to answer him, to take the bait. When she didn't, he filled in the dead air, the awkward silence that had settled over the phone between them. "Cara, where are you?" he asked her.

174 Deborah J. Wolf

Cara followed the short corridor back toward the visitors' room. Hazy smoke filled the room where her children sat at the other end. On the way she studied the addicts, the alcoholics and drug abusers, those who had lost control of their lives and couldn't find any part of themselves that existed before. She wondered if she was all that different, really. She wondered if people looked at her and wondered when she'd be back to her old self again.

"I'm with Katie," she said simply to him, and that was enough for him to know that she couldn't see him now, not now and not for a while. She was leaning against the door of a janitorial closet, waiting for him to say something. She wasn't sure what it was he might say to her, when he finally broke the silence.

"Stay strong, Cara. Call me when you can."

She clicked off after that, hanging on those words.

When will I see you?

16

Jack eyed Cara carefully, looking her up and down.

"What?" Cara asked, finishing a peach. She chased the syrup with a napkin, slurping up the juice. Jack was dropping off the kids, lugging their backpacks and overnight bags into the house.

"Nothing, nothing," he answered, dumping the load on the floor. "You look, um, well, I guess you just look different is all. Did you change your hair or something?"

Cara's hand went to her hair, running her fingers through it. "No, no, nothing." She was immediately suspicious. It wasn't like Jack to stop and engage in meaningless chitchat. His usual modus operandi was to drop and run, usually with Barbie in the front seat of an idling car. But Jack looked like he was ready for coffee, maybe even breakfast.

"How was your weekend? Anything interesting going on?" he asked her, and her bullshit indicator went on.

"Fine," she answered him. "Yours?"

"Fine, fine. Plenty to keep us all busy, of course."

Jack was fishing, waiting for her to come clean.

Cara busied herself unpacking Claire's backpack; stuffed animals and a sweatshirt, a book and her lunchbox.

"Cara?" Jack asked. "Are you, well, I'm not quite sure how to ask you this, so I guess I'll just come right out with it. Are you *dating* someone? I mean, I know it's not really my business and all, but the kids mentioned it this weekend. And I figured, if so, well, I should probably know about it."

Cara put one hand on her hip and balanced herself against the kitchen counter. She didn't know whether to laugh in his face or throw him out on his ass. "Well, you're right about one thing, Jack. It is none of your business. But let me get this straight, *you* figured that if *I* was dating someone, you should probably know about it?"

He nodded. "For the kids, of course. In case they bring it up or something."

"For the kids," Cara replied, tilting her head as if she was thinking about how much sense that made.

"Yeah, Cara." He narrowed his forehead. "In case they ask. What would you like me to say to them? I should probably have some sort of answer about whether or not their mother is dating someone . . ."

"God, Jack, that's unbelievably thoughtful of you. Too bad you didn't clue me in when you started dating. It would have made things so much easier to explain to the kids then. Oh, right, that would have been a little awkward, I guess. Since we were still married and all." She walked away from him, disgusted. The kitchen was clean, spotless, in fact, the way it always was after a weekend without the kids. There were no dishes in the sink; no crumbs left scattered across the countertops, but Cara whipped out the bottle of disinfectant anyway and started scrubbing away at the granite.

"C'mon, Cara, how long are you going to hold it over my head? How long are we going to go on bringing everything back to what I did to you? I'm sorry, Cara. I've said it, I don't know how many times. Saying it again isn't going to change anything. You know what, forget I asked. Forget I wanted to know if you were getting on with things. I figured that maybe you *were* actually getting on with things. And, quite frankly, I was going to be really happy for you, really I was. I thought that maybe you were seeing someone that was going to make you happy again, Cara. It wouldn't be such a bad thing."

The louder Jack talked, the more Cara scrubbed. She worked each tile, scrubbing at the grout until it looked as if it had been bleached. His voice was grating on her, pitchy and whiny and consistently nagging. She would have liked it if he would just leave.

"Getting on with things, Jack? You think I haven't moved on? You think I'm sitting here pining away for you, crying for you every night?" She stared at him from the other side of the island, a small prep sink in between them. She wanted to tell him about David just to prove a point, just to wipe the sympathetic "poor Cara" look off his face, but then she didn't see much point in it, anyway. It wouldn't change anything, certainly not what Jack had done to her.

Jack pushed his sunglasses on top of his head and placed his hands, palms down, wide apart on the countertop. "Cara . . ."

"Don't start, Jack. Do yourself a favor and stop there. Stop before you get yourself into a situation where you can't afford to do anything but lie to get out of it."

"Cara," he said, more calmly, his voice even.

She ignored him, hoping he would leave, disappear, vanish, dissolve.

"Cara, please."

"What, Jack? What is it that you feel is so vitally important that you have to tell me? What is it that will help you clear your conscience? Go ahead"—she opened her arms wide—"go ahead and get it off your chest."

He took a deep breath, willing himself to find an extra dose of patience. "Cara, honestly. I don't care if you're seeing someone. I don't care if you're not. All I'm hoping is that somehow you can see through to the end of this. I'm just, I'm just . . ." He struggled to find the words that he wanted to say. "I'm just hoping you can heal from this. I hate to think the wounds are so deep that they might not ever heal. That's all."

He stood before her, exposed. He hadn't meant to touch her most sensitive nerve and bring her to a boil but that's exactly what he'd done.

Cara set the bottle of disinfectant down with a thud. The paper towel she'd used to scrub the countertop was shredded. *She wouldn't cry.* She'd promised herself that over and over again. *She wouldn't cry.* Damn, Jack was infuriating. The last thing she needed from him now was his sympathy.

She studied the countertop, the intricate detail the tumbled marble made. She and Jack had argued about the tiles. He'd wanted something far more simple and she'd spent hours meticulously picking out the exact tiles, the color and the unfinished, rough edges—part of what made the kitchen so warm and inviting.

"Just go, Jack. Please, just go."

She didn't want to share anything with him, not anymore. She didn't want to confide in him the relationship she'd started with David for fear he'd make a judgment about it. She didn't want to know that he thought David was too young, or that she was too old, or hear him say that everyone needed a rebound and that it was just good for her to be back out in the dating scene again. She certainly didn't want his advice about how to talk to the children about her new *boyfriend*.

He picked up his car keys, jiggling them in his hand, and paused, waiting for her to say something else. When she didn't, he turned and left.

Cara felt as if a storm had filled a river, backing up at a dam, ready to burst forth. She paced the kitchen like a caged animal, back and forth, back and forth. Upstairs the kids were arguing; Will and Luke ganging up on Claire, banging on her door and tormenting her. Claire cried for her—*Mama, Mama*—screaming with a vengeance that Cara knew meant she was all right, just in need of attention, of being rescued. Cara took the stairs two at a time and stood on the landing.

"Will, Luke, Claire. Get your butts out here this minute!"

They appeared in unison, each of them with their mouths open and cries of mistreatment springing forth.

"Stop!" Cara yelled at them. "Stop it right now. I've had enough. I am sick and tired of listening to the three of you argue with each other. Do you hear me?" She stomped up the remaining stairs and stood towering over the three of them.

Will crossed his arms over his chest, angry. His eyes were just slits, narrowed and studying her as if he wanted to lash out at any minute. Luke held back, cowering. He wasn't used to his mother yelling, certainly not as much as she had been lately.

And Claire was insistent. Determined that she'd been wrongly accused, she began to argue with Cara. "But Mom, you don't understand. It's not my fault. I wasn't doing *anything*. The boys won't leave me alone."

"Zip it, Claire. You're just as much to blame as your brothers."

"Am not."

"Claire, I said, ZIP. IT."

"She's such a pain, Mom. All she ever does is bug the crap out of us. She has to be right in the middle of everything we're doing."

"That goes for you too, Will. ZIP. IT."

They stood in front of her, her three youngest charges, waiting. She was on her own here, outnumbered and exasperated.

"Which one of you told your father that I was dating someone?" she demanded, her hands on her hips. She figured that if she caught them off guard she'd know right away, that the guilty party wouldn't be able to look her straight in the eye. "Come on. Which one of you told him that Mommy had been seeing someone? He really had no right to know, no need to know. So which one of you thought it was so important that you had to tell your father about it?"

Will shook his head and pulled his baseball cap down low over his eyes. He scoffed under his breath, "Yeah, right."

"What did you say, Will?"

"Nuthin'."

"No?"

He tipped his head up so she could see his eyes, so that they were eye to eye. "No," he answered her, more clearly.

Luke's tiny voice piped up, sounding smaller than Cara had ever heard him. "Are you, Mom?"

Cara was tired, exhausted even. Her kids had been home less than an hour and she was already running referee. "Am I what, Luke?"

He swallowed hard, and stared at the toe of his shoe. "Dating someone? Do you have a boyfriend?" His voice was so small Cara almost had to strain to hear him.

She dropped to her knees in front of him, grabbing him by the shoulders so she could hold him at arm's length and be certain he wouldn't run from her. Luke was wearing his favorite pair of jeans and a T-shirt from Spring Training. His lips were rimmed in purple popsicle. She grasped his hands and held his arms open wide so she could look at all four foot nine inches of him. The last time they'd been to Disneyland—nearly two years ago—he'd been devastated that he wasn't tall enough for the Orange Stinger, a giant swing that circled the inside of a make-believe orange. Now Cara was sure he'd make it, sure he'd be tall enough, but that the ride would still leave him nauseous.

"Oh, Luke," she said to him, and he collapsed against her chest. She kissed the top of his head over and over again, a million tiny little kisses that ran over his sweaty forehead and around the top of his ears. "Oh, honey, it's okay."

Luke was crying, silently dropping hot tears against her tank top and bare arms. She held him tight to her chest; hugging him from behind until she was certain he couldn't breathe or even wriggle free.

"Lukey, Lukey, sweetie, it doesn't matter. Really, you can't get upset about all of this. I promise you that nothing else is going to change. Oh, sweetie, come on, take a couple of breaths, honey, just take a couple of breaths and breathe."

He gulped giant breaths of air, hiccupping and trying to catch his breath, and then tried to be very brave, nodding his head. His bottom lip quivered and his body shook and Cara's heart went out to him. He'd been so invisible, little Luke, fading into the background. Claire had been so inquisitive that it was impossible to miss her. Will's antics had caused her nothing but headaches, days of grief. And, of course, Katie had required all her strength. But Luke? He'd gone so long without being noticed, without needing her that she'd practically forgotten he was there at all.

Will stood behind him, his right hand stoically placed on Luke's shoulder as if he was supporting him. Cara hadn't seen him like this in a long while, so grown-up-looking, so mature. Cara looked from him to Claire and back again. Claire was sniveling but silent, one leg crossed over the other as if she had to go to the bathroom. There was no way Claire was moving, no way she would dare break the moment.

Luke pressed the palms of his hands deep into his eye sockets and rubbed them hard. Cara felt as if she owed him an answer, as if she owed all of them an answer.

Cara sat back on her heels. "Hey, you guys," she said softly, and pulled Luke down into her lap. She reached for Will's hand and pulled him down next to her, under her right shoulder. Claire settled in next to her on the other side, nuzzling her face against Cara's left breast. "So, yeah, okay, I am seeing someone. He's someone I met at work and his name is David. And he's far, far from being my boyfriend or anything remotely that serious. He's just someone that I enjoy spending some time with sometimes, you know, when you guys are over at your dad's house and I'm on my own."

She waited for one of them to say something but they were soundless, subdued. Luke held himself as still as he could and Claire ran her fingertips up and down Cara's arm as if she was thinking of something she might want to say, but couldn't quite put it together.

"I really don't want you to worry about this, you guys. Nothing around here is going to change. It's not as if I'm going to make you spend a bunch of time with him, or even meet him if you don't want to. Okay?" She wasn't sure they believed her, not even a little bit, and who could blame them. The only data point they had was Jack, and any promises he had made them about life not changing could be disputed in a flash. "Okay?" she asked again, looking from Claire to the boys, hoping she might find a little something in each of them that would make her feel better.

Cara wasn't in the mood for anything in particular to eat. Actually, she didn't have much of an appetite at all. Katie was due home in a week, Cara had been called twice this week by Will's principal about his behavior, and Jack had called to complain about the amount of spousal and child support he'd been assigned to pay Cara and the kids.

"It's the new house, Cara. Well, with a second mortgage, and the baby due in just a few weeks and Barbie on bed rest now, the expenses are really adding up. I'm sure you can imagine what it's like."

"Yeah, it must be a bit tight," Cara answered, not really listening, or trying, for even a second, to imagine what it must have been like.

"Well, after all, you are working now, Cara. Surely you can get by on just a little less a month. Maybe for just a few months."

She paused, waiting on him, anger mounting. She couldn't believe he wanted her to let him off the hook. He had no right to ask, none whatsoever. And since the last time she'd seen him he'd been so inquisitive about her personal life, she had no desire to give in.

"No. I really don't think so."

"But, Cara."

"No. Sorry, Jack, but I don't see how it would work for us."

"Can't you at least hear me out? I mean, maybe we could work this out amicably in some way, just for the time being."

"Amicably?" she asked, with emphasis. Then, *"AMICABLY?"* she shouted. "Are you fucking kidding me?"

"Cara," Jack warned, assuming he could speak to her the way he had, in the tone he had always used.

"What?"

"Be reasonable about this. Can't you stop and think about this from my side? Just once?"

"No."

"Why not?"

Cara remembered the day Jack had left, the way he had packed his suitcase and clothes in his car and driven off down the street, Cara running after him. She remembered what it was like to feel emptiness, really feel it to her core, and know there was nothing she could do to change his mind. She thought about all he had taken with him, and the things he'd left behind, turning them over to her willingly so that she would be faced to deal with them alone.

"Because, Jack," she answered him, "I wouldn't have any idea what *your side* looks like. I wouldn't have any idea how to stop and think about this."

Summer in San Francisco had never been colder; it had never left Cara feeling more damp and chilled at the core. It wasn't just the weather, the gray, overcast days that settled on the city like a goose down comforter, it was the feeling that this was it, this was the way it would remain for the rest of her foreseeable future.

"Cara," David said to her, "your mood leaves a little to be desired."

She was frowning and she hadn't even realized it. They sat across from each other at a small round table, the restaurant bustling around them with activity. Cara usually liked this place, the quaint Mediterranean market at the center of the Ferry Building. She and David often walked from the office to the building to have lunch or a cup of coffee or sometimes a drink after work if she had time and Jack had the kids. But today she wasn't in the mood for anything on the menu, not even the seafood stew, which was one of her standbys. Today she wasn't in the mood for the rush of people, the noise or the activity.

"Sorry."

"What's bothering you so?" David believed in long, slow lunches. And since he'd had almost no time with Cara lately, in his opinion, they were off the clock and due some time together. If need be, they'd make up for it later.

Cara shrugged her shoulders noncommittally, the way Katie would have if Cara had been asking the questions. Everything seemed so desperate.

"Cara. It isn't that bad; it can't be. Katie's due home in a week. You'll start putting the pieces back together. You'll see; it'll start feeling like you've got your sea legs again."

She stared back at him, annoyed. How could he know what it would be like when her daughter came home, the dynamic shifting once again in their house? How could he have any idea about how to put things back together? David didn't have any understanding of what it was like to get a phone call from Kate's probation officer or Will's principal. He'd never worried about getting a child's homework done or school project completed, or about getting home in enough time to make the first pitch. David didn't have a seven-year-old daughter who questioned everything, or an eight-year-old son who questioned nothing, for fear of the answer. He didn't have an angry ten-year-old or a rebellious seventeen-year-old. He wasn't saddled down by a mortgage or encumbered by PTA meetings and baseball commitments; he didn't have to deal with the guilty feeling of leaving his kids with a nanny every day, knowing he wouldn't see them again until just before bedtime.

"How would you know, David?" she snapped at him. "How would you know what it's going to be like when Katie comes home?"

He placed the dainty butter knife on his bread plate and cleared his throat.

"Look, David, it's not that I don't want my life to have some peace in it. Trust me, there's nothing more that I'd like. But it doesn't appear it'll be that way for a while, and your breezy, easy, it'll-be-better-soon attitude really isn't helping." She ran her hands through her hair and tucked the wispy ends back behind her ears. Compounding it all, she was due a haircut. And a wax, for that matter.

She'd laid into him hard, her sarcastic voice firing off before she knew what she was saying. She'd meant no harm, and she certainly hadn't meant to distance him from her, but that's exactly what she'd done.

"Cara, let it go. It doesn't have to be perfect. It may not even be close to perfect, not now and not for a while. But it will get better. I can promise you that. There's something on the other side of all of this for you," he said softly, sweetly, to her.

She listened to his voice, the calm rhythm his words took. He reached across the table and touched her arm, laying his palm over her elbow. She was tense, incredibly rigid and locked. She couldn't remember being this tightly wound in a long time.

"I'm sorry," she apologized. She didn't figure on such sensitivity from him, certainly not when she'd first met him, and not even much later, even now, as she got to know him better. She never would have considered David someone who could calm her so easily. And yet here he was, bringing peace and order to her life.

He waved her off, shaking his head. "There's no need to apologize. None, whatsoever."

Cara took a deep, cleansing breath and sat back against the small chair, trying to relax. Around them, waiters dodged in between the tables as if in an orchestrated play. She looked across the table and smiled weakly.

"Cara, how's Mel?" he asked her and she prickled at his question.

Mel had been into the agency only the day before, and Cara had avoided her at all costs. She was there to meet with an art director, a planning meeting for a website they were designing, and although it wasn't an account Cara worked on directly, it was odd that she'd avoided the meeting altogether.

"Fine, I suppose," Cara answered him, vaguely. "Um, I wouldn't know, really. I understand she was in yesterday but I must have missed her." She hunched her shoulders benignly enough.

"She asked about you, you know."

"*She did?*" Cara asked, surprised.

"Mmm-hmmm," he baited, waiting to see what she would do with this piece of information. He could tell she was rolling it around in her mind, unsure of how to handle it.

Cara waited, hoping he might go on. When he didn't, she asked him, smugly, "How did the planning session go?"

"Cara," he said to her, and she looked up at him. "You and Mel have been friends for a long time. A long, long time. When are you going to put this whole thing behind you? I'll bet there's a part of you that misses her something fierce."

Cara didn't want to admit it, but he was right. She had missed Mel a great deal. This stupid argument had gone on longer than any other squabble she'd ever had with her best friend. And, truth be told, she needed Mel now, maybe more than ever. She could have used Mel's unabashed confidence, her bigger-than-life personality. She would have given anything for an afternoon of laughter, of easy conversation that was possible only with the one person she'd known practically all her life. She would have liked to have heard a few of Mel's stories, listened to her go on for a while about Garin. There were no two ways about it; she just plain needed her.

Cara shook her head. "I can't call her, David. I just can't. There's so much that I just can't overlook. There's just so much, that well, she never shared with me, that she . . ." Cara trailed off, lost. She'd been over it so many times in her head, so many scenarios over and over again. She'd been so angry with Mel, so disappointed in the way Mel had hidden so much from her.

"Cara, what is it you are so afraid of? That maybe she's right and that maybe, just maybe, you might be wrong?"

She eyed him carefully. She expected such a comment would set her off, like a match to dry leaves. But it hadn't. Because of the way he'd said it, as if he was honestly trying to help her comprehend what it was that was holding her back, what it was that kept her from picking up the phone and throwing the whole stupid argument out the window.

It took a minute before she could muster the courage to answer him. Then finally, quietly, Cara asked, "David, what if I am wrong?"

"I don't think it's so much about who is right and who is wrong, Cara. I think, at this point, I think it's just about forgiveness."

17

Nearly a week after she'd been home, Katie sat in front of an Absolut bottle for an hour and a half. The voices in her head kept taunting her, slowly and patiently prodding her. She had no choice but to pray. She didn't pray often, but in this case it felt both familiar and necessary. There had been a lot of praying in rehab. She shrugged off the Serenity Prayer—she was sick to death of the damn thing—and opted instead to speak with God directly. She thought maybe she'd have better luck if she could have a few of her own words with Him.

You wanna drink, Katie. Go ahead, you deserve to drink. No one knows what it's like being here. No one knows what it's like living here. Go on, Katie, you can have just one. Honestly, no one will ever know.

"God, please keep me sober. God, don't let me drink this bottle. God, keep these fucking voices out of my head."

C'mon, Katie, you can have just one and quit then. You know you want just one drink. It'll make you feel a little better; it'll help you through the afternoon. You can handle just one drink.

"God, you know I can't do this without some help. Please, please get me through this. God, help me through this. I can't stand it here, I can't stand my life. It would be so damn much easier if I could just have one drink. But God, please don't let me drink. Please, please, please don't let me drink."

She hated the sound of her own voice, begging for help. She hated how helpless she sounded, how completely lost she was. She thought about calling her sponsor, Sarah, but she knew Sarah would want to come over. She knew all the logic Sarah would use on her, and she wasn't in the mood for any of it. She knew Sarah would encourage her to go straight to another meeting. And she wasn't in the mood for another meeting, either.

When she heard the grinding of the garage-door opener and her mother's car pull in and idle, she got up from the table and put the bottle back in its spot in the bar. Her mother's presence was the most sobering thing in her life.

C'mon, Katie . . . It won't hurt you. It's just one little taste. You could use just one little swig. She'll never know.

"SHUT UP!"

"Katie? Honey? Are you okay?" Cara's voice rang out from the butler's pantry before she came into the kitchen where Katie stood with her back against the countertop, her eyes closed to everything around her.

"In here, Mom," Katie answered reluctantly. She was exhausted from arguing with herself; in no mood to deal with her mother now.

"Oh, hi, honey. How're you feeling? What time did you get up? How's your morning going? Did you have some breakfast?" Cara was in her face, bombarding her with questions one right after the next before Katie ever had the chance to answer. She reached over and tucked Katie's hair behind her ears, pushing it back. Katie hated it that way; she had always hated it that way.

Katie sighed and shrugged her shoulders. "I'm fine."

Her brothers and sister were at their father's house. Katie had refused to go. Anyone would have thought it crazy to have even asked. She hadn't seen her father in three months; she certainly wasn't going to start now. It was bad enough that she had to be here with her mother, 24/7. Cara had hardly left her alone for a minute. The fact that she'd convinced her mother that she'd be okay while she went out to run a few errands this morning was practically a miracle.

"I thought we'd head out before lunch and do some shopping. And I've made you an appointment for a haircut. We've simply got to get that hair under control." She pushed at Katie's hair again, cupping it to shape the bottom. Katie pushed her hand away.

"I like it this way. I don't want to cut it."

"Just a trim, honey. We'll just give it a little shape. It could use a little shape."

"I don't want to cut it."

"Really, Katie, it'll look so much sweeter when we give it some life. Just the wee ends here and there." Cara reached over once again to fluff Katie's hair with the ends of her fingertips. Katie caught her at the wrist and held her tight, her fingers encircling Cara's plump wrist.

"I. DON'T. WANT. TO. CUT. MY. HAIR."

"Katherine," Cara whispered, stunned, spiraling backward. Cara's breath caught in her throat and scarlet blotches appeared on her face and arms.

"You're not listening to me. Don't you get it, Mom? I don't want to cut my hair. I don't want to cut my hair. I don't FUCK-ING want to cut my hair." She crossed her arms over her chest and hunched her shoulders, pulling away from her mother and retreating to the corner of the kitchen.

"Okay."

"Fine."

"You have an AA meeting this evening. Seven o'clock." Cara's chirpy voice had gone flat, dead. She said this matter-of-factly, without question. It was a statement and not a question. It was a fact, not an option. She left no room for negotiation.

"Fine."

18

Melanie had broken the news to Cara first. She was pregnant; seventeen and pregnant. It was the week before graduation, steamy and muggy and humid. Mel had been fighting the nausea for three weeks, trying desperately to keep her breakfast down and take her finals.

It hadn't exactly been a surprise to Mel. When Dermott raped her, Mel had the feeling she'd never be able to shake it off. Now she was certain of it.

What to do with the baby was never in question for Mel. She dismissed abortion immediately, never even contemplated adoption. Despite the circumstances surrounding how she got pregnant, there was a part of Mel who thought maybe she was supposed to have this baby, a part of her that thought maybe this was her way of getting back her family. Her mother had left her, abandoning her without even saying good-bye. Surely Mel could do better than that.

"Are you crazy, Mel?" Cara pleaded with her. "You can't have a baby. You're seventeen. And, my God, Mel, this is Dermott's baby. He *raped* you."

"I'm well aware of what he did to me, Cara," she snapped, defensive and angry at the same time. "I know how this happened."

"Well, then, why the hell are you even thinking about this? Why would you even contemplate it?"

"I'm not thinking about it. It's done. This is what I'm doing."

Cara was furious. Mel was just getting started, they all were. They were about to graduate from high school, go on and live their lives—really live their lives for the first time ever. Mel had a future she needed to consider. Sure, she didn't have all the advantages that Cara and Leah and Paige had—she wasn't heading off to a university the way her friends were—but there were still plenty of opportunities she could have looked at. Cara's parents had already told Mel she could stay, even after Cara left. There was junior college, a job, a life. But not with a baby. Not with a child. Not at seventeen.

"But, Melanie, you've got to think this through. God, Melanie, he raped you. This baby happened because he attacked you."

"Again, Cara, I was there. I know what happened."

"But how can you even fathom this? How can this be something that you would want?"

Mel whipped her head around and squared Cara off, towering over her. They'd come to the park to talk and the sun was hot, blistering on the skin. Cara had been sitting on a chipped picnic table, hunched over and resting her elbows on her knees.

"Look, Cara, I don't expect you'll understand this. I don't expect you'll ever be able to get your arms around any part of this. Your life has been virtually untouched, unscarred. You have no idea what it's like for your mother to walk out of the house and never come back. You have no idea what it was like to be left."

"But, Mel, you've got to . . ."

"No, wait, Cara. You think you know what this has been like because you've been here with me through it. You and your family have been over-the-top generous. You've taken me in. Your mother has single-handedly held Dermott off so that I could stay here. But this, Cara, no one knows what this feels like except me."

Cara sat on the table quietly tracing the graffiti with her index finger, waiting for Mel to finish. The anger she had felt only moments before had subsided. Mel stood in front of her, pleading for her sanity, reaching for survival.

"No one gets to make a decision about this but me, Cara. Do you understand that? No one."

Cara nodded slowly. It wasn't as if she was agreeing with Mel, certainly not about her decision. She opposed Mel's decision to her very core, there wasn't anything redeeming about it. But Mel was right about one thing: it was her decision. Only a few weeks shy of her eighteenth birthday, there wasn't anyone who was going to stop her, not on this one.

When Mel gave birth she was on her own, alone and frightened, in the sterile and colorless maternity ward at the general hospital that the counselor at Planned Parenthood had instructed her to go to. The aloof and hardhearted doctor on call that night delivered Isabella in record time, lecturing Mel about getting pregnant again while he sewed up her episiotomy. She turned her head away and drifted off, letting the pain medication run thick over her muscles, and watching the nurse sponge off her daughter and wrap her tightly in a blanketed cocoon.

Mel had prayed for one thing, and that was that her child resembled no one but herself. She'd been blessed with a girl, and the resemblance to Dermott was difficult to detect, though if Mel stared long enough at Isabella's face, as she had the entire first day she was in the hospital, Dermott appeared out of nowhere, taunting her like the Devil, hanging there in front of her the same way he had the day he'd raped her. Isabella was striking; olive skin, long eyelashes, a perfect, heart-shaped face. She possessed only one noticeable feature of Dermott's that couldn't be denied. Mel had spotted it right off, and in the years that followed, she grew out Isabella's thick hair and rarely permitted her to wear it pulled back or tucked behind the long, thin ears that made Melanie cringe.

19

When Katie left, she carried what she could in her worn black duffel bag and blue backpack. She hadn't completely unpacked in the two weeks that she'd been home so it didn't take a great deal of effort to load the duffel and her backpack again, shoving the corners with T-shirts and sweats, folded, faded jeans and a couple of sweatshirts. She took her iPod and her cell phone, but that was about it.

After the train she'd taken had pulled into the Fourth Street station she called Mel. The city sky was bright blue, sparkly, and she found herself swimming against a crowd filing into the ballpark where the Giants were ready to start a double-header against the Padres.

She'd left no note for her mother, no card or message for Will or Luke, or even for Claire, who had been following her around for the last few days as if she was trying to make sure that she wouldn't leave again.

Katie didn't know what it was about home that she couldn't take anymore, just that she couldn't stand to be there. It was as if when she was there she was choking and couldn't get a breath to save her life. It was as if someone was squeezing her so tightly that she couldn't move. It was as if someone was holding her and wouldn't let her go, wouldn't let her run. Nothing was like it should have been, nothing felt familiar anymore.

Katie had planned her escape, plotting every little detail. She strode out of school after second period, hitchhiked home, picked up her bags and was on her way. She spent the hour on the train to the city feeling like she might as well have been three states away.

Mel's assistant answered the phone on the second ring. Mel was in the middle of a shoot with a temperamental hand model who spent more time rubbing lotion across his knuckles and cuticles than he did on camera. The caretaking of his hands—his lifeblood—was more than a little disturbing.

Gloria, Mel's trusted right-hand apprentice, had the good sense to whisper in her ear. "It's Katie," she said through a cupped hand. "And she's in San Francisco." Melanie took the cell phone from Gloria and excused herself, covering her left ear so that she could hear better. Over her shoulder, she saw the hand model cover his goods in a pair of pink chenille socks to keep them warm, dry and protected.

"Katie?" Mel asked. "Where are you? What's going on?"

"At the train station. Um, look Mel, I need you to do me a favor. I need a place to stay, just for a little while. I can't stay at home anymore. And, well, I don't know where else to go. I don't know who else to call." Katie was breathless, full of information and brimming with details before Mel could get a word in edgewise. "If I can't stay with you, well, I guess I understand, but I can't go home. I just can't; not anymore."

Mel took a deep breath. "Where does your mother think you are?" she asked her.

It wasn't all that important to her, really. She'd take Katie in in a heartbeat, no questions asked. But she figured she better know what she was up against. And she had a hunch that, given it was sometime around noon on a Tuesday afternoon, Cara had no idea that Katie was standing in the middle of San Francisco somewhere.

"School, I guess."

"So you didn't tell her you were leaving. Did you at least leave her a note?"

"Yeah, sure. I told her I'd call her later," Katie fibbed. She'd worked up the story in her head, the intimate details so that the lie tumbled easily out of her mouth without a second thought, without even stumbling. Mel never would have guessed that she was lying.

"Where exactly are you?" Mel asked her again. "I'll send Glo to pick you up in the van. I'd come myself but I'm right in the middle of a shoot."

Katie breathed a huge sigh of relief. Mel would have her; she knew it. It had been the right decision to come. She looked around her at the people shuffling in and out of the station, people of all races, genders, ages. They ignored her and went about their business. She pulled the hood of her sweatshirt over her head and hunched down lower, dragging her duffel closer to her. She blended right in with the other teenagers, those who should have been in school as well. She wondered who they were, if they were as lost and lonely as she was.

"I came up on the train. I'm right at China Basin, over by the ballpark. I can wait here if you need me to. Tell Gloria to take her time."

"She'll be there soon. Just wait right out front; don't go anywhere else, okay? Just wait right there." Mel hesitated, fiercely protective and having little understanding of what kind of shape Katie was really in. The last time she'd seen her had been a few days before she was due to go home. She had seemed eager then, ready to go at last. And she seemed strong. Strong enough to get through what was ahead of her. But this Katie, the one who had called from the train station, was different. Clearly something had happened, otherwise why would she be here?

"I'll be fine, Mel."

All things considered, Melanie wasn't so sure.

The agreement that Cara and Katie had struck was that Katie would be allowed to stay home afternoons on her own so long as she called Cara as soon as she got home. No friends, no car, and absolutely no drinking, but it was a first step in regaining her freedom; the first step in repairing the damaged trust.

When Cara hadn't heard from her daughter by three o'clock—their daily check-in time—she called home. When Katie hadn't returned the call fifteen minutes later, she called again. Then she left a voice mail on Katie's cell phone. By half past the hour, in the middle of an input session for a new client, her mind was wandering. At four o'clock, she panicked, excused herself and drove straight home, alternately calling the home number, Katie's cell phone and a multitude of Jack's numbers—office, cell, home—all of which led to one voice mail box after another. Cara frantically tried to re-create the conversation she'd had with Katie that morning. Had she forgotten a commitment? Was her daughter at school? Working on a special assignment somewhere? Had she given her permission to do something after school and forgotten about it? And if so, why the hell wasn't she answering her cell phone?

By dinnertime, panic had given way to horror. Katie was gone. Her closet and drawers had been emptied of her favorite outfits; her favorite stuffed animal—an old, ratty pink pig—was not in its normal spot on her pillow. Her toothbrush and comb and blow dryer had disappeared. Without a doubt, Katie was gone.

Cara called Jack again, frenzied. He answered on the second ring, agitation seeping into his voice. "I've been in a meeting all afternoon, Cara. What in God's name is so damn important that you have to call my cell phone every half hour?"

"You mean you knew I was calling and you couldn't pick up the goddamn phone?" she screamed at him. "You've got to be kidding me, Jack?"

"What is so important?"

"Katie's gone. I have no idea where she is but she's gone. Her duffel and backpack aren't here and she's taken some of her favorite things."

"Gone where?"

"Goddamn it, Jack, do you think I'd be calling you if I had any idea where our daughter was? I have no fucking idea. Do *you* know where she is? Has she called you?"

"No, Cara, you couldn't possibly think that she'd be with me. She isn't even speaking to me."

Cara wanted to scream at him. *And whose fault is that?*

"So you have no idea where she's gone? No idea whatsoever?" Cara asked.

"No, Cara. I don't know where she is. Have you called her friends' houses? She's probably just spending the night somewhere and forgot to tell you."

"I don't think so, Jack. Maybe you don't understand me. Her things are gone. *She's gone.* This isn't a sleepover; this is for real."

"Cara, get real. Where would she go? She's not just going to up and leave. She just got home from rehab. She's clean for the first time in months. She's back in school and she's hanging out with her friends again. She's around here somewhere. Have you called her cell phone?"

Cara wanted to throw the phone across the room. She wanted to take it and chuck it as far as she could. She wanted to bang it on the countertop until it broke into a million little pieces. "Do you think I'm a complete idiot? Of course I've called her cell phone. She's not answering it." Cara paced the kitchen floor, running her hand through her hair until it stood on end.

"How about her sponsor? Have you called that woman? What's her name?"

Sarah. Her name was Sarah. Cara had her number printed on a folded-up Post-it note, buried in her wallet. She hung up the phone and went to dig it out, punching out the numbers as if she was making the only call she got from her jail cell.

"'Lo?" a young woman's voice carelessly answered from the other end. Cara had met Sarah only once, a few weeks before Katie had been released from the facility. Sarah was twenty-three and wore all black. Black T-shirt, black jeans, black high-top tennis shoes, black eye makeup. She was stick straight, no hips or breasts on her, and if you weren't looking carefully enough, she could be misconstrued as a fourteen-year-old boy. She'd had her ears pierced in three places and tattoos up and down her arms. Her hair had been dyed as black as ink and she wore it in a page boy cut that she combed straight around her ears.

"May I speak with Sarah, please?"

"Yeah, this is her," the voice answered.

Cara had been unimpressed at the center, aggravated that someone in a position of authority had thought that pairing this unpolished drunk with her daughter would be a good idea.

"Oh, um, hello, Sarah. This is Cara Clancy, Katie's mom."

"Oh, yeah. Hi."

"I was just calling because, well, I don't suppose you've heard from Katie today, have you?" Cara wasn't altogether sure that Sarah would have told her either way; she wasn't sure what the code of ethics called for in situations like these. But she was desperate, so she added, "Sarah, please, if you have heard from her, I really need to know."

"No. No, I haven't heard from her."

"Oh. Are you sure?"

"Yeah, I'm sure. The last time I talked to her was on Sunday. I saw her at our AA meeting."

"Did she say anything to you about going somewhere? Maybe to a friend's house or something?"

"Mrs. Clancy? Is Katie missing? Don't you know where she is?"

Cara was in no mood to discuss this with someone she barely knew, much less had little respect for. She certainly didn't need Sarah's help if she didn't know where Katie was. "Um, well, I'm not really sure, Sarah. Maybe you could just have her call us if you hear from her. Or you could call me yourself. Anytime. If you hear anything at all, just give me a call, okay?"

"Sure, Mrs. Clancy, sure."

An awkward silence hung between them. Cara didn't see how Sarah might help them any further, yet she didn't quite want to let her go, either. She didn't want to admit it, but talking to Sarah gave her a feeling of some sort of connection to Katie. Even if she didn't know where Katie had gone, Sarah might have known what it was that forced her to go.

"Mrs. Clancy?" Sarah asked. "Are you still there?"

"Uh-huh, yes. Was there something else? Something that Katie might have said to you?" Cara was immediately hopeful. She would take anything. Even the smallest detail might help her find her daughter.

"Did you call her friend? You know, the one in San Francisco? Actually, I think maybe she's your friend, but she used to come see Katie all the time at the center. I can't remember her name, but she's a really pretty lady, really tall and thin . . ."

MELANIE! Of course! God, Cara was so stupid. How could she not have put it together? How did she miss it?

"Sarah, you're a genius, that's got to be it. Look, just in case I don't connect with her, and she calls you, please have her call me. Just so I know she's okay, just so I know where she is. Okay?"

"Sure, Mrs. Clancy, sure thing."

Cara hung up the phone, setting the receiver back in its cradle for only a minute before picking it up again and checking for a dial tone. She dialed nine of Mel's ten numbers, area code plus her home phone, all but the last number. She held the phone in midair, cursing herself, cursing Katie. She hadn't spoken to Mel in almost three months. It had to be some sort of record. What in the world would she say to her now?

Mel, hi, it's Cara. I'm looking for Katie. Is she there?

Let me talk to Katie, Mel.

I know she's there, Mel. You can't hide her away forever.

Give me back my daughter, Mel.

She contemplated calling Leah. Or Paige. Certainly she could talk one of them into calling Mel for her, just to check on Katie. On second thought, Leah would never call her. Leah was so tired of the disagreement she and Mel had been harboring that there was no way she would make the call. And Paige wasn't likely to involve herself in anything controversial.

Maybe Jack? Surely he'd make an exception and call Mel. She dialed Jack's number, waiting.

"Hello?" Barbie's singsongy voice chirped through the receiver.

Damn. She hadn't counted on Barbie. Barbie with her swollen ankles and out-of-control hormones.

"Um, hi, Barbie. Is Jack there? I need to talk to him about Katie."

"Oh, hi, Cara," Barbie said, mispronouncing Cara's name for the nine millionth time. There was no hope; no way would Barbie ever get it right. "No, no, Jack's not here. He went out to pick up dinner. Did you hear from Katie?"

The last thing Cara wanted to do was have a conversation with Barbie, certainly not about Katie. "No. No, not yet. Listen, could you just have Jack call me? I have a hunch about where Katie might be."

"Sure, Cara. I'll have him call you when he gets back. Anything to help track our girl down."

Cara was seething. *Our girl.* Jack had spent no more than five minutes with Katie in the last three months, never mind Barbie. She had no right to refer to her daughter that way. Barbie was right in the middle of having her own baby. What did she need with Cara's children?

She couldn't take any more. "*Our girl? OUR GIRL?*" Cara was fuming, ready to burst. "She's my girl, Barbie, not yours. She's my little girl, my baby. You've got your own damn baby on the way. And I'll be damned if you ever hear me call her, 'our' anything. So, I'll beg your pardon if this seems a little out of place to you, but I'd appreciate it if you could hold off the 'our girls' until you have one of your own, okay?"

Cara was sure she'd hear about her outburst later, and that Jack would be furious with her and come unglued, but she couldn't help it; not this time, not when Barbie had been so presumptuous. Cara had had enough. She'd been forced to share her children with Jack, and that she could understand. They were, after all, his as well. But they weren't Barbie's. She'd had nothing to do with them, nothing other than helping to tear their family apart. And as far as Cara was concerned, she didn't have to share them with her.

"I'm sorry, Cara," Barbie whispered.

From the other end of the phone, Cara could tell that she was crying, small, quick hiccuplike breaths coupled with sniveling. It should have left Cara feeling satisfied, as if she'd made her point, but it didn't. She simply felt guiltier, as if she'd been in the wrong to say anything in the first place.

"She's my girl," Cara said again quickly and firmly. "Not yours." She clicked off then, not sure of what to do next.

Screw it, she thought. Screw. It. Enough of this madness.

Cara picked up the phone again and dialed Mel's number without hesitation. It rang once, then twice, before Mel picked up on the third ring.

"Hello, Cara," she said calmly.

"Hi, Melanie," Cara answered her.

"I suppose you're calling for Katie?"

"Oh, my God, Mel, is she there?" Cara wailed, immediately grateful that she had picked up the phone.

"Yeah, of course she is. Didn't you see her note? She told me she left you a note letting you know that she'd be up here with me for a few days. She came up this afternoon."

"No. No note," Cara said curtly, just relieved that she'd found her. Finally, she'd found her. "Look, it doesn't matter. All that matters is that she's okay. Oh, thank God she's there."

"She took the train up. I swear she told me she'd left you a note, Cara. Otherwise, I'd have called to let you know."

"You would have?"

"Of course, Cara, of course. My God, you must be sick with worry."

"Is she okay? Does she seem okay to you?"

Melanie took a deep breath and walked into the sunporch, the small enclosed area off the back of the kitchen. The room was cluttered with books and drawings, treasures that Mel had kept through the years, things that made her feel connected to something, despite her lack of an anchor of any sort.

Mel had just finished with the hand model when Katie arrived at the studio, wide-eyed and hesitant. Katie dropped her bags at the same time Mel opened her arms wide. When Katie reached Mel, she melted against her chest, leaning into her. After a minute Mel pulled back and cupped Katie's chin in her hand. "Are you okay?" Mel asked her, looking deeply into her eyes, looking for some sort of answer, some sort of clue.

Mel didn't let Katie go until she saw her nod her head slowly. Even still she didn't believe her. Katie wasn't all right, far from it. Her eyes were glassy, her hands shaky. Mel didn't know how Cara could miss it, the telltale signs of weakness that crept over her body and stained every pore. And if you couldn't miss it, she didn't understand how Cara could stand to ignore it.

Mel wouldn't lie to Cara, not now, not with so much at stake. As much as she'd like to reassure Cara that everything was going to be okay, as much as she would have liked to have Cara back, really back, as her closest friend and confidante, she wouldn't lie to her about Katie.

"She still needs a great deal of work, Cara."

Those weren't the words Cara was prepared to hear. Mel's summarization left Cara feeling like a failure, unfit. She was prickly and irritated. How would Mel know what kind of shape Katie was in? Who made her qualified to make a judgment about it? After all, the rehab facility had checked her out. Weren't they the experts? Didn't they know best? Cara cleared her throat and waited.

"She's been fine, Melanie. She's been home for a couple of weeks and she's been fine. We haven't had a single episode, not a single problem." Cara's voice was cold and had an edge to it. She really didn't want to argue with Mel right off, not the first time she had talked to her in months, but she couldn't help but take personally what Mel was saying to her. She couldn't help but feel as if she was to blame.

"Yet."

"We haven't had a single problem at all, Mel. Can't you look at the bright side of things? Can't you give some credit where credit is due?"

"Something brought her here, Cara. There's a reason she's sitting in the guest bedroom at my house and not in her own room at home. You have to at least admit that."

Cara opened her mouth to argue with her, but nothing came out. She waited Mel out but Mel remained quiet on the other end of the line. The silence that hung between them was painful. It left a dull ache in the center of Cara's chest.

Finally, in a small voice, Cara asked her friend, the person she had most counted on for as long as she could remember, "What should I do, Mel?"

"Let her stay, Cara. A week or so, maybe more if it suits her. Just for the break, so she can get her bearings again." Mel had rehearsed the words carefully as if they were a piece of music she was playing, the tempo tricky and just so.

"But she's only just come home," Cara pleaded. "I've only just gotten her back."

Mel held strong; she had Katie's best interest at heart. "It might be nice for her to have some time, Cara, some space to acclimate again. And it might be a good idea for her to do that in a place where she can just be herself."

Cara teared up, her ego bruised. "And you think that's with *you?* And not in her own home? With people who love and understand her? With us?"

Mel waited on Cara, patient and quiet. Katie had snuck up on her, blending into the door frame, waiting. She didn't move; Mel even wondered if she dared breathe.

"But the kids need her. I need her. And she needs us. She does, doesn't she? She needs us?"

From behind Mel, Katie's voice was strong, distinct. "Tell her I want to stay, Melanie. Tell her I won't come home. If she makes me, I'll just leave again."

Cara could hear her clearly. She could hear every last syllable her daughter enunciated.

"What? What was that, Mel? Is that Katie? What's she saying? Oh, c'mon, Mel, let me talk to her."

Mel held the phone out at a distance for Katie but she was unmoving.

"I won't do it for you, Katie," Mel said to her, shaking her head. "Talk to your mother. Tell her for yourself what you want to do."

Katie took the phone, holding it up to her ear gingerly as if she was expecting Cara to come unglued at any moment, obscenities flying through the connection.

"Hi, Mom," she said, resolutely.

"Katie," Cara said simply. "Oh, honey, are you all right? I was so worried."

"I'm fine," she answered plainly, simply. She couldn't stand the way her mother's voice dripped syrupy sweet as if she was adding heaping teaspoonfuls of sugar to tea.

Cara stood and stretched her back. She was stiff and tired and her body ached with worry and stress. Her daughter was trying every last bit of patience that Cara thought she contained; every last ounce of empathy was draining out of her as she stood there.

"What is it, Katie? What is it that you want?" Cara urged, short on understanding. She had tried too much, so hard, and every time it felt to her that they were right back at the beginning, starting over again and again.

"Half a bottle of Absolut and a Sprite to chase it," Katie answered.

"Don't be absurd, Katherine. Don't fuck with me anymore. I'll come and haul your ass out of Mel's house so fast your head will spin." Cara spat the words through the phone line, meaning business. She'd had more than enough, more than she could deal with. "You want to try me on this one?"

"No," Katie answered her honestly, panic gripping her. Her mother was mad, angrier than she had heard her in a long time.

"Then let's try this again. Tell me what it is that you want. What is it that will make you happy? 'Cause from where I'm standing, Katie, I'm at a loss as to what we need to do to make all this right, to make your life look a little bit better so that you don't jump off a bridge again."

"I want to stay here."

"Come on, Katie, be realistic. You've only just gotten home. You should be at home with us."

"Please, Mom."

"But, Katie . . ."

"I won't come home. I can't do it anymore," she said with some finality, taking Cara by surprise.

Cara hadn't expected Katie to react so strongly, to draw a line in the sand so quickly. It was clear that Katie had been thinking on this. It was clear that she'd had enough.

"And if I let you stay with Mel? Will it be better then? Will it be what you need to finally get a grip on all of this?"

Cara wasn't convinced, not anymore than she would have if Katie was at home. As much as she hated to admit it, she was near giving up on her daughter once and for all. But she also didn't know if she had much of a choice. And she wasn't willing to tempt Katie on this one. Bringing her home right now might mean losing her again. Losing her forever.

"Jack, we need to talk about Katie." She had left the message on his voice mail, urgency growing in her voice. "I need you to call me when you receive this message. Call me right away." She was rarely so insistent with him, but this time she wasn't letting him off the hook. She wouldn't be blamed for this later. This was a decision they'd make together.

Cara had only just moved Katie home. The last thing she expected was to be packing the rest of Katie's things—those she hadn't been able to fit in the duffel or backpack she'd taken with her—and hauling them to Mel's house. Of all places to go; Mel's. Cara should have guessed it; it was so damn obvious. Katie knew Mel wasn't exactly top of mind with Cara right now and she knew

Mel would have her. Mel would never turn her back on Katie. Not ever.

When Jack called, the first thing he said to Cara was, "Maybe it will do her some good, Cara. If she thinks life at Melanie's is going to be so much better than living the posh life she's had at home, then let her go. She'll figure it out soon enough. Tell Mel her program isn't negotiable. She can stay there but someone will have to haul her back and forth to all her damn therapy sessions and AA meetings."

"It's completely inappropriate, Jack," Cara interrupted him, insistently. Cara sat Indian style in the center of Katie's bed, photographs and letters spread out before her. She'd called in sick to work and spent the morning in her daughter's room, alternately snooping and organizing, occasionally stopping to cry. She was due a shower, wore no makeup, and she desperately needed to shave her legs.

"If Mel thinks it's so easy, let her deal with Katie for a while. I'm telling you, Cara, Katie will realize how lucky she's had it in a few days and she'll be banging on your front door."

"She's *our* daughter, Jack. We can't just pawn her off on someone else, least of all Mel."

"Look Cara, you're the one that's always telling me how difficult this has been, how much energy and time and effort it takes to make sure Katie is doing the things she needs to be doing. All I'm saying is that maybe it's time you took a break. Maybe Mel can get through to her. Maybe she can figure out what's so goddamn difficult about her life that she has to solve it by cracking open a beer in the middle of the day. That's all. Just give her a chance; you may be surprised. Christ, Cara, I'm late. I can't talk about this anymore. I've got three back-to-back meetings this morning that will make this little problem look like a cakewalk. I suggest you send Katie's stuff up to the city and take a little vacation."

Cara hung the phone up without saying good-bye. She didn't have to; Jack had hung up first, clicking his cell phone closed with a harsh snap.

"I suggest you send Katie's stuff up to the city and take a little vacation."

Venom burned in the back of Cara's throat.

Let Mel take her, she finally said to herself in exhaustion. She was weary, frightened and alone, and spent from packing. She'd arranged everything she thought Katie would want, everything she could possibly fit into the two suitcases that were propped open on the floor of Katie's room. She pulled back the covers and crawled under the sheet and blankets on Katie's bed, pulling herself tightly into a ball and rolling her body toward the wall. She shut her eyes tightly to the world around her. The scent of her daughter was on her everywhere, mixed with that of the Tide detergent she used to religiously wash Katie's sheets once a week. Everything felt unsteady, unsure. The room spun as if she was drunk, leaving her disoriented.

When she'd had enough, she got up and stripped the bed of all its linens. She removed the sheets and blankets, the comforter and mattress cover, and rolled them into a giant ball, heaving them into the hall outside Katie's room. She opened the windows wide, letting the strong afternoon breeze push against the screen and blow the curtains freely, wildly. Later she would come back with two large garbage bags, the vacuum, and a new bottle of Pledge and scrub the room clean, but for now she wanted nothing more than to let the wind whip through the room, the force of oxygen, plentiful and abundant, to rush against the walls, through the carpet, over the furniture.

On Mel's doorstep, Cara set Katie's suitcases one right next to the other. On top of these she placed Katie's pillow and a coat that would have been horribly wrinkled if it had been folded and stuffed into one of the bags. Cara had no intention of staying and so she stood on the third step down from the top, keys in hand, and double-parked in the street, ready to wave quickly and bolt. She was just there to drop off Katie's things; she didn't want to have to look at her daughter and realize she had failed her.

Mel answered the door to the flat, took one look at the bags, then at her friend who was ready to sprint, before she put her hands on her hips and said to her, "Cara, get your ass in here, you just can't drop all of this stuff off here and leave." Melanie stepped outside. She was thin and tall in jeans and a tank top, the bones of her angular shoulders jetting out from beneath the cotton shirt. She was in the middle of shooting a back-to-school fashion spot for a kids' store and from the studio below Cara could make out the sounds of children's whiny voices, clients with expectations that weren't being met.

"You're shooting; I don't want to stay."

"I'll take a break. Look, Katie's not here right now," Mel told her. "You can come in without seeing her."

"No. It's fine, Mel. She can stay with you for a while. Just promise me you'll keep her on her program, okay? Just promise me that." Cara's voice cracked then, to think of her daughter here in the flat with Mel, smiling, maybe, for the first time in a long time. Katie's words echoed in her head, *"I won't come home. I can't do it anymore."*

"She's at a meeting now, Cara. Bella took her."

Cara cleared her throat, trying to gain her composure. "Well then, see. You're off to a good start, Melanie." She took the bottom two steps then, leaving Mel still standing alone in front of the open door amid the pile of luggage she had so carefully, so meticulously packed. "Tell her she can call me anytime she wants. You know, if she wants to talk to me."

"You can't just go, Cara. Please?"

From the street, Cara shook her head and swallowed back the inadequacy that she felt. She had failed with her daughter, time and time again. She was leaving the mothering to someone else, someone who'd been raised, even, without a mother.

It wasn't like Mel to get emotional, but just the sight of her very best friend had left her feeling sentimental. "You can't just leave her without some sort of plan to see her soon. It's important, you know. It's important that she knows she has your support. It's the only way she'll come home again."

Cara turned to face her then, standing on the street with her glasses pushed up on her head. She felt disheveled and disoriented, unaware of how she had made it here, how she could have possibly gotten to this point. The wind whipped at her hair, and stung her cheeks. She hadn't thought about Katie coming home, about what it would take for Katie to want to be with her again. She had only considered what it felt to lose her, how letting her go had a sense of physical pain for her.

"Cara," Mel said again, her voice changed this time, less authoritative. "She will come home. You do know that, don't you? She'll be back, I promise."

Mel had poured out every last drop of alcohol in her house, drained every bottle and emptied the entire top shelf of her bar. She had toted a case of beer and two large crates of wine next door to her neighbor's house. She threw out the olives, the cherries, the limes and the mixed nuts for fear that any of these might spark something in Katie that would make her want to take a drink.

The stench of the liquor running down her kitchen sink made her queasy and restless and reminded her of unpleasant days with Dermott.

When she was finished she sat Katie down and spoke to her calmly.

"There's one rule, Kate, that's it."

"Okay."

"No drinking."

Katie stared at her, not sure what to make of Mel's point. It was pretty obvious, wasn't it? "Okay." She brushed by the warning as if it was a passing comment.

"There are no substitutions to this rule. No grace period, no warnings, no second chances. There is no drinking in my house or anywhere else while you are living in my house."

"All right, Mel, I get it."

"You are done drinking. I know you might want to drink. I know you might think that it's okay to slip up because I'll be there to catch you and I'll understand that you needed to drink. I know you think that I'll support you. And I will. But I won't let you live here. And I won't take you home to your mother or your father, either."

Katie looked away, embarrassed. She hadn't expected a lecture from Mel. Mel had always treated her like an adult. Mel had never addressed her from her soapbox, speaking to her in a tone similar to one Katie might have heard from her mother.

"I will call your probation officer and I will turn you in. I will tell him that you have been drinking and driving and causing undue harm to yourself and to those around you. I will recommend they put you back in a lockdown program. And I won't see you again until you can look me in the eye and tell me you are sober."

Katie was wordless then, tears welling up in the bottom of her heavy lids. She swallowed hard and nodded her head.

So far, three weeks in, Katie had kept her end of the bargain.

20

Garin left a voice mail on Cara's cell phone; his voice was strong and confident and it surprised Cara to hear from him.

"Hello, Cara, it's Garin."

He stopped and took a breath. She could hear him exhale deeply into the receiver as if he was searching for the right words.

"Look, I know you don't see eye to eye with the way Melanie and I have been living our lives, and I guess in your position, I can understand that, as much as Mel would kill me for saying so. But look, Cara, I need your help. Mel needs your help. Her father has passed on. Dermott, I mean. He died the night before last. Mel's mother called to let her know and, um, well, quite honestly, Cara, she hasn't been the same since.

Look, I can't get there right now. It's nearly impossible. I've got a number of family obligations that I need to deal with and it's just not in the cards. Besides, I'm not entirely sure that I'm the one who could help Melanie through this, anyway. But she needs you. She needs you and Leah and Paige more than ever. From this distance I can't really tell what kind of shape she's in but it doesn't look very good. She's crumbled, and, well, frankly, I don't know what to do to help her. Not from here, anyway.

Look, Katie gave me your number. I know she's staying with Mel right now and I'm sure that's been really, really hard for you. If nothing else, you should probably check on Katie and just make sure she's okay. Mel's not really in any kind of shape to be making sure that she doesn't slip up or anything.

Can you call me, Cara? I need to confirm that you've received this message. I need to know that you'll reach out to her. That's all I'm asking, Cara, is that you reach out to her."

Cara slowed the car, then stopped it altogether in the deserted parking lot of an old grocery store and turned off the engine. Kids on bikes and skateboards raced around her car, using the lot as a makeshift course. She played the message again, listening to the tone of Garin's voice, the rise and fall of his breath coupled with panic.

He'd had the good sense to call, to reach out to Cara. For Mel, of course. But also for Katie. And for that she was eternally grateful.

Dermott gone, after all these years. Melanie hadn't heard from him, not after he'd finally left town. And for all their history, Cara and Paige and Leah had finally just stopped asking. As far as they knew, he'd been gone for a long, long time.

But this was official word. And from Bea. Melanie would be in no shape to take care of Katie. Hell, Melanie would be in no shape to take care of herself. Mel hadn't heard from Bea in years, not at least that Cara was aware of. She couldn't imagine what it must have been like, that phone call.

Dermott gone.

Cara drove to the city on automatic pilot, watching the sun transition through the fog and dance on the shimmering bay. At Mel's flat, she stood on the sidewalk and stared at the building, remembering the anger and hurt that had consumed her the day she walked out Mel's front door and down the steps and into the street, fury sweeping over her.

Katie answered the door, dressed in jeans and a crisp white shirt, as clean and clear-eyed as Cara remembered seeing her in a long time.

"Garin called. He told me about Dermott."

"She's in her bedroom, Mom. She went in there yesterday afternoon around four, just after her mom called. And she hasn't been out since. Bella came last night and we both tried to get her to eat something or get up or even talk to us, but she's just in there lying on the bed or sitting in the chair in the corner staring off into space. It's like she's a zombie or something. I don't get it. It's not like she was even close to her mom and dad so it's kinda weird that she would have such a strong reaction about the whole thing. Isabella's really, really worried."

"Where's Bella now?"

"She had to go to work. She didn't want to leave, but I told her I would keep an eye on Mel. But she's starting to freak me out, Mom. She just sits there and stares off into space, just kind of glassy-eyed and not at all with it. It's like she doesn't even know I'm there. I've never seen her like this. Mel's always so full of life, so sure of everything."

Cara placed her purse and jacket on the bench in the hall and started to take the stairs to Mel's room. "Would you make me some tea, Katie? Strong and hot and black."

Cara knocked softly on Mel's door before opening it. Inside, the room was dark, the blackout shades drawn until they touched the edge of the windowsill. Cara waited for her eyes to adjust and searched the room for her friend, leaving the door cracked to let in the light from the hall.

Melanie sat in the corner chair, her knees pulled up to her chin and her head buried in her arms. Her hair was loose and fell around her shoulders in long sheets. She looked to be very uncomfortable but she never moved when Cara entered the room, never looked up to see who it was. She wasn't crying, but she sat very, very still.

"Mel?" Cara whispered, because whispering seemed more appropriate. "Mel, honey?" She went to her and draped her arm around Mel's back. "Come on, sweetie, you can't sit in here by yourself all day."

They sat together for a few minutes, getting used to each other again. It had been a long time since Cara had been this close to Mel, close enough to hold her tightly, close enough to feel her breathing. The room was dark and quiet and cool. The duvet had been turned down and folded neatly at the end of the bed, but the sheets and blanket remained untouched as if Mel had had every intention of getting into bed but never quite made it. Cara rubbed her back and shoulders, encouraging her over and over again until she finally uncurled herself and stretched, turning instead to lay her head down in Cara's lap.

"He's gone, Mel. He can't hurt you anymore."

"I don't get it, Mom. Mel hated Dermott. She never talked about him. And I've never really heard her talk about her mother, either." Katie had made the tea as her mother had requested and was waiting for her in the kitchen.

"Lotta history, Katie. Long before your time, a really, really long time ago."

"Will she be okay? I mean, really okay?"

"Eventually."

Cara took the tray and started up the stairs again, her legs heavy and slow. She stopped, turning to address her daughter. "Katie?"

"Yeah?"

"I just want you to know you can come home, you know, whenever you're ready. I know that it's important for you to be here right now, that you feel like this is the place where you can be at peace with your treatment and make some good progress. And, well, from the looks of it, I'd say you're doing fairly well at that. But when the time's right, well, I just wanted you to know that you can come home. I'll be there. I'll be there waiting for you."

Katie blinked back tears that burned at her eyes. "Okay," she replied softly, almost a whisper.

"Okay," Cara answered her.

Melanie had been sleeping for a couple of hours, fighting the demons that crept through her dreams. Cara sat in the chair near the bed thinking about the time that had passed between them, the silly argument that had left them each on one side or the other.

"What time is it?" Mel asked her, blinking her eyes awake slowly.

"Nearly two."

"Katie will be leaving for her meeting soon. She likes to go on Sunday afternoons. She says there's more redemption at AA than at the Vatican."

They made their way down the stairs together, leaning on each other like women far older than they were. Katie had scrawled a note and was just leaving, collecting her things and huddling them together in her daypack.

"Remember what I told you, Katie. When you're ready, okay? Whenever you're ready to come home, I'll be there," Cara told her and then pulled her tight against her chest, her arms wrapped around Katie's tiny back. She felt Katie give in to the embrace, just a little, enough so that Cara knew that her daughter was still in there and that together they had a chance to start over again.

After Katie was gone, Mel moved about the kitchen listlessly, dazed and glassy-eyed. She took two teacups from the cabinet and set them on the countertop but she couldn't remember why she'd gotten them out. She went to the refrigerator to pull out the milk but only stood in front of the open door staring at the contents, unable to recall her purpose. Finally, Cara took her by the elbow, leading her to a chair and encouraging her to sit down.

* * *

After a while Leah arrived, bringing with her strength and courage and perspective. And then Paige, with a Crock-Pot of chili and two dozen oatmeal chocolate chip cookies, still warm and tightly wrapped on a pretty ceramic plate. Mel took one look at the plate of cookies and dissolved into tears, burying her head into the crook of her arm.

"You made all this? For me?" Mel muffled through her elbow.

"I, I didn't know what else to do, Mel," Paige answered her. Her body had betrayed her; she was enormous now, deliberate in every move. "Mel, I am so, so sorry."

Someone had died. It meant that it was practically a holiday in the kitchen for Paige. It didn't matter that it was Dermott; she'd have done it no matter who had gone. It was part of her DNA, embedded within the fabric of who she was.

"Oh, Paige," Mel answered her.

Over steaming tea, Mel recounted the conversation she'd had with Bea in a haze of details that ran in long, run-on monotone sentences.

"Dermott's been with my mother for the last three years."

"What?" Leah asked her, disbelief ringing in her tone. "You're kidding."

"No. No, I'm not. Three years. She's been harboring that man for the last three years. He's been living in her house; she's been taking care of him all this time. After all of this, after all that he's done to us, and she took him back. No questions asked."

"But, but I don't understand. How could that be? After all this time? Mel, are you sure you understood her correctly?"

"Yeah." Mel looked at her coldly. "Yeah, I got it. All of it. He went to live with her after he was diagnosed. Chronic pancreatitis. Shocker, I know. I mean the man drank himself through more bottles of Jack Daniels than you'd find at a distillery."

"And Bea took him back? I can't believe it," Cara said simply.

"You can't?" Mel asked her, deadpan. "C'mon, Cara. She'd been waiting for him all these years. That's why she left in the first place. She figured he'd come looking for her one of these days, that in reality, he couldn't live without her. And then she'd have the last word, the upper hand. I guess she was wrong about that."

"How so?"

"Well, shit. The man died on her. After all this, all the years of arguing, the years of cheating on her. After failing the child she left him to take care of, like I was a trade-off. After finding his way back to her and giving her three shitty years of his disease, three shitty years of watching him die a little bit every day. He got the last laugh, I guess. He got the final say." She lit a cigarette, sucking deeply on the end of it. Mel never smoked inside her flat; this was definitely an exception.

They were quiet, contemplative. Mel had every right to be bitter; she'd lost so much. First her mother, then her innocence. She'd had so much stripped from her, so much taken away.

"She wants me to fly back there. To Nashville. She thinks I owe it to Dermott to come and say good-bye to him. She thinks I should be grateful for the years he cared for me after she left."

"*You?* She can't possibly be serious. She thinks *you* owe it to *Dermott* to fly across the country."

Mel nodded her head slowly, drawing on the last of her cigarette before stubbing it out in the ceramic bowl she was using as an ashtray. She exhaled, blowing the smoke away from the table. "Yep."

Leah was disgusted, vocal. "Mel, my God. Has she lost her mind? She can't possibly think that you would fly across three time zones to attend the funeral of a man who *abused* you, after your mother walked out of your life and left you with him. She thinks you owe this to Dermott. I suppose she thinks you owe it to her, too. Mother of the Year. Shit. What gives her the right?"

"I'm going, Leah."

They all stopped, frozen. "What?" Cara asked her. "You can't possibly be serious, Mel. You can't go?"

"I'm going, Cara."

Mel could be headstrong, but this was ridiculous. She hadn't seen her mother in over twenty years, maybe closer to thirty.

"Bea doesn't know what happened after she left. She doesn't know what Dermott did to me. You can bet your life that Dermott didn't tell her."

"You don't have to prove anything, Mel. There's no unfinished business, nothing that needs to be dug up and rehashed. You've got a good life now. You've raised Bella to be a beautiful woman. It's not your job to go back and pick up the pieces from all of that. There's nothing left that needs to be tended to," Leah lectured.

"Look, Leah, maybe you think this is crazy and, shit, I'll admit it, there's a good chance that you'd be right. Dermott certainly doesn't deserve my sorrow; and he definitely doesn't deserve my kindness, either. Bea left me with him and this is how he repaid her, how he repaid both of us. But if nothing else, Bea should know that the man she spent waiting for all those years, the man she spent caring for until his last dying breath, well, he wasn't the man she thought he was. She deserves to know that." The tears came quickly for Mel, raw with emotion and sick with the memories.

Leah shook her head. "She doesn't deserve that. She doesn't deserve to know anything about your life. She left. She doesn't deserve anything from you. Not now, not ever."

"Maybe it's not for Bea, Leah. Maybe the desire to tell Bea about what Dermott did to me isn't for her, after all," Mel shouted. "Maybe it's for Bella. Did you ever consider that? Maybe it's important for me to tell Bea about Bella. She exists, you know. Dermott took everything that I had, everything that I was, and destroyed it. But he gave me Bella, too. He gave me a child, a family that I didn't have. He replaced what I had lost; he replaced what I'd had with my mother. Only now I was the mother.

How could I possibly feel any sadness for this man who set my life in motion and forced it down this road? How could I feel any empathy whatsoever for his lifeless body, especially after all these years? And yet I do, Leah. I mourn for his being gone, for the life he pissed away in a bottle of alcohol and for the years he and Bea were constantly at each other, for the family they pissed away. I mourn for his inability to know what to do with me, for the fact that he couldn't manage to keep it all together. And Isabella? My beautiful daughter who was brought into this world through such hate, through such distaste for anything resembling love? God, I mourn for the fact that she'll never know her father. His pathetic life wasn't worth her time or energy, but God, how unfair to be dealt those cards. She had no choice in the matter, she never got a say about that."

The room was dead quiet, still. With shaking hands that she couldn't control, no matter how hard she tried, Mel lit her third cigarette in less than fifteen minutes. She was chain-smoking, lighting one right after the next so that a haze of blue smoke hung thick in the small kitchen. Finally, Cara reached over and propped open a window. Then she went to sit next to Mel, sharing a kitchen chair with her and holding her at the elbow to steady her.

"You should go," Paige said slowly, breaking open the silence that had settled across the room. She spoke to the room, not necessarily to Mel herself. She spoke to them all, and to no one, in a voice that was recognizably her own, but sounded even stronger, more assured than anyone knew she could be. Gone was mousey Paige, the apprehension that normally hung at the end of every sentence. "You should go, Melanie," she said again, and smiled at her friend. "You owe that to yourself. You owe that to Bella."

21

"I won't have you go alone," Cara said to Mel, firmly. Mel was pulling clothes from her closet, refolding and laying them across the bottom half of her suitcase. She would go for four days only. She had decided and purchased the ticket overnight. "I'll go with you. I haven't been anywhere in God knows how long and David owes me one. Christ, he can hold the agency together for a few days."

"I can't ask you to do that, Cara."

"You didn't."

Cara had the office manager book her flight and phoned Jack to tell him he would need to take the kids for the weekend. He and Barbie had moved into a new house with plenty of space for *all* of his children. There was no reason to think he couldn't manage them for a few days.

Her only real concern was Katie. Cara was reluctant to leave her, but Isabella promised to stay with her, promised to keep an eye on her. Even Leah vowed to make regular visits to Mel's flat, checking in on Katie and swearing to call Cara the minute she suspected anything was wrong. In the end, though, it was Katie herself who guaranteed Cara she would stay on her program. She had approached her mother and looked her in the eye—really making strong contact—for the first time in as long as either of them could remember.

"I promise you, Mom, with everything I have. I know how important this trip is for Mel. And I know it's important that you feel like you can go with her. I won't drink. No parties or driving or crazy binges. It's the first time in a very long time, but I can honestly tell you that the desire is gone, really gone."

"Are you ready to come home yet, honey?" Cara had asked her much too eagerly, pushing Katie's hair away from her face, then pulling it back the way it was, the way she knew Katie liked it in the first place.

"I'm getting there. Maybe we can talk about it when you come back."

Cara hugged her tight, resolving not to force her, for every time she did, it felt like Katie ran from her.

"Deal."

Mel and Cara left on the red-eye. Their flight was crowded and cramped, making it nearly impossible to sleep. Melanie stared out the porthole window, watching the million tiny lights, houses and businesses on the Peninsula disappear behind them. She heaved a sigh and ordered a Rum and Diet Coke.

"Do you know what you'll say to her? I mean, first off? Have you thought about it?" Cara asked her, while flipping through a magazine.

"No."

"It might be better that way. It probably wouldn't matter, anyway. Even if you rehearsed the first line. No telling where it'll go from there."

"No."

"We can turn around if you change your mind, you know. We can get right back on the next plane and come back."

"No, Cara. I need to do this. There's no turning back now."

The plane touched down in Nashville near seven o'clock in the morning. Outside dark, pregnant clouds hung thick in the sky, threatening to break free at any minute. Mel and Cara made their way through the terminal to the rental car counter in less than ten minutes. Mel handed the clerk her driver's license and credit card and was settled behind the wheel of a LeBaron in record time.

They maneuvered their way through the city, and then onto the interstate, south to Shelbyville. Homes dotted the miles along the way, brick ranchers with acres of open space on either side of them, landscape that they weren't used to seeing. Cara's home was older, and much smaller, and in the summer when the windows were open, she could make out the dinner conversation coming from her neighbor's kitchen, not more than 100 feet away. Mel's flat shared walls, one tiny apartment lined up next to the other.

"Of all the places in the world to go, how'd she end up here?" Cara asked, checking the directions Mel had printed and handed to her to navigate.

Mel shrugged her shoulders. "Guess it was just the last place she stopped. Once she stopped running."

"Are you going to put that thing out?" Cara asked her, coughing, choking on the residue of Mel's third cigarette. She held the lit butt outside the open window, but smoke snaked its way inside the window and hung on the fabric of the seats.

"Maybe. Probably not before we get to Bea's house."

Bea's home, as it turned out, was an eleven-hundred-square-foot double-wide trailer with rusted aluminum siding and waist-high weeds that covered the back end of the unit. Out front, two plastic green chairs sat facing each other in the dust. A chained boxer greeted them, barking furiously and noisily in an out-of-control fashion.

They parked in the dirt lot next to the trailer and Mel leaned over to check the address on the paper again.

"This is it," Cara said to her and she nodded.

Mel sucked in the last of her available oxygen and opened the car door without any hint of hesitation, charging forward on the property as if she owned it. It was as if she was to hang back and wait on her decision, she just might turn the car around and speed off.

"I can wait here. If you want, that is," Cara called after her, opening the passenger door with more caution, slowly and methodically. She stepped out of the car and onto the hard, dry dirt. The land desperately needed the rain that looked promising.

"Do whatever you want, Cara. You can stay there or come with me. It really doesn't matter."

Cara was hoping to have been invited, included. Instead she watched as Mel stomped up the three metal steps that led to the door of the trailer and pulled back the screen door. She knocked loudly, her knuckles rasping on the peeling wood, and let the screen slam shut in front of her.

Bea was quick to answer. Rail-thin and wrinkled over every inch of her body, she wore a cheap white blouse that hung much too loosely on her concave chest and left her looking like a skeleton. Her gray hair looked like the sun had set in it a long time past; all that was left were fleeting streaks of color that had once shone. Her cheekbones were sallow and sunken from too many cigarettes, and her lips were pressed into a thin, hard line.

"Mama?" Melanie couldn't help but ask.

Bea pushed open the screen with her right arm, and then cleared her throat, coughing up the phlegm that had settled in her chest.

"Melanie. It's about time you dragged yourself home."

Mel was sinking, stuck in quicksand. Her legs were weak at the knees, incapable of inching forward. Cara could see that without help she would go down, succumb to Bea's cruel words in a minute.

Home?

Home was where she had come from, where she had started out last night when she kissed Isabella good-bye at the airport. This was not home, no part of this place belonged to her.

Bea stared at Melanie, waiting on her to make a move. Instead, Cara stepped forward and caught her attention.

"Cara? Is that you? Did you come all this way with Melanie? Well, you two come on in and I'll fix you some lemonade. Too hot to be standing out here gaping at your mama. 'Sides, those clouds are gonna break free any minute and you're gonna get soaked if you're standing out here." Bea's voice had changed in an instant—sweeter, and more contained—when she realized she had company, real company.

Cara approached the trailer slowly, carefully and considerately. She looked at Melanie, waiting for her friend to come to life, hoping that if Mel had anything left she'd dig deep inside and find it right here and now.

"It's good to see you, Bea," Cara tried, filling the empty, uncomfortable space that hung amid the three of them. She took Mel's hand and tugged at her, dragging her along, propping her up as she stepped hesitantly inside. They'd come to make a point, to finish what had been left so long ago. They weren't going away empty-handed now. "Lemonade would be perfect, just fine."

"It has been a long time." Melanie struggled to find the words, waiting for them to come to her. She had expected she'd know just what to say, exactly the points she wanted to make to her mother. *Her mother.* She was standing in front of the woman who she'd called her mother all her life, for no particular reason other than she'd never adopted a more fitting name, something that might have worked better, something slightly more appropriate.

God, Bea had aged. Her outside appearance, any signs of beauty or femininity, anything soft at all, had long been replaced by signs of a hard life. Her hands had aged horribly, rough, leathery skin atop crooked, bony fingers and short, unkempt, ragged nails. She stooped when she walked, limping on the left side as if she needed to have a hip replaced or her knees had gone bad.

Inside, the trailer was cramped and cluttered, filled with dusty knickknacks and neglected, shabby furniture that desperately needed to be replaced. The windows were full of grime, the curtains tacky and threadbare. Mel looked around in awe, struck by what a pathetic life her mother had led.

Bea emptied an ice tray and then poured lemonade into three large unmatched glasses, slowly and purposefully. With her back to Mel and Cara, she said, "I expected you would have come out to see us sooner than this."

Cara could feel the tension build in the small space, pushing on the trailer walls until it wanted to burst forth and blow out the dirty windows. She watched Melanie's eyes grow small, just slits, really, and a crease formed at the spot above her nose where her eyebrows would have come together had she not had them waxed and manicured every few weeks.

"Well, I figured you would have come back by now, too. But I guess we were both wrong," Mel said.

There she was, Cara thought. There was the friend she knew, the woman she'd expected.

"I've been taking care of your father, Melanie. Three years that man has been ill, right here in this trailer. It took everything we had just to keep us going. I worked all day to earn enough money to pay for his medication, stayed up half the night tending to him."

"He was not my father."

Bea was quiet, thinking on her words. "No, no I suppose not. Not technically, anyway, though he might as well have been."

"No. He was not my father."

"Now I know that Dermott had his issues. Believe me, I know. You don't think I went about my business because life had been a bed of roses with him, do you? Of course not. But he always kept a roof over your head. Until, that is, as I understand it, you got all smart on him and moved out. Thought you could do better staying with your friends, is what I understand." Bea glanced sideways at Cara, standing silently in the corner. "No harm, of course, Cara, but really Mel should have just stayed put. There was no need for her to burden your family with one more mouth to feed. So sweet of you and your mama to take her in. Joanie was always such a doll baby."

Melanie had had enough. It took everything she had not to

completely lose it and shake her mother senseless. At some point she became aware that she was gaping, flabbergasted at Bea's version of the story. She couldn't even imagine where to begin.

Mel stood abruptly, tall and commanding at once. "Why did you leave?"

"Oh, for goodness sake, Melanie, you've just gotten here. Do we have to go through all of this now? When it's been so long since we've seen each other?"

"Why, Mother? Fill me in on the details. I mean, if you don't mind, that is."

Bea sighed. "It's all such water under the bridge, Melanie. So many years that have gone by now. Do we really have to revisit the past like this?"

Mel held firm, her feet planted on the floor. On this subject she wasn't willing to budge; she saw little room for negotiation, so she waited Bea out.

"I told you, Mel. Dermott was a good man. But he had a wandering eye. Always had, I knew that. But at some point you just get tired of being disrespected, I guess. At some point, you just realize that it's time to go. I finally knew it was time to go."

Mel couldn't stand it any longer, everything in her wanted to come spilling forth. Every birthday and Christmas her mother had missed; every secret she had kept. "But you left *me*, Mama. *You left me.* You up and packed your bags and dropped out of sight and we didn't hear from you for years. We never even knew where you went. What kind of mother does that? Who in their right mind leaves her daughter to fend for herself? You knew Dermott was incapable of taking care of me. My God, Mother, he had moved out. I had to call him on the phone and drag his sorry ass home. And let me tell you, he was not fucking pleased about it, either. I don't know where he was or whom he was with then, but it did not please him to have to move home and take care of a sulky, stubborn teenager that wasn't even his to begin with. For God's sake, who does that to their own daughter?"

Bea wrapped her hands around one of the glasses, running her palms up and down against the condensation. She stared intently at the lemonade, at the ice cubes that were melting quickly in the steamy, unbearable heat.

"I didn't have a choice. You were too young to understand that then, but I didn't have a choice in the matter."

"Everyone has a choice. You had a choice. You just chose something else. You picked to leave. You picked to leave and leave me with him. I don't know how I can ever forgive you for that. I don't know how I can ever forget what it was like to be left. Do you have any idea about what it feels like to be left?"

"Yes, Melanie. I know exactly how that feels." Bea's voice was small, weak, but caustic and cynical. Even all these years later, she was resentful and bitter. "It was all I could do to leave you there. I had no job, no life, no one to turn to and no place to live. I knew if I left you that you'd have food and a roof over your head. If I'd taken you with me, I wasn't even sure I could give you those things. Imagine what it must have been like for a mother to wonder how she would be able to feed her children. Imagine what it must have been like for me to wonder where we would have slept that night. I hadn't worked in years. I had no job, no income of my own. When I left, I went to a shelter for a couple of weeks. Then, later, when I was able to scrounge up enough cash, I went to Atlanta to see my sister, and then finally here to Nashville. I had already lived a life of nothing with you, long before Dermott rescued us. I couldn't bring myself to do it again. I had every intention of coming back for you, really I did. But by the time I tried, you were living with Cara. And I knew you'd be better off there. I knew that Joan would take better care of you even than I could myself."

"You never should have left me," Melanie said again, hurt rising in her voice. She shook her head back and forth, angry that her mother wouldn't accept responsibility for her actions, even now. "What could have possibly been that bad, so horrible that you would leave me with him?"

"Oh, Melanie, it's so long ago now. So very long ago that it all happened that it's not worth drudging it all up. I've buried it, moved on. When your father came back here, he was so sick. What could I do? He didn't have anyone to take care of him. He didn't have anything in his life. Even after all he'd done to me, I couldn't turn him away. He needed someone to take care of him. And Dermott and me? It didn't take long before we made peace with our war. It was so long ago and so much had passed between us. None of that was important. What was important was that we could set it aside. What was important was that after all this time, we could set it aside."

"There are some things you can't set aside, Mama, no matter how much you try," Mel answered. There was a hard, controlled edge to her voice that she fought to keep in control.

"Oh, sugar," Bea started, and then stopped when she saw the look on Mel's face, a reaction to the affection in her tone. "Melanie, please," Bea pleaded with her, but Mel wasn't quick to soften.

"I think you owe me an explanation, Mother. At least that much. You owe me some sort of an explanation, if you can even find one."

"I can't give you one, Melanie. No matter what I tell you, after all these years, you won't understand it. And, at this point, it may not be important. Dermott is gone now. With him went all the sins of his past, all the years that fell between us like a sharp sword. In the end, I forgave him for what had come between us, and he forgave me for leaving. There was nothing more than that. There was nothing left unsaid, nothing left unfinished."

Melanie turned on her heel and set down her bag on the worn table. She dug through the contents, pulling out her keys and wallet, her sunglasses case, until she found what it was she was looking for. She held the small photo album, a portable, purse-size version littered and stuffed with photographs of Bella. Tears streamed down her face, her cheeks heated and splotchy.

"And for this? Were you able to forgive him for this?"

In her shaking hand she held the page open. In the shot, Bella was five, maybe six. Her face was sprinkled with freckles, her brown eyes large and untamed. She'd lost her first two teeth, a gaping hole in the middle of the bottom row.

Bea stepped forward to look at the photo, pushing her glasses to sit on the top of her head. She was nearsighted but up close her vision was nearly 20/20. She stared at the photo, intent, looking for recognition in the face of the little girl who was staring back at her.

It was true that Isabella had resembled her mother; she always had. If nothing more, Bea should have seen her own daughter in the photo, a resemblance far too obvious to set aside. But Melanie had chosen this photo for a reason; there was no closer shot that resembled Dermott more than this one. Something about the way the camera had captured Bella, as if proving out her paternity once and for all. And yet at the same time, her features resembled Mel's. Her eyes held the same inquisitiveness that Mel's often had, her smile, the confidence.

"Who is this?" Bea asked, calmly controlled. She held the photo between her thumb and her forefinger, gripping it tightly. She couldn't take her eyes off the child, familiarity slowly dawning on Bea.

"Her name is Isabella. She's my daughter."

Bea swallowed hard, shock registering on her face, but careful not to let on. She sat in the shaggy recliner in the corner, one leg tucked up under the other, and flipped through the album Mel had brought, stopping to study each shot, Bella frozen through the years. "She's beautiful, Melanie. She looks like a really nice little girl. I wish I'd have known."

"She's no little girl; not anymore, anyway." Mel was not done with her, distaste had settled on her tongue and she was determined to spit it out. "And you've had no desire to know about this little girl. You had no desire to know anything about your own daughter, never mind the child I have raised."

"That's not true. I always wondered about you, Melanie. I always prayed you were safe and cared for."

"But I wasn't. There wasn't anything of the sort going on, Mother. Home was hell. You should know; you ran from it."

"That was different. I didn't have a choice."

"Neither did I. You left me there without any sort of choice. There was nowhere I could go, nothing I could do."

They squared off like two cocks ready to move in for the kill. Bea looked through the last of the photos and folded the album closed, handing it back to Melanie.

Mel shook her head, refusing to take it. "The photos, they're for you. I brought them for you to keep."

"Oh. Oh, no, I couldn't, Melanie. She's your daughter; you should keep these."

"She's your *granddaughter*. Don't tell me you don't see it, Mother. You sit there and look through these photos and you're listening to me tell you that life was surely no picnic in Dermott's house and you're going to pretend that you don't even see it?"

Bea had, of course. And Melanie knew it. Bea had tried to hide the shock that registered on her face every time she took in a new photo, but it was near impossible to camouflage. Melanie had chosen specific shots in which Bella had more often resembled her father than she did her mother. Mel knew that Bea saw it and she wasn't willing to let her go. Not on this one, not this time.

"I know you can see it, Bea. I know you look at those photos and wonder how in the world my daughter, my own flesh and blood, looks so much like *your husband*. How in the world could Isabella have managed to look so much like Dermott when I'm clearly not related to him? It's not as if he was *my* father."

Bea finished the last of her lemonade and swallowed hard. Her stomach jumped and lurched, turning over. "Don't be ridiculous, Melanie." She delivered the words flatly, with little emotion at all as if she wasn't willing to give it even a minute's consideration.

Mel was ready for her; she had expected as much. She picked up the photo album from where it sat on the small, Formica kitchen table and opened it to a shot of Isabella when she was just two or three. "Here, Mother, look at Bella's chin. You can see it plain as day, there's no denying it. Bella has Dermott's chin, strong and square and forceful." She flipped forward a few pages. "She has his ears, too. You can see them here, large, full earlobes that weigh down her whole face. This is one of those rare times she wore her hair pulled back. She hates it pulled back off her face because she can't stand those damn ears. Dermott's ears. She got those. She got his spitfire temper, too, though we've worked hard to keep that in check."

"Wait a minute, Melanie. Help me understand just what it is you are suggesting."

"I'm not *suggesting* anything. I'm telling you plain and simple that this child, this twenty-two-year-old beauty of a child who is smart as a whip and quick and funny and interesting as all get-out was the result of your husband's actions. He raped me, Bea," Melanie pleaded. "You left me there and he repaid you by hurting me."

Bea's bony arms shook; the loose skin flapping back and forth. Her hands were incapable of grasping anything and she had to lean on the side of the table for support. She desperately wanted a cigarette and she fumbled with the broken zipper on her worn leather purse before she ripped it open and rummaged through the contents, pulling out an empty pack. She was low on cigarettes, tight on money.

"I'm sorry, Melanie, but I just can't believe that you would accuse Dermott of something so horrific, something so monstrous. Dermott would never have done something like what you are saying. Never."

"I'm not accusing him, Mama; I'm telling you what happened. You didn't have to be there to know that what I'm telling you is the truth. Look at her, Mother," Melanie screamed and thrust the album at her mother again. "Look at her. You can see it in every ounce of her. I didn't think it would be so obvious. You know, at first, when she was so little. I would spend hours at night with Isabella on my lap, just staring into that big, beautiful face, looking for signs. And I swear they weren't there, not at first, anyway, not visibly. But then they'd appear, just right out of nowhere, haunting me like a bad dream. Imagine what that must be like, Mama, to see something you despise so greatly in someone you love so much."

Bea was rummaging through drawers, pulling out pens and index cards and rubber bands. She was desperate for a hit of nicotine; she was an addict searching for a fix. She coughed up a good amount of phlegm, spitting it into the handkerchief she kept shoved in the pocket of her jeans.

Finally, Melanie could stand no more, her mother wouldn't look at her, wouldn't talk to her. Mel pulled a pack of Camels from her own purse and slid them across the countertop at Bea. The pack stopped short in front of her and she yanked out a cigarette quickly, cupping her hands around it to light it and sucking in deeply on the hit, the poison settling in her lungs and calming her immediately.

"Listen," Melanie started again, more calmly this time. "I didn't come here for anything other than to make sure you knew who you've been dealing with all these years. Isabella's a wonderful young woman, much better than I ever professed to be at her age. She's poised and bright and has a wonderful future ahead of her. I couldn't be more proud of her. And she's mine, Bea. Make no mistake about this; she's mine. I chose to bring her into this world, despite the violent, horrific way she came to be. I've done my best by her, and she's got a great start.

"So, like I said, I'm not here for anything other than to make sure you understood just who Dermott was, just what he was capable of. You can cry over him and bury him in the ground and pray for his soul, but before you do all of that, before you send him on his way, I thought it was important for you to realize just who he really was, just what he had really done. I don't think you had any idea of whom you were leaving me with, what he was really like. But now you know, okay? Now you know the nightmare that I had to live through all those years ago."

Bea smoked the last of her cigarette until it was nothing more than a nub and wanted another one immediately. She refrained from taking a second from Melanie's pack. Instead she popped two pieces of Trident into her mouth, letting the peppermint flavor seep into her teeth and the back of her throat. Instantly she coughed wildly until her cheeks and neck burned bright, blotchy red spots. Melanie waited on her, a hand on her hip, the other hand tapping her nails on the countertop.

"Look, Melanie, I've known who Dermott was all along. I've been well aware of what he was capable of. I'm not sure what you're out to prove here, but I can tell you that he was not a man who would have raped someone, never mind the child that he was supporting, the child he considered to be his own. I may not know everything about that man, but that I can tell you unequivocally. Dermott Paulson certainly did not make a habit of impregnating teenage girls."

"Are you telling me that you don't believe me?" Melanie seethed between clenched teeth.

Bea shook hard, her entire body convulsing and trembling. She wasn't sure what to make of her daughter, the brazen accusations that she had confessed like loaded weapons. She shook her head hard at Melanie, the deep crease of a frown worn into her jaw muscles. She'd have liked very much to have covered her ears and blocked everything out around her, but she knew that would only infuriate her daughter further. Instead she sat and leaned back in the worn, threadbare recliner that Dermott had taken to sitting in for hours on end the last few months of his life. It smelled of his body odor, his stench, sweet and pungent the way Bea had remembered him when he moved in with her. She had been so glad to have him back; she'd known he'd come on his own one day, and he had, showing up on the cement-block stoop that backed to the side door of her trailer. She knew right away that he was sick, that the years of alcohol and nicotine had finally permeated their way through his bloodstream and his soul, polluting both. She knew that he came back to her because he had nowhere else to go, no one else to take care of him. And yet she hadn't cared, not one bit. He was back, and he was reliant on her, to make what was left of his miserable life just a bit more bearable.

They'd long since buried the past; they never even discussed it after Dermott moved in. Dermott certainly wasn't going to reclaim it, and Bea had no desire to hold him accountable any longer for what he had done to her, the rage that had overcome her when she'd found out so long ago that he had been sleeping with Mirabelle Anderson, that he had moved out so that they could be together.

And now here was Melanie. Long, lost Mel. Waking up what had long been put to bed. Showing up on her doorstep as Bea had asked her to do, but with news that Bea was in no way prepared to digest.

She closed her eyes and shook her head, pushing the photo album across the table in denial. "No. No, it can't be. It just can't be."

22

Bella had promised her mother that she would stay at the house with Katie while she was visiting Bea. It was the compromise that they'd finally worked out after Isabella had turned Melanie down for the hundredth time on her offer to fly to Tennessee and meet her grandmother. Bella had no desire to meet the woman who had started the firestorm that had erupted into her life, and quite frankly she didn't understand what it was that was dragging her mother there, either. But Bella knew better than to push.

Bella opened the door to her mother's flat, two grande extrahot lattes in hand for Katie and her. Katie's bags were packed and stacked just inside the front door.

"Katie?" Isabella called out to her, tossing her keys onto the front table.

Katie popped out of the bathroom, toothbrush in her mouth and foaming at the edges. "Hang on," she gurgled, and ducked back inside to spit. She emerged a minute later, wiping at the corners of her mouth with a hand towel. "Hi."

"Hi," Bella answered her and handed her the hot coffee gingerly so that she wouldn't burn her hand. "What's all this?" she asked, motioning toward the pile.

"Goin' home. My dad's coming to pick me up in about an hour," she answered without any signs of bitterness or distress.

"Your dad? Really?"

"Yeah. It's time. I've been here long enough."

"My mom would tell you to stay. You know that, don't you? You don't have to leave just because she's gone to see Bea. You can stay here as long as you like."

"I know," Katie answered, nodding her head. She believed her, too. Melanie had told her as much a few nights before while she sat sorting through old pictures of Isabella to take with her. Katie had approached her quietly, unsure still of what she wanted to do. Mel had patted the floor next to her, encouraging her to sit with her.

"I'm thinking of going home, Mel," Katie had said to her, quick breaths pushing the words out for her.

"Do you think you're ready? I mean, you've stayed on your program and been amazingly dedicated to your own health, and I'm really, really proud of you. But do you think you're ready? You know, to deal with everything at home? Your mom? And your dad, too?"

Katie thought on it a minute. She had done some serious soul-searching on the matter and been back and forth over the scenarios. She wasn't entirely sure she was ready to deal with any of it, but she also knew that she wouldn't know if she could do it until she tried. "It won't be easy; I know that. But it's time, you know. It's time for me to go and face everything that I left, everything that I left in such shambles. Until I can do that, until I can tolerate a day without a drink in a place that makes me want to have one, then I won't really know if I can do it or not."

Melanie nodded her head. "That makes a lot of sense, Katie."

They sat for a few minutes together, shuffling through the stack of photos. The shots were, for the most part, pictures of a time before Katie was born. Isabella was just a baby, then a toddler and a full-fledged little girl. The photos were worn at the edges, and had been handled once too often.

Katie picked up a photo, holding it at the edges and staring at it. "Is this Isabella?" she asked Mel.

Melanie turned her attention to the shot, an afternoon tea party they'd had in the park. Bella was four. She nodded her head.

"Huh. It doesn't even look like her."

"She looks like her father in that shot," Mel answered, and took the photo from Katie, placing it on the top of the pile to take with her.

Cara played the message twice, listening to the hesitation in Jack's voice.

"Cara? Katie called. She wants me to pick her up from Mel's house. Um, I'm not really sure what I should do with her, you know. Well, it's been a long while since Katie and I have had any sort of a conversation, never mind have her in the house, and, you know, given how far along Barbie is, I'm just not sure that it's a very good idea right now. Could you call me, Cara? Let me know what you think I should do. It's really inconvenient, as you might imagine. It'd just be a whole heck of a lot better if you were here to deal with this, Cara."

She called Katie instead.

"Honey? Your dad says you want him to come get you? Is everything okay?"

"Yeah, Mom, yeah, everything's fine. I'm just ready, I think. I'm just ready to go home."

"But sweetie, do you want me to come and get you? You haven't spent any time with him in months. I can be on the next plane home, honey, really I can. If you're ready to come home, I can come and get you. You can come home. Really come home." Much as she hated the idea, Cara would leave Mel if she needed to. After all, this was her daughter, her Katie. Mel would understand.

"No, Mom, it's okay. I need to do this on my own with Daddy. I need to make sure I can get through this."

Cara started to interrupt. She started to find an excuse for Jack, a reason for Katie. She started to fit the broken pieces back together, filling in the chips with as much caulk as it would take to hide the cracks. But then she stopped, realizing that this was exactly what Katie needed, that at some point she'd have to come clean with everyone around her, but, more importantly, she'd have to come clean with herself.

It was just like Katie to start with Jack.

23

Shelbyville boasted an assortment of two-star hotels with indoor pools and complimentary home-cooked breakfasts that smelled like overcooked oatmeal and burnt bacon. Mel drove past three of them before she reluctantly pulled into the Best Western Celebration Inn and Suites, unloaded the rental car and lugged her suitcase up a flight of stairs. She was exhausted from the afternoon with her mother and bone-tired from the flight itself, and she wanted nothing more than to sleep. It should have come as no surprise that the worn polyester bedspread was stained and the sheets were coarse and overbleached. Still, she dove under the covers and was asleep in fewer than five minutes, refusing to let the events of the day play over and over in her mind, haunting her.

Cara had little tolerance for sleep. She felt as if she owed it to her friend to stand watch, guarding her closely. She took her cell phone and retreated to the lobby.

Leah answered on the first ring, punctual and all business.

"Did you see her? Did you get to talk to her?" Leah asked without hesitation.

Cara reclined the best she could in a chair that wasn't meant for lounging. She stretched her legs in front of her and settled in. "Yeah. Yeah, we saw her. First thing this afternoon, as soon as we got off the plane. Mel wouldn't have it any other way, Leah. It was as if she was possessed. We picked up the rental car and went straight to her house. Well, if you could call it that."

"Details. Every last one of them, Cara. Don't leave anything out."

Cara recounted the specifics of their visit, doing her best to paint the bleak picture for Leah. She answered every question that Leah asked her, every time she interrupted and stopped her cold.

"It wasn't pretty, Leah. Not at all."

"Sounds downright ugly, Cara. Where's Mel now?"

"She's sleeping. I told her to just put everything out of her head and get some rest. She never slept on the way out and I think she's just exhausted now. And, Christ, we're holed up in the most desolate-looking hotel in Shelbyville, Tennessee. Quite frankly, our prospects of this trip looking up are pretty damn weak."

"When will you be back?"

"Friday. Maybe sooner if we can't find anywhere slightly more upscale than Papa John's pizza to eat. How's Paige doing? Have you seen her?"

"Big as a house. My God, she's huge. You two better get back here before she births this child. She'll never forgive you if you aren't here and I'll never let you live it down if you miss it."

"We'll be home. Friday."

In the hotel gift store Cara stopped for coffee and the paper. She longed for the pink section of the *Chronicle* and would have killed for a copy of the *New York Times*. She settled for a wrinkled copy of the Nashville *Tennessean*.

She found the obituary on page 6B. *Dermott Paulson, 67.*

There was a photo, Dermott much younger, years before alcohol and a reckless life had claimed his good looks. His chin was strong, his eyes dark and inset. His hair was thinning but he wasn't bald. He wore a plaid button-down shirt.

Cara remembered seeing the photo, a long time ago, and then

earlier that afternoon on Bea's tabletop. It made her shiver, like something had crawled across her skin.

Dermott Paulson entered into peace on Saturday, September 17th after a long battle with cancer. Dermott is survived by his loving wife of thirty-seven years, Beatrix Paulson, and his daughter, Melanie Marie Paulson of San Francisco, CA. Visitation and viewing will be held at the McCullum Family Funeral Home on Wednesday, September 21st from 4 to 8 p.m. Memorial services will be held on Thursday, September 22nd at 11:00 a.m.

Cara read the notice again before she folded the section of the paper in half and then in half again and tucked it in her bag.

In the room Melanie was propped up in bed watching an episode of *The Ellen DeGeneres Show*, the sound barely audible. She was brushing her hair; long, full strokes that ran from the top of her head to the middle of her back.

"You know what I like best about this show? Her dancing. She just doesn't give a fuck, you know what I mean? I mean she's not that great of a dancer. I know everyone thinks she is. And that's just because she stands up there every episode, sure as it's going to snow in New York every winter, and lets loose. Really? She's not that good. She just doesn't give a fuck."

"Well, you gotta give her credit for that," Cara said, nodding her head. She took a seat on the end of Mel's double bed, next to where she had curled her legs up. "How was your catnap?"

"Fabulous," Mel said, punching one of the pillows to fluff it. "If, that is, you don't count the scratchy sheets and stained bedspread with God only knows what on it. You saw that *20/20*, didn't you? I can only imagine what's on this thing. Imagine who's slept in this bed," she said and shivered.

Cara blanched. "God, Mel, don't even go there. I'll never be able to sleep in this bed tonight."

"Garin called. He woke me up, actually."

"Oh, really?"

Mel nodded her head. He had woken her out of a sound sleep, so groggy when she first answered the phone that she wasn't even sure of who it might be. It had taken her a few minutes to register his voice, to recognize it as his. His tone was laced with concern, his voice worn with worry.

"My God, Melanie, are you all right?" It was all he could ask her. It was all she had needed to hear.

"I brought you something," Cara said to her, changing the subject and gingerly removing the section of the newspaper she had stuffed into her bag.

Mel sat up, crossing her legs Indian style. She took the paper from Cara and unfolded it, her brow furrowed.

"It's Dermott's obit," Cara said, matter-of-factly. "Page six."

Melanie flipped open the paper and stared first at the shot, studying it intently for the longest time before she turned her attention to the announcement.

"His daughter?"

Cara nodded her head, unsure of what she should say. "I guess Bea felt she had to include you, huh?"

Mel hugged her knees and pulled her legs close to her chest. "I remember when my mother had that photo taken. She dragged Dermott and me to Sears to get a family portrait done. She made me wear that white smocked blouse that I really hated. I must have been in kindergarten or first grade. We got all dolled up. Bea kept telling us how much fun we were going to have, that we could make a day out of it. She had these grand plans to do some shopping and have lunch downtown before we had the pictures taken. Then she wouldn't let me eat anything because she was so afraid I would spill on that blouse. God, you would think she would have had something somewhat more recent. Dermott's gotta be thirty-one or thirty-two in this shot. Honestly, she couldn't come up with anything after that?"

"She really wanted you all to be a family, Mel. It was a long time ago, but she always wanted you to be a real family."

Mel nodded her head, glancing at the paper again. "It was all Bea had wanted. She always thought she could find a way for us to be a happy little family, just picture perfect."

"And then she left?"

"And then she left," Mel answered her, matter-of-factly. "But you know, Dermott was already gone by then. He'd given up on the idea that we'd be the ideal family unit long before that."

Cara sighed and looked away, wanting to change the subject. "I talked to Leah."

"Oh?"

"She desperately wants to be here; I can hear it in her voice."

"Someone had to stay home. How's Paige doing?"

"Leah says she's ready to go any minute. We'll never live it down if we miss this, you know. Never, never, never."

"Cara?"

"Hmmm?"

"About Garin. I wanted you to know that I'm sorry about not telling you about him, all that time. It wasn't fair; I understand that now. I see how that must have looked to you, how that made you feel."

Cara shook her head slowly. "It's done. It doesn't matter anymore."

"I never meant to hurt you. You know that, don't you?" Mel's voice was soft, sincere.

It reminded Cara of a time when her friend wasn't quite so hard, so scarred by the events of her life. Mel sounded very much like she did when she was younger, before she had become the person she was today.

"Yeah, Mel. I know that."

24

Cara had avoided being left alone with Bea since they'd arrived; dodging her like a fly would a swatter. She had no intention of being dragged down into the details of why she'd left so long ago. Cara didn't want to hear the excuses Bea felt she needed to pawn off on someone, anyone, who would take the time to listen to her. But try as she might Cara wound up on Thursday face-to-face with Bea in the small kitchenette off the reception room at the mortuary. The air in the small room was stale, stagnant, and Bea had Cara backed into a corner by the old rattling refrigerator.

"I suppose Melanie won't ever understand the reasons why I left when I did," Bea started in, without letting the opportunity slip by.

They were washing dishes now; Cara stacking clean plastic tumblers they had used to serve tea and lemonade and the serving spoons on a towel on the countertop, Bea drying.

"No, Bea, I don't suppose she will. It's been a long, long time. Mel's had a long life of trying to make sense of it all. Surely you can't fault her curiosity."

"No, I guess not."

Cara watched her, the way her eyes jetted back and forth over the top of her glasses and watched for Cara's reaction. There was nothing affectionate about Bea anymore; she lacked any compassion that may have been there at one time. She was too thin and too angular and too used up. Her face was wrinkled and permanently hollow at the cheeks. Her hair was brittle and dry.

"You have no idea what kind of solace it could provide Melanie if you would only help her understand what happened all those years ago, why you had to go. All her life she's been trying to figure out what kind of mother just up and leaves her husband and her daughter. And why you never came back. Can't you imagine what it has been like for her to live with this, for her to spend her whole life wondering why you never came back? Surely you can understand that. Look at what's she's been through. Everything that happened with Dermott, raising a kid on her own?"

Bea stopped drying and leaned against the cracked tile countertop. She shook her head as if she was still chasing away the truth, refusing to hear it. But her eyes softened, just a bit, watery. She stared ahead, lost in memory, quiet and contemplative, still. She grasped Cara's arm tightly at the wrist. "I want you to know, Cara. Someone should know. Someone should understand what happened all that time ago."

"Go on, Bea," Cara encouraged, and reached to close the door to the foyer, keeping it cracked a bit so she could watch for Mel. Last she'd seen, her friend had gone out for a well-deserved smoke. She'd endured a full day of introductions to Dermott and Bea's friends, people that had milled about and asked her if she was Dermott's daughter. Chances were she'd be gone for a while, probably a long phone call with Garin, maybe a walk around the block. Cara knew she had some time, she hoped to use it wisely. "Go on," she said again to Bea.

Bea continued drying the plastic cup, rubbing it with one of the frayed dish towels they'd found in the closet. "Your mama was there, of course, when Dermott and I got married. She never liked Dermott, not from the get-go. She thought I'd be better off on my own, that Dermott was a lousy excuse for a husband and that he'd be out cheating on me in no time. But your mama, she'd never known what it was like to raise a little girl on her own, to have to struggle through every day wondering how you were going to provide for her, how you were going to get a better job. Melanie was five when I married Dermott. I'd had five years of being on my own. I needed someone. I needed someone in the worst way. Dermott might not have been the ideal partner, but for me he meant safety and security, someone I knew would make my life, and Melanie's life, a little better."

Cara had heard all the stories, the endless chitter-chatter of comments about Dermott Paulson all her life. "I know my mother never cared much for him, Bea. I know Leah's mother never cared much for him, either. Mirabelle was always much more vocal about it. As a matter of fact, Mel used to say that if Mirabelle could have had Dermott run out of town, she would have taken up a petition and solicited the signatures herself."

"Hmmm." Bea snorted loudly and abruptly. "Sounds just like something Mirabelle would have said, Cara. Trouble was, Mirabelle was always a good liar."

Cara eyed Bea carefully, her brow furrowed. "Bea?" she questioned. Cara was testing the water, suddenly and acutely aware that she'd poked her nose too far down the path to turn back now.

"Mirabelle Anderson's been fooling everyone her whole life, Cara."

Cara's senses prickled, her intuition heightened. Something made her want to run, leave the small, confined kitchen quickly before anything else would be let out of the bag, free to roam the four walls around them. But more than that, something made her want to stay. Perhaps if she knew the truth, she could help Mel understand what had set her destiny down this path, where everything had gone so terribly wrong.

Cara approached Bea carefully, waiting on her before asking, "What do you mean she was a liar? What's Mirabelle got to do with all of this? What's Mirabelle got to do with Dermott?"

"Mirabelle Anderson and my husband were lovers, Cara. They carried on for years."

Cara stumbled backward, bracing herself against the wall.

Over her head, a small rectangular window had been slid open but there was little air circulating throughout the room. She felt dizzy immediately, sick. A loud ringing settled between her ears, numbing her.

"But, but, that's impossible. Mirabelle couldn't stand Dermott. She never let Leah near your house because she had such a dislike for Dermott."

"Oh, no, it's quite possible. And I'm here to tell you it was true. I didn't know about it right off, of course. But a couple of years into it I figured the two of them out. And then I caught them. Red-handed, so to speak. Dermott had been trying to get Mirabelle to leave her husband, and I caught them on the phone one night. He was pleading with her, Cara, begging her to leave and marry him. But Mirabelle wasn't a fool; she was never going to do that. She'd married well, she had everything she'd ever wanted, everything she'd ever needed taken care of for her. She even had a husband who ignored the affair she'd been having. But marry Dermott? Never. That would have been far beneath her, far below her standards. Dermott never understood that. He never saw himself as less than Mirabelle. And he could charm that woman. Charmed the pants right off her."

"I, I just can't believe it. *Mirabelle and Dermott?* It just doesn't make any sense. I can't even fathom it."

"When I finally confronted Dermott, he told me that he was done with Mirabelle for good. I think he knew deep down inside that she was never going to marry him. And when it came right down to it, Dermott was an old-fashioned guy, you know. He liked the idea of providing for a woman and giving her what she needed, but Dermott never could have pleased Mirabelle, not in a million years. Anyway, I guess after that they figured if they couldn't be together, they'd concentrate on hating everything about each other, and so they did. Just out and out hated each other."

Cara shook her head, trying to clear the headache that was building at the base of her skull.

"A few years went by, you know, me and Dermott we did okay,

then. It wasn't paradise, God, far from it. And Dermott had plenty of affairs over the years, Cara. I wasn't stupid. I knew he had a wandering eye. I knew he was out messing around. I also knew that they meant nothing to him. I knew the only woman he truly wanted to be with was the one who had turned him down cold. Mirabelle was the only person I couldn't compete with, the rest were just whores."

"But you and Mirabelle were friends; you'd known each other for years. Didn't you confront her? How could she do that to you?"

"I guess there are some things girlfriends just don't talk about, Cara. And this was one of them. Mirabelle and I went way back. We had been friends as long as I could remember. Just like you and Melanie." Her words caught Cara like a punch to the gut, quick and hard. She was standing on Mel's front steps again, listening to her friend confess about the affair she'd been having with Garin.

"I'm sure his wife thinks so . . ."

Mel's words mocked her, laughing.

"When I caught them, I told Mirabelle that I'd be happy to let the entire town know about her relationship with Dermott. See, I knew he wasn't the prominent doctor her husband was, and that he didn't have anywhere near the money that her mama and daddy had, and that he didn't run in the social circles that she did. And I knew that letting her little secret out would hurt Mirabelle more than anyone else. She had a reputation to protect, an image to keep up. And Dermott didn't figure into that any way you cut it."

Cara took a deep breath, absorbing what she'd heard. *Mirabelle? And Dermott?* Implausible, crossed her mind. Impossible, even. She watched Bea carefully, every move she made, the meticulous way she stacked and shuffled the cups just so. She didn't figure Bea had any reason to lie about the past, especially with Dermott gone. But it was almost too unthinkable to believe, too unrealistic to imagine.

"Dermott didn't take too well to my butting in, of course. He never blamed Mirabelle for leaving him; he blamed me for breaking up his little fantasy. But I had my daughter and a roof over my head, and well, hell, I could endure pretty much anything beyond that. As for Mirabelle, we found our way back, somehow."

Cara took a deep breath, stunned. She leaned against the countertop and shook her head in disbelief.

Even now, all these years later, you could hear it in Bea's voice, how much she must have hated Dermott for doing this to her.

"But what happened, Bea? What made you finally leave?" Cara placed a hand on Bea's arm, quite near her wrist. The older woman jumped, startled.

Bea stared through the partly open door, into the sterile hall where a few people were still milling about. Most had come from Bea's work, a paper mill on the far side of town where Bea handled the office administration. They didn't know Dermott, had met him only once or twice before his cancer had become so debilitating that Bea had to cut her hours down to twenty a week just so she could take care of him.

Her eyes appeared dead, lifeless. "I'm not sure when, really, that they started seeing each other again. Dermott was drinking a lot then, and you know Mirabelle always liked to tie one on. It was a tough time for her, her marriage had really begun to unravel, her mother had died suddenly, things weren't as easy as they'd been. Anyway, it doesn't matter now. The fact of the matter is that they were together again. At first I didn't believe it, you know. I had forgiven Mirabelle; we had moved on. But I was wrong. I was always wrong about these things. Mirabelle did everything she could to hide it from me, but in the end even that was impossible.

"He wanted a divorce, Cara. He came to me one day and just told me straight up that he was in love with Mirabelle and that he wanted me to give him a divorce. He thought he'd finally convinced her to leave her husband and he'd gotten an apartment and he wanted me to just sign away my life with him. I mean Dermott wasn't perfect, far from it. But he was all I'd ever had,

all I'd ever had to count on. You know, Mel's daddy was gone before I even had the chance to tell him that I was pregnant. And
here was Dermott telling me that he was done, too."

Bea's voice was unsteady and shaky. Cara listened to her and
thought of her own life, her own situation with Jack, the way he'd
discarded her for someone else.

"I couldn't, of course. Not willingly. I was angry with Dermott,
angrier still at Mirabelle. Furious, actually. I was sick to my stomach to think about the lies that woman had told, one lined up
right after the next. I told him the answer was no; that I wouldn't
give him the divorce he wanted and that I wouldn't make it so
easy on the two of them. I told him I wouldn't go down without a
fight. A fight for every stinking dollar that he had and then some
of Mirabelle's, too. I didn't care. I tried everything, Cara, really I
did. I would have given anything to make sure that those two
didn't end up together."

"Bea?" Cara stopped her suddenly. "Did my mother know?
My God, did Joan know about all of this?"

"Truth be told, Cara, I have no idea. But I don't think so. Not
right away, anyhow. But then Dermott moved out. In the end,
you know, he made his choice. He picked her over us and he left.
You might remember Mel telling you about that. He had rented
an apartment and he packed up his things and he left. Oh, I don't
think Mel ever realized why he'd gone, or who he wanted to be
with, but one day we came home to an empty closet and a note
with his new number, no explanation, no apology. Just a note and
his new number."

"God, Bea, I had no idea. All these years and none of us ever
knew."

"I moped around for a week or so. I never left the house, that
whole time. All I remember, really, was crying. That and Mel
coming in and out of the house every now and then, to and from
school, sort of surviving on her own. She didn't get it, really. She
kept good watch over me, but she didn't have much to say about
the whole thing. She never really had a lot to say about it.

"I knew there was really only one thing I could do to make

sure that Dermott and Mirabelle wouldn't be together. There was no way Mirabelle would take Melanie. She'd barely wanted Leah, and, Christ, compared to Leah, Mel was like a wild animal. She was untrained, unrefined, unkempt. I loved her to death, but she certainly wasn't Mirabelle's cup of tea, and she'd certainly put a crimp in her style. It was a gamble, but I had to take it.

"I left one morning just after Mel had gone to school. I packed everything I could, every stitch of clothing, every pair of shoes, just to make a point. I figured that Mel would call Dermott and Dermott would be forced to come home. And I figured that once he got home, he'd come to his senses and call me. It was cruel and selfish, I know that now, but it was all I had. And by that time, well, I was a little out of my tree, anyway."

"But Dermott never called you," Cara whispered, her eyes distant and focused on the past. They had been in ninth grade, the start of their freshman year, when Mel had come to school, devoid of makeup or any signs of life, really. She was pale and sorrowful, fear and worry washing over her in giant waves.

"No. Dermott never called. I knew he could hold a mean grudge. And I knew he had to be very, very angry with me for leaving. But still, I figured Dermott didn't want to deal with a daughter on his own, especially one that wasn't really his in the first place. At least with me around, there was someone to take care of Melanie. He had to call eventually, I figured he just had to."

"It was hell for Melanie then, Bea. It was pure hell living in that house," Cara said, not willing to let Bea off the hook. "Dermott got really, really mean, really, really fast."

"He was mad, Cara. Mad at me for leaving. Mad at Mirabelle for turning her back on him. I had been right about Mirabelle; she didn't want anything to do with raising another child, certainly not someone like Mel. There wasn't any way she was going to get all wrapped up in the problems he had at home. He thought he'd finally won, that he was going to finally get her to come and live with him, and in the end she never moved out, she just wouldn't do it. My plan worked; they wouldn't be together."

She heaved a sigh then, relief pouring out even now. "But I never realized the toll it would take. I never counted on Dermott holding out for so long. Or what he might have done to my girl."

"He was drinking a lot then. Mel used to tell us that he'd come home from one bar or another drunk every night. Dermott had women over all the time, crazy sluts who would follow him home and treat Mel like she was a second-class citizen. God, those were some bleak days, really, really dark."

"It wasn't easy for me, either, Cara. I had no job; no place to go. I shuffled from one place to the next trying to figure out what I could do, where I could go to start over. I kept thinking that if I could just settle down in one place and save a little money, I would send for Melanie. And then Dermott could have whatever he wanted with Mirabelle; they could live whatever life they decided worked for them. By that time I'd realized how foolish I'd been, and how badly I wanted my girl back. Dermott and Mirabelle could go to hell. Melanie was all that really mattered to me then. I never should have left her; never."

"What happened?"

"By the time I finally got settled, Mel had left; she'd moved in with you. I felt like such a failure. Your mother was the one to tell me, actually. Dermott wouldn't take my calls. He told me to fuck off, that I'd dug my own grave. And to be honest with you, he wasn't half-wrong. I'm the one who walked out; I'm the one who left. It was what Dermott did to Melanie that drove her away, but it was my fault for leaving in the first place."

"My mother knew where you were? All that time? But she never told Melanie, Bea. Why didn't she tell her?"

"I have Mirabelle to thank for that, of course. Mirabelle convinced your mother that someone like me didn't deserve her child back. Don't blame your mother, Cara. She had Mel's best intentions in mind. And she was probably right, anyway. I'm the one who had left; I'm the one who abandoned my daughter. Thank God for your mother, thank God she kept her."

Cara was speechless. She slumped against the kitchen counter, her legs tired and her lower back aching. It was a lot to digest, the years that had passed them by, and the questions that for so long had gone unanswered. And her own mother had known all along, all this time, where Bea had disappeared to. And yet she'd not said a word. She'd kept Mel safe and sheltered, but she'd never handed her back over.

Cara thought about Katie, the way Mel had taken her in without any hesitation, without any question. She'd known what Katie had needed, automatically, even when Cara couldn't fix what was wrong for her. Mel had said to Cara, *"She'll be back, Cara, you realize that, don't you? She'll be back."*

"Why haven't you told Melanie, Bea? How could you go this long without telling her? All these years she's been left wondering, recovering, actually. So much happened to her then, so much of what shaped her life. *Dermott raped her.* Don't you understand that? Dermott took all that anger he had for you, all that frustration and poured it into one fateful day. Everything changed for Mel when you left, everything you left in your wake."

Bea shook her head, turning away. She busied herself at the sink, steam rising from the full blast of hot water she'd forced on at the faucet. She was scrubbing an already-clean pan, a glass dish that a casserole had been brought in. Her back arched, her shoulders set at an angle, she was unmovable, unshakable.

"Bea?" Cara tried to no avail. "Bea?"

Outside the propped door, voices rose and swirled in conversation, people leaving, others arriving, lives carrying on. Cara studied the foyer, on the lookout for Mel.

"Bea, please," Cara said again, a little more urgency in her voice. Nothing.

Cara supposed this was the end of their conversation, at least for the meantime. She wondered what Bea expected her to do with the information, the secrets, she had imparted on her. She wondered if it was Bea's intention that Cara be the one to tell Melanie the truth, to confess all the secrets that she had so carefully tucked away. Cara removed the apron she was wearing, lifting it over her head and folding it into a compact square that she left on the countertop next to the sink where Bea continued to scrub at the pan, determined to work away the very last of the residue.

Outside, humidity hung like a wet blanket and the greasy smell of fried clams from Long John Silver's drifted into the parking lot. Cara walked the lot, dodging in between cars to find Melanie.

Smoke was swirling around Mel's head when Cara approached, remnants from the cigarette she was holding in one hand while gesturing wildly. She was on her cell, her voice low and soothing, and Cara figured she must be talking to Garin until she heard her say into the receiver, "Get as much rest as you can; you're going to need it. We'll be home on Friday, don't worry so much about everything. I'll bet you have a month's worth of casseroles in the freezer, don't you? A whole month's worth."

Mel clicked her cell phone shut and stubbed out her cigarette against the cement curb. Cara offered her a hand, pulling her to her feet.

"Paige?" Cara asked, surprised because it wasn't like Mel to spend a great deal of time on the phone with their friend.

"Yeah," Mel nodded, crushing the last of her cigarette with the toe of her stiletto.

"Is she okay? Is everything okay?"

"She's fine. She wants us home," Mel said, linking her arm in Cara's. "She doesn't want to have this baby without us there. God, Cara, can you imagine having a baby at forty-two? Your *first* baby? I barely had enough energy when I was a teenager and she's going to have a brand-new baby. Seriously, I don't know what she was thinking. This has got to be the most ridiculous thing some-one would do. *Forty-two?*" Mel looked at her sideways, rolling her eyes.

They walked back toward the brick building, the streetlights sputtering on one right after the other on the expressway. Gnats danced in the shadows; across the street, bats began to dodge be-tween the trees in an empty field.

"We've got to hightail it out of this crap-ass piece of town, Cara. I'm done with it."

Cara shuddered despite the much-too-warm night. She was done, too. She'd heard enough, been privy to more than what she'd planned for. She and Mel stood outside the main glass doors to the mortuary and stared out at the single-file line of cars on the highway, people leaving town. Commuters going home for the night, passing through Shelbyville without blinking.

"Tomorrow," Cara said, rubbing her arms, and then turned to look at Mel. "Let's go tomorrow instead of Friday. We can leave in the afternoon, after the service. There's nothing to stay here for anymore."

Mel took a deep breath and let it out in a burst. "There was nothing to come for in the first place."

As far as Cara could tell, nothing good could come from telling Mel about Dermott and Mirabelle. Just like her own mother, Cara decided to keep Bea's secret—a secret that could have revealed so much. It was all ancient history now, buried with Dermott, Cara thought as she reached forward to throw a handful of dirt on Dermott's grave. Good riddance.

On takeoff, Cara studied the ground below. The people, cars, houses, fields, rivers, lakes, all getting smaller and smaller until they disappeared altogether, blurred by distance. Lies left behind.

Instead, she concentrated on her children, her family, the life she had to go home to. All of it came clearly into view when they landed. She thought about pulling Katie into her arms, her daughter stiff and rigid because she was unsure about what it meant to be home again. She thought about breaking up an argument between Will and Luke, a silly spat that would have sent them screaming at each other over Cheerios at the breakfast table. She thought about tucking Claire into bed, the sweet strawberry smell of her just-shampooed hair, and Claire's endless stream of questions about Jack and Barbie's new baby. She thought about how overwhelming it had all felt when she left and yet how welcoming it all looked as she was headed for home.

"Do you feel better, Mel? Was it what you wanted?"

"Nah."

"No? Oh, honey, why not? It was such a long way to go to come back feeling like you hadn't made your point."

"I wasn't searching for vindication, Cara. Not really. I never really believed Bea would be able to stomach the truth, anyway."

"Why did you go then?" Cara asked.

Mel thought on her question, turning it around in her head. "Dunno, actually. I really don't. Something called me there; carried me. Maybe I thought there would be an answer, some sort of reason why. I guess I thought that after all this time, what with Dermott finally gone from all our lives, finally Bea would be able to be straight with me."

"Would it have mattered?" Cara asked tenuously, careful not to let on what she knew.

"No. Probably not."

They touched down just before seven. At Baggage Claim, near the carrier that was spewing luggage piece by piece onto the conveyor belt, Garin stepped forward through the crowd and simply said, "Mel."

Melanie looked nothing like herself. She wore no makeup and her glasses were perched on the end of her nose. Her hair was limp and lifeless and she was dressed in an old, unflattering sweat suit. Lines crept around her eyes, making her look older than she felt, and she already felt ancient. She needed a bath, a long, hot, soak in deep water. And she craved sleep, equally as deep.

But he stood in front of her, clean-shaven and mesmerizing, still and reassuring. He wore jeans and a white oxford, a black belt, sunglasses. His hands were sunk low in his pockets.

Mel took two small steps forward and he caught her in both arms, low at the waist until she collapsed against him.

Cara heard him say to her, "You're home. You made it home."

And Cara thought about how much he really must love Mel, in his own way, in a way that worked for them.

They parted after that, Mel and Garin going north to the city, and Cara in a taxi set out for home.

Home. She longed for every aspect of it as if finally being here wasn't even enough. She'd lived her entire life here, knew the intricate characteristics of neighborhoods that ran into the neighborhoods that bordered others. Every aspect of who she was had been developed here, save for the few years she'd spent in college when she lived in Southern California. Her marriage had started and ended here, her children had been born here.

Home.

She flipped open her cell phone and called Leah.

"Hello?" Leah's voice sang through the wire, clear, confident.

Nothing good could come from sharing her secret with Leah, either. "Hi, sweetie."

"Are you home?" Leah asked her, breathless.

Cara sighed, "Yes. Thank God, yes."

25

Katie wanted a drink. It hit her first thing in the morning and the feeling was so familiar that she fell back in step with it, like a habit that she indulged in without even thinking about it. She went immediately to the bar, which had been emptied out. Then to the refrigerator. Cara had dared to keep a bottle of wine—just one, a Pinot Grigio, not one of Katie's favorites—on the top shelf. It had been opened and recorked, and stood ready to be drunk. Her mother had only had one small glass; three-quarters of the bottle remained untouched. Katie lifted it from the top shelf in the refrigerator, grabbing it around the neck like she wanted to strangle it. She pulled out the cork and let the pungent smell from the bottle waft under her nose.

She drank from the bottle, tipping her head back and closing her eyes the way a teenage boy drinks from a milk carton after football practice. The wine gurgled in the bottle and dripped down the sides of her mouth, back along her chin and down her neck. She drank the whole thing in one long gulp, coughing only at the end when she came up for air. She placed the bottle down on the countertop with a hollow thud and looked around the kitchen, waiting for someone or something to strike her down.

Everyone had told her how proud they were of her. Everyone. Her mother, her friends, her teachers. Even her father, as he thrust the keys to the car at her. His voice had been muffled and very low, but pride seeped through his words.

She'd let them all down. She'd done it purposefully and without too much consideration, the way she knew was habit for her. She knew she should have called her sponsor but she dismissed that thought immediately, too.

Katie leaned back against the bar stool and stared down the empty bottle. She had been sober a long time; forgetting what it felt like when alcohol did its trick on her, the way it came over her. The words on the label jumped and jumbled around her, effects of the wine settling in and numbing her brain, singeing it at the ends. She hadn't had a drink in over three months; she had the ninety-day pin to prove it.

The first few days with her father had been okay. Jack was walking on eggshells, carefully watching over everything she did. She didn't mind, not much, anyway. She was ready for a little attention from her father. Her brothers pretty much ignored her, but Claire was all over her, plump with love and admiration. Even Barbie, so enormous that she could barely get around anymore, was tolerable. In the end, coming to stay with her father seemed like the right thing to do.

When her mother came home, Katie went, too. She went back to her bedroom and back to school and back to her life. And everything about that seemed slightly off kilter; just enough so that she couldn't pinpoint what it was that was missing. But something was definitely missing.

"DAMN IT!" she screamed, bolting out a shriek that shook the windows. "Damn, damn, damn." She went to the small guest bathroom and folded herself into a ball on the floor. The tiles were cool and hard on her knees and elbows, but she lay there anyway, hugging herself. She wanted to throw up, to rid her body of the alcohol.

It was the alcohol that had been missing. She knew it. She'd figured it out the day before when she got up and got dressed. The feeling had been there again—that missing feeling—where she didn't feel quite herself. It was the same feeling that had been following her around since she got home, like she had missed someone's birthday or forgotten an important assignment at school. She couldn't shake it, couldn't quite figure out how to chase it away. When she was done dressing, she stood in the middle of her bedroom, thinking what it might be before she pushed off the thought and reached for her backpack, unzipping the middle section and looking for a beer or a thermos of vodka, whatever she might have stashed there.

And that's when she knew. It was like yesterday, the way she went looking, the bad habit slipping on her like a silk glove. That's when she knew that it was the alcohol that had been missing, gone from her life like a friend who had passed on, a friend she desperately longed to have back.

When it was there, when she stood in the kitchen in bare feet, her jeans slung low across her tiny waist, the bottle poised at her lips, she felt like her old self again. Even as she crouched over the toilet, forcing herself to throw up, dabbing at her face with a clean washcloth to clean up the vomit that had splashed back at her, she felt once again like herself.

She'd grown to hate this version, this image. Familiar as it was, she'd grown to despise the person she'd left behind.

Cara found her there, an hour or so later. She'd been out running errands, the boys to their baseball games, Claire to a playdate. Cara came into the house in a hurry, laden with groceries she'd picked up and a leaking plastic jug of milk that she set in the sink. She spotted the empty wine bottle sitting on the countertop and froze; sweat brimming above her lip and at her armpits. She wasn't ready for this, not again.

Cara dropped her keys on the kitchen table and walked calmly through the house.

"In here, Mom," Katie called when she could hear her tennis shoes padding across the floor. "I'm in here."

"Sorry, Mom," Katie said, bowing her head. She was washing her face, running an ivory washcloth over her neck and around her lips. Residue from vomiting stung the back of Katie's throat and she desperately wanted to go and brush her teeth. Instead she cupped her hands under the faucet and lifted the water to her mouth, rinsing and spitting.

"What happened?" Cara asked her, a whisper barely escaping her lips.

It was the last thing she expected, to come home to this. But Katie's drinking, whenever it started again, always surprised her, always left her wondering how it was she had missed the signs, again.

Katie met her mother's eyes through the reflection in the large bathroom mirror. Cara stood just behind her, to the right and over her shoulder. It reminded Katie of the way a guardian angel would stand next to you, watching over you. Disbelief registered on Cara's face. Katie wondered why she was so surprised, why she wasn't angry, screaming and dragging her away. It might have been easier if her mother was angry, if she'd given Katie something to yell back at.

"I drank your wine. The whole thing. I drank the entire bottle start to finish in about a minute and a half." Katie watched for the expression on her mother's face to change, for disappointment to come creeping back in.

"But why?" Cara asked her.

Katie turned and faced her mother. She was almost her same height now, just an inch shy, but they came eye to eye anyway. Her mother stood very close to her, blocking the doorway so that it would be very difficult for Katie to run past her if she wanted to; she didn't.

"I thought I needed to. I can't explain it, really, but ever since I came home, here to the house, something has felt like it was missing, like it was supposed to be there and it wasn't. And then yesterday I went looking for something to drink. I went looking in my backpack for something to drink because it just felt like that was what I was supposed to do. There was nothing there, of course, but just looking for it, just like I used to do every day, well, it just felt like that was part of who I was, of what defined me.

WHEN I'M NOT MYSELF 263

"I couldn't chase it away, Mom. That feeling just kept following me around all day. So this morning, when I got up, I just gave
in to it. It just felt like that's what I was supposed to do. There
wasn't any reason, really."

Cara wanted so badly to take Katie in her arms. She wanted to
wrap Katie's rigid, tense body with as much warmth and comfort
as she could, but she knew that wouldn't solve anything, that
doing so would only leave Katie feeling like she wasn't being listened to, that Cara hadn't heard her.

Cara understood what her daughter was saying. For the first
time, she really understood her. It wasn't much different, really,
than what Cara had felt herself, the days after Jack was gone,
when she'd reached across the bed for him in the morning or
picked up her cell phone to call him about something ordinary,
what to have for dinner or where she'd be when he got home. It
was a hard habit to break. Identifying it as such was the first step.

"How did it make you feel, Katie? After you drank the wine.
Did you feel better? Did you feel more like your old self?" Cara
was careful with her questions, cautious not to upset Katie. She'd
seen this movie before; she didn't want Katie pushing past her
and stomping out the front door.

Katie shrugged her shoulders. "I remembered what it was like
to drink like that. It felt just like it always did; it felt good."

They weren't the words Cara wanted to hear, not at all. They
were the words she had feared, the words that she didn't know
what to do with.

"But then," Katie continued, "I realized that I didn't particularly like that person. Even though it felt familiar, like something
that fit me perfect, it wasn't who I wanted to be. It wasn't what I
wanted to be. Not anymore. I can't be that person anymore,
Mom, I just can't." Her face dissolved, her lips trembled, and her
shoulders shook. "I made myself throw it all up, Mom. I couldn't
stand it. It was like poison in my body. I didn't want to drink it
anymore, I just couldn't." She covered her face with both hands
and stood there sobbing in front of Cara.

Still, Cara held back from taking Katie in her arms. She wasn't entirely sure she trusted her, not one hundred percent. She wanted to believe her, God, she wanted to believe her, but she wasn't completely convinced.

Cara dug her hands into the back pockets of her jeans. She wanted Katie to own this, all of it. She wanted only to be on the sidelines, as coach, to help her figure this out. So she asked her, "What do you want to do, Katie?"

It took Katie a minute to catch her breath. She was crying harder now, so hard that she had to sit down. She lowered the toilet seat lid and took a seat; her arms crossed at the chest she doubled over, rocking back and forth. Cara handed her the Kleenex box, plucking one out. She took it and balled it up in her hand, wiping one eye, then the other.

"I don't know, Mom. I was thinking I should go back to the center, you know, and check myself back in."

"That's one option, yeah. You can do that. If you want."

She looked up at Cara. Her face was blotchy and her eyes were rimmed in red. "You're not going to make me?" Katie asked, sniffling. She had half-expected her mother to haul her out of the bathroom when she found her and insist that she do just that.

"No, Kate, I'm not. You have to do something; you can't just let this go. But I'm not going to make you go back there. And, quite frankly, I think you're on to something."

"How do you figure?" Katie wiped the back of her hand across her nose and cleared her throat.

Cara slumped to the floor and leaned against the wall, pulling her knees up to her chest. "I remember when your father left. For the first few weeks, I didn't know which end was up. I didn't know what normal was supposed to feel like because nothing, and I mean *nothing*, felt normal anymore. It was as if I were a completely different person, that I had been forced to be someone that I had no idea how to be. Everything around me was changing and I couldn't get my arms around any of it. It was the most surreal feeling, quite frankly."

Katie nodded her head and listened intently.

"I don't remember, really, what happened, or I guess when it happened that I started feeling like my old self again. Only it wasn't my old self at all. It could never be my old self. When your dad left, he took part of my identity with him. So much of who I was was built around who I was with your father. I had no idea who to be without him."

"But you figured it out, Mom, didn't you? You figured out how to move on."

"Yeah. Yeah, I have. But it's not who I was, Katie. I had to be okay to be someone new, someone different. And that's what you have to do, love bug. That's what you have to do. There's a new girl in there who can get through a day without downing a bottle of wine before nine o'clock. She's just as pretty and smart and sassy and everything as you are, but she doesn't need a six-pack, or three or four shots of vodka because it's part of who she is. She's defined by other things, other characteristics that the people who know her, really know her, love about her."

Katie took a deep breath, shuddering. She caught her reflection in the mirror, stopping to really look at the person staring back at her. She was without makeup and her hair was disheveled, sticking up this way and that. She turned her attention again to Cara, looking down at her from where she sat. "Will you help me, Mom?" she asked. "I really, really need your help."

Cara wanted to scream, *What do you think I've been trying to do? All this time. What do you think this has been like for me, Katie?* But she knew that wouldn't help, not in the least. And besides, this was the first time Katie had asked for her help, the very first time.

"Of course," she said to her daughter, lifting her body from the floor and holding her hands out to Katie. Katie took them and Cara pulled her up from the toilet, into a warm embrace that kept them there together, wrapped tightly in each other's arms, for a long while.

26

A call bolted Cara awake. Panic washed over her in the thirty seconds before she managed to grab the phone and bark into the receiver, her heart pounding with fear that something had happened to her daughter. It was Paige.

"Meet us at the hospital, Cara. Please. I know it's the dead of night, but I really need you there. I can't do this without you guys. Call Leah for me. And Mel, too, if you think she'll come down from the city."

Cara could tell Paige was in pain. Her breath was quick and she was insistent, almost frantic.

"Mel will be there, sweetie, without a doubt. We all will. Calm down, honey. Is Dennis taking you to the hospital?"

"Uh-huh, yeah."

An hour or so later, they walked into her hospital room; Cara, Leah and Melanie arm in arm. Paige was peeing, squatting on the toilet with the door open, *Jerry Maguire* playing on the small television screen above her bed.

" 'You had me at hello,' " Melanie said to her, smiling and quoting the movie verbatim before she got a good look at Paige.

Paige stood, lifting her hospital gown to adjust one of the wires from the fetal monitor that had been disconnected so she could use the toilet, then settled the gown back over her enormous belly.

"Oh, my God, Paige. You are fucking huge," Melanie exclaimed, gasping.

"Melanie!" Leah admonished. "For Christ sake, she is about to give birth."

"Ain't no way that thing is coming out without a little help. My Lord, what have you been eating? Are you sure you're not having twins?"

To their horror, Paige lifted the gown again, pulling it straight up over her rock-hard belly and then letting the gown fall, cascading over her like a tent.

Mel closed her eyes and shook her head as if she was trying to shake off the image. "Let me say it again," she started. "Thank God it's you and not me."

"Paige, c'mere, sweetie," Cara crooned, encouragingly. "Let's get you back to bed. Just ignore the self-centered bitch with the twenty-two-inch waist. She can't remember what it was like to be basking in the glow of childbirth, ready to bring a beautiful little baby into this world."

Paige waddled to the bed and hoisted her butt on the edge of the mattress. "It's okay, Cara. If they don't frigging get this baby out of me soon, I'm going to reach up there and take care of things myself. I mean it was all fun and games when we started this nonsense nine months ago, but this is ridiculous. I'm sort of over the basking and glowing part, quite frankly. Let's get on with the show."

"Where's Dennis, Paigey?" Leah asked, her voice syrupy sweet and soothing.

"Ice chips. He went for more ice chips." Paige grunted this out during what appeared to be a fairly significant contraction.

"Ice chips," Mel stated. "There are exactly zero good reasons to chew on ice chips at a time like this. How about a shot of tequila, Paige? Vodka? Scotch? My God, the kid is cooked already. There's nothing you can do to hurt it at this point."

"Don't think I haven't thought about it."

Dennis bounded into the room, two plastic cups full of ice chips along with a pink plastic pitcher of what appeared to be more. "Hey, sweetie, how're you doing? Everything okay?" He was singsongy and light like he'd been dipped in sugar, but if you looked closely, you could see him cracking at the edges with concern.

"Did you bring the scotch, Dennis?" Mel chided immediately.

"Huh? Scotch?" Dennis looked puzzled. "Oh, you're kidding. Funny, Mel, that's really funny."

"Whoa, buddy, loosen up. It's a baby. She's going to be fine."

Dennis was already at Paige's side, scooping ice chips with a spoon and ladling them into Paige's open mouth. "I can do this myself, Dennis," she said, taking the cup and spoon from him. "I'm not sick, I'm just in labor. God help me if I ever decide this would be a good idea again."

It was Cara who suggested coffee and Leah who gently nudged Dennis toward the door. "Just a few minutes, Denny. Let's take a break. She's nowhere near ready to go yet, so you've got plenty of time." They led him to the door, guiding him by his elbows, one on each side.

"Are you sure, sweetie? I'll just be down in the cafeteria, if you're okay here. Are you . . . ?" But he never got the rest of the words out. The door swung open, then shut, and Dennis found himself on the other side.

Paige breathed in, then out. Deep, calming breaths that sent shivers down her spine and instantly made her feel better. Her water had broken, just before eleven when she'd gotten up to pee for the nine hundredth time of the day, and that had sent Dennis into a flurry of activity, most of it meaningless and repetitive. He had loaded the suitcase into the car and then came running back into the house searching the bedroom until Paige had asked him what he was doing.

"I'm looking for the suitcase, Paige. Where did you put it?"

She stared at him, exasperated already. "You just put it in the car," she said, gritting her teeth.

"Oh."

He'd driven too fast to the hospital, setting off an argument between them about getting the baby killed even before it had a chance to live. And at the hospital he'd turned into a raving lunatic, demanding a private room for his wife as soon as they walked in.

His attitude was nothing like his usual calm, sweet demeanor. And the crass way he was ordering those around him didn't suit him. It wasn't until Paige had been checked into the room he'd insisted they give her, and hooked up to the fetal monitor, that he calmed down. Now Paige was just glad to be rid of him for a few minutes. Just glad to see the girls.

"You're home," Paige said, reaching at once for Cara and Melanie's hands. "You made it."

"Thank God, yes," Mel answered her and sidled up to the bed, pulling her body up on the high mattress. "Four days in that god-forsaken country inn with bad sheets and towels like sandpaper. It was heinous."

"It was good that we went," Cara said, filling in the quiet space that had settled on the room, no one knowing what the right questions were to ask, what the right answers were to offer. "In the end, it was the right thing to do."

They let it go then, fading away from them like a distant memory.

Mel had been back to work for two days, making up for lost time, shooting two a day. She had called her mother once, a sense of duty falling on her like a heavy cloak, and when she hung up the phone from that conversation she knew it would be a long time before she and Bea spoke again. There was nothing further for them now, nothing left that Mel felt she needed to tell her or that she somehow needed to hear from her. Mel had been resolved to the fact that those words would never be muttered aloud.

David had greeted Cara on Monday morning with hot chai tea, an armful of work and a soft smile. "Cara, I'm so glad you're back," he said to her quietly. "I've missed you."

She was checking the e-mails that had piled up while she was away. She looked up at him from her computer. "Me, too," she

answered. And what passed between them was a quiet understanding that Cara would fill him in later on the details of her
trip.

Cara had packed away the knowledge she had, the secrets she
now kept, like an old quilt that had served its purpose but was
too worn to be of use anymore. She had decided that there was
no point in telling Melanie or Leah about Dermott and Mirabelle's
affair, the reason Bea had left and never returned. Some things
just deserved not to be cut open and dissected. Some things just
deserved to be left alone.

Paige delivered her daughter in record time. By seven in the
morning they were laughing, holding baby Ella and trying to figure out who she looked more like. She had Dennis's fair skin and
blue eyes, translucent and icy and not likely to change the way
most newborns' eyes did. But she had Paige's dimpled chin, her
long fingers, her sweet, pinched mouth.

Paige was exhausted, soaked in perspiration and worn from
the quick delivery. The delivery room nurse showed her how to
breast-feed Ella, positioning her just so. Ella cried and fought for
a minute, then latched on like a champ.

Cara and Leah convinced Dennis to go for breakfast and followed him toward the door. "You coming, Mel?" Leah asked, looking back at Melanie still poised on the side of the bed watching
Paige and her new daughter intently.

"I'll be down in a few minutes. Go on ahead," Mel urged.

Ella had fallen asleep while nursing. When they were gone,
Paige sat running her index finger over the top of the baby's head.
Ella had fine peach fuzz, guaranteed to fall out but likely to grow
back in soft, reddish blonde curls like her father had.

"She looks just like her father," Melanie stated, saying it out
loud for the first time.

"Yes."

Melanie lifted Ella from Paige and placed her in the makeshift
cradle, the plastic rolling crate that had been positioned next to
Paige's hospital bed. The baby yawned wide, her mouth forming

a perfect round circle *O*, and then settled into the hospital blankets she was wrapped in.

"What was it like, Mel, when you had Isabella? You were all by yourself then." Paige reached for Mel's hand and held it tightly. She didn't often have the chance to be alone with Mel, certainly not at a time when emotions were running so high.

"Nothing like this, Paige, not at all. It was so long ago. God, it feels like a lifetime ago."

Mel watched Ella sleep, the rise and fall of her tiny chest, the way her hands had wrestled free from the tightly wrapped blanket to find her mouth. She sucked on two fingers—her pointer and middle finger—and cooed contentedly.

"Are you glad you went, to see your mom and to say good-bye to Dermott?" Paige asked.

Mel shrugged her shoulders and shook her head resolutely. "I don't know. I didn't have much of a choice, really. At least that's how it felt. I guess I could have let it all go. And maybe I should have. But it didn't feel right to do that. It felt like I needed to be there, for Isabella and for me."

Paige nodded her head, understanding.

When Cara and Leah made their way back into the room, they came with cups of steaming coffee and extralarge frosted cinnamon buns, the icing melting.

"Please tell me you didn't actually eat one of those things," Melanie said to Cara, pointedly. "There's like nine million calories in that thing. And more trans fat than your body could ever absorb."

Cara smiled. "You didn't think I got rid of my favorite pair of jeans, did you? Just because you made me buy that loincloth of denim that barely covers my crack."

Mel eyed her suspiciously. "Not the pleats, Cara. Please tell me you've gotten rid of those godforsaken pleated pants. They are so not you."

Cara smiled devilishly, knowing how to get to Mel. "I'll make you a deal," she said.

"What?"

272 Deborah J. Wolf

"I'll get rid of the jeans on one condition."

"Anything."

Cara nodded toward Paige and Dennis. "See our friends here? You're on dinner. A casserole, Melanie. One with cooked carrots and stewed potatoes, or pasta and hamburger. Something full of nutrients that will fill their bellies and keep them alive for a few days." It wasn't in Mel and Cara knew it. She wouldn't take the bet on principle alone.

Mel blanched and swallowed hard, shaking her head. "Fine," she answered and dove into the cinnamon bun, licking her finger-tips.

27

David suggested they take in a ball game. "There is nothing better than a ball game, Cara. It's just what you need. And, my God, we never get weather like this in San Francisco. A ball game it is."

Cara had been to plenty of baseball games; Little League had been a rite of passage for Will and Luke for as long as Cara could remember. But she hadn't been to a real ball game—peanuts and beer and a seventh-inning stretch—in a long, long time. And David was right; the weather in the city couldn't be beat. She was suddenly overcome with a sense of spring fever, feeling young and free. She did something she had never done before; she called Jack and fibbed. *"A last-minute meeting,"* she told him, *"a career-making opportunity."* He whined that Barbie was too far pregnant, too moody, but she held him off, waiting out his tantrum with silence on the other end of the phone. He just had to pick up the kids and get their homework done; she'd done it for him plenty of times.

David had season tickets. Not just any season tickets; three rows up from the field, first base side. The crowd around them swelled and welcomed them like the sea swallowing its prey.

"We've been in these seats for a while," he explained. "Ever since they built the new park."

It was Wednesday and they weren't the only "South of Market" executives who'd cut out early to enjoy the afternoon. Still, Cara felt overdressed in a peach linen blouse and black slacks. David held her beer while she settled into the hard folding chair and when he handed it to her she drank the top quarter of it without stopping.

"What else can I get you, Cara?"

"Absolutely nothing," she answered him, pulling on her sunglasses and rolling up the sleeves to her blouse. It was near seventy and clear, almost unheard of in early May in San Francisco. And Cara meant what she said; there was absolutely nothing else she could think of that she needed at that very moment.

The Giants batted through their order twice in four innings but couldn't score until Ray Durham knocked one dead centerfield for a three-run homer, sending Cara and everyone around them cheering, whooping it up, on their feet. Cara threw her arms in the air and David lifted her at the waist until she practically came right out of her four-inch heels.

"Woo-hoo!" they shouted, "Yeah!" and toasted each other with what was left of their beers.

In the end, the home team lost, coughing one up to the Mets when they couldn't convert the runner on second in the bottom of the ninth. A collective sigh was heard through the park, right on the heels of the sharp strike called by the umpire. Cara watched as the crowd heaved disappointment, then gathered their belongings and headed outside, flooding the busy city streets with defeat.

David took her hand and led her up, then down, the stairs until they exited onto Third Street and Willie Mays Plaza. He looped his arm over her shoulder in a friendly, brotherly way and pulled her close, kissing her on the cheek. "You win some, you lose some," he whispered in her ear.

"That's very adult of you." She smiled.

"Oh, Cara, you can't win them all," he quipped.

"Nice. How many more of those you got?"

"A million."

"I figured."

The sun hung high in the afternoon sky, still warming the city. They walked together, falling into step, their fingers intertwined. Cara didn't want to leave; she loved the way the city smelled, the way it moved around her, carrying them along.

"We're having dinner, yes?"

"God, I hope so. I'm starved."

"Cara?" He stopped her on the street, jerking her around so she faced him. "How in the world can you be hungry? Where did the *Say Hey! Willie Mays* sausage and garlic fries go?"

"God, David, that was hours ago."

They made their way north a few blocks to COCO500, where David wormed his way into a table in the back of the restaurant and ordered them each a Mojito.

"I wouldn't have pegged you for a baseball fan, Cara. You did okay out there," he added, commenting on her steel-trap knowledge of the right plays. "I've been to plenty of games with women who talked my ear off during full count of a tied game."

"And?"

"And, I wanted to kill them. God, it was so annoying. A complete deal breaker."

"I'll bet," Cara said, pausing to sip her drink. "And just who are these so-called women?"

David rolled his eyes. "I'm sure that I've forgotten," he answered her and leaned in, resting his elbows on the small table that separated them.

"Uh-huh," Cara teased. "I'm sure that you have not."

"Honestly, Cara, do you think I'd rather be sitting at this table with some twentysomething with no innate knowledge of what a ninth inning pop fly can mean to a major league pitcher who is staring his first no-hitter in the face? Or do you think I'd rather be sitting here with you?"

"Admit it; you're just happy I'm back."

"I'm absolutely thrilled that you're back. I've lost my touch with Stewart; you've stolen his logic. He won't listen to anyone's reasoning but yours."

"Did it ever occur to you that maybe I'm just right?"

"God, no. Never."

Cara propped her chin in the palm of her hand, satisfied. She loved to banter with David, the easygoing, quick wit that kept each of them on their toes. She loved the way he volleyed one-liners back and forth with her, engaging her all the while.

David cupped his hand around the back of her head and pulled her face close to him. "And even if you were—right, that is—do you think I'd let you get away with it?"

He kissed her then, his lips lingering very close to hers afterward. She took in a deep, sharp breath, startled by the way he surprised her.

"You haven't told me about your trip yet, Cara," he said to her when she sat back, taking him in.

Cara stretched her arms over her head and yawned. Her once-crisp linen blouse was wrinkled beyond recognition. She sipped the last of her Mojito before she answered him. "Oh, it was quite an adventure, my God . . . so much to cover."

"I'm not going anywhere, Cara. Let's hear it." He closed the menu and flagged down the waitress, ordering a smattering of small plates: marinated olives, goat cheese, oysters on the half shell. He looked at her for approval and she nodded her head. "We'll start there," he said to the waitress, dismissing her as quickly as he'd called her over.

"Well," she started, leaning back in her chair, getting comfortable. "I think it was good that we went. I wasn't so sure, certainly, when we were there, but all things considered, it was good for Mel to put a few things to bed, finally and completely. She hadn't seen her mother in thirty years."

David's eyes grew large over the top of his glass. "What? You've got to be kidding. Why not?"

"Oh, David, there's too much to tell. I'd have to start at the beginning and that was obviously so long ago that much of it isn't relevant anymore, not really, anyway."

"I'd say it's probably very relevant, Cara. It was Melanie's life."

"Yes." She paused. "Yes, you're right. It was very relevant. It had everything to do with who she's become."

"I'm sure."

"And how about you and Mel? Things had been distant for a while now. Were you able to put some of that behind you and heal a bit?"

Cara thought about how she should answer that. She hadn't told David everything that had passed between her and Mel; even though she'd held her opinions core to who she was, somehow she felt foolish admitting them to him, as if he might find her naive or childish.

"We were, yes. I think I finally realized that Mel and I could be the very best of friends, certainly the very oldest of friends, and still have our differences. Different opinions, different lives, really. It's funny, but we practically grew up right next to each other, you know. And yet we were worlds apart. We still are today."

Their food arrived along with another round of Mojitos, and then truffle-mushroom pizza that David had spied on the menu and ordered on the fly.

"Mmmm," Cara moaned, diving into the warm goat cheese. "Really, really good."

"Cara?" David asked and waited until she looked at him.

"Hmmm?"

"Think you'll ever get married again?" he asked her, leaving her midbite and more than a little surprised.

She stopped chewing and stared at him. It was just like him; a question to throw her off her game. She finished the cheese and drank some water, squirming in her chair, shifting from one side to the other. She avoided his eyes and couldn't imagine what had possessed him to ask her. She hadn't considered it herself, not since Jack left, not wanting to tempt fate.

"God, David, where do these questions come from?"

"Don't know. Why?"

"Because that has to be the *last* question I would have thought you would have asked me."

"Why?"

"Um, well, I guess because I hadn't even considered it myself, not yet, anyway. And I can't imagine what about me getting married again would be so entertaining to you."

"I'm just curious. Hypothetically speaking, of course. Would you ever get married again? It's a simple question, really. I would think you'd have a pretty good idea about it, actually, having done it once. I would think someone like you, with four children and a house in the burbs would be a prime candidate."

She couldn't help but feel a bit self-conscious. It was the first time he'd pointed out what she had so readily always known was the biggest difference in their life paths. She was forty-three-years old with four kids and a significant mortgage. He could kiss her good-bye on a street corner and pack his bags overnight for an extended assignment in Paris. There was nothing to keep him here; he was anchored by little, if anything.

"I think I should be insulted," she told him, wearing her life's choices like a badge of shame.

"Why?"

"You make it sound rather fatalistic, as if it's my only option."

He laughed openly, warmly. "No, Cara. You make it sound as if it's your only option. I was only curious."

"Oh."

"And contrary to popular belief, I don't think of marriage as fatalistic. Not even close."

"Okay, smart-ass, your turn. Would you get married? Ever?"

"That's not the open question on the table. The question on the table is would you ever get married? Again."

"Okay, fine. Here you go. I have no idea, actually. I haven't thought about it, not once since Jack left. My divorce will be final next week and I still can't get my head around the fact that it's actually over. Not in the, *"Oh, Jack, I really want you back; I can't believe you ever left me*" way, but in the *"Hmmm, you really aren't married anymore"* way.

"I get that."

"You do?"

"Sure, absolutely."

Cara finished her second drink, sucking it back and letting it dull the base of her skull. She would have to call Jack soon and tell him to keep the kids for the night and she hoped that he wouldn't ask her where she was or what she was doing. He had no business knowing and it shouldn't matter to him, anyway, but she wondered if maybe it did. Not because she couldn't come retrieve their children, but because he really wanted to know where she was and what she was doing.

"I should call Jack," she slurred, sleep creeping in and settling over her. "You're going to have to take me home, at least for a while. I can't drive."

He snuck a smile at her and laughed, paying the bill at the same time. "Okay, Cara."

Cara's heels might have been mistaken for tap shoes as she *click-clacked* across the sterile, freshly mopped lobby floor. The hospital reeked of too much antiseptic and made her stomach lurch. Katie's panicked call had come in on Cara's cell phone just after midnight.

"I have to go. It's Barbie's baby," Cara said; shaking off the headache that pounded at her temples. She fished around the bottom of her bag for her car keys.

"You can't drive, Cara." He rolled toward her, and sat up on the edge of the bed, pulling a T-shirt over his slight frame. In the shadowy room, his image bounced and danced on the wall, chased by the headlights from a car that passed the flat.

"I'll be fine," she answered him, attempting to stand in her heels but failing radically, shifting and shimmying unsteadily.

"I'll take you, Cara," he said to her and pulled on a pair of black square-framed glasses that she hadn't ever seen him wear.

He'd removed his contacts and needed them for driving. In the unfamiliar light, he looked like a stranger to her. He pulled on a pair of jeans over the black boxer briefs he was wearing and buttoned them from the bottom up, then slipped on a pair of flip-flops.

Cara closed her eyes and shook her head, cursing herself for drinking too much. *Dear God*, she thought, *who am I kidding?* David looked as if he was all of twenty-three, stumbling in from a study group in the university library. She would have him drop her at the front door of the hospital. She would call a cab to get them home later. She would take the train up sometime tomorrow to collect her car.

"You can't take me, David. Really, it's too much to ask you to do."

He came to her side and embraced her, wrapping his arms around her back so that she couldn't move. Cara's arms hung limp at her sides. She couldn't imagine what she was in for, a trip to the hospital while Barbie was in labor. She should have listened to Jack in the first place; Barbie was far too pregnant to be dealing with all of this. And now Jack would be furious with her for being so inconsiderate. And for what? A night out with David.

"I want to take you, Cara. It's okay; I don't mind. I don't want you driving. Not like this."

She thought of Katie, the countless nights her daughter had gotten behind the wheel of a car and somehow stumbled home, and she knew she couldn't, moreover that she wouldn't, do this. "Okay," she answered him, the muffled sound coming from where her face was pressed against his chest. "Thanks."

They walked the block to his car in silence, avoiding any sort of conversation. Cara was all nerves, full of endurance and awake. She couldn't imagine what lay ahead of her. Barbie's baby, Jack's fifth child, was due to make his or her entrance any minute. An undeniable surge of energy overcame her. She felt the need to fly in and rescue her children, an overwhelming sense of protection as if she needed to keep everything in their lives frozen in time, as it were.

*   *   *

When they arrived at the hospital, David respectfully pulled into the roundabout and let her off. It wasn't the right time to meet her children and, God, she couldn't imagine what it would be like for Jack and him to come face-to-face. He left the car idling and went around to open the door for her, pulling her to her feet. She was a mess, the remnants of her professional look long gone. Everything about her was wrinkly, deep creases pressed into the fabric of her black pants and suit jacket.

"How will you get the children home?" he asked her. He was standing very close, towering over her, and he jingled his keys in one hand, turning them over and over again.

"I'm sure I can take Jack's car. I'll figure it out." She ran her hands through her hair, trying to bring it to life a bit. "I'll need the morning off, and I'll take the train up to the city later so I can pick up my car." She stepped away from the car then and closed the passenger door firmly. "Thanks again," she said, nodding at his BMW, "for driving me. I really shouldn't have been on the road."

He smiled at her and leisurely kissed her on the forehead. "It's okay, Cara. Be well, okay? Everything will be fine."

She turned, taking him in one last time. He filled her frame, his presence so easygoing and calm. "David." She stopped and stood staring at him. "I would. Get married again. Maybe, some day. If it was right."

He ran his hands over his day-old stubble and through his hair, then crossed his arms across his chest and leaned against his car, laughing. "Yes, Cara. I knew that about you. I had an idea."

They were sitting together on the chipped tile floor of the labor and delivery ward halfway down the hall, outside Barbie's birthing room. Katie was cradling Claire in her lap while she slept. Will and Jack were sitting on the other side of the hall, brooding and thumb wrestling. Cara saw the four of them from a distance as she ran in her heels, *click-clack, click-clack, click-clack,* echoing all the way, her black wool coat open and flapping behind her.

Katie's frantic, adrenaline-charged voice rattled off the details in double-time with barely a breath in between. "She's in labor, Mom. Daddy says we have to stay out here but that the baby should be born soon."

Claire woke sleepily and reached out her arms to Cara. "Mama." Cara lifted her easily, and buried her nose in Claire's strawberry-scented curls. "Barbie's gonna have her baby, Mama," she whispered, piercing right through Cara. "Isn't it great? She's gonna have her baby tonight."

"I know, sweetie," Cara answered her, and blinked back the tears. She had no idea where to go, the ground beneath her feet foreign. She had no idea where to take her children, or if she should stay at all. Technically, she had left them with Jack to-night. Technically, she'd had an *emergency* that required him to step up and take responsibility for the four of them. Technically, she should have been home.

Or out with David Michel.

Or curled up on a bar stool with Mel and Paige and Leah, martinis and a pack of cigarettes between them.

Anywhere but here.

Oh, how she longed right this minute for her friends. Mel, whose rock-solid advice would guide her, so she'd know exactly what she should do. Leah, who would lovingly take her in her arms and wait with her no matter how long it took, reminding her of what a strong woman she was. Paige, who would clasp her hand and cry with her, letting the tears come in great, giant floods until she was drained dry, giant concern heaped on top of her like a pile of blankets.

Cara stood in the middle of the hall, blinking against the bright fluorescent lights. On the other side of the door, she could make out Jack's strong voice. Jack's encouragement, the rise and fall of his delighted pitch, his reassuring support, the undeniable optimism. She felt as if she was miles away, years away, and Jack was encouraging her. Jack with his unfailing pride, his determination.

She felt him there with her, all over again. She knew there was no greater sense of accomplishment for him than the birth of his children, these four, and the fifth one now, this one coming into this world, coming into this crazy family he had created.

Cara stood with her children huddled around her, supporting her. She was sure they must have been holding her up; certainly she couldn't muster the strength to stand on her own accord.

"Cara." Jack's voice shook her awake and she turned to face him. He wore scrubs, and a cap and mask, but his eyes were unmistakable. He looked her in the eye; the first time she could remember him doing so in a long, long time.

"How is she?" Cara asked on automatic pilot and pulled her coat closer to her chest. She didn't want Jack to see her dressed this way, in a crumpled suit that left her looking suspicious.

"She's okay. They're going to give her an epidural now and that should help ease the pain some. She wanted to do it without the drugs, but it's just too intense. I don't know why you women have to be so brave, so . . ." He stopped then, realizing perhaps the inappropriate nature of his revelation. Jack cleared his throat and shuffled his feet, staring down at the floor briefly before he looked at her again. "It was good of you to come," he said simply.

"Katie called me. I can take them, if you'd like." Cara studied the span of the wide hall, both north and south. The ward was relatively calm. "Or I can stay."

"Would you? Oh, Cara, really? There could be a million complications and, well, I guess I'd just feel better having everyone here with us."

Everyone. Cara nodded her head slowly, unsure why she was doing so. Perhaps she felt the need to be with her children. Perhaps she felt that leaving now would have been callous. "We'll be down the hall. There's a room with a couple of couches and a TV. We'll be in there. Come for us when you know where things stand. I'll stay with them; we'll be fine."

Luke and Will were asleep in minutes, having argued about who got which couch and then collapsing on top of each other. Their hands curled into each other, their heads touched. Cara crept down the hall and found two blankets. She draped one over each of them. Claire was right behind them, excitement over-whelming her only briefly until Cara told her it could be hours before Barbie had the baby and promised that she'd wake her the minute they knew what had happened.

Only Katie kept pace with Cara, kicking off her shoes and curling her legs up on one end of the last remaining sofa. She and Cara sat facing each other and huddling under a warming blanket that Cara had turned up from one of the delivery rooms.

"They wrap you in these blankets after you've had a baby, but they're warm, as if they had been taken right out of the oven. There's nothing, really, that feels better than that. I was so cold after I delivered you, so very cold and awed and overwhelmed. Your body doesn't know which end is up, really."

Katie yawned fully and snuggled farther down on the couch so that only her eyes and nose looked out from under the blanket. "It's kind of weird, huh, Mom? I mean, you being here and all."

Cara nodded. "A little, yes."

"Do you think it's going to be a boy or a girl, Mom?"

"Kate, I think that's one of life's greatest surprises. I'd hate to guess, especially at this point when we're so close. Let's just hope that the baby is okay and that the delivery isn't too hard on Barbie."

"That's nice of you to say, Mom."

"What?"

"About it not being so hard for Barbie. I don't know, after all this, I guess I would have thought you would just kind of hate her or something."

"Oh, Kate, honey . . . It's, well, it's so much more complicated than that." Cara sighed and pulled her knees up to her chest, hugging them tightly and wrapping her arms around her legs. An old air-conditioning unit rattled in one of the corners and churned out small gusts of chilled air that filled the room and kept Cara's blood racing. After a minute, Cara said, "I guess I did, you know, hate her for what she did to our family, for taking Daddy away from all of us, from all of you."

"Yeah, I know. Me, too."

"What changed your mind?" Cara asked her.

"I don't know. I guess I just figured that she didn't exactly take Daddy away, you know. I mean Daddy went. He went willingly. I don't know why, but he did. I used to think it was because he didn't like us anymore, that he didn't like having a family and a bunch of kids around all the time, but I guess that's not it. I mean he's starting all over again with a whole new kid."

"Oh, Katie, I don't think that was it at all. Daddy loves you. A lot, you know."

"Yeah, well, I figured I couldn't hate him forever."

Cara pulled her daughter close to her so that Katie's head rested on her chest and their breathing became steady and even together. She waited while Katie began to doze off, the weight of her head becoming heavy and significant on Cara's chest. Cara thought about who she'd become, the transformation this year, and wondered how she'd ever gotten here. It wasn't so long ago that Jack had left, and she'd been devastated, lost.

She thought maybe Mel was right, that Cara's very job was to start over, to take everything she knew about her life with Jack and do it the right way this time, to be someone different from who she'd become with him. She thought about her new career, the clothes and shoes and handbags that defined who people assumed she was when she walked down the street. She contemplated the changes in her hair, the monthly waxes that Mel had her addicted to, the person she'd become when she was with David.

She gazed at Katie and wondered how they'd survived the year together, how Katie had realized the changes in her life that needed to be made. Surely if Katie could do so, Cara could as well.

She turned the anger she'd had for Jack over in her mind again and again, and balanced that with her decision to sit here now, her own breathing measured and relaxed, while his new son or daughter came into this world only a corridor away. She felt an intimacy for Jack she hadn't been in touch with in a long, long time. She no longer desired him, no longer needed him, but only wished for him a goodness that seeped through his every pore and ran the course of his body. She hoped he'd found what it was he'd left her in search of, that his desires would be achieved, his sense of delight fulfilled. She wasn't at all sure Barbie was the answer, but she realized it wasn't her place to figure that out.

She had given herself a gift; she realized that now—the ability to heal from what had been dealt to her, the ability to move on. She had to do this herself, she knew. She had to let go of what she thought her life was supposed to look like in order to accept this new one, this life where she sprawled on the couch, her children around her, waiting for Jack's child to be born. The sweet taste of independence melted in her mouth like a first bite of pie, and she wanted more.

Jack rounded the corner to the waiting room just before four AM. His eyes were bloodshot and tired, the tiny capillaries broken. He surveyed the room and pulled the green surgical cap from his head, standing sheepishly in the door frame and unsure of what to do next.

"Well?" Cara whispered, unwrapping her legs from Katie's and straightening to stretch her stiff back. She had been dozing off, falling into a fit of dreams that kept jolting her awake.

"It's a boy." It was all Jack could manage, all he knew how to deliver at that moment.

Cara stood, shaking her legs out and pulling one of the blankets around her shoulders. The air conditioner pumped cold air into the room and shook her alive. His news woke her immediately.

"Oh, Jack." She walked to him and stopped short of embracing him.

He studied her hard, as if he was looking at her again for the first time, aware that she had become someone different. She had ditched her coat and stood in bare feet, feeling shorter but more powerful than ever. She stood in front of him without pretense, shamelessly and willingly.

"I, I don't know what to say, Cara. I'm a little, well, I guess I'm just a little overcome with everything." He looked around the room, studying each of his children as if he wasn't sure who they were. "Should I wake them?" he finally asked her, uncertain.

"Never wake a sleeping baby, Jack, you know that."

He smiled at her then, comforted. "Right."

"You go." She stood on her tiptoes then and kissed him on the cheek. "You go, and we'll be here. I'll be right here with the kids."

He turned then and walked away from her, down the hall until he disappeared from her sight.

A CHAT WITH DEBORAH J. WOLF

While on vacation the other day, I picked up Jodi Picoult's new novel, *Nineteen Minutes*. I am an avid fan of hers, and probably would have bought the book regardless of whether or not I'd cracked the cover and read the first page. But I'm often particularly taken with the beginning of a book, and usually will buy it if I find the first few lines particularly intriguing, as I did with her new novel.

The first line of *When I'm Not Myself* followed me around for days before I sat down and typed it out on the keyboard. There it sat before me, the first line of my second book. I quickly learned that writing your second book is nothing like writing your first. Whereas the first book flowed in long, lyrical sessions, the second sputtered out in fits and starts. It took a while before the rhythm stuck with me.

I had set out to write a story about women's friendships, and at the center of this novel, you find the deep, long-lasting, enduring relationship between Cara and her three friends, Leah, Paige, and, in particular, Melanie. Cara and Mel have known each other the longest, but that's not to say their lives have traveled the same path. I wanted a story where we could look at the judgments women—even the best of friends—make about one another, the things they are willing to forgive and those that they have the hardest time setting aside.

I'm blessed by the friends in my life; amazing, unbelievably strong females who have known me for years and those with whom I've more recently had the pleasure of building a relationship. My best friend came to covet that position on the first day of Mrs. Yamamoto's seventh-grade math class thirty years ago. We've survived junior high, high school, college, life post-university, first apartments, first jobs, weddings, first babies, second babies (and in her case, a third), heartache, heartbreak, and, most recently, fortieth birthdays together. Our lives are nothing alike anymore, and yet I am constantly astonished by the core of our friendship, the years that have solidified the bond between us. I shudder to think what life would be like without her.

It turned out that my first book, *With You and Without You*, was readily embraced by countless book clubs. I have been fortunate to have been invited to discuss the story with women of all ages, races, and beliefs. These discussions taught me that while reading a story is a very independent, personal experience, discussing it offers an entirely different perspective.

During these discussions, I learned a couple of things about my writing. I learned that the thing readers most often praise about my writing is my character development, which is, perhaps, the biggest compliment I could ask for. I find the stories I like best are those in which we lose ourselves in the characters. For me, the women in this book exist in one form or another, even beyond the voice in my head. They're my best friends, my confidantes, and my heroes. They represent some of the things I like best about those around me, and some of the things I like best about myself.

I've also learned that in reading this book you may have a very different relationship with them than I did. You may not agree with what they've done, or how they've reacted, or even with who they are. You may question their actions, disagree with their motives, and become frustrated with their choices. You may think of their conduct as unacceptable. There were times when I did as well.

I suppose that's the point. For they are not characters I created, but only those which I allowed to develop. Their stories are not mine to write, but theirs to tell. Being allowed the great privilege to do so is my greatest joy.

I sometimes say that I am called to write. What I mean by this is that I am physically drawn to sit down and start telling a story, one that just grows and brews and brims until it has no choice but to escape from the tips of my fingers onto the keyboard. Before me, it appears on the screen, and sometimes, just like turning the pages of a really great novel, even I'm surprised to uncover what happens next. It's really quite thrilling, actually.

Recently someone asked me what my third book would be about. Mind you, I'd barely finished editing *this* book, so the thought of sitting down to another blank computer screen was more than a little unnerving. I mentioned this to a friend of mine, complaining that I'd like to just enjoy the moment, even if it's for only a minute. In his very kind way, he replied, "Maybe they're just curious because they like what they've read so far and they want to know what they have to look forward to."

Truth be told, I do have an idea for a third book. And quite frankly, I can't wait to write it. I started, and shelved it, about a year ago. I'm not someone who can read more than one novel at a time, so I know I certainly can't write more than one at a time.

I can tell you this about it. The characters are like none I've ever explored before, not in any depth. First off, they're men. And although they're struggling with their own lot in life, not unlike the female characters I've had the opportunity to develop before them, I suspect they'll do it in a way like nothing I've had the license to investigate before. And that sounds like a great deal of fun.

Thank you, thank you, thank you, sweet reader, for taking the time to spend with Cara, Mel, Leah and Paige. I hope you were able to laugh with them and cry with them. I hope they touched some part of you or reminded you of someone remarkable in your life. Even more, I hope you'll share them with someone you think will enjoy them.